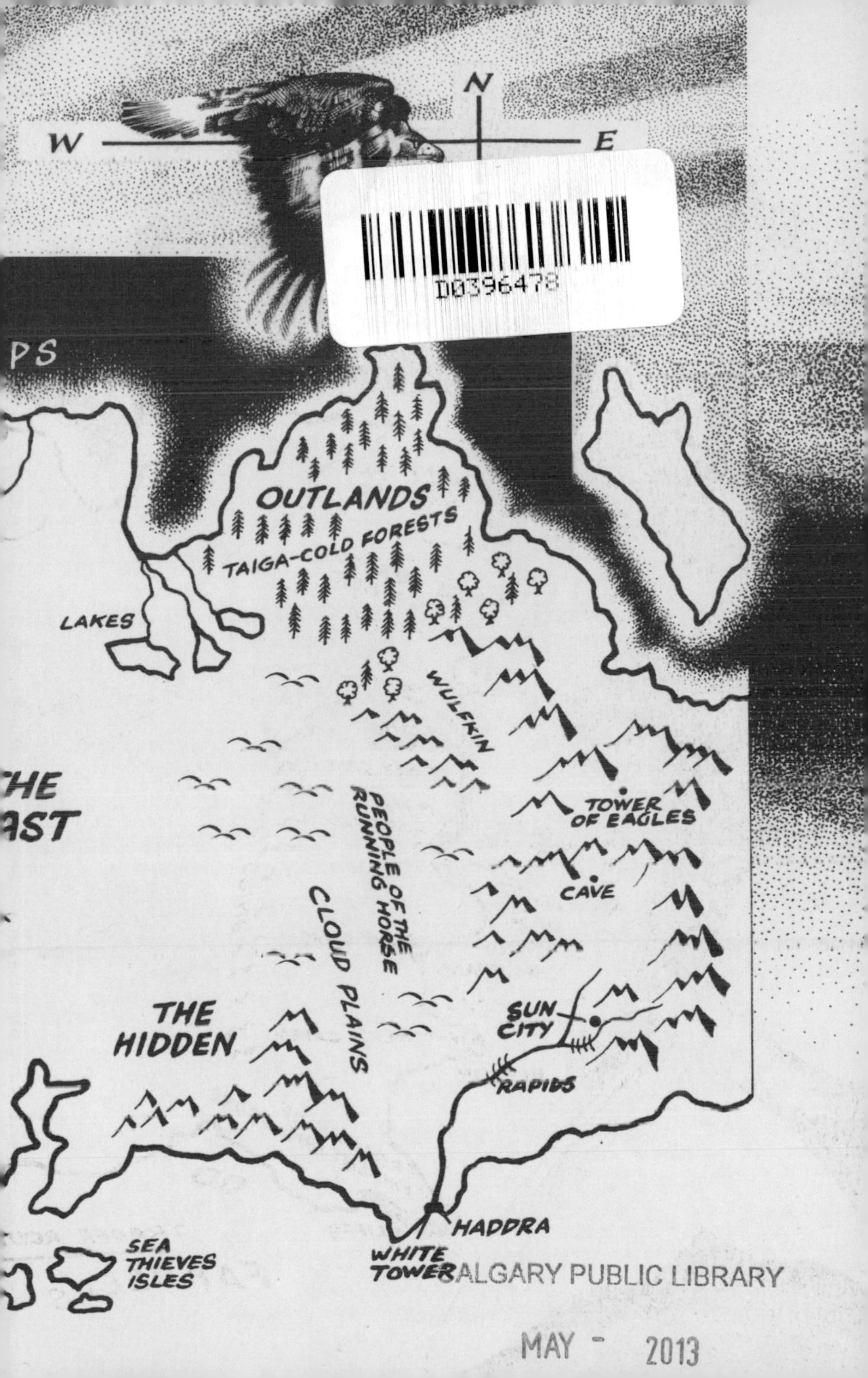

D0396478
CALGARY PUBLIC LIBRARY
MAY - 2013

Sun Catcher

Sun Catcher

SHEILA RANCE

Illustrated by Geoff Taylor

First published in Great Britain in 2013
by Orion Children's Books
a division of the Orion Publishing Group Ltd
Orion House
5 Upper St Martin's Lane
London WC2H 9EA
An Hachette UK Company

1 3 5 7 9 10 8 6 4 2

Text copyright © Sheila Rance 2013
Illustrations copyright © Geoff Taylor 2013

The right of Sheila Rance and Geoff Taylor to be identified
as the author and illustrator of this work has been asserted.

All rights reserved. No part of this publication may be
reproduced, stored in a retrieval system, or transmitted,
in any form or by any means, electronic, mechanical,
photocopying, recording or otherwise, without the prior
permission of Orion Children's Books.

The Orion Publishing Group's policy is to use papers
that are natural, renewable and recyclable products and
made from wood grown in sustainable forests. The logging
and manufacturing processes are expected to conform to
the environmental regulations of the country of origin.

A catalogue record for this book
is available from the British Library.

ISBN 978 1 4440 0620 9

Printed in Great Britain by
Clays Ltd, St Ives plc

www.orionbooks.co.uk

For Dave, Sian and Penny

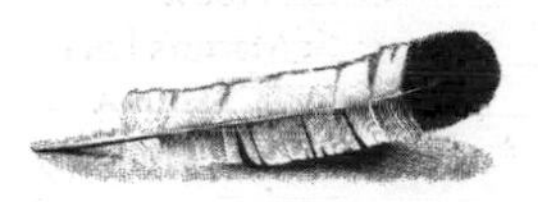

Maia held her hand over the silk. She closed her eyes and listened. Nothing. She touched the silk and a tiny swirl of colour seemed to twist from it and curl around her hand. Tareth had told her that the silk held the dreams of the moon-moths who spun the cocoons. Dreams for the taking. Dreams that became voices when he boiled the cocoons with crushed sea shells and wove the threads into singing silk. Silk so precious, so powerful, that it was kept secret from the Cliff Dwellers. From everyone.

One

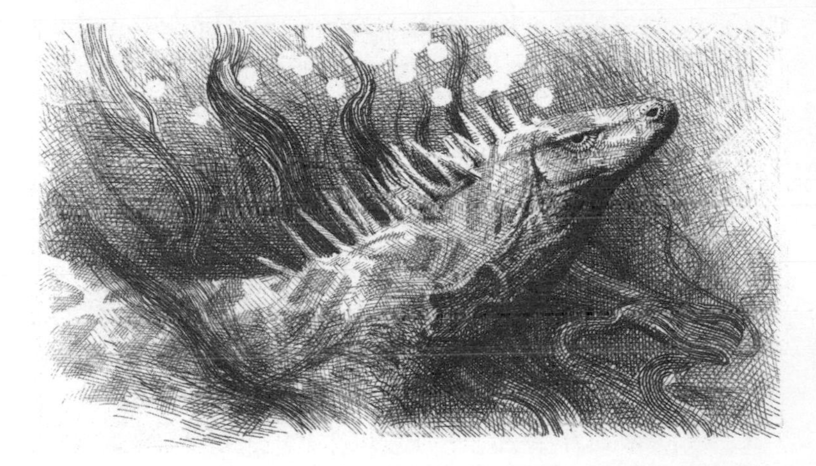

The huge lizard trawled through the garbage surging on the edge of the incoming tide. Maia gagged and tried not to breathe in. The storm had swept stinking debris around the headland and into the cove. The lizard must have followed it in, leaving its family in the sea fiord where the Untouchables would be sorting the storm waste. Nose deep in the floating rubbish, the lizard gobbled pieces of rotting carcass.

The gang of half-naked children gathering seaweed along the tide line yelled and hurled handfuls of pebbles at the lizard. The missiles bounced off its scales. The lizard raised its head, trails of seaweed festooned its jaws. The Weed Master, a tall dark-haired boy in a ragged tunic, scrambled onto the smooth rock at the far end of the beach. Waving his arms and shouting abuse, he lobbed rocks at the scavenger. Ignoring him, the lizard stirred up more stink as it raked its long claws through the swill, trawling for the flat bottom-feeders.

The Weed Master howled a challenge and hurled another rock. The lizard hissed and swung round, its crest turning red.

Maia felt her own anger kindle. The lizards were not supposed to trespass into the weed beds, but if it was hungry . . .

'Leave it alone!' she yelled at the boys still leaping at the edge of the sea spinning stones across the water. They turned, sensing a new target.

'Lizard lover,' yelled the Weed Master. Razek. Trust it to be him, thought Maia. Razek, the handsome bully. Razek, Elder's nephew who, with his widowed mother, was forever finding excuses to invade her cave.

'Leave it,' shouted Maia. 'What harm is it doing?'

'Lizard lover! Stink mother! Flame Head!' chanted the boys.

It was an insult too far. No one else in this dark-haired tribe of Cliff Dwellers had her red hair. It was one more reason why she and her father, Tareth, would never belong. The Cliff Dwellers had not killed them when Tareth's boat was wrecked and he was swept ashore, a red-haired child strapped to his back. They had taken them in, tolerated their strangeness. Tolerated them because Tareth was useful. And now, with a new moon and her Naming Day imminent, they would decide if she could be useful too, despite her red hair. She knew what Razek planned for her, if he could persuade Elder. She had seen it in his eyes. But if he thought she would ever agree to be hand-fast . . . Maia killed the thought. She grabbed a handful of sand and stones and hurled them at Razek.

'Weed slimers,' she screamed.

Razek yelled with fury as the sand and stones hit their mark. 'You're fish bait, lizard lover,' he roared. 'Get her. Chuck her in with the lizard.' He rushed towards her.

Maia stood her ground. Then, before Razek reached her, she turned and scrambled across the sand and up the cliff path. She reached the entrance to the cave and turned to grin down at her pursuers.

'Carrion collectors,' she spat. 'Gull bait!'

She was safe. Tareth and her home cave were close. They would not dare to trespass in the weaver's cave. Not with Magnus, the yellow-eyed sea-eagle, on his perch outside.

Maia reached into her woven bag and held out a shellfish. The eagle glared at her as she emptied the limpets she had prised from the rocks and dropped them near him. Magnus leapt from his perch, the silk jesses on his legs bright strands of colour against the limestone ledge. Delicately he started picking over the shells.

Tareth would take him hunting before sun-sleep. They would launch the dugout and row far beyond the headland. The eagle would fish and later, if the moon was bright, while the Cliff Dwellers dreamed, Tareth would dive into the dark sun-deeps to collect the shells he crushed to make his weaving colours. And, as always, she would kneel above in the boat, counting the heartbeats and the iridescent ribbon of bubbles drifting to the surface, waiting for his gasping, exhausted return.

Maia shivered. She hated the moon track. Hated waiting alone until Tareth's head broke the surface of the water and he dragged himself into the dugout, his skin bright with the gleaming sea-jewels which drifted in vast trailing shoals, turning the sun-deeps silver. She was afraid the water would keep him. She was too old to sleep snuggled safely in her furs as if she was still a child. He needed her to help him. If she was not a coward, terrified of the sea, she would dive for him deep beneath the moon track. If only she could breathe like a fish, dive deep like the lizards, tumble and fight in the waves like the weed boys. But she couldn't. She sank like a stone in the water. She was useless.

Maia looked over the sun-deeps. She could see the huge lizard swimming strongly into the bay, its head held out of the water. Safe. She spun into the coolness of the cave.

She could hear the scrape of the wooden sledge as Tareth pushed himself across the floor, throwing the weft rod through the warp as he worked at his loom. The spicy smell of fish stew made her mouth water. Had Tareth had time to cook small salty dumplings to go with it? Maia felt a stab of guilt that she had spent time dreaming on the headland, watching the wind patterns on the water and hunting for the lizard scrape with its clutch of eggs, instead of gathering the roots that she had been sent to find. But she had found the eggs. She hugged the thought to herself. And she would do better tomorrow. She would cook Tareth the flatbreads and baked seabird he loved, to go with the roasted roots she would collect early before she went back to the scrape. Before she stole a lizard egg. Maia felt her heart jump at the thought.

'Maia,' Tareth called.

At the sound of his voice, the sea-eagle flew to the entrance of the cave. Tareth turned to watch and the eagle feather bound into the end of the braid in his dark hair brushed his shoulders.

'Magnus.'

The eagle strutted into the cave and perched at the foot of the sledge. Tareth leaned forward to caress its head. The eagle bobbed with pleasure. Then spread his wings over Tareth's twisted leg, lying useless on the sledge, so that Tareth could stroke the plumage on his back.

Tareth looked up at Maia, noticed her stormy expression and sighed.

'We have a guest,' he warned.

'Maia.' A short, plump woman in a saffron coloured shift stepped from the gloom. 'I brought Tareth some fish stew. I made too much for just Razek and me.'

Selora! Maia was suddenly less hungry.

'And blueberry flatbreads. Fresh baked, as you like them.'

They were Maia's favourite. She would often burn her mouth gobbling the hot, bubbling treat straight from the bake-stone before her breath had time to cool them. Her mouth watered. Maia scowled at her own weakness. What did Selora want? It was the second time this moon-set that she had invaded their home. The last time she had come with her broom and had swept the cave. She had dared touch the mounds of wool and bundles of threads lying on the floor by Tareth's loom where he could reach them as he worked.

Interfering, gossiping Selora. She'd be better occupied

keeping her headstrong son from stoning lizards than cooking and cleaning the Weaver's cave. There were more important things to do than sweeping floors: cliff-climbing for gulls' eggs, honey-hunting in the bee-cleft, cocoon-gathering in the high, treacherous moth-garden. No one else could scramble up the cliffs, finding the invisible hand and footholds she had made, not even Razek and his weed boys.

Tareth sighed again as he read the emotions chasing across Maia's face.

'Selora has made berry flatbreads for your Naming Day,' he chided.

Maia gritted her teeth. 'Thank you, Selora.'

Selora swished her skirts and sidled round the end of the sledge, wary of the eagle. 'And perhaps we may join with you to celebrate Maia's name giving.'

'No,' groaned Maia, under her breath.

Tareth glanced at her. 'Maia will be pleased to share her Naming Day. You and Razek are welcome.'

'No they're not,' thought Maia. She glared at Tareth. What was he thinking? It was her Naming Day. The day that marked her thirteenth star-shift. She should be the one to choose who she shared it with. And she chose Tareth. She'd never choose to share blueberries or anything else with Razek.

Selora was always trying to get Tareth to take an interest in her son. Did she think Tareth would take him on as weaver apprentice or gift him their cave? Maia almost laughed. As if Razek would exchange his life as Weed Master to work at a loom. She hid her grin behind her hand. But Selora was not looking at her. She was watching Tareth as he gently stroked his eagle.

'Thank you, Tareth,' Selora's smile was triumphant.

'It'll be good to have company,' said Tareth.

Maia frowned at him. Everyone knew that Selora was ripe for another mate. Once Razek became hand-fast, his mother would leave their cave. Was Selora planning to move in, to become her new mother?

'Never!' thought Maia fiercely. She didn't need a mother. She had Tareth. She needed no one else. She had no memory of a mother, no memory of anything before the caves. It was as if there had never been a has-been. Yet sometimes Maia heard Tareth whispering strange names as she lay listening to him weaving long after he thought her asleep. Whispers that seemed like dreams and were never repeated at sun-wake.

'Sun-sleeps are lonely when the young leave,' agreed Selora. 'And Maia will soon be hand-fast.'

Maia felt her stomach churn. Hand-fast? Not yet. No way.

'Not yet, surely?' said Tareth.

'The girls often leap the hand-fast fires on their Naming Day,' said Selora comfortably. 'Seeker will come to speak with you, Maia. He'll tell you which man has chosen to leap with you.'

Maia's eyes narrowed. 'But I'm not a Cliff Dweller,' she said. 'And I've other things to do on my Naming Day.'

'As does everyone.' Razek strolled into the cave.

He had smoothed his hair, noticed Maia, until it was as glossy as a raven's wing.

'We've driven off the lizard, but the weed beds will need cleaning,' announced Razek.

Unasked, he stooped to pick up one of the woven bags Tareth and she had stuffed with leaf-fall.

'Sea-rise hasn't washed the storm scourings away. The beds will have to be cleaned.'

'Razek will have to summon all the Cliff Dwellers to help,' said Selora proudly.

Razek nodded. 'Everyone will be needed in the weed beds. Even girls.' He glanced at Maia. 'With the exception of the Weaver, of course.'

Maia felt as if she had swallowed a sea urchin. She choked on prickles of anger. How dare Razek suggest that Tareth wasn't needed. Did he think Tareth's twisted leg made him unable to work in the kelp beds? He would paddle the dugout to the deeps at the edge of the levee. Everyone knew it was the most dangerous place to work since a sudden sea-surge could drag you out and drown you. Tareth never shirked any of the communal work. He always worked harder and longer than any of them.

'Thank you, Razek,' said Tareth mildly. 'It's good to know you can do without me.'

A rush of blood stained Razek's face. 'Weaver. I didn't mean . . .' he mumbled.

'And I've other work to do,' said Tareth.

'And so does the Weaver's daughter.' Maia glared at Razek. 'I'm sure you can manage without me too.'

Maia felt Tareth look at her. She held her breath, but he didn't ask her what her tasks were though. He'd given her none. After a storm everyone was supposed to help collect any scourings that the Untouchables and their lizards had not harvested before it drifted into the weed beds. But she wanted to return to the lizard scrape. She had to be there when the eggs hatched. And they were hard now. Another sun-sleep and she could be too late.

She shivered at the thought of what she was planning to do. Stealing a lizard egg was forbidden. The lizards belonged to the Lizard Keeper.

'I've berries to collect,' she said. It wasn't a lie. She did have to climb to the thorny garden, just not before the next sea-fall.

'I'll help harvest the berries once the weed beds are cleaned,' offered Razek. He glanced at Maia. 'If Maia will take me.'

Maia took a breath, but Tareth forestalled her and shook his head.

'It's a job for small hands,' he spread his own long fingers wide. Shadows like feeding herring danced across the walls. 'The berries cluster among thorns. My hands, and yours, are too large.' He smiled at Maia. 'And the cuts fester if you're scratched. You could lose a finger, if Healer cannot drain the poison.'

He didn't say that he had an earthenware jar of cool, green salve that drew the poison and healed the seeping cuts. Maia felt a jolt of triumph. He didn't want Razek to be shown the way up onto the cliffs. The moth-garden, its entrance guarded by the thorn bushes, was their secret. Soon she must collect the hidden cocoons before the moon-moths chewed their way free and spoiled the silk.

'And Maia climbs like a squirrel. The path is long and dangerous.'

'I'm not afraid,' said Razek.

'Nor was I,' said Tareth. 'A mistake.' He glanced down at his leg. 'A wise man knows when it's good to fear, eh Magnus?'

He stroked the sea-eagle's breast. The eagle blinked its fierce amber eyes.

'I must fly Magnus. He's growing lazy.' The eagle lowered his beak to gently scratch Tareth's hand. 'I'll hunt him across the cliffs at sun-wake.'

Selora shivered. 'Then I'll not go gathering mushrooms.'

'He'll not harm a Cliff Dweller,' said Tareth. 'But he'll attack a stranger.'

Maia glanced at Tareth and wondered if he could see the secrets behind her eyes. Did he know about the lizard scrape and that she'd planned to take the eagle there?

Would Magnus find the Untouchable boy who had watched her and attack him?

Two

Kodo saw the lizard swimming slowly towards the sandspit and the sun-deeps beyond. He recognised the crimson crest. It was Doon. She must have escaped through the holding nets again. The storm had carried its stinking quilt of flotsam along the coast. Doon would have smelled it and wanted first pickings. When she was hungry, it took more than the nets to keep her in the compound with the other lizards. Kodo groaned. He was supposed to have checked the nets at sun-wake, after the storm. He would be in trouble again.

He wondered if he should paddle after her to shepherd her back to the others. But, something had upset her. Her raised crest was a warning. If Doon was red-angry she could turn on him and sink his dugout with one sweep of her tail.

He sat and listened to the water slapping softly against his dugout. The setting sun threw a net of gold across the still water. He dipped his paddle into the sun-deeps, breaking the perfect lizard-skin sheen of the water and held it aloft, saluting the flaming sky and a skein of birds flying home to roost, a dark arrowhead against the sunset.

She had been there again. The flame-headed girl. Near the lizard scrape. He had hidden behind spiky gorse bushes and watched her. He had waited as the sun slowly measured out the passing sea-fall, burning his skin with licks of fire until he'd thought he would melt. But he hadn't dared move in case she saw him. Fire was dangerous and so was she. She should not be at the lizard scrape. It was his place. The Untouchables' place. And because he'd been stunned by the sun and Flame Head he hadn't checked the lizard eggs. More trouble.

Ootey would want to know if the soft shells had hardened, ready for hatching, and if he'd laid his ear against the eggs to listen for the faint tapping of the tiny hook-like tooth battering against the shell as the baby lizard struggled to break out. But he couldn't, not while she was there.

Kodo shivered as the drops of water ran from his paddle and dripped onto his hot, sunburned skin. He was afraid; afraid of the Cliff Dweller, even if she was a girl. Afraid, even though she lay as still as a basking snake in the grass at the edge of the lizard scrape. So still that she could have been asleep. He'd been too afraid to leave his hiding place. He was an Untouchable. Nothing. No one.

His fear gave way to indignation. The lizards, the eggs, the lizard scrape belonged to the Lizard People.

Kodo sighed. Now he would have to slip away from the

stilt village before sun-wake to check the eggs. He would have to find his way through the cold, eerie mists hanging over the water before they were burned off by the rising sun. He didn't dare think about what would happen if the eggs hatched before he carried them back to the hatchery. If the gulls found the slithery newborns as they tumbled from their shells.

Kodo flinched, already feeling the weight of his grandfather's stick across his back if any hatchlings were killed. Yes, that's what he must do. Go early, before sun-wake, taking the warm, sand-filled hatching basket with him, and bring the eggs back.

The golden surface of the water split as his fisher-bird surfaced, a fish flailing in its beak. The bird hopped onto the prow of the dugout, dropping its catch. Kodo leaned to scoop it up and drop it into the keep-net. For a young bird, Tuctuc had done well. The fisher-bird spread its wings to dry, posing like the figureheads on the traders' ships which sailed up the river with the sea-rise.

Kodo laughed. 'Big dreams for a small fisher-bird.'

He had dreams too. One day he would become a trader, would sail a boat along the river to trade with the stilt village. How proud his mother, Jakarta, would be. Even old Ootey's complaints would be silenced.

He thrust his paddle into the water and sent the dugout skimming towards the thin wisp of smoke curling above the cluster of stilt houses at the far end of the sandbank. The sluggish sea-rise bumped him gently against the net platform of his home.

He could hear Jakarta singing. No sound of grumbling.

Good. Ootey wasn't home yet. He tied the dugout to the bone mooring ring and, grabbing the keep-net and his fishing spear, scrambled onto the net platform, avoiding the swags of fishing nets hanging there to dry. Tuctuc flapped onto the mooring post and started to preen his night-black feathers.

His mother looked up as he padded barefoot into the smoky hut. It smelled, as always, of fish and rope, resinous wood and baby. His mother unlatched the child from her breast and laid it in the cradle of woven hazel wands. She fastened the edges of her tunic together, the gold of her stab pin glinting in the firelight.

The pin was her hand-fast gift. After Kodo's father had died she had treasured it. Ootey had wanted to trade it for nets and the timber posts the traders brought to the Solstice Gathering. Jakarta had won that argument and kept her pin. One day, Kodo promised himself, he would trade for a pair of gold earrings to match the pin.

'Where have you been?'

Kodo gave her the dripping keep-net. 'The bird fished well.'

'You think that will help Ootey forget that you haven't mended the nets?'

Kodo grinned. 'Perhaps if Grandfather has to use his breath to cool baked fish, he will have none left to scold.'

Jakarta scooped the largest fish from the haul, killed and gutted it and laid it on the hot flat stone on the hearth. 'You expect too much, little fisher.'

'Not if he has the baked roots I can smell cooking and hot chay for his aching bones.'

Jakarta placed two more fish on the stone. Kodo's mouth watered as the fish sizzled, the skin blistering brown and crisp. His mother spread herbs over the fish skin. The remembered smell of the summer horse meadows tickled Kodo's nose.

'Did you bring the eggs?' she asked.

Kodo hid his hands behind his back and crossed his thumbs. 'They were still soft,' he lied.

His mother pushed a basket closer to the hot stones on the hearth. 'Ootey thought they would be ready. I've been keeping the basket warm for you.'

Kodo squatted beside the hearth and stirred the sand in the reed basket. It slid warm and soft through his fingers.

'I'll go at sun-wake and collect them.'

His mother looked at him. Kodo wondered if she'd guessed that he'd lied about the eggs.

'If you take them after sun-high, it will be a poor clutch,' she said.

Kodo picked up a woody stem of rosemary. He pushed it deep into the fire. The sudden swirl of smoke made his eyes water.

'I saw a Cliff Dweller. The flame head one.'

He winced as his mother grabbed his arm. 'And . . . ?' she asked fiercely. Disturbed by her voice, the baby stirred in the cradle.

'And . . . ?' echoed Kodo sullenly, rubbing his arm.

'Did she know you were watching? Spying?'

'I wasn't.'

Kodo wished he'd said nothing about the girl. At least his mother was too upset to ask where he'd seen her. Flame

Head shouldn't have been at the lizard scrape. The storm would be nothing to Ootey's rage if he learned that a Cliff Dweller had found the clutch of eggs. For his own sake, he would say nothing.

'Did she see you?' demanded Jakarta.

Kodo showed her his arm. It was criss-crossed with a mesh of red scratches from the bushes. 'No. I hid.'

'Good,' said his mother. 'Stay away from the Cliff Dwellers.'

Three

The summons of the conch shell skittered along the cliff-face, fracturing the drifting mists. Magnus shuffled irritably on his perch. Maia huddled deeper into her sleeping furs trying to ignore the noise. Trust Razek to call all the Cliff Dwellers out so early. Well, she wasn't going to jump to obey the summons he was bellowing through the conch shell. It was her Naming Day. A day to spend as she pleased. And she'd made plans. She'd make Tareth a cup of warm chay to chase away the sun-wake chill when he woke and then she was off. Off to the lizard scrape to see if the eggs had hatched. She had to make the journey to the Watcher after sun-high, so she must hurry.

She had filled a sack with the things she needed: the flint knife Tareth had made and taught her to use, a chunk of sticky honeycomb, double-wrapped in leaves to stop it oozing into the bag, two apples from their dwindling store, a handful of nuts and a baked root saved from their meal. She had hidden the last blueberry flatbread on the stone ledge behind the pottery jar stuffed with chunks of golden honeycomb. She'd eat that instead of the seed porridge she would make for Tareth's breakfast. She would leave the porridge keeping warm by the side of the fire and slip away before he woke properly and asked too many questions about how she was going to spend her day.

Maia wriggled out of her sleeping furs, threw herbs and a lump of weed curd into the blackened metal pot, tipped in a beaker of water and set the pot over the fire. Grabbing a handful of hair and twisting it behind her head, she knelt and blew at the embers until she had a flickering flame which she carefully fed with strands of dried weed and then a few thorn sticks. At least Razek's summons had wakened her. She would have longer to hike to the lizard scrape and steal a hatchling.

She tiptoed into the cool dimness of the store cave where she had hidden her sack, retrieved it and found the blueberry flatbread, stuffing it greedily into her mouth. Selora was a good cook. It must be what made Razek taller than most of the weed boys. He was man height already.

Carefully measuring fistfuls of seeds and oats from the pottery urn into a dented cooking pot, she carried it and her sack into the cave.

She could see Magnus strutting outside, waiting for Tareth to wake and feed him. He would frighten off anyone who came near. She didn't want any witnesses today. She thought about the curly-haired boy she'd seen hiding in the bushes. The Untouchable would be scared of the eagle. He would stay away if he saw Magnus spiralling on the updrafts above the lizard scrape.

She dropped her sack among the sleeping furs, where it couldn't be seen by Tareth if he woke, and stirred the warming chay. The smell of melting curds and summer herbs tickled her nostrils. Moving the chay aside, she pushed the porridge pot over the flames. If she were swift, maybe she could gulp down a bowl of porridge before she left. She might have to share part of her packed meal with a ravenous baby lizard. She pulled out the bone stirrer, blew on it and licked, scalding her tongue in her haste.

'Maia.'

Maia almost dropped the stirrer. Tareth had propped himself up on one elbow and was watching her across the cave.

'Up so early?' His gaze swept across her tumbled furs.

For a moment she thought he'd seen the bulge made by her sack and guessed what it was. Tareth always saw the things she wanted to hide. But he was looking beyond her to the entrance of the cave where Magnus was preening his tail feathers. He smiled.

'Early risers, both of you.'

The conch wailed again. Tareth grimaced. Pushing aside his furs he hauled himself into a sitting position and pulled on his tunic.

'I see Razek's impatient.'

He swung himself onto his sledge and propelled it across the floor to the rain-filled stone cistern at the back of the cave. Dipping in his hands, he splashed water over his face.

'But perhaps he can wait until we've eaten the porridge I can smell.' The sledge skidded back across the stone floor. 'And hot chay,'

He watched as Maia poured chay into a beaker. 'I'd promised myself that today you'd be allowed to sleep and that I'd cook for you.'

Maia grinned. 'No one could sleep late with Razek bellowing like a bull seal.'

Tareth wrapped his hands round the pottery cup and lifted it in a toast.

'The sun's greetings, a wind's blessing and the earth's song be yours.'

Tareth's invocation sent a shiver down Maia's spine. Today she would find her chosen name. She wasn't sure she was ready for that. Not ready for the changes, the decisions, the responsibilities which must follow the choosing and taking of a name as surely as sea-fall followed sea-rise. Definitely not ready to choose a partner to leap with her over the hand-fast fires.

Quelled by the gravity in his tone she touched her forehead with her cupped hand, 'And to you, Father.'

Tareth scooped porridge into bowls. 'How are you intending to spend the rest of sun-wake?'

So he did know she'd lied to Razek about collecting berries. Maia blushed. 'We need more rush lights. I thought I'd go to the marshes,' she said. 'And perhaps see the horses.' When she was not roaming the beaches or exploring the limestone caves and scrubby uplands beyond the cliffs, the marshes with their herds of horses and the floating huts of the Horse Guardians were her favourite place. As a result their cave was always well-stocked with the tough reeds Tareth made into slender glows.

Tareth stirred the porridge, sniffing the steam with pleasure. 'Too far.'

'Not if I leave now.'

'And avoid the weed bed cleaning?'

'I could take Magnus for company,' she suggested innocently. 'He could hunt across the marsh. You said he's getting fat and lazy.'

Tareth shook his head. 'Not even a Naming Day will excuse you from cleaning duties, Maia. The weed beds come first. You know that. The Cliff Dwellers depend on the beds.'

'But we don't,' protested Maia. 'You are Weaver. The silk and shells are our concern. Not seaweed.'

But she could sense the inevitable, could see it in Tareth's eyes. If only the blaring conch hadn't woken him too. Her day was going to be ruined all because Razek wanted to play Weed Master and boss everyone about.

'Weed beds,' she sulked. 'What difference will I make? He has the weed boys and the rest of the Cliff Dwellers to help. He doesn't need me.'

Tareth sighed. 'If you tried a little harder . . .'

'What? To be like them? To grow webbed toes? To think of nothing but weed?

'Green, red and brown. Kelp in the dark-deeps, red in the sun-deeps, green near the shore,' she chanted, reciting the lessons drilled into the cave children.

'Be like them and never, ever want to leave the cliffs? To think going to the Solstice Gather is a great adventure?'

Tareth's lips twitched as he bit back a grin at the look on her face. 'Webbed toes? Is that the fate of our Weed Master? To grow frog feet? Poor Razek. Should we warn Selora? She might be less puffed up about her wonderful son, the finest and youngest Weed Master ever, if she knew what awaits his feet.'

Maia felt her bad mood evaporating.

'He spends his life paddling.'

Tareth's failed attempt to hide his grin encouraged her to make one last try to get her own way.

'No one will miss me. And it's my Naming Day.'

Tareth gave in, but only a little. 'I'll speak to Razek and arrange for us to finish working in the weed beds early. We must visit the Watcher after sun-high. No one will expect you to avoid that.'

Maia pulled a face. On their Naming Day, everyone visited Sabra, the terrifying old woman in the sky-high cairn guarded by four bleached skulls and a ragged flock of red-legged crows. If she was in the mood, Sabra read her stones. If she was pleased with your gift, if your name had been well-chosen, good would come. If the Watcher had no name for her, she'd run away and work in the Marsh Lords' holdfast. Or, better still, learn to care for the horses on the marshes. Just as long as the Horse Guardians' floating huts didn't make her feel as if she was in Tareth's boat and seasick.

'But,' continued Tareth, 'even Sabra must wait until we've done our part. We owe the Cliff Dwellers our lives. Help in the weed beds is little enough by way of payment.'

'Collecting storm waste?' snorted Maia. But she knew when she was beaten.

'Collecting storm waste,' agreed Tareth firmly. 'After all, weren't we washed up in a storm too? Who knows what the waves have carried to shore this time.'

Four

Kodo stretched his aching back. Ahead of him, his grandfather Ootey worked tirelessly, repairing the lizard net. He was a hard taskmaster. He had tumbled Kodo from his sleeping mat at sun-wake and barely allowing him time to eat the cold fish wrap Jakarta had made, had loaded him with bone spikes, hanks of rope and bundles of twisted cord, and hustled him from the hut.

Behind him, the village lay in the sea mist. Wisps of smoke seeped from the reed-thatched roofs. A few women were already awake and tending their cooking fires. Stomach rumbling, Kodo wished that his grandfather was like the other Untouchables and that he, Kodo, was still swaddled in sleep, while Jakarta blew the embers of the fire alight and the hut filled with the smell of porridge. But the lizards always came first. Ootey was determined that the roving Doon would have no chance to escape from the enclosure again. So before anything else, they would have to repair the lizard nets.

'Stop dreaming, boy,' bellowed Ootey. He twisted and knotted thick cords across a tear, his gnarled hands deft and strong as he tugged the knots tight. He pulled, testing the repair and grunted. 'That'll hold.'

'Till next time,' muttered Kodo to himself.

No net, not even Ootey's cunningly crafted one, could hold an adult lizard determined to escape. Kodo could hear the reptiles waking. Doon was grunting. No doubt she had stuffed herself full to bursting during her escape. She would be off her feed and wanting to sleep. Kodo hoped Ootey would remember that he was going to collect the lizard eggs and not expect him to work in the floating rubbish beds with an unwilling Doon.

'She'll be too idle to work at sea-rise,' grumbled Ootey.

Kodo hid a grin. Ootey's complaints were always predictable.

His grandfather glowered at him. 'You should have checked the nets after the storm, boy. The lizards are always restless in bad weather. They'll break through the nets if they can.'

'Sorry, Grandfather.'

'Too late to be sorry.' Ootey frowned. 'You'll never make a Lizard Keeper if you don't understand them, boy.'

'No, Grandfather.' Now was not the time to tell Ootey that he didn't want to look after the lizards. He wasn't like Ootey, content to breed and train them to pull the net booms out into the sun-deeps to collect the sea-drifting flotsam. He was going to find a place on a traders' ship, to become a trader himself one day.

Ootey cleared his throat and spat. 'She'll have got the taste for freedom now. But once she has the hatchlings, she'll be content.'

Kodo slipped his netting spike into his belt. 'I'll go and collect the eggs.'

'Net first,' said Ootey. He handed Kodo a coil of rope. 'We need to check the far net too.'

Kodo suppressed a groan, slung the rope across his shoulder and slipped into the water. Dragging in a deep breath, he sank below the surface and, kicking strongly, swam down to the seabed. Water roared in his ears, salt stung his eyes. The net, strung with streamers of weed, swayed in the current. Kodo clung to it and pulled himself across the knotted web, feeling for breaks. None.

His feet reached for the sand, ready to kick up to the surface. A burst of bubbles and a warble of sound swirled around him as Doon arrived and bumped against the knotted ropes, bouncing Kodo off the net. He drifted away.

Doon blew a stream of bubbles after him. She wanted to play. Kodo swam back to the net. Reaching through it, he scratched Doon's bony eye ridges. Her rumble of pleasure trembled across the current. She pushed her nose through the net. Kodo lowered his face to hers. Their air bubbles mingled and spun upwards. Kodo gave her nose a pat and lungs bursting, arrowed upwards. As he surfaced, gasping for air, he felt the water surging round his feet.

Doon broke through next to him, reared into the air and flopped back. Kodo saw a flying wall of spray hit Ootey, soaking him to the skin.

'Aahhh!' roared Ootey.

Kodo paddled in and dripped ashore. Ootey was still spluttering with rage. 'The sooner she has young to look after the better.'

Kodo could hear Doon's belly rumbling as she waded out of the shallows. It sounded like lizard laughter. His own stomach growled.

'Far net's fine. I'll fetch the eggs,' said Kodo. He could jog back to the hut, collect the egg basket and escape for the day. 'It's time to put them in the hatchery.'

Ootey twisted water from his tunic. 'You'll feed the lizards. Then you can line the hatching circle with dry sand. After that you can put Doon in the hatchery.' He wiped his wrist across the water dripping from the end of his nose. 'Then you can go and fetch the eggs.'

'But Grandfather, it'll be gone sun-high.' Kodo thought of the hot slog across the rocks to the lizard scrape. Would any of the eggs have hatched in the heat? He knew he should have carried them home. If only he hadn't been frightened away by the flame-headed girl.

'The eggs will be hot,' he added. He might not want to be a Lizard Keeper, but even he knew that it was better not to move eggs that were close to hatching. A sudden change in temperature wasn't good for them.

'Then you can wait with them until the sun cools,' said Ootey. 'Get your mother to line the carrying bag with fur before you leave.' He squelched across the lizard pound and set off towards the village. 'Don't stand there dreaming. The sooner that lizard has her eggs, the better.'

Five

Tiny fish nibbled Maia's toes. Green weed curled round her calves. She felt the tide-sculpted sand ridges beneath the soles of her bare feet. They made it hard to balance as she hooked a bundle of feathers and bone out of the water.

Maia shoved the dripping, slimy mass into the bag slung across her shoulder. Gingerly she pushed it off her stick. Her fingers curled into claws, trying to avoid touching the stinking waste. She didn't dare imagine what she had just scooped from the weeds with the forked dredging stick Razek had given her.

She straightened her aching back. All around, the weed boys were bent double fishing out bits of debris. They were working faster than her. What had been a straight line of weed cleaners stretching across the weed beds was now a broken wing of sullen children.

Further away Maia could see the adults moving across

the deeper weed beds. Women with their skirts caught in their belts showed flashes of bare leg and giggled as they paddled through the weed. Snatches of song wafted across the water. Amazing, thought Maia. But perhaps being knee-deep in water under a bright sun was better than being confined to a smoky cave.

The smell of weed smoke hung on the air, mingling with the mouth-watering smell of baked fish. She turned to see Selora, cooking on a bake-stone set up at the edge of the beach. Close by, a black pot of steaming chay sat over one of the fire-pits Tareth had dug before paddling his punt out to the deeper waters at the edge of the levees.

Other women were making flatbread. Patting the dough flat between their clapping palms, they twirled each handful in the air as if they were Gather jugglers, then tossed them onto the baking stone. Maia's mouth watered. She could hardly wait for Selora to bang on the black cooking pot and summon them to eat. It seemed forever since she and Tareth had broken their fast.

Tareth was stretching over the side of his dugout, hauling a huge, dark bundle from the sea, struggling to pull it onboard. Even at this distance she could see his back arch with the effort. She ought to be helping him. Maybe she should climb onto the low stone wall and go out to him. She hesitated. It would mean scrambling past Razek, standing like a Marsh Lord, watching them work.

The swill surged round her knees, disturbed by someone approaching.

'What's the matter, Flame Head? Is the work too hard for the Weaver's daughter?'

'Not if it's easy enough for the Salt Holder's daughter,' retorted Maia as Laya, black-haired and beautiful, even with her mouth twisted in a smirk, waded up to her, skirt trailing in the sea. Didn't Laya care that the salt would stain the deep blue cloth? A blue which took Tareth hours to brew.

Maia sneered. 'Why are you here?'

She knew that the wealthy Salt Holder's only daughter thought the weed cleaning beneath her. Laya always behaved as if she were a Marsh Lord's lady. Once Maia had thought she might be a friend to go exploring caves, climbing cliffs and battling the weed boys. When she'd suggested it, Laya had looked at her as if an Untouchable had dared spit at her.

'I thought you hated the weed beds.'

Laya preened. 'Razek asked father and me to help.' She glanced towards Razek, saw him watching and waved.

Razek ignored her. Maia grinned. In his own way, Razek was as arrogant as Laya.

'And you always do what Razek wants?' mocked Maia. 'Poor, sad Laya.'

Laya flushed. 'So why are *you* here, Flame Head? You're not a Cliff Dweller.'

'Razek doesn't have to ask us for help. We know when we're needed.'

Laya glared and flailed her stick in the water, flicking weed and scraps over Maia.

'Sorry,' she smirked.

'You will be when I push you in,' threatened Maia.

'You wouldn't dare,' said Laya, but took a step back in case.

Maia dropped her stick and grabbed Laya's shoulder. Laya screamed.

'Maia! Laya!' roared Razek from his vantage point on the levee wall. 'Keep up.'

Maia scowled. She thought about the fuss there would be if she dumped Laya in the storm-swill. Thought about how angry Tareth would be. Thought about being hauled in disgrace to see Elder. Heads were turning in her direction. Reluctantly she let go and picked up her floating stick.

'Lucky for you,' she muttered.

'And for you, Flame Head.'

Laya fell into step beside her. She kept just out of reach of Maia's stick. They trawled slowly forwards in silence. Maia snared the corpse of a bloated squid. A foul smell filled the air.

Laya was looking green. 'I didn't think it would be like this.'

'What did you think it would be like? Why did you come?'

'Razek,' muttered Laya.

'Razek?'

'I wanted to see what it's like to help in the weed beds.'

'You want to be a weed boy?' Maia stared at Laya in disbelief.

'Razek isn't a weed boy. He's Weed Master. And one day he'll be even more important. He'll be Elder.'

'Razek? Elder? Never ever.'

'Yes he will. And when he is . . .'

'If he is,' mocked Maia. 'When he's really ancient.'

'He's the youngest Weed Master ever,' said Laya, sounding just like Selora. 'Everyone knows he's going to be Elder. Even father says so.'

'And that makes it true,' scoffed Maia.

'Father's always right.'

'Always? Can he tell the to-come then? Does he know what will happen? Like Sabra.' Maia closed her eyes and swayed in a mock trance. 'Razek the weed boy,' she wailed, 'will lead us all!' She opened her eyes. 'Has your father been to see the Watcher? Has she read him Razek's runes?'

'Can she?' asked Laya.

Maia shrugged, suddenly worried about her own visit to the Watcher. Would Sabra know that she had made fun of her?

'All the Cliff Dwellers say she knows the to-come,' she added.

'Razek will be elected Elder,' said Laya, lifting her chin in a way that made Maia wish she had pushed her under the sea. Laya thought she was so special. 'And we're going to be hand-fast.' Her eyes challenged Maia.

Maia stared at her in astonishment. 'Says who?'

'I do. And father. Razek and I will leap over the fire together.'

Disbelief and relief warred in Maia's chest. Razek would ignore her then. Selora would be so puffed up with her son becoming hand-fast to the wealthy Salt Holder's daughter that she would be too important to become Tareth's mate. Maia felt the warm glow starting in her stomach grow into a grin. And Razek would find himself hand-fast to a beautiful hornet. Laya was probably as bossy as he was. They deserved each other. She started to laugh.

Laya thumped the water with her stick, spraying them both with water and weed. 'What are you laughing at?' she demanded. 'Stop laughing.'

But Maia couldn't.

'Stop it, stop it,' screamed Laya.

'Laya, a cave mate!' hooted Maia.

With hysteria came relief. She'd been so afraid that her Naming Day fate would be the same as the other weed girls. That Tareth would tell her she was to be hand-fast. That her chosen partner would be Razek.

She glanced towards her father.

Something was wrong. He was in trouble. As she watched, the dugout tilted, standing on end. Tareth, encased in weed, was struggling in the embrace of a sea-beast that was half in, half out of the boat. His free arm rose and fell, desperately striking at the writhing creature. The mass seemed to heave itself higher, growing arms, a head. Tareth was being dragged into the sea. Something flashed in the sunlight. A knife.

'Tareth!' screamed Maia.

Throwing off her bag, she plunged forward. Ropes of weed wrapped round her ankle. She lost her footing. Fell. Water flooded into her screaming mouth. Frantically Maia thrashed against the slimy weeds. Gasping, swallowing water, gagging, panicking, she broke free and surfaced.

'Tareth,' she croaked.

She could see Razek running along the levee towards Tareth. She staggered to her feet and waded through the stinking filth that was oozing from her abandoned sack.

Laya was screaming at her, backing away from the raft of debris. Maia ignored her.

'Tareth!'

Horrified, Maia saw the weed monster collapse and smother Tareth, dragging him into the water. The dugout shuddered, rose like a finger pointing to the sky and sank.

Maia floundered to the levee and hauled herself up onto it. She didn't feel the stones and shells scraping flesh off her hands and shins. Then she was running towards the frothing whirlpool that had swallowed Tareth, the dugout and the weed monster.

Razek got there first. Tareth's head appeared. His arm. His shoulders, dark with weed, broke the surface.

Razek was on his knees, reaching. He grabbed Tareth's flailing hand. The water boiled as Tareth surged out of the sea and lay gasping on the embankment.

He rolled over, plunged his arm underwater and tugged at something. The sea-beast's bulk broke the surface. Maia could hear Tareth calling urgently to Razek. Together they hauled the bundle onto the side of the levee. It lay there, inert, streams of water draining from the glistening weed.

Tareth started pulling aside the weed. Maia saw Razek flinch in horror.

'Tareth.' She laid a shaking hand on his shoulder. 'You're safe.'

He coughed, salt water dribbling from his mouth. 'Thanks to Razek.'

The beat of wings announced the arrival of Magnus as he dropped like a stone from the sky. He folded his great wings and hopped clumsily towards Tareth.

Tareth coughed. 'Not this time, old friend,' he rasped.

The eagle ruffled his feathers and started picking over the weeded monster. A wave broke over the levee. The weeds lifted and moved as if alive. A foot appeared. The water bubbled and groaned through the weeds, giving the creature voice. A furred forearm flopped free.

Maia gasped and reached for her knife. 'What is it? Is it alive?' she asked.

Tareth shook his head. He looked at Razek. 'We'll need the others to carry it ashore.'

Razek nodded. He stood and faced the beach. Cupping his hands to his lips he whistled. The sound carried across the weed beds. Maia saw the weed boys scampering towards them. A group of men ran across the beach.

Razek crouched beside Tareth. 'They're coming.'

Maia tried not to look at the mound. But her eyes kept flicking back to it. It smelled of wet hide. Was it a man or a beast? The foot she had seen wore a boot. The arm was that of a bear. The glint beneath the weed was metal.

She looked at Tareth. She had never seen him look so grim. His eyes were like smouldering coals. If he stared any longer at the weed mound, it would burst into flames.

Razek cautiously poked the body. 'What is it, Weaver?'

'Trouble,' said Tareth curtly.

Six

The muttering of the Cliff Dwellers swelled round Razek and Tareth like the noise of an incoming tide. Razek, on his knees, was pulling aside the ropes of bladderwrack tangled round the body on the sand. Maia twisted her way through the crowd and crouched next to Tareth.

'What is it, Weaver?' asked Razek.

'A man from Khandar,' Tareth said.

'Khandar?' queried Elder.

Tareth hesitated. 'A land I once knew.'

'A man?' Razek exposed the bear arm. The hair was matted and thick with sand and weed. A silver arm-ring glinted. 'Or a beast?'

The crowd gasped, swaying back from the body like weed in a surging tide.

'A dead man,' confirmed Tareth. 'From a distant land.'

Elder nodded as if he had known as much. 'No doubt. And swept from his ship in the storm.'

'This won't be the last of them.' Tareth twisted to scan cliffs and the coastline. 'And his beast will be somewhere close. It will come looking for its master. It will kill.'

The crowd groaned as Razek pulled more weed from the dead man and they saw linked metal discs sewn to a leather tunic, gleaming with salt crystals.

'He is Wulf Kin,' said Tareth.

Elder summoned up the courage to touch the bronze discs. 'A wealthy people.'

'Warriors,' said Tareth. 'They sell their skills to the highest bidder.'

Razek had pulled a short curving blade from a studded scabbard. He ran his finger along the edge of the knife.

'Well paid work to have such a weapon.' His voice was laced with envy.

'Usually poisoned,' said Tareth. Razek dropped the knife as if it was red hot. 'And they hunt with wulfen.'

He glanced up at the men standing around him.

'You'll need to search for the body of his beast . . . his wulfen. It will be better for us if it drowned. If it's survived, it will come searching for its master. It's more bear than dog and as vicious as a she-lizard defending her hatchlings.' His eyes searched the cliff again.

Maia followed his gaze. She could see Magnus wheeling in the updrafts. What could the eagle see? This strange beast Tareth was describing, this wulfen?

She felt a chill feather her skin, as if a whisper of air had brushed across her arm. The name awoke echoes in her mind.

A memory of firelight whispers when Tareth thought she slept while he wove the moon-moth silk. Khandar. Wulf Kin. Dreams dissolved in sunlight. Words never spoken in the light.

'There are enough goats on the cliffs to feed it. But you should warn the herders and the Horse Guardians. I've seen . . . heard,' Tareth corrected himself smoothly, 'that they'll even prey on horses. And they'll kill a grown man.'

The crowd muttered. The cooking women had joined them, Selora pushing her way to the front. A woman was sobbing softly. Selora put her arm around her. 'Are none of us safe? Will we be ripped to pieces by beasts?' she demanded. More women began to wail.

Maia glared at Selora. Did she have to panic everyone?

'We will tell the Watcher,' said Elder, struggling to regain authority. 'She can send messages to the Marsh Lords. They will hunt the beast. If it hasn't drowned, like its master.'

He glared at Tareth as if the body of the Wulf Kin as well as his momentary loss of authority was the Weaver's fault.

'No one will go out alone,' he ordered. 'The children will stay close by. They are not to leave the weed beds until we've heard that the beast is found or dead.'

Tareth nodded. 'They don't like water. You'll be safe in the weed beds.'

Maia suddenly thought of the boy from the lizard scrape. Would his village be safe? The lizards must be too big to fall prey to a wild beast. They would protect the village. Her nose winkled as she remembered the time she had sneaked close enough to the village to smell it. The stink of the Untouchables' harvest and the smoke from the burning waste would be enough to keep any danger away.

But when the boy returned to check the lizard eggs, would the beast be lying in wait?

Maia fingered her knife. There was no way she was going to listen to Elder and stay close to the weed beds. She had to return to the lizard scrape. Soon, before the eggs hatched. The beast would not catch her. She could climb like a mountain goat. And she would slither like a hidden snake through the grasses. It wouldn't find her. Maia chewed her lip. And if it did? She slammed her mind shut on the half-thought. She had her knife. She would take Magnus. Tareth's eagle would be more than a match for a wulfen.

She glanced at Tareth. He was white round the mouth. The struggle in the water had been too much for him. She should have been in the dugout helping him. But she was too afraid of the sun-deeps beyond the sea-wall. She'd allowed Razek to bully her into staying with the children because she was afraid of the sun-deeps. She flushed with shame.

She remembered the horror of seeing Tareth dragged under the water. She remembered the flash of silver. She glanced at Tareth's belt and saw that the black hilt of his knife was missing.

Maia frowned. She relived the moment when huge arms had seemed to embrace Tareth. She could see his hand beating at the bulk as the dugout pitched in the swell. Had Tareth been holding his knife then?

She forced herself to look at the corpse. Had it been dead in the water since the storm? Was that fresh blood oozing from beneath the armpit where the gleaming metal scales ended?

'Maia?'

The dark stain was seeping into the fur beneath the armour. It had turned the tunic sodden, blacker than night. Was fresh blood black?

'Maia,' commanded Tareth.

She dragged her gaze to Tareth. His hand lay over his empty dagger sheath. His eyes were sending her a message. Maia swallowed.

'Weaver, I got them.' A small weed boy broke through the crowd and dropped Tareth's crutches by his twisted leg.

'Thank you,' Tareth grabbed the crutches and hoisted himself upright. 'I thought I'd have to crawl across the beach,' he grinned. 'Come Maia. If Elder thinks it's safe, you and I'll take the message to the Watcher. She's expecting us.'

'No one must be alone,' said Elder pompously.

'We won't be alone. We'll be together. And,' added Tareth, as Elder opened his mouth to protest that a lame man and a girl would be no match for a wild beast, 'the eagle will fly with us.'

As if he had heard Tareth's words, Magnus screamed. The challenge bounced off the cliff. The eagle swooped lower, shrieking again.

Elder shivered. 'You know best, Weaver.'

Tareth nodded and turned away. Maia got to her feet and held out her arm as the eagle came diving in. She bit her lip as his talons curved round her forearm, raking her skin. Not for the world would she cry out in front of the others.

The eagle turned his head, his bright eye glaring at her. She forced her lips into a stiff grin.

'Good landing, Magnus,' she gasped. 'Next time cut your toenails first.'

The eagle shuffled his wings, easing his vice-like grip on her arm. He bobbed his head, stretched up and glared at the crowd of Cliff Dwellers. Maia noted with satisfaction that they edged away from her. That would show them that she and Tareth were able to take care of themselves. She braced her arm and turned to walk up the beach.

'Weaver,' said Razek. 'The stranger. What should we do with him?'

Tareth glanced at the dead man. From his expression, Maia thought he was going to tell Razek to throw the body back into the sea.

'In his homeland, his kind burn their dead,' he said. 'Then leave the pyre to be scattered by the winds to the mountains.' His eyes narrowed as he stared out to sea. 'He's far from home. The sea wind will have to suffice. It will be a going of sorts.'

Elder looked unhappy. He glanced at the pyramid of driftwood and weed that the cooking women had been slowly building on the beach. 'The hand-fast fire should not be used for death.'

'Nor should a dead stranger be at the feast, when we leap through the fire,' added Razek. He glanced at Maia. Did she know about Laya's boast that she would leap with him across the fire before sun-sleep?

'What are we to do, Weaver?' he asked.

Tareth adjusted the crutches under his arms. 'Carry the Wulf Kin to the cliff-top and light his death fire there. The wind will carry away his leavings. It would be a kindness he would not have given you. The Wulf Kin leave their prey for the scavengers. They don't care how their victims pass to the Otherworld.' He looked down at the corpse. 'He's been dead for days. His fire can wait for sun-wake.'

'Burn a body?' Elder shook his head at the thought of such disrespect. 'We will be judged by our dealings with the dead.'

Tareth shrugged. 'Fire is their chosen way,' he said.

'The stranger shall not lie in the Bone Caves,' decided Elder. 'He isn't one of us. But, he shall have his fire if that is the way of his tribe.' He glanced at the muttering crowd. 'He has been dead for days. His death fire can wait until sun-wake,' he announced.

Tareth bowed his head. 'As always, you are wise and strong, Elder.'

Elder smiled wryly. 'And, as always, your words show me the way, Weaver. Give my greeting to the Watcher. Tell her that we must speak soon.'

He studied the Wulf Kin. Flies were already settling on the waxen face and buzzing in the mounds of seaweed strewn beside the dead man.

'Soon. When this trouble is past. We'll look for her messenger birds and hope that she will tell us that all will be well for the Solstice Gather.'

Seven

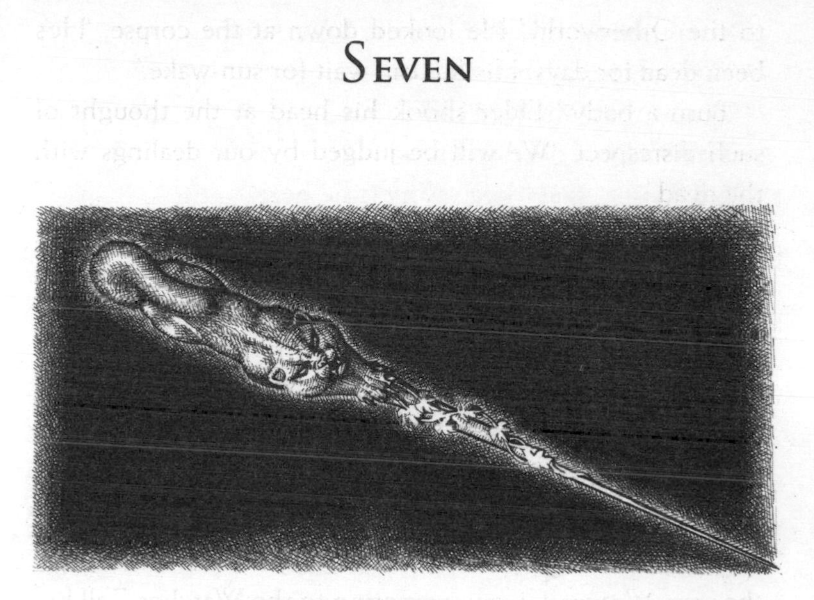

'Well?' said Maia. She lowered her arm so that Magnus could jump onto his perch. She licked the talon scratches on her forearm. Being an eagle perch hurt.

Tareth hauled himself out of the basket in which he had swung hand over hand up the cliff-face.

He stooped to caress the head of his eagle. 'Well?' he mimicked.

Maia frowned. Surely she could be trusted with his secrets? After all, on the beach, he had told Elder that she was still going to the Watcher. That meant he thought her strong enough to cope with any danger that lay on the cliff-top track.

'You've lost your knife,' she said.

Tareth turned, his eagle feather fluttered.

'A pity. It was a fine blade. The sun-deeps claimed it. I'll have to barter for another at the Gather.'

Maia tried again. 'Who are the Wulf Kin?'

'Warriors from Khandar.'

'I know that. You told Elder that.'

'That's all you need to know.'

'No it's not,' said Maia. 'Why is he here?'

'I can't ask. He's dead.' Tareth propelled himself into the cave, leaving a trail of seawater.

Maia took a shaky breath. 'Dead . . . because you killed him?'

'He died in the weeds. The sun-deeps killed him.'

Maia shut her eyes. 'After you stabbed him?'

There was a long silence. Maia screwed up her face trying to make the words she had just said disappear. Eventually she opened her eyes. Tareth had turned his back on her. He was unlacing the thongs that fastened his tunic.

'The Wulf Kin drowned.' His voice was muffled as he peeled off the sopping garment.

'Find dry clothes. Sabra isn't expecting water-logged rats.'

Maia went into the sleeping cave. Shivering, she wriggled out of her soaking clothes and burrowed in the chest of woven hazel wands for dry clothing.

'A clean tunic, Maia,' called Tareth. 'And a kirtle, not boy's clothes for your Naming Day.'

Was she expected to scramble up the cliffs wearing a skirt, thought Maia crossly. Did he think she was Laya? Was this to be her fate now? To be bundled in skirts, to bind up her hair and put away the freedom and clothes of childhood?

She didn't have to go to the Watcher. She wouldn't go. She would refuse to leave the cave. She would stay hidden until everyone had forgotten her and her Naming Day. Her life was ruined.

Naked as a gull's egg, she dived under the sleeping furs. Her feet hit the sack she'd hidden earlier. She would never get to the lizard scrape now. She pulled her feet up, hugged her knees to her chest and sulked.

'Maia!'

She lay still under the furs.

'There's nothing to be afraid of. Surely you don't believe the stories that the Cliff Dwellers tell to frighten naughty children?'

'I'm not afraid,' she muttered.

'Then don't behave as if you are. The Cliff Dwellers will be waiting to sing the start of your Naming Day walk. Will you let them think you're afraid? Afraid of what the Watcher will choose for you?'

Maia could feel her breath warming the dark beneath the furs. Her face was burning. She wasn't afraid. She wasn't cowed by the stories Selora and the other women told. Tales of a black-hearted hag who hung wicked children in the trees round her cairn. And then left them there as bait for her red-legged crows.

'I'm not afraid,' she repeated.

'Good.'

'And the to-come is mine to choose,' she claimed rashly.

She lay still until she heard Tareth leave the sleeping cave. She sat up.

Tareth had left a new blue skirt and over-tunic at the end of her sleeping bench. Gleaming on the soft fabric lay a silver stab-pin. Maia thrust the furs aside and picked it up. A snarling wild cat entwined in a flowering vine lay in her palm. Her finger traced the curve and swirls of silver. It was a gift beyond price. Her hands trembled. The wild cat looked as if he would leap from the flowers into her hand.

When she stepped hesitantly into the cave Tareth was sitting on his sledge, wearing his best black tunic, untying the leather fastenings of his back-sack.

'I'm ready.'

Tareth glanced up at her. 'So I see,' he said drily.

Maia blushed. 'I wasn't afraid. I didn't want to dress like a girl, like Laya,' she confessed.

Maia swished the long skirt as she had seen Laya do, when she had sat in their cave, taking care that her fine clothes did not touch the floor.

'Nor such a fine dress,' she said.

A tiny smile twitched at the corner of Tareth's mouth. 'You are the Weaver's daughter. She'll be jealous.'

Maia grinned. 'She'll be spitting sparks.'

She felt a surge of relief. Tareth had forgiven her.

'Thank you for the gift.' She touched the pin which fastened her tunic.

'There's one more. The clothes may be like Laya's, but she'll never wear eagle feathers.'

He held up two eagle feathers. Strands of silk thread were bound around the quills. This was what she had most desired. She crouched beside the sledge. Tareth fastened the feathers in her hair. If she turned her head she could see the tips touching her shoulder.

'Magnus gave them willingly . . . with barely a shriek.'

'Then I'll collect more limpets.'

'We'll need a gift for the Watcher.' Tareth lifted down the honey jar and peered inside. 'We've used more than I thought. We may as well take the whole pot. Sabra has a sweet tooth. You'll have to collect more honey soon, Maia.'

And visit the lizard scrape on the way to the honey cliff, thought Maia.

She watched Tareth check the seal on the jar. He tightened the twine holding the thin leather skin across the neck of the pot.

'With luck she'll be pleased with your gift and read you a good Naming Day.'

'Will she tell me if my father lost his knife fighting?'

Tareth's busy hands stilled. 'If you ask her, she'll tell you, yes.'

Maia sighed. Suddenly she wondered if she really wanted to know the truth about the struggle in the sun-deeps. Once she knew, everything would change. But she couldn't stop, not now.

'Or yes, you did?'

Now Tareth sighed. 'You are just like her. Stubborn. Inquisitive. Too knowing for my peace of mind.'

Like who? Not like Sabra, the wizened Watcher? She was ancient. There was no way she was like her. Tareth was trying to distract her. Well, she wouldn't be distracted.

'Tell me about the Wulf Kin. Why is it better that he's dead? And his beast How d'you know so much about them?' She took a deep breath. 'Where is Khandar?'

The name resonated in her head, and whispered round the cave. A name from her half dreams when the rhythm of the loom and Tareth's murmurings had lulled her to sleep. Khandar was important. 'Who am I like?'

Tareth rubbed his hand across his face. He groaned softly.

'It will hurt less when you tell me,' said Maia wisely. 'Start with Khandar. Tell me about Khandar.'

Tareth glanced at his eagle. Maia thought that he looked as if he was seeing somewhere other than the cave.

'Khandar is the land of eagles. A mountain kingdom. Beyond the high plains they call the Cloud Plains, because after snow-melt, they are covered with white flowers. And because when the snows return to lock the land in the sleep of wolf-walk, the plains seem to billow like the clouds in the sky.

'Herds of horses, so swift that they seem to fly, roam the pastures. Their coats gleam like copper and gold in the sun.

'The queens who rule are buried on the high plains. The tribes believe that each queen becomes a star and they look for them in the night sky to guide their journeys.

'Khandar is our land. The Eagle People's. It is where you were born.'

Maia stared at him. 'Where I was born?'

She felt as if she had been punched in the chest. She had always known she was different from the Cliff Dwellers. That she had been washed ashore in a storm. Now she came from a fabled land. A land of majestic horses, eagles and queens who became stars.

'And the Wulf Kin?' she asked

Tareth nodded. 'And the Wulf Kin.'

She saw shadows darkening his eyes. She felt cold. Tareth

was afraid. He looked up and smiled and she wondered if she'd imagined it.

'You. The silver wildcat . . . and the dead Wulf Kin,' he said. 'All from Khandar.'

She touched the brooch. 'But . . .'

'Later,' said Tareth. 'The stories can come later. First you must see the Watcher.'

The line of women waiting outside the cave started to chant, a high wailing sound of greeting and departure. Maia hesitated.

Tareth glanced over his shoulder. 'Come,' he commanded. 'It doesn't do to keep Sabra waiting.'

Maia straightened her shoulders, lifted her chin and stepped into the sunlight and the Naming Day song.

Eight

Tareth crashed to the ground and lay winded, staring at the sky.

Maia scrambled round the rocks strewn across the winding animal track and dropped down beside him. She handed him her leather water pouch.

Tareth raised it eagerly to his lips, squeezing the leather bag as he gulped down the water. A dribble ran down his cheek, glistening like a snail trail. He wiped it with the back of his hand and passed the bag back to Maia. She drank thirstily. The water was warm and tasted of tannin, dark and bitter.

It had been a long, hot climb. Heat bounced off the rocks. She shaded her eyes and looked out across the sea far below, flat and empty. Up here she had eagle sight. She looked back the way they had come. The cliff-top shimmered in the heat haze.

Maia looped the thong of the bottle through her belt. She watched anxiously as Tareth heaved himself to his feet. He had fallen several times slipping on loose scree. She chewed a strand of her hair as she turned to look along the way ahead. She could pick out the track disappearing in the distance. A dark shape pulsated through the heat haze, flowing and retreating, moving towards them.

Maia squinted, but the shape still looked like a writhing curl of smoke. High above her Magnus screamed a warning and plummeted, mobbed by four red-legged crows.

'Something's coming,' she warned.

Suddenly a flock of pigeons flew overhead. The sound of wind flutes tumbled from their feathers. Maia shielded her eyes, staring up in delight. A tiny gourd sprouting miniature reed pipes was tied on each bird. As they wheeled around her the pipes sang in the wind.

'It's Sabra,' said Tareth. 'And her birds. She has come to meet us.'

The pigeons swirled round Maia, swooping above her head. She felt as if she was in a circle of song. Laughing, she stretched her arms and spun with them until the birds, the sea and the cliffs twirled in a streaming kaleidoscope of colour around her. She stopped and the world continued spinning. The pigeons fluttered to roost on the boulders, their wind flutes murmuring.

'Sabra,' called Tareth. He put his hand to his forehead in greeting.

'Weaver.' A voice harsh as a corn crake calling in the marshes broke the fluted music spell. 'So this is the child.'

The world steadied around Maia. A stick-thin woman

dressed in long, black robes was standing next to Tareth. Maia stared. She was taller than Tareth. Her face and hands were burned brown, her skin as ridged and wrinkled as the sand at sea-fall. Her dark hair was tightly pulled back, so that her face looked like a skull, thought Maia. A silver disc swung from one ear, a bone from the other.

The woman lifted her arms and whistled shrilly to the crows taunting the eagle. Silver bangles clashed on her wrists. The flowing sleeves of her robe fell, billowing like wings, away from her skinny arms. With her black eyes she looked like a crow herself.

Magnus thumped to the ground, raising a puff of red dust. A crow fell from the sky and landed on Sabra's outstretched hand. She stroked its head with a bony finger and tucked it inside the sleeve of her robe. Maia could see its beady eyes. The rest of the flock wheeled away, calling to each other.

Magnus hunched his wings like a grumpy old man rocking by a fire, and eyed the plump pigeons at Maia's feet.

'Control your bird, Weaver,' rasped the Watcher. 'My pigeons are too precious to be dinner for a scrawny eagle.'

'Careful, Sabra. You'll offend his dignity.' Tareth dropped his crutches and lowered himself onto a boulder. 'Your crows have already ruffled his feathers.

Sabra laughed. Even her laugh was like a crow's croak. Did she have red legs like her crows too? Surreptitiously Maia sneaked a glance at the tall woman's ankles as Sabra hitched up her robe and squatted beside Tareth.

'Sit,' Sabra commanded. 'Don't you want to know what awaits you?' She grinned at Maia, baring broken, yellow teeth.

'Can anyone know?' asked Maia. She was half-repelled, half-fascinated by the old crone.

Sabra shook back her flowing sleeves, her bangles clashing and jangling, and pulled out a bundle of feathers. Curly red talons and a curving beak swung from the bundle. Tiny red stones filled each eye socket. Maia stared in horror. It was a bag made from a filleted bird.

'So, they call you Flame Head.' Sabra glanced at Tareth. 'Fire only by name? Or fire by nature?'

Tareth was silent.

Sabra's sharp black eyes examined Maia. 'Have you chosen your name, girl?'

'No.' Maia touched the silver brooch. She had hoped that Tareth's gifts meant that she would be named after the wild mountain cat or an eagle. But she wasn't going to tell this inquisitive old crone.

'I'm tasked with seeking her true name,' said Tareth. 'I need guidance, Watcher. Perhaps the stones will grant Maia a fitting name.'

'Perhaps,' said Sabra. She upended the bird-bag, spilling a stream of smooth stones onto the ground.

Maia took a step closer.

Each stone had a design scratched into its surface. As Maia stared, the symbols seemed to slide and change, becoming leaping animals and shifting shapes. Fascinated, Maia moved closer. Some glinted with specks of silver mica or glistening fool's gold. They sparkled in the sun, tempting her to touch them. Every stone was a different colour.

One was blue, speckled like a thrush egg, another green as water in a rock pool, another the burnt ochre of baked earth. There was a rose stone, the colour of the cliffs as the sun set above the rim of the deeps, another dull grey like a sky in wolf-walk, and one as black as storm clouds. The smallest stone was a white breaking wave.

A turquoise stone flecked with gold made Maia feel like smiling. She stared at the black disc and felt as if a cloud had passed across the sun.

'Do the stones speak to you?' asked Sabra.

Maia shivered and looked away from the black stone. 'Stones can't speak,' she muttered.

'Come. Sit and choose a stone,' said Sabra.

Maia sat. She stared at the stones. She could see the runes clearly now. They were just lines and swirls. Crude patterns scribbled on to make the stones seem magical.

Tentatively she touched the turquoise stone. It was ice cold.

'Is that the one?' demanded Sabra. She sounded disappointed.

Maia shook her head.

'Then choose. And hold the stone.'

Did it matter which she chose? Maia frowned.

The turquoise was obviously the wrong choice, yet it made her feel happy. Should she pick the pink rock, the colour of the evening cliff? She liked that one. Did the stone with the bird-foot runes represent her place with the Cliff Dwellers? If she chose it, was she destined to roost like the gulls and stay forever with them?

Should she pick the storm-black stone? Or did the black rock bring darkness and danger? She thought about the dead Wulf Kin and shivered. The rune on the stone rippled. The black stone seemed to sneer at her. She wouldn't be intimidated by a rock. She would pick the black stone and face down the strange, dark fear.

Maia hesitated. The green stone, lying close to her knee, seemed to call to her with the sound of the sun-deeps. If she chose that, maybe she would overcome her terror. Maybe bury her infant memories of drowning, roped tight on Tareth's back as the storm waves roared and broke over her head. Yes, the green was the one.

She reached out. And pulled as the moon pulls the tides, her hand found and clutched the dull, grey pebble.

Burning pain scorched her palm. She almost screamed. The ferocious stare of the Watcher made her bite her lip. She would not cry out. But the pain was searing her skin. She tried to drop the stone. Her fingers were welded to it. Tears filled her eyes. The stone was burning a hole through her hand. She felt a scream ballooning in her mouth. She bit down on her bottom lip. She would not let this old woman and her evil stones beat her. Never. Ever. But the scream was building.

Then, suddenly, the pain was gone. Sabra had grasped Maia's hand in hers. It was like being held under cool water. And the water washed the pain away.

Maia's breath escaped in a sobbing sigh. Her eyes were stinging with unshed tears. Her hands were shaking, but she had not cried out.

And then Maia realised that it was not her hands that were shaking. It was the Watcher. Her whole body was shuddering.

Sabra's head fell back. Her eyes rolled. Her mouth opened. A terrible baying cry exploded from her mouth.

Maia tried to pull her hand free so she could cover her ears, and block the blood-freezing scream. She stared at their clasped hands in horror. A tiny tongue of smoke curled between the Watcher's fingers.

Her body jolted as if struck by lightning. She went limp. She dropped Maia's hand and slumped inside the folds of her dusty, black clothes.

Maia could see a burn on the palm of the Watcher's hand. The bird sheltering in her sleeve tumbled into her lap. The air smelled of singed feathers.

'Tareth?' Maia said.

He looked as ashen as she felt.

'Is she dead?' whispered Maia.

With a sigh like the wind passing through dry leaves, Sabra slowly lifted her head.

'Not yet. Not this time.' The crow in her lap shook out its singed feathers. It hopped away and sat preening on a rock.

The Watcher glared at Tareth. 'You could have warned me, Weaver,' she said.

Maia was still staring at the burn on Sabra's palm. She turned over her own hand. Her skin was scratched and dirty, but unmarked.

She turned her hand to show Tareth. 'I don't understand,' she whispered. 'I felt pain. I saw the smoke. Why am I not burned?'

Tareth stared at her, shocked.

'Why?' Maia turned to Sabra who was scratching tufts of moss from the rocks.

'Because the stone knew you,' she hissed. 'And I took the flame for you. I spared you the pain of that knowing.'

'Knowing?' Maia couldn't believe her ears. 'How can rocks know anything?'

The Watcher frowned. 'Has he taught you nothing?' She looked at Tareth. 'You have failed her, Weaver. She has no control. She has no idea what she can do.'

Tareth came out of his trance. 'So it seems. It was a gift I hoped she would never know or need.'

'You're too soft for your own good. Or hers when you hid the truth from her.'

Sabra glared at Maia. She pointed to a patch of tall weeds growing in the shade of a rock. 'Make yourself useful. Fetch that leaf. I need to bind it against the skin.'

Maia did not move. Anger was replacing shock. How dare this old crone trick her into picking up a burning rock? It served her right if she had burned her hand.

'Why did you do that?' she demanded. 'What are those . . . pebbles?'

The Watcher sucked in her breath. 'Quick, I've taken the fire for you. Bring me the weed.'

Maia hesitated. But Sabra was rocking with pain, her pigeons clustering about her feet, their soft coos burbling like water bubbling over rocks. Maia spun on her heel and tore a handful of the tall weeds. Green sap stained her fingers, numbing her fingertips. She thrust the weeping leaves at Sabra.

Sabra spat into her blackened hand. The gobbet of spit hissed. Sabra grimaced and crushed the heal-leaf into her palm. She shovelled the scattered stones back into the feather bag. Maia noticed that she first flicked the dull grey stone carefully aside with her hooked fingernail, separating it from the others. But the stone seemed inert now the runes were burned black across the surface. The Watcher peered at it, her finger tracing the pattern, hovering above it, not touching the stone.

She doesn't dare, thought Maia. Sabra was afraid of the power of her own stones.

Maia examined her own burn-free palm. Would she risk touching the stone again? Sabra was watching her.

'The Cliff Dwellers named you well, Flame Head. A fire child.' She spat on a second leaf and twisted it over the first.

'My name's Maia,' said Maia defiantly. 'The weed boys call me Flame Head to annoy me.'

'Then they've even less sense than I thought,' said the Watcher. 'It's not wise to anger a Sun Catcher.'

Tareth tensed. 'What did you call her?'

He glanced at Maia then quickly turned away again. As if he can't bear to look at me, thought Maia.

'The stone knew her?' asked Tareth.

'As you knew it must,' said Sabra coldly. 'The stone has spoken her name, Weaver. But you knew the name that was waiting for her. You didn't need the stones to tell you.'

'I hoped that I was wrong.'

'Foolish hope. She was born to be what she is.'

'But she is different,' protested Tareth. 'That way . . . that life is no more. Maia's a Cliff Dweller. As am I! She cannot be Sun Catcher. The sun-stone is lost . . . hidden.' He looked from Maia to the Watcher. 'I stole it. And never spoke to anyone about the has-been to keep her secret from those who might listen and would harm her. Hid her from Elin. From Urteth. Without the sun-stone she cannot be the Sun Catcher.'

'She's a Sun Catcher,' said the Watcher implacably. 'The stones don't lie.'

Tareth bowed his head. 'Then they will seek her,' he muttered. 'And I have failed.'

Sabra got stiffly to her feet. The pigeons rose and circled round Maia. The wind flutes on their tails caught the breeze and notes tumbled round her. But there was no giddy pleasure for her in the wind music now.

'If the news from the weed beds is true, they have begun already, Weaver.'

Sabra put her fingers to her lips and whistled two shrill notes. As one, the crows rose and flew. Maia noticed the crow with singed feathers struggling to keep up with the others. Sabra watched them depart. When they were mere dots in the sky she stooped and swiftly flipped the grey stone into her bag.

'Come,' she said. 'Come Maia, Sun Catcher. Come Tareth, Warrior Weaver. The crows will seek out the missing beast, if it still lives, and bring me news.'

She turned and strode off along the cliff-top, her black robes flying, her pigeons circling overhead.

Maia turned to Tareth. 'A Sun Catcher? What does she mean?'

'It's your name. The name the stones have given you. If you choose to take it,' said Tareth bitterly.

'Choose.' exploded Maia. 'I don't choose to listen to . . . an old woman. Or a lump of rock. How can a stone tell me who I am?'

Tareth shook his head. 'You must ask Sabra.'

Maia frowned at him. Surely now he could tell her the truth.

'What did you mean? What life is no more, Tareth? Who is Elin? Who is Urteth? Those names . . . it's as if I have heard them before.'

Tareth got to his feet and set off after the Watcher. 'Come.'

He seemed to be moving with more vigour, as if trying to put a safe distance between them.

'Why did she call you warrior?' called Maia after him.

'Come,' repeated Tareth.

Maia clenched her fists. Why wouldn't he answer her? Why were there so many secrets? She felt anger race through her, a bright echo of the pain she had felt in her hand. She would make him tell her the truth.

'Does a warrior kill a drowning man?' she shouted. 'Is a warrior frightened of an old woman's ravings?' There, she had said it.

Tareth stopped. He swung round. Maia had never seen him look so angry.

'If the Wulf Kin had lived, he would have killed you, Maia. And then killed those who sheltered you. It's their way. Is that what you want? The death of the Cliff Dwellers? Did you want him to live to kill? '

They glared at each other.

'I did not,' said Tareth. 'For you . . . to keep you and the Cliff Dwellers safe, I would willingly stick a knife between the ribs of a drowning man.'

Maia felt as if her world was falling apart around her. Tareth had killed a man. Her mind veered from the thought. If she didn't think about it everything would still be all right. But images and words jabbered in her head like restless gulls wheeling and calling above a midden.

Old women spoke in riddles.

Stones burst into flames.

Had Tareth killed a man?

What was a Sun Catcher? Who could ever catch the sun?

Tareth had killed a man.

A woman like a crow.

Burning hands.

Tareth had killed a man.

Nothing made any sense.

Flame Head. Sun Catcher. A knife between the ribs. Stones. Secrets. Death.

STOP.

Maia clapped her hands over her ears to end the chattering in her head.

'Maia?'

She made herself look at him. He looked the same as ever. 'The Wulf Kin?' she asked.

This time, his gaze did not waver. 'The Wulf Kin died in the sea, Maia,' he said.

Maia shivered. She wanted to believe him. She had to believe him.

'The Watcher is crazy.' she whispered.

Tareth's anger left him as quickly as it had come. 'I've often thought so,' he said.

Maia desperately tried to put the world back as it had been. Tareth was still Tareth. No matter what. And she . . .

'I'm still Maia, the Weaver's daughter.'

Tareth nodded.

Relief washed over her. Everything was as it had been. Nothing had changed. Then he spoiled it.

'After all, who would believe that a weaver with a twisted leg is a warrior?'

Maia's hands clenched into fists. Her mouth felt as dry as the sand in the lizard scrape. 'I would.'

'Then you'd be mistaken,' Tareth said abruptly. 'I'm a crippled weaver. Now come. There are things I must discuss with Sabra.'

Maia watched Tareth disappearing into the heat haze. He was so sure that she would do as he wanted that he hadn't even glanced back. She glowered and scuffed her feet in the red dust. She didn't want to follow. She didn't want to have anything more to do with the Watcher. They were treating her like a child. They could keep their secrets, she didn't care.

She picked up a rock and hurled it over the cliff. Her plans for her Naming Day were ruined. No one had asked what she wanted. She'd been sent to clean the weed beds. She'd been hustled from the beach just when things were getting interesting. Everyone would know more about the mysterious drowned man than her. Razek and the weed boys would be full of the gossip. Even Laya would know more than she would. Her father, the Salt Holder, would speak to Elder and he'd tell Laya everything. It wasn't fair.

And then, she'd been taken to see a crazy woman who spoke with stones that burned. Maia hurled another rock. It clattered down the cliff-face, disturbing nesting gulls. They spiralled on the air currents, screeching. Maia scowled. So what if Tareth had made her new clothes. So what if Selora and the cliff women had honoured her and sung her on her way. It didn't mean anything. The gulls blurred as angry tears smudged her eyes.

She rubbed her fist across her eyes. All she had wanted to do on her Naming Day was to go to the lizard scrape.

So why shouldn't she go?

The idea popped unbidden into her head. She was as close to the lizard scrape as she was to the Watcher's cairn. All she had to do was turn the other way.

Maia looked along the path. She could still see Tareth and beyond him the fluttering black shape that was the Watcher. They were too far away to stop her. The Watcher's spying crows were flying far ahead of her. Magnus was . . .

Maia glanced round. Magnus was still sulking on a boulder.

Before she could change her mind, Maia turned and headed down to the goat track that meandered below the shoulder of the cliff and dropped steeply along the gully to the lizard scrape.

She whistled. Magnus took off and soared lazily after her.

Nine

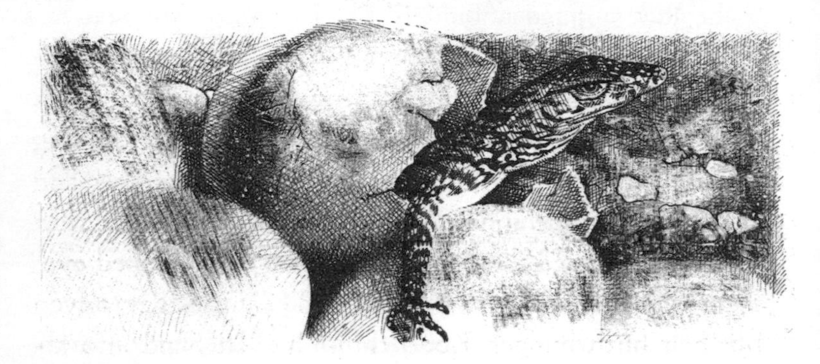

Maia could see the empty dugout drawn up on the sand at the edge of the water. Was she too late? She skidded down the scree. An avalanche of small stones bounced off the rocks. Maia winced. Whoever was there would have heard that. Recklessly she slid down the steep overhang and dropped onto the sand, sprawling on all fours.

She wriggled across the sand, keeping close to the rock face until she could peer over the tumbled, wave-rounded boulders.

The boy was on his knees. He was singing. As Maia watched he lifted his hands, holding up a large shell and poured water over his head. Then he lowered the shell and dipping his fingers into it flipped drops of water in a shining arc across the mound of sand that covered the lizard eggs. Maia craned forward to watch. The sand was moving. The mound was writhing. The boy stopped singing. He rocked back on his heels.

Kodo's song died in his throat. He was too late. The lizards were hatching. Two tiny brown hatchlings were scrabbling across the clutch of mottled eggs. Their claws scratched and clicked against the unhatched eggs. They butted them with their nose, tapped them frantically with their hooked eye-teeth. They would break the shells and eat the eggs, driven by their birth hunger. Kodo thrust his left hand into his pouch, feeling for the last crumbs of the fish wrap Jakarta had given him. He had to feed them to save the hatchlings still in the eggs. He dropped a pinch of fish and bread flakes on the sand. He leaned forward to grab the wriggling hatchlings. A rush of wings brushed past. Talons extended, Magnus grabbed one of the tiny lizards, pinning it in his claws, he caught the second in his beak.

Both Kodo and Maia heard the crunch of bones as the eagle crushed the lizard in his beak.

'No!' yelled Kodo. He flung himself across the mound. Boy and eagle tumbled in a flurry of sand and feathers.

Magnus screamed in outrage. He released the pinioned lizard. His talons raked Kodo's bare chest as the boy reared away from him. Kodo cried out and squirmed to one side as the eagle stabbed at his face. Kodo threw up his hands to protect his eyes.

'Stop! Stop, Magnus. No!' Maia rose from her hiding place.

Kodo was on his knees, reaching for his knife. He lifted it high and lunged, then fell as Maia took a flying leap and crashed into him.

'Don't!'

She grabbed Kodo's knife hand as she slammed into him. They rolled over and over in the sand, scratching and kicking.

Magnus half-flew, half-hopped closer, making deadly stabbing runs at Kodo. Maia twisted away from the furious eagle. They rolled across the injured lizard, burying it beneath them.

'Stop, Magnus!' she gasped. Somehow she was on top of the struggling boy. She pinned his arms into the sand.

'I'm sorry. It's my fault. He didn't mean to. He doesn't understand. Stop!'

Kodo tried to buck Maia off. 'I'll kill him. He's eaten a hatchling,' he sobbed, spitting sand from his mouth.

'I didn't mean to hurt the lizards.'

'I'll kill him.'

'I'm sorry.' Maia was babbling, her eyes stinging with tears and sand. 'He's a hunter. He doesn't understand.'

'He's killed a hatchling.' Tears of anger furrowed Kodo's sandy cheeks.

'I'm sorry. It's all my fault. I shouldn't have allowed him to come.'

'He shouldn't be here. You've no right to be here. The lizard scrape belongs to the Lizard People.'

'I know.' Her grip on Kodo's wrists relaxed. He pulled free and pushed her hard.

Maia sprawled in the sand. The tiny lizard crawled from beneath the swirls of sand they had kicked up. Listing sideways, dragging its injured legs, it zig-zagged uncertainly towards the shade of the rocks. Maia saw Magnus' head swivel. His wings opened.

'No!'

She closed her hand around the lizard and slowly slithered out of range. There was no telling what the irritated bird might do next. She sensed the boy getting to his feet behind her. The eagle screamed and took flight.

Maia watched him until he was a dot in the blue sky. She realised that she had been holding her breath.

'Tareth would kill me if anything happened to his eagle. I could have broken his flight feathers.'

'Ootey will beat me when he learns that a hatchling has been killed.'

'Ootey?'

'The Lizard Keeper . . . my grandfather,' Kodo looked at the Flame Head. She didn't seem so scary now, crouching on the sand, her hands cupped round the new lizard. Not so frightening now that her ferocious eagle had gone. 'Tareth?' he tried the word out. It felt strange on his tongue.

'The Eagle Keeper. The Weaver. My father,' said Maia.

So the eagle was not hers. Kodo squared his shoulders, feeling braver all the time. 'I would have killed him.'

'If you could,' mocked Maia. The boy was slight, dark-haired, his eyes still wide with anger and fright. His mouth looked as if it was more used to smiling than being clamped as it was now in a tight line. 'He's a fighting eagle.'

'He killed a lizard. There's a price to pay for that.'

'Price?' said Maia. 'He's a hunter.' She opened her hand. 'And anyway this one's safe.'

Kodo glanced down at the hatchling. 'It's better dead. It will be no use.' He held out his hand. 'Give it me.'

Maia covered the lizard with her other hand. 'No.'

'It'll die soon.'

'I'll care for it.'

'Cliff Dwellers don't care for lizards.' Kodo stared at her. 'I'll finish what the eagle began.'

'No.'

Kodo thought she looked as fierce as the eagle that had fought for her. But he wasn't scared of her.

'It's better dead, Flame Head. It will be no use. It'll never work with Doon. She will know its weakness and kill it. Better to finish it now.'

Maia took a deep breath and damped down the anger growing in her. She was in the wrong. She shouldn't have come to the lizard scrape. She shouldn't have planned to steal a lizard egg. It was her fault that one hatchling was dead and another mortally injured. But this boy had no right to call her by her hated nickname.

'My name is Maia,' she retorted. 'The Weaver's daughter. I'm not like the Cliff Dwellers. And I will keep this one from death.'

She gently ran her finger across the lizard's head. It tried to escape.

'See, it's still moving. Its skin is broken but that will heal.'

She closed her hand round the lizard so that it could not escape and shrugged off her sack. She pulled out the leaf-wrapped honeycomb and dipped her finger in the sticky ooze. She smoothed the honey across the broken skin.

'This will mend the tear. Tareth always uses it to heal cuts. And binds the deep ones with spider-web.'

Kodo stepped closer and tentatively put his finger in the honeycomb. 'Honey heals?'

Maia nodded. The hatchling's hind leg looked strange. She wanted to ask the boy if Magnus had broken it, but if she did he would only say it should be killed and this was maybe her one chance to keep a lizard. If she could take it to Tareth, he would know how to mend it. She looked at the boy. Magnus had gouged a long scratch across his chest. She held out the honeycomb. 'Put some on the eagle scratch. If you're lucky it won't leave a scar.'

Kodo did as he was told. Then sucked his sticky fingers. The honey was delicious. He glanced at Maia from beneath his lashes. She was frowning at the lizard. He quickly stuffed the rest of the honeycomb into his mouth, chewed and swallowed. He eyed the sack. Did she have more in there? He saw Maia watching him and blushed.

'If I have no scar who will believe that I fought an eagle?'

Maia grinned. 'No one. And it's better eaten than worn.' She pulled out a second leaf-wrapped package. She handed it to him. 'A lizard's price?'

Kodo took the package. He bit into the comb. Honey trickled down his chin.

Maia laughed. 'I can show you where to get more.'

Kodo nodded. 'That would be a fair price.'

'So I can keep the lizard?'

'It will die.'

'And will you forget to tell the Lizard Keeper that Tareth's eagle ate his lizard?' Maia was just beginning to realise what trouble there would be if her trespass and Magnus' actions at the lizard scrape were discovered.

Mention of his grandfather reminded Kodo that he still had a task to do. Carefully he picked up the broken shells and slipped them into the pouch on his belt. There must be no litter left in the scrape or the next egg-heavy lizard would not lay there. He brushed the sand from the remaining eggs and lifted them gently into the fur-lined basket Jakarta had given him.

Maia got to her feet. 'Next sun-high,' she said. 'I'll show you the honey cave.' She pointed to the top of the cliff above the lizard scrape. 'Sun-high. There.'

Kodo placed the basket in the bow of his dugout, pushed it into the shallows and stepped aboard. He waved his paddle in agreement.

Maia glanced down at the lizard she held. She had got her way. Sharing the honey cave was a small price to pay.

The dugout was sliding swiftly across the smooth sea.

'What's your name?' she called.

A dark cormorant bobbed up from the sea and flew onto the prow of the dugout. Laughter drifted across the water.

'Kodo. The Fisher-Bird's Keeper. And Honey Hunter after sun-sleep!'

Ten

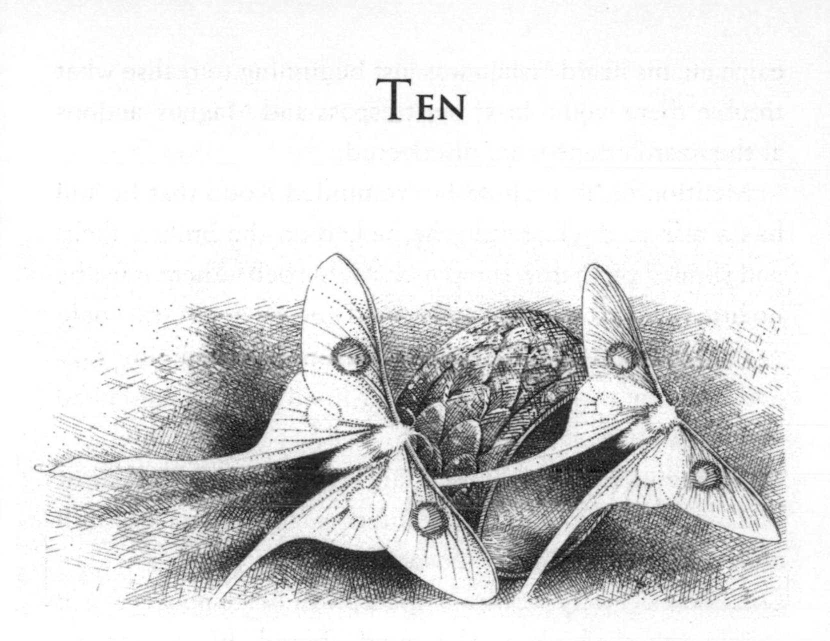

The sun was sinking towards the distant edge of the sea as Maia jogged within sight of the path down to the caves. Two figures were silhouetted against the sky. Tareth and the Watcher.

Maia slowed to a walk. She tucked the leaves containing the baby lizard more securely inside her sleeve. The couple were talking and bending over a long bundle at their feet. As she approached, Maia realised that the mound must be the corpse of the Wulf Kin. The Cliff Dwellers had laid him on the cliff-top to await his death fire.

Maia glanced down to the bay. She could see the piles of wood built into waist-high pyramids. Figures were moving around a huge pot straddling a fire. Even from here she could smell fish stew. Her stomach grumbled. She hadn't eaten for ages. Maybe she would go down to the beach, just to share the hand-fast meal. She didn't have to leap over the fire. She could avoid Razek. But first she had to get past Tareth and hide the lizard. She wanted to choose a good time to ask him to help heal the hatchling. She wasn't going to say anything while the Watcher was with him.

'Maia.' Tareth had seen her. 'Where's Magnus? Where have you been?'

Maia shrugged. 'Hunting. He was hungry. He was with me earlier on the cliffs.'

Tareth's eyes narrowed as he gazed at her. Maia looked away and stared instead at the corpse. She swallowed as bile rose in her throat. The Watcher folded the coarse cloth covering the body at her feet across the water-bloated face. She stood up, her bangles jangling.

'I'll recognise his kin if they pass.' She looked at Maia and flicked her fingers against her forehead. 'Sun Catcher.'

Her gaze dropped to Maia's sleeve. Maia forced herself not to close her hand protectively over her wrist to clamp the sleeve there. Surely the Watcher couldn't see through cloth?

'I didn't think that you ever left your cliff-top,' she said.

She heard the hiss of Tareth's intake of breath at her rudeness.

The Watcher ignored her. 'I will come and speak with Elder.'

'Stay to witness the hand-fasting,' suggested Tareth.

The Watcher nodded. 'And share some of that fish stew. The scent of it on the wind makes me wish for company.'

'That too. And I'm sure Maia will want to ask you about the stones,' added Tareth.

Sabra glanced at Maia. 'I'll speak about what I know. But much of her story is yours to tell, Weaver,' she said.

She twitched the folds of cloth hanging from the shoulder of her robe to cover her head and turned away. With a final jangle of bracelets and a waft of peppery spice from her robes she disappeared down the cliff path.

'Well?' demanded Tareth. 'Didn't you hear Elder say no one was to walk alone while we search for the wulfen? Where did you go?'

'I didn't want to spend my Naming Day with the Watcher.' Maia felt the lizard stir in her sleeve. She clasped it with her hand. 'And I wasn't alone. Magnus flew with me.'

'So he did,' agreed Tareth. 'Now you wear eagle feathers, it seems Magnus has divided loyalties.'

Maia could not bear the hint of jealousy in Tareth's voice. 'He came because he was looking for the wulfen. He flew high along the cliffs. I was glad of his company. But he's not my eagle.'

Tiny lizard claws scratched her wrists. Perhaps her to-come was to be different: to roam with a lizard, to persuade the Cliff Dwellers that a lizard was valuable in the weed beds.

'I went to the lizard scrape,' she confessed in a rush. 'I saw the eggs hatch. Magnus . . . Magnus attacked . . . killed a hatchling.'

Tareth struck his forehead with his clenched fist. 'As if we don't have enough trouble.'

'There's more,' said Maia. She felt in her sleeve and drew out thc bundle of leaves. 'I brought an injured lizard with me.'

Carefully separating the bundle, she held out her palm so that Tareth could see the hatchling. 'I put honey on the eagle tear, but I think it's broken its leg. Can you heal it?'

'A lizard? Here? Do you want the Cliff Dwellers to cast us out, Maia? They loathe the lizards. Only Untouchables live with lizards. What were you thinking?'

'It's hurt,' said Maia.

Tareth looked down at the lizard. It did not move. 'It will die, Maia.'

That was what the lizard boy, Kodo, had said. 'No. I need him to live.'

Tareth looked at her in surprise. 'Why?'

'I need it to dive for me. To fetch the shells. The Untouchables train their lizards to work. So can we. It will help fetch the shells.' She looked at Tareth. 'I'm afraid of the water. I'll never be able to dive deep and collect the shells for you.'

'That's my task,' said Tareth. 'Not yours.'

Maia bit her lip. How could she tell him that she was afraid for him? How could she tell him that she saw him find the dive beneath the moon track more difficult each time he made it? That she was afraid that she would be left alone in the dark boat beneath the wheeling stars, swallowing her fear and watching in vain for the trail of silver bubbles that marked his underwater trawl along the shell bed.

'I'll teach the lizard to fetch the shells so that you don't have to.' She looked down at the lizard panting on her palm. 'Can you heal it?'

'I'm not a Lizard Keeper, Maia. Nor are you.'

'Please.'

Tareth gently ran his finger along the lizard. It twitched. 'Maybe the silk will help.'

He covered the lizard with the leaves and closed Maia's hand round the bundle. He held her hand for a moment longer. 'I know what you fear. And yet I found us a home on the edge of the sun-deeps.' He sighed and dropped her hand. 'Your mother never liked water either. She would ride out of her way to avoid crossing a river. Luckily Khandar has few.

'Take the hatchling to the cave and line a basket with the spoiled silk cocoons. If they don't heal it, they will ease its passing. I'll come once I've finished here.'

'Khandar?' The name he whispered in the dark. Her mother? Maia's heart leapt. Was Tareth going to tell her about their past at last? Maybe the story was to be her Naming Day gift.

'Am I old enough to hear about the has-been? I've heard you whisper names in the dark when you weave the silk.' She saw Tareth flinch. Saw that once again he was going to turn her questions aside. 'I thought I was dreaming. But sometimes you call out in your sleep too.' She tried to ignore his frown. She swallowed. 'Tell me . . . about my mother? Am I like her? Was her hair red too?'

Tareth hesitated.

'Tell me.'

'Those stories are for firelight and not for the dead Wulf Kin to hear.'

'But . . .'

'Not here.' Tareth gave her a gentle push. 'Go. Tend to the hatchling.'

Maia went. When she turned to glance back at Tareth he was on the ground beside the body. He had thrown the cloth back. She could see the gleam of bronze, the glint of the wide silver armband on the furred forearm. She shivered. Tareth pulled the armband from the corpse's arm. He began to search the body. He looked up and saw her watching.

'Go, Maia,' he repeated.

The cave was a sanctuary. As she raided the weaving cavern for the soft bundles of waste silk, Maia tried to scrub out the picture of Tareth's hands scavenging across the corpse. She shivered. Tampering with the dead was forbidden. It was cliff law. Tareth would not break it. A tiny voice niggled in her head. Tareth was not a Cliff Dweller. He was a law unto himself. A man of secrets.

She grabbed some of the silk waste that Tareth had put aside to stuff the quilted coats he was making for the cold of wolf-walk. Colours seemed to run from the silk through her fingers like smoke. Maia tumbled the stuff into a basket. Carefully she lifted the lizard from its bed of leaves and placed it in the silk, tugging the floss over its body. Maybe the silk would dream the lizard well.

She held her hand over the silk. She closed her eyes and listened. Nothing. She touched it and again a tiny swirl of colour seemed to curl around her hand. Tareth had told her that the silk held the dreams of the moon-moths who spun the cocoons. Dreams for the taking. Dreams that became voices when he boiled the cocoons with crushed seashells and wove the carefully chosen threads into singing silk. Silk so precious to Tareth that it was kept secret from the Cliff Dwellers. From everyone.

'Dream well, hatchling,' she muttered.

She heard footsteps. Not Tareth's halting approach. She pushed the basket into the shadows.

'Razek.'

Razek hesitated at the entrance to the cave. His hand was twisting the fish-scale silver wristguard on his left arm. His eyes seemed to search the shadows behind her. Maia got to her feet and crossed to the entrance to prevent him from coming any further.

'What d'you want?' she asked abruptly.

'They're building the hand-fast fires.'

Did he think she was sightless and stupid? 'I saw them.'

'And it's your Naming Day.'

Maia stared at him. 'So?'

Razek stopped twisting his wristguard. 'So you can leap through the fire. You can be hand-fast now.'

Maia frowned at him. 'If I choose to be.'

'I have spoken with Elder and with Tareth,' said Razek. He took a step into the cave.

Maia held her ground. 'You speak to them every day,' she stalled. 'You've been speaking to us all today, ordering us about, telling us how we must clean the weed beds.'

She watched anger flare in his eyes. 'I spoke to them about you, Flame Head.'

'That isn't my name.'

'So what name did the old woman find for you?'

Maia clamped her lips tight.

'Was it Sea Witch?' taunted Razek. He glanced at the silver brooch pinned to her tunic. 'Or Sea Cat?'

'What concern is it of yours?'

Razek looked at the eagle feathers and the strands of silk bound in her hair. 'Or did she call you Sea Bird, Flame Head?'

'If she had I'd fly far from you and the weed beds,' retorted Maia.

To her fury he grinned down at her. 'So. You didn't like the name she found for you?'

Over his shoulder Maia could see red light spilling from the sun as it slipped towards the rim of the sun-deeps. If she was a Sun Catcher, could she catch it and hold it there? Hold on to the light. She squinted at the horizon and the sun slipped a notch lower. No one could catch light. She looked down at her hand. A trail of lizard slime from the injured hatchling, scratches from her slide into the lizard scrape, broken nails from her struggle in the sand with the boy were the only marks. The burning stone might never have happened.

'My name is Maia,' she said haughtily. 'I don't need another name.'

Razek ignored her. 'I didn't take the old woman's name either,' he said. 'I am the Weed Master. I need no other name. Not until I become Elder.'

He pulled the wristguard from his arm and held it out to her.

'This was my father's. It's mine because I'm Weed Master now. Mine to give. I choose you to leap the hand-fast fire with me, Maia.'

'But you don't like me,' whispered Maia. 'I don't like you.'

'We are the same then. And there's more than liking between us. It happened when my father dragged you and

Tareth from the sun-deeps many star-shifts ago. It's the same now.' He held out the silver wristguard. 'Take it. It's yours. And give me . . .' he looked at the silver cat. Maia saw him reject it. He glanced at her hair. 'Give me an eagle feather and we will be hand-fast. And we'll jump through the fire for everyone to see.'

'Razek.' Maia protested. 'I . . .'

Razek grabbed her hand, turned it over and put the silver band into her palm. 'Take it. Wear it.' He saw the dark lizard blood on her hand. His finger scratched at it. Razek's nose crinkled. 'Is that . . . ?'

Maia pulled free. She took a step back and held out his gift. 'I don't want to be hand-fast. Not with you. Not with anyone.'

Razek's head was up like a Marsh Lord's hunting hound scenting the wind.

'Is that . . . ?' He stepped round her and strode deeper into the cave. 'Lizard?'

Maia grabbed at his tunic, tugging him to halt. 'Not lizard,' she hissed as she swung him round to face her. 'Lizard blood!'

Razek pulled himself free. 'You've brought a *lizard* here?' He spotted the basket in the shadows. He crouched and upended it. Silk wadding and dozing lizard tumbled out. The hatchling lay stunned on its back, its belly as pale as the silk littering the cave floor. Its tiny talons flexed. Feebly its forelegs waved in the air as it struggled to right itself.

'Lizard spawn,' spat Razek.

Maia dropped to her knees, turned the basket over and shovelled the silk back. She picked up the lizard, returning it to the bed of silk. 'It's dying.'

Razek glared at her. He got to his feet. 'This cave stinks. You . . . you stink of lizard,' he said coldly.

Maia cocooned the lizard in the silk. 'Perhaps the stink will convince you that you and I will never be hand-fast.' She stood and held out the wristguard.

Razek spun on his heel. 'Wash the stink of lizard off you before you come to the fires.'

'I wouldn't be seen dead at the fire!' Maia yelled, but he had gone.

She looked at the wristguard in her hand. Had he stormed off without it because he thought she had contaminated it with the lizard blood? She glared at the silver band with its chased fish-scale pattern and hurled it into the pile of sleeping furs.

'You will go. You will not skulk in the cave as if you were ashamed,' Tareth had said.

Maia watched the dark figures hand-in-hand springing across the fire, scattering bright sparks as they stamped in the embers and remembered Tareth's words. She could see Sabra, a black shape beyond the dancing sparks talking to Elder. There was no sign of Razek. She had only come for the food, she told herself.

A shower of sand thudded into her.

'Hey. Careful.' She flinched and juggled the bowl, almost tipping fish stew over her new clothes.

'What have you done now, Flame Head?' Laya, hands on her hips, flounced up to Maia, kicking sand as she walked, and stood scowling at her.

Maia made a show of brushing the sand from her skirt. 'Be careful where you're putting your great feet. You'll spoil my new skirt.'

Laya barely glanced at the beautiful cloth. 'Razek is . . . furious.'

'What's that to do with me?' Maia picked up her bowl and spooned the rich stew into her mouth. She was pretty sure that Razek had not gone running to Elder with tales about the lizard in the cave. If he had, Elder would have sent for her.

'You must have done something. You always do. You always make Razek angry.'

'Poor Laya,' said Maia heartlessly. 'Is Razek too upset to leap over the flames with you?'

'You told him not to,' stormed Laya. 'I asked him and he walked away.'

'Since when has Razek taken any notice of what I say?' asked Maia.

'Since . . . since . . . you grew your hair so long,' snapped Laya.

Maia gazed at her in disbelief. 'My hair? Razek? Oh Laya, little do you know.' She started to laugh. 'Razek thinks I'm a lizard lover.' She watched Laya's eyes widen with disbelief and hope. 'If he thinks about me at all, that is,' she added, suddenly taking pity on the Salt Holder's daughter, who had so much and hoped for so much more. 'He says I stink of lizard.'

'Really?'

Maia nodded. 'Really. And I never think of him at all if I can help it,' she added for good measure. 'Lizard-loving Flame Head, that's me. Razek and I always fight.'

She ate more stew. 'I'd say we didn't like each other at all.'

Laya perched beside her.

Maia moved to make room for her.

Laya carefully folded her skirt around her ankles and cradled her knees, rocking with anxiety. 'Why is he so cross?' she asked.

Maia bit her tongue.

'Maybe it was the stranger,' said Laya. 'It took ages to finish cleaning the weed beds after they had carried the body to the cliff-top. Everyone wanted to talk about it. '

Maia wanted Laya to talk about it. To tell her what had happened once she and Tareth had left to visit Sabra, but she wasn't going to ask.

'He didn't have to walk away when I said we should jump the fire,' grumbled Laya. 'Father likes him. Razek should be pleased when the Salt Holder's daughter says . . .' She stopped and swallowed hard. 'He shouldn't have walked off.'

'No,' agreed Maia.

Laya looked at her suspiciously. 'You're being kind.'

'No I'm not,' denied Maia. She looked at Laya and grinned. 'Well, maybe.' She lifted the hem of her skirt. 'D'you like it? Wouldn't you like Tareth to weave you one?'

Laya tossed her head. 'As if I'd wear anything you wear, Flame Head.'

Maia saw the Watcher approaching. She needed to speak to her. She didn't need Laya listening.

'If Razek won't leap with you, you and I could leap together,' she teased.

Laya glowered at her. 'You're making fun of me.'

Maia slipped her hand into her pocket and pulled out Razek's wristguard.

'Razek's angry because he lost this in the weed beds.'

She tossed Laya the band. 'Tareth found it,' she lied. 'He told me to give it back.'

Laya caught the wristguard. 'I'll do it for you, Flame Head.'

'Thought you might,' said Maia.

'And I'll make him jump through the fire for it,' declared Laya.

The Watcher folded her long legs and sat on the sand beside Maia. They watched Laya hurrying back to the figures milling around the beach fires. Maia drew in a deep breath, smelling the strange scents of Sabra's robes. Maybe she had a remedy that could help an injured lizard. But first . . .

She stared at the figures by the fire. She saw Razek move from the dark to speak to Selora, her plump shape unmistakable against the bright fire. She saw Laya tripping across the sand to join them. She took a deep breath.

'Tell me about Sun Catchers,' she said.

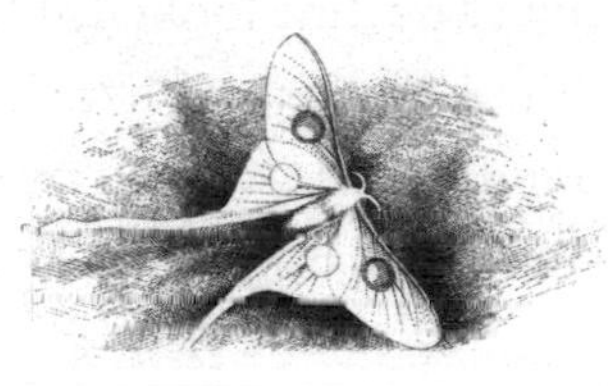

Eleven

The Watcher plunged Maia's hand into the sand. It was like being pinned beneath Magnus' claws. Maia longed to tug free.

'Feel,' said Sabra. 'It grows colder in the darkness. Just as the land grows cold in the dark of wolf-walk. Then, the Catcher brings warmth to the land so that life begins again. In the high mountains where they live, the Sun Catcher traps the sun and warms the valleys.'

'How?'

The Watcher released Maia's hand. 'With the sun-stone.'

Maia thought about it.

'I don't have a sun-stone.'

Sabra shrugged. 'I know only that your destiny is to be a Sun Catcher.'

'The Cliff Dwellers don't need a Sun Catcher,' Maia objected.

Sabra pulled the bird-bag from her sleeve. The stones rubbed against each other. It sounded to Maia as if they were chuckling.

'The Cliff Dwellers will need you.'

Maia felt as if she had fallen from a cliff. 'Need me?' They had never needed her.

'But you won't stay in the weed beds,' said Sabra.

'Will Elder send me away because of the lizard?' panicked Maia.

The Watcher looked at her. 'What have you done?'

Maia told her.

The cave was still in darkness. In the first grey smudge of light creeping across the ledge linking their cave with the other dwellings on this level of the cliff village, she could see Magnus hunched on his perch. Soon sun-wake would flood the entrance to the cavern. It would be cold on the cliff-top for the death fire of the Wulf Kin. That must be where Tareth had gone.

Reluctantly, Maia pushed down her sleeping furs and rolled off her mattress. The stone floor was chilly beneath her bare feet. She grabbed her crumpled clothes and scampered across to the fire. Before he had gone out, Tareth must have blown the embers into life and left a covered pot of chay to simmer. The smell was just beginning to seep from under the lid.

On the far side of the hearth, close to the warmth, was the lizard basket. Beside it lay a bundle of wilted leaves; the Watcher's knit-bone remedy. Maia pulled on her clothes, reciting Sabra's instructions as she hopped on one foot and tugged on her soft sheepskin boot.

'Crush the leaves, steep in hot water and try to get the lizard to drink it.' Then she had to mix the mashed leaves with the red mud to make a poultice to smooth over the injured limb. And confine the lizard.

Maia pulled on her other boot. The Watcher had managed to part the herb women from a handful of leaves and kept her need for them secret. No way would the women spare knit-bone remedy for a lizard. They would have rushed in with their grinding stones and pounded it to death.

Maia crouched beside the basket and lifted the hank of silk. No colour seeped through her fingers. Lizard slime soiled the bedding. The hatchling lay still. Maia touched it. It did not move. Its skin was dull. Its tiny jaws locked in a rictus grin. Shreds of silk were tangled in its teeth as if it had been eating the bedding.

The lizard was dead.

Slowly Maia replaced the silk padding. No need for the Watcher's leaves.

Outside Magnus gave a harsh call. Maia brushed the back of her fist across her eyes.

'You wanted him dead!' she cried.

She rose and grabbed a worn cloak of Tareth's. Twirling it about her shoulders she ran from the cave and along the path to the cliff-top.

Tareth was not alone. Elder stood beside him. And Razek.

Maia slowed to a walk. As she drew closer Elder gestured to Razek who crouched and took a smouldering fire-fungus from a pot at his feet. He blew on it. When it was scarlet, he lit the bundle of dried weed tied to the top of the long stick he was carrying. The sea wind caught the glowing weed. It burst into flames. They roared and crackled. For a moment Razek stood, dark against the fingers of light streaking across the sky, his head crowned with fire, his face smooth and stern, his cheek bones and nose the colour of beaten copper in the flames. He looked unreal, as if he wore the bronze and gold killing helmet of the Marsh Lords. Maia shivered.

At Elder's signal, Razek plunged the flaming stick deep into the heart of the pyre.

The flames roared higher, tossing sparks into the pillar of smoke spiralling from the mound.

Elder raised his arms and turned to face the climbing sun. 'Go well, stranger.'

Razek repeated the gesture and the words.

Tareth leaned heavily on his crutches and watched the flames. Maia joined him. At his feet lay the Wulf Kin's bronze and leather cuirass, his armband, a curved sword and a dagger.

'Do we bury them?' Elder asked.

'That or cast them into the deep,' said Tareth.

'I'll wait until the fire dies and throw them away,' said Razek.

Elder nodded. 'So be it.'

Tareth turned away. 'This wind is cruel on old bones. There's chay heating in the cave. You're welcome to share it.'

Together they moved off. Maia watched Elder lengthening his stride to keep up as Tareth swung between his crutches.

Razek was examining the pile of metal. 'Fine work,' he murmured. He slipped off his jerkin and piled the weapons and mail into it. He lifted the armband and turned it towards the sun. 'Pure silver.'

Maia wondered if he would really throw it all away.

'Tareth says that the weapons are passed from father to son,' she said.

Razek nodded. 'As my father gave me his weed knife and his silver wristguard.'

'Or to the daughter, as her hand-fast price, if there's no son,' challenged Maia.

'Better than throwing it away.'

Maia let her breath out. She was right. Razek had no intention of getting rid of the Wulf Kin hoard.

'You must do what Tareth says. Elder agrees that nothing should be left of him.'

Razek frowned down at her. 'Why did you come?' he demanded.

'Why did you?' countered Maia.

'To watch the stranger depart. To assist Elder with the fire. One day I will be chosen Elder, as my uncle was. I need to know how to do these things.'

'Then do as Elder says and throw the stranger's bronze and silver into the deep.' She held out her hands. 'If you can't, then I will. The Wulf Kin's beast is still free. Maybe he'll come looking for his master. Maybe he'll scent his armband. It will lead him here.'

Razek smiled. 'There's no sign of the beast. It's dead too.

Elder thinks Tareth's wrong. He thinks the beast has drowned.'

Maia shrugged. 'I hope so. But we shouldn't keep anything that the Wulf Kin owned.'

'I'll do what must be done, Flame Head. And,' Razek glanced over his shoulder, 'unless you want Elder to find it, you'd better move that stinking lizard. Even the smell of chay won't hide the stench.'

Maia stared at him. 'Why didn't you tell him I'd found a lizard?'

'I may yet,' said Razek. 'Or I may kill it myself. It doesn't belong here.'

'Nor does the Wulf Kin's silver or his weapons,' retorted Maia. 'And if you try to kill the lizard, I'll stick you with your own weed knife.'

Razek laughed. 'D'you think you could stop me?'

Maia clenched her fists. 'You'll have no need to dirty your hands killing a hatchling. It's already dead.'

'And will stink all the more. Run and hide it, Flame Head. Maybe you should build it a death fire too. Or ask the Untouchables how they deal with the passing of a stinking lizard. Except they mustn't know that the Weaver's daughter dared steal one of their lizards, must they? And let it die. Poor Maia,' he taunted. 'What a storm awaits when you are discovered. But don't worry. I'll keep your secret . . . for now.'

'Tell who you like.' stormed Maia. She wiped out the sudden terrifying vision of being hauled before Elder, women hissing, weed boys jeering and Tareth's shame. 'I hate you.'

Maia slipped into the cave. Elder was seated, his hands cradling a clay beaker.

'A good end,' he was saying. 'And no sign of the beast, Weaver.' He stretched his legs out to the fire and almost nudged the lizard basket with his toe.

Maia stepped past him, grabbed the basket and headed for the sleeping cave. Razek was right. The smell of lizard was stronger. She saw Tareth lean forward and vigorously stir the chay. It splattered over the edge of the pot and hissed onto the hot stones of the hearth. Steam and the smell of herbs and scorched milk filled the cave.

'More chay, Elder?' asked Tareth.

Maia vanished into the sleeping cave as Elder creaked to his feet.

'Kind of you, Weaver, but the Cliff Dwellers will be waiting for me. I must tell them that the Wulf Kin's fire burned well.'

Maia heard him leave. Heard Tareth pour chay into a beaker. 'Maia?'

She returned to the fire and put the basket at Tareth's feet. 'The lizard's dead.'

Tareth watched her across the rim of his beaker as he drank. 'And now?'

She shrugged.

Tareth sighed. 'The lizard belongs to the Lizard Keeper, Maia.'

Maia stared at the splodges of chay burning black on the hearth. The smell was horrible. As bad as a lizard's death. She would have to scour the hearth clean. She stared into the flames until her eyes felt as hot as the fire.

'Silence is no answer, Maia.'

'I'm sorry.'

'That's a start. But it may not be enough.'

'Then I'm sorry for that too,' muttered Maia.

'We must take gifts,' said Tareth. 'What's the value of a hatchling.'

'Two hatchlings. Magnus ate one,' she mumbled.

'Let's hope the Lizard Keeper doesn't have a taste for roast eagle then.'

Maia looked up. She saw the tiny quiver tug at the corner of Tareth's mouth. She felt a slight lifting of her gloom. He wasn't still cross with her.

'Perhaps a gift of cloth would be welcomed,' said Tareth.

'And the lizard boy liked honey,' remembered Maia. 'I put it on his cuts. He licked it off.'

'Then you should show him the honey cave,' said Tareth. 'It might make up for the loss of his lizard. You'll need to visit the bees soon. We took the last of our honey to Sabra.'

Maia looked at him suspiciously. Had he guessed that she'd decided to meet Kodo to take him to the honey cave? Had told him to meet her above the lizard scrape at sun-high?

'If you say so,' she muttered.

'I say so. And the sooner the better. Before the Lizard Keeper comes to accuse the Cliff Dwellers of stealing his lizards.' He poured her some chay. 'Drink and then go and load the dugout. And attach the outrigger. We'll take the saffron cloth and the blue. A colour for each hatchling. We'll have less to trade at the Gather but . . .' he shrugged. 'Bring a pot for the honey.' He frowned. 'And the lizard basket.'

Maia groaned. Wasn't it punishment enough to have to go and admit to the Lizard Keeper that she had stolen from the lizard scrape? Did she have to suffer sun-deep sickness too?

Maia gulped down her chay. It scalded her throat. It was likely to be the least of her troubles.

Twelve

Kodo watched the red sail approaching. He flexed his stinging shoulders. Ootey had not spared him when he had counted the eggs in the hatching sands. Nor spared him the extra task of collecting the lizard-spoil since sun-wake. As the sun hitched higher in the sky, its rays had burned through the lotion Jakarta had smoothed across his beaten shoulders as he lay face down snivelling in the net hammock. Now his shoulders felt as hot as the grated root she used to spice her fiery fish stews.

Kodo screwed up his eyes and squinted. He could see two heads in the boat and an eagle wheeling high above the sail. One head was the colour of fire. Kodo groaned. Why was Flame Head coming? Wasn't he in enough trouble? He had lied to Ootey. Now the beatings would begin again. He shuddered as he remembered his return to the stilt home;

remembered Jakarta's concern when he had hidden in his hammock; remembered Ootey roaring until he woke the baby and she screamed. Jakarta had been like a cooling stream trying to calm the baby, appease Ootey and soothe Kodo's cuts.

'Leave him!' Ootey had shouted. 'The boy must take his punishment like a man, not a wailing child.'

Jakarta's hands had been gentle. The lotion stung. She had ignored his grandfather. 'He won't be able to work if his back is raw.'

'He'll work,' shouted Ootey. 'Am I to be the only one to work? Must I do everything? Useless boy.'

'Is it his fault gulls killed the lizards?'

'He should have collected the eggs before any hatched. The boy's a dreamer.'

Jakarta had rubbed the lotion across his shoulders, the long strokes swinging the hammock, as if he were the baby to be rocked to sleep.

'You're too hard on him.'

'And you're too soft, woman. He'll never make a Lizard Keeper. Letting gulls take a lizard!' Ootey had stomped off in disgust.

Now Ootey would learn that it wasn't gulls. Unless he could stop the girl. Persuade her to tell the same story. Kodo dropped the scraper, squelched across the lizard-spoil and left the pound to join the gaggle of naked, shouting children who had seen the approaching boat and were running to the water's edge. Adults were coming too, walking slowly, shading their eyes to make out the approaching boat. One man had brought his long, pronged lizard trident. Kodo saw another peel off from the group and run to fetch his. Did they expect trouble? He saw Jakarta come out of their hut with the baby in her arms and stand on the net platform. Ootey followed her. Grabbing his trident and pulling a net from the holding pegs he crossed the walkways between the huts and stepped down onto the beach.

Kodo groaned aloud and walked to the shallows, surrounded by a crowd of children. The adults spread in a new moon crescent behind them. Kodo watched a dark-haired man drop the red sail. The boat lost way, rocking on the ripples of sea-fall. He saw the girl jump into the water. She took a bundle the man was holding and waded towards the beach. He met her wide-eyed gaze across the distance separating them. Her face was white. Without meaning to, Kodo stepped forward. The children, silent now, parted in front of him and he stepped into the shallows. The girl stopped. She looked at him and tried to smile. Kodo could see that she was afraid. She licked her lips and looked past him, searching the crowd gathered on the beach.

'I have come to see the Lizard Keeper,' she cried.

The crowd on the beach muttered.

'I have a gift for the Lizard Keeper.'

Kodo turned to look at the crowd clustered on the shore. No one had moved. They seemed frozen to the spot. Even the lizards in the compound were silent.

Behind him Kodo heard the girl clear her throat.

'A gift and a story.'

Kodo felt the stirring of anger. Were his people afraid of a girl? He turned to face her.

'Ootey is Lizard Keeper.'

Ootey strode forward still carrying his net and trident and stood beside Kodo.

'And he is not used to Story Tellers from the cliffs. You name us Untouchables. Cliff Dwellers don't come here. Not unless they bring trouble and moans about the lizards with them.'

The girl took a step closer. Kodo felt Ootey tense beside him, but at least his grandfather didn't raise his trident to threaten her.

'I am Maia. Daughter of Tareth, the Weaver.' She held out the cloth. 'We live with the Cliff Dwellers. They have given us shelter. But we are from elsewhere. I have a gift and a story for the Lizard Keeper.'

Ootey was looking at her from beneath his brows. He glanced beyond her to the bobbing out-rigger. Kodo saw the dark-haired man raise his hand, open-palmed, towards his suspicious grandfather.

Ootey grunted and glared at the red-headed girl. 'And why does the man sit there still and send a girl?'

'The story is mine. My father will wait for me until it's done. He was hurt in a fall from the cliffs many star-shifts ago and must use sticks to help him walk.'

Ootey thrust the net and trident at Kodo. Surprised, he just managed to hold out his hands in time to grab them.

'I am the Lizard Keeper. I'll hear your story.' Ootey gestured to two men in the crowd. 'Fetch the man so that he listens where we can see his eyes.' He looked at the saffron and blue cloth. 'And we'll see why a Cliff Dweller brings so fine a gift.'

The two men waded to the outrigger. Kodo saw the eagle

spiralling down. He heard the man whistle and the eagle widened the circle of its flight.

'Grandfather,' Kodo warned.

'Will the bird attack?' demanded Ootey.

'Not unless you attack us,' said the girl boldly.

Unexpectedly Ootey laughed. 'Come in peace then.' He lifted his hand. 'The men will help you ashore,' he called to the dark-haired man.

Two men carried Tareth to the dry sand above the edge of the water. The girl, her arms sagging with the weight of the cloth she still held, followed them. She walked past Kodo and didn't even glance at him. Kodo saw her nose wrinkle. He glanced down at his arms holding the bundle of nets. He was streaked with lizard spoil. He was Untouchable. He turned and splashed out of the shallows and met Jakarta crossing the sand.

'Kodo?' Jakarta called.

He brushed past her. Reaching their home he dumped Ootey's net and spear on the net platform. Flame Head had pretended not to know him. She had come to his village. She would expose his lie. Return the injured hatchling he'd let her take. Ootey would banish him. Jakarta wouldn't be able to protect him this time. And he was stinking of lizard spoil just as the Cliff Dwellers always believed.

Leaping down from the net platform he jogged back to the sea, avoiding the cluster of people now crowding about Ootey. The girl was standing, her pile of yellow and blue cloth at her feet. Jakarta would love the colours. Would Ootey take the gift?

Kodo shook his head to block his thoughts. He plunged

into the water, grabbing handfuls of sand to scrub himself clean. The salt stung his skin. Kodo gasped and scrubbed harder. It was good to feel pain this time. It would make what was to follow easier to bear. He tugged off the strip of material tied round his waist and furiously flayed it against a rock until the water swirled with dirt and ran clear again. At least now when he was shamed, he would not smell of lizard spoil.

Wrapping the cloth around his waist Kodo jogged across the sand and found a place at the edge of the story circle. Jakarta, sitting on the fringes of the group, smiled at him. He was forgiven. It might be his last chance to say goodbye. Kodo went to sit with her. Ootey, of course, was sitting in pride of place, the dark stranger with a twisted leg at his side. As Kodo sat and the muttering of the crowd died away, the girl began her story in a high, clear voice.

THIRTEEN

'I'm going to be sick,' thought Maia.

She swallowed an acid hiccup. It burned her throat. Her knees were trembling. Sweat trickled down her back and yet she was icy cold. She looked at the old man sitting in front of her. So this was Ootey, Kodo's fearsome grandfather. He was as wrinkled and weathered as the rocks around the lizard scrape. His eyes beneath jutting eyebrows were storm clouds as he glared at her with growing impatience.

She took a shaky breath and held out her hands, fingers spread wide.

'There was a great storm as many star-shifts ago as I have fingers on my hands,' she began. 'A storm that drowned the weed beds. It swallowed the lizard scrape and gobbled the lizard eggs. The waves were so great, that it seemed that even the stilt village would be washed away and everyone with it.'

The crowd muttered. Maia saw Ootey nod.

'There was such a storm,' he said.

Her voice grew stronger. 'The storm wrecked a ship, and spat a man and a child into the weed beds. Two strangers from a land of eagles.'

She tugged one of the eagle feathers from her hair and held it up. The silk strands that Tareth had twisted in her hair on her Naming Day came free and sang in the breeze. She felt a movement in the crowd, as if they were leaning forward to listen. She captured the strands in her free hand and tucked them into her tunic. She didn't want the silk whispering. This was her story. She stuck the eagle feather in the sand at the old man's feet.

'They were found by the Weed Master. He thought them dead, but the child cried. So he carried the man with the child tied to his back to the Cliff Elder. They spoke together and agreed that the incomers could live, since the great storm had spared them. The strangers became Cliff Dwellers. And this was good for the village since the man, Tareth, was a weaver.'

She grabbed two handfuls of cloth and lifted her arms so that she held waterfalls of yellow and blue.

'A fine weaver,' she added. She saw the old man look from the cloth to Tareth and nod again.

'The child and Tareth were happy with the Cliff Dwellers. But he still remembered the land of the eagles, so he caught and trained his own eagle. And the child watched and waited until she too would be old enough to fly an eagle.'

Maia saw the old man's eyes widen with surprise. 'For it is a custom among those people that men and women are the same,' she added.

She heard a murmur of surprise from the crowd. 'A sensible idea,' a woman called out. There was a ripple of laughter. Ootey frowned.

Maia lowered her arms so that she was standing in a swirl of yellow and blue cloth.

'But the wait for an eagle was long. And the child grew impatient. She started to search the cliffs for an eagle's nest, but all she found were gulls and crows. And as she strayed further from the village she saw many things. A marshland roamed by horses; the stone holdfast; the fierce Marsh Lords. And then she saw huge, sea-creatures ridden by men and boys. Beautiful, red-crested lizards.

'And she wished that she too could swim with lizards. Could dive deep and search for shells.'

Maia looked at Tareth and voiced her fears. 'For the storm had stolen her courage, and she was afraid of the deeps. She hoped the lizard could make her strong, as the Lizard Keeper is strong. She wanted a lizard to dive for the shells the Weaver needs for his dyes.'

The crowd muttered. Eyes that had smiled when she said the lizards were beautiful became hostile, because everyone knew that the lizards belonged only to the Untouchables, just as the horses belonged to the Marsh Lords. Maia crossed her thumbs and rushed on.

'So the girl continued her search for her eagle, but she looked for a wild lizard too. And one day she found a lizard scrape. The sun was hot. And the hatchlings were breaking from their shells. A boy was gathering them. His dugout was pulled up on the sand. The girl hid and watched. She saw him put the eggs into a basket and crawl across the sands to collect the tiny hatchlings as they wriggled towards the sea. And then, like a bolt from the sky, an eagle fell on them.'

The crowd gasped. She could feel Tareth's eyes boring into her. Was he worried that her story might incite them to harm Magnus? Somehow she had to protect the eagle and Kodo too.

'It killed the hatchlings and attacked the boy who tried to protect them. He fought bravely. The eagle savaged him. But the boy drove him off. And the rest were safe.'

Maia felt the crowd stir as they looked at each other to see who had fought the eagle. She suddenly wondered if the boy had told his grandfather what had happened at the lizard scrape. Would her story make more trouble for him? It was too late to worry now.

'The girl called the eagle and fled from the lizard scrape. Sabra, the Watcher, who sees everything, spoke with the girl, telling her that the boy who had battled with the eagle to protect the hatchlings was Kodo, Ootey's grandson.'

The crowd sighed. She saw the old man sit taller. She hoped it was pride not anger stiffening his spine. Those close to him were turning to look. Others nudged each other and pointed their tattooed thumbs across the circle. The lizard boy must be there, behind her. Her hands clenched. She was almost done. Her half-truths had been told.

'He battled bravely. But two lizard hatchlings were dead. So there must be a reckoning.' She laid the cloth at the old man's feet. 'It is the wish of the Eagle People that the Lizard Keeper, Ootey, and his grandson Kodo, accept this gift in place of the hatchlings.'

Maia turned and looked at the crowd. She saw Kodo

staring at his feet. Someone thumped him on the back. Kodo looked up. He seemed dazed. She saw the woman next to him touch his arm. He got slowly to his feet.

'Is the gift a fair exchange?' she asked the crowd.

A few nodded. Others looked past her to the old man, as if waiting for his reaction. Maia turned back to face him.

'I shouldn't have led the eagle to the lizard scrape,' she said. 'It was wrong to wish for a lizard. Will you take the cloth in exchange for the hatchlings?'

She watched Ootey purse his lips and suck his teeth.

'It's a fine story,' he mused. He looked at the cloth and then towards Kodo. 'My grandson fought bravely?' he asked.

Maia nodded.

'I wouldn't want to fight a fully grown eagle,' said Tareth. 'Only a brave man would come between an eagle and his prey. You must be proud of him.'

Ootey grunted. 'The lizards are not to be exchanged for cloth. Fine though it is.'

Maia's heart sank.

'But as a reckoning for eggs just hatched?' he scratched his chin then nodded. 'I accept your story and your gift.'

He lifted his hand and beckoned impatiently. Kodo walked across the circle and stood next to Maia.

'You didn't tell me of your battle with the eagle,' Ootey said.

'No, Grandfather.'

Maia could see the slight trembling of the boy's hands. He stooped and pulled her eagle feather from the sand and held it out to her.

'It was a good telling,' he said.

Maia twisted the feather back into her hair and gave him a swift grin. The boy's eyes were still wide with shock.

'A talent of the Eagle People,' said Tareth drily. Maia couldn't meet his gaze. He knew she had adapted the truth.

Tareth smiled at Kodo. 'My eagle will remember his tussle and think twice about raiding a lizard scrape. So will Maia.'

He turned to Ootey. 'Honey would sweeten her tale. Since Maia trespassed at the lizard scrape, she should share the secret of the bees' cave with Kodo.'

Maia watched the old man consider the idea. Finally he nodded.

'A fair exchange,' he grunted.

Maia and Kodo breathed sighs of relief. They had escaped Ootey's anger.

Fourteen

'Why didn't you tell Ootey about taking the hatchling and its ending?' asked Kodo, gazing down at the tiny, silk-wrapped lizard Maia had placed in his hand.

Maia shrugged. 'It made a better story without that part,' she said.

Kodo frowned.

Did he think she was a liar as well as a thief because she hadn't admitted to stealing a lizard? Well, she didn't care what he thought.

'And anyway it made you sound braver,' she said crossly. 'I'm only giving it back because Tareth said we ought to ask how it should pass. He didn't want to offend the Lizard People.'

Kodo cupped his hands around the tiny bundle. Maia swallowed. It was her fault the lizard was dead.

'And you'd have got into more trouble if I'd told him that I'd taken a lizard,' she added shrewdly.

Kodo sighed. 'So much trouble that there wouldn't ever be enough honey to save me.' He looked down at the empty pottery jar at her feet, next to a basket and a rope.

'Thought so,' said Maia. Kodo looked as downcast as a moulting eagle. She grinned at him. 'And he'd have yelled at me. Tareth was cross enough. Your grandfather looks as if he could get crosser than a red-crested lizard.'

'Worse,' said Kodo.

'So I won't tell him a different tale if you don't. And Tareth won't change the story now.' She frowned, knowing that when they were alone, Tareth would take her to task. She put the thought of that aside. 'All we have to do is take your grandfather some honey to soothe his temper. He liked the story and the cloth.'

She was suddenly practical, her mood changing like gorse-fire, jumping from bush to bush. 'So, what do we do with the lizard?'

Kodo told her. It took them out of their way but Maia didn't protest, just suggested they leave the honey-hunting gear tucked out of sight and followed him down the cliff path.

'It mustn't be in the laying cove,' he told her as they scrambled over a rock fall. 'Or Doon won't use the same scrape and I'll have to follow her to find the new place. I've told her the hatchling died.'

'You speak to the lizards?'

Kodo nodded. 'It's easier in the water.'

'Tareth talks to Magnus. And the eagle understands him. He understands me too,' she added quickly as if Kodo wasn't going to believe that she could communicate with an eagle. 'Soon I'll have my own eagle.' She touched the eagle feathers in her hair. 'A sea-eagle. I've been looking for nests. I haven't found one yet.'

'Sometimes I see them flying out to the deeps when I'm with the lizards,' Kodo told her. 'I could tell you . . . if you want.'

'Thank you.'

Maia helped Kodo dig a deep hollow at the fringe of low water, scooping out the water with a shell as an occasional tiny wave flooded the hole.

'It's best if the water always covers it,' he said.

Maia watched as he covered the bundle with sand and placed a smooth flat stone over the place. Facing over the shallows towards the sun-deeps he whispered the parting words. The lizard was young, it had no stories other than its time in the egg and its hatching so the telling was brief.

'I'm glad Tareth gave it silk to lie on, even though it didn't heal it,' said Maia when he had finished. 'It will have brought dreams.'

Kodo looked at her in surprise. 'Dreams?'

She shrugged the question aside. She had said too much. The whispering silk, the moon-moths and their hidden moth-garden were secrets. Maybe when Tareth finally shared them all with her she would take her place as a weaver too and could forget the Watcher's story and stones.

She turned away from the sea and ran up the beach. 'Come on. The best time to find honey is while the bees sleep. They'll be flying now. We might get stung,' she looked back over her shoulder. 'Are you frightened?'

'No!' he protested. 'I'm not scared.' He stooped and touched his palm to the stone, smoothing his tattooed thumb twice across the surface. Then he chased after her.

Maia swung high on the cliff above him. The bee-cleft was like a teardrop in the rockface. She reached up, a basket balanced on her hip, and prodded the nest with the long stick in her hand. With a deft flick she knocked a honeycomb free and caught it in the basket. Bees buzzed around her head. Maia ignored them. She climbed a little higher. Swinging her stick, she hooked another comb. This time she failed to catch it.

'Look out!'

The honeycomb tumbled from the sky, a dark blob surrounded by flying bees. It fell near Kodo's feet. He scrambled to get it, brushing the bees away with a large leaf, got stung several times, yelled and dropped it in his basket. He sucked at his hand trying to get at the small, black barbs.

Maia worked her way across to a larger cleft in the rocks. Wedging her basket against the cliff-face, she pulled a fire-fungus from her waist pouch. She rested it at the entrance of the nest and blew gently on it. A trickle of smoke drifted into the nest. The thread became a small cloud. She waved her hand to waft the smoke into the cleft. Bees started swarming.

'Come,' she called. 'Bring your stick.' Bees buzzed around her head like smuts of ash dancing round flames.

Kodo spat out a bee-barb and retied his loin cloth so that the knot was to the side and tucked the bee-stick through the knot. Next time he was going to wear all his clothes and Ootey's knitted hat.

When they were back on solid ground, Maia cut a comb in two and sucked honey from her piece as she passed the rest to Kodo. She lay back in the warm, grassy hollow. Kodo's eyelashes fluttered as he chewed blissfully, sweet stuff dripping from the corner of his mouth.

'Good,' he mumbled.

Maia grinned. 'Good for cuts too,' she said and rubbed her sticky fingers over a graze on her elbow.

'Better to eat,' said Kodo.

Maia wrapped three large leaves over the opening of the pottery jar propped against the pile of rocks she had gathered to support it. She pulled several tall, grass stalks, twisted them together into a cord and tied the cover in place.

'Ootey's,' she said. 'We should go.' It was a long scramble back to the stilt village.

Kodo stood stretching his arms wide like his fisher-bird drying its wings. He picked up a stone and hurled it into space. It fell short, thudding into a thicket of gorse. The bushes trembled. A creature squealed.

'Rabbit,' said Kodo. He bent to grab another stone and crept towards the bushes.

Maia was staring at the gorse. 'Too big. A wild goat, maybe.'

The bushes shook.

A rabbit shot out and ran towards them. Kodo shouted in triumph and flung himself forwards to tackle it.

He heard a growl.

'Kodo!' screamed Maia as a beast erupted from the bushes. Its claws slashed at Kodo, missing his head by a hair's breath. Yelling, Maia hurled a rock. The wulfen checked, half-turning towards her, fangs bared, small eyes gleaming.

Kodo rolled over and over towards the cliff edge.

Maia hurled another rock. It thudded against its skull. The beast shook its head. Swags of saliva dripped from its snarling jaws. Kodo lurched to his knees and tried to crawl away. His movement distracted the beast. It reared, towering over him. Kodo screamed.

Maia yelled. Her world narrowed to black fur and a gaping red mouth. She saw Kodo lift his arm to ward off snapping teeth. Heard him shriek. He was going to die! Her desperately flung stone ricocheted off the beast's snout. As another found its mark, the beast roared and sprang.

Fifteen

Maia felt the scalding chaos of fury roar through her as fire cut her heart in two. Pain and flames licked at her. She was burning.

The beast roared.

Kodo screamed.

Maia tore at the rocks beneath her bleeding hands, ripping them from the ground. She staggered to her feet. Her eyes were on fire. She was going blind. She squinted through the red, roaring light. The beast was a towering, writhing shape, in the blood-red light searing her eyeballs. She couldn't see Kodo. The stones scalded her hands. She was consumed by fire. She was going to die. Kodo was going to die. She screamed and hurled rocks. The smoking missiles thudded into the beast's pelt. She could smell smouldering fur. It bellowed and knocked Kodo aside to face her.

It was going to charge.

Maia clutched at her chest. The pain would kill her before the beast ripped her limb from limb. If only she could see clearly. If only she could tear the flames from her eyes she could see where to leap, where to plunge the knife.

She reached for her knife. The dagger sheath was empty. She dropped to her knees, scrabbling for another rock.

Above her the clouds split and a blade of sunlight speared down.

Maia raised her arms. Her fingers stretched towards the golden strand. It wavered, splashing across the rocks, streaming towards her. Maia flinched as it hit her.

She staggered to her feet. Bright tentacles of light curled round her. The fire in her eyes was turning to molten gold. She would go mad with the pain. She flung up her hands to block out the light. The molten gold ran through her fingers. Her skin was flowing from her bones, dripping into the light, becoming the liquid light. She was breathing light. She clawed at it. It was like gathering and reeling the silk threads from Tareth's cocoon in the boiling pot. She was being wrapped in a cocoon of light. She couldn't breathe. Couldn't move. Couldn't think.

The beast leaping towards her was rimmed with gold. Flames shot from the tips of her fingers. Fire roared from her hands and hit the beast. A raging torrent of red and gold blasted the earth and engulfed the wulfen. It crackled and spat and swallowed it. A blackened smoking lump crashed to the ground at her feet. The earth hissed, boiled and splintered. Stones shattered. A sliver sliced her cheek open. Maia screamed and fainted.

The cool breeze brushed across her face. She could hear gulls calling. Heard a rush of feathers, the cry of crows, the sound of wind flutes. Reluctantly she tried to open her eyes. Her lids were glued together. She rubbed her eyes with her torn fingers. She squinted through her scorched eyelashes, peering about like a newly hatched lizard. The light was grey and misty, everything was blurred. A sob rose in her throat. She swallowed it and tasted fire. Her head hurt. Her chest felt as if it had been crushed in a rock fall. Maia blinked at the mist above her. Tears ran from the corner of her eyes and down her cheeks. Her vision wobbled and seemed to clear a little.

A sob that was not hers bubbled through the silence. Kodo?

Maia coughed and sat up. A pigeon fluttered beside her. She squinted at it, trying to focus. The red blob on its tail was a tiny carved flute. Sabra's bird. She would be somewhere near. Maia rubbed her eyes again. She heard another groan and moved her head stiffly towards the sound.

A pile of grey ash lying across a gleaming black pool at her feet was stirring in the breeze and being blown across the rocks. Beyond it a hazy figure was rocking and moaning. Kodo. Maia felt a rush of joy. He was hurt but alive.

'Kodo?' she croaked.

He lifted his head. He looked at her, eyes wide with horror. 'You threw fire at the beast.'

The wulfen. Where was it? Maia looked at the pile of ash.

'The fire burned me!' Kodo whispered. 'You burned me!'

Maia heard a jangle of silver bracelets. She breathed the waft of dusty herbs.

'A Sun Catcher burns all who threaten her world, lizard boy,' announced a familiar voice.

'Sabra?'

'Greeting, Sun Catcher.' Sabra's robe brushed Maia's arm as the old woman squatted beside her. 'The crows called me. But I came too late. So the wulfen is dead.'

A red-legged crow hopped across to the black pool and pecked at it. Its beak clicked against the surface. Sabra's bony finger touched the solid pool. She looked at Maia.

'You have pulled down the sun. You have melted sand and bone with your anger, Sun Catcher. Earth and the beast have become one.' She scooped up her crow and tucked it inside her sleeve. 'Truly you are to be feared.'

Maia shivered. 'The fire came. It hurt.'

She looked at the Watcher. Sabra seemed as if she was sitting underwater. Fretfully Maia rubbed her eyes. She held her hands close to her face. They were scratched and bleeding but there was no trace of burned, blackened skin. Yet she had seen, had felt, fire blast from her fingers.

'I don't understand,' she said.

Kodo was shuffling away from her. 'You burned me,' he repeated.

'You're alive,' retorted Sabra. 'And the creature is dead. You were lucky, lizard boy. She cannot yet control the fire. You could have melted in the flames like the beast.'

She turned to look at Maia. 'Although since the boy lives, you must have already started to learn the secrets of sun-fire.'

Maia dragged in a deep breath. It was like swallowing knives. 'Melted?'

The Watcher was pulling leaves from a pouch on her belt. 'Come,' she said to Kodo. 'Heal-leaf will calm the burn.'

Maia watched Kodo crawl towards the Watcher. He wouldn't look at her as he held out his arm. His fear hurt as much as the raw burn in her chest. She coughed and tasted smoke and fire on her tongue. She watched as Sabra wrapped a long leaf around Kodo's forearm and bound it in place with a soft twist of stem. If she chewed the heal-leaf would it ease the pain in her chest?

'I'll make a poultice,' Sabra glanced at Maia. 'It will soften the pain.'

Maia nodded. 'Good,' she whispered. She blinked at Kodo, trying to get him in focus. 'I'm sorry,' she said.

Suddenly Sabra's face was next to hers, her hand under her chin forcing her head up. The light stung. Maia could feel tears gathering in the corners of her eyes.

'Can you see, Sun Catcher?'

Maia nodded. Fat tears oozed from the corner of her eyes and rolled down her cheeks. She closed them against the light. 'As if I'm in water. My eyes are full of smoke.'

She felt the Watcher's fingers pushing open her lids. First one eye, then the other. Sabra leaned even closer. Her breath brushed across her face. An old woman's breath. Maia tried not to wrinkle her nose at the smell. Tried not to wrench her chin out of Sabra's pinching hold.

Finally Sabra let her go. 'There's no cloud,' she said. 'You will see clearly again. I'll find eyebright. It will help.'

Maia grabbed Sabra's arm as she started to get up. 'When?'

Sabra brushed Maia's hand from her arm. 'I'll find eyebright. You can help, lizard boy. Look for a white flower and plant no higher than your thumb. It grows beneath the rocks.' A crow called. Maia felt the Watcher become rigid.

'Someone comes,' she hissed.

'When will I see clearly?'

Even with her blurry vision Maia could see the Watcher's frown. 'Sunlight is fierce. Bright and strong. No one should look at the sun. But the Sun Catcher must.'

'So . . . ?' Maia demanded.

The crow called again. Maia heard Kodo scrabble to his feet.

'Horses,' he said.

Now Maia could hear the jingle of harnesses, the thud of hooves on the soft turf along the cliff-top. The Watcher was gathering her robes, ready to depart.

'Come with me, boy. Say nothing unless you have to. And then play the fool.'

'Stay here,' Sabra told Maia. 'And cover your hair.'

'Why?'

'Questions! Always questions. No time now. The Marsh Lords are coming. They'll have seen the fire!'

Maia got to her feet and stood blinking. 'Tell me!'

'Hide your hair. The Lords do not need to see you and link you with fire. Quick boy. We'll meet them on the cliff-top.'

Maia heard Kodo's gasp of pain as Sabra grabbed his injured wrist. 'Remember. Agree with anything I say. And hope they do not see the black pool and wonder what happened here.'

She turned to Maia. 'Find sand. Cover the dark stain. Stay here.' She hesitated. 'The Weaver said that the Sun Catcher's eyes become covered with a cloud to protect them from the light. The cloud is thick. The Sun Catcher cannot see through it. But they don't need to see because they can feel the sun on their skin and can still catch the sun. Blindness is the Sun Catcher's fate.'

She shoved Kodo ahead of her. 'Climb, boy.'

Sixteen

Kodo felt the old woman's hand planted firmly on the base of his spine as she pushed him up the track.

'Move,' she muttered. 'We don't want them to dismount and search the cliff. A pool of black glass will be difficult to explain.'

She shoved harder and whistled. Three crows took off from the gorse bushes either side of the track. Calling to each other, they flew ahead and arrowed over the top of the cliff.

Kodo heard a startled shout and then, gasping, his legs trembling with effort, he was up and over the edge himself standing in a mêlée of wheeling grey horses, sleek hounds, swooping crows and metal-clad men who shone in the sun. He froze. A brindled hound snarled and thrust its head in Kodo's stomach. It must be able to smell his fear. Kodo's knees buckled. The Watcher pushed through the snorting horses to stand by him.

She flung her hand in the air and the crows stopped swirling around the ears of the squealing horses. Reined in tight, the horses stopped snorting and stamping their huge feathered feet. Kodo winced as a massive hoof crashed to the ground, lizard claws away from his foot. A hound the colour of wet sand sniffed round the feet of the Watcher.

'Greetings, Lords.' Sabra flicked her fingers against her forehead. 'Call off your hounds before they scare the boy to death. He has frightened himself speechless already.' She cuffed Kodo. He staggered and his ears rang. 'The foolish boy set the gorse on fire.'

Now that the world was still, Kodo could see that it was not an army surrounding him but merely two riders in gleaming helmets and mail jerkins on tall, dappled horses. He twisted to look behind him. Not two but three mounted men. The third was leaning forward in his saddle and peering over the cliff.

'A large fire for a small boy.' The voice sounded metallic, booming within the helmet. 'We thought it was the beacon. There have been rumours of Sea Thieves along the coast.'

'Not raiders, children playing,' claimed Sabra. 'And they had controlled the fire before I arrived. The boy singed his arm. '

One of the riders pulled his helmet from his head and rested it on his thigh. He ran his hand through his sweat-flattened hair. Kodo could see the silver thumb ring on his right hand. He stared at the brown curling tattoo, just like the one on his own thumb, partially hidden beneath the silver band. Kodo felt dizzy. Was it possible? Was this Marsh Lord an Untouchable?

Then the Lord's dark eyes were boring into him. 'What is a lizard boy doing so far from the stilt village?'

Kodo licked his lips. He glanced at Sabra. She had taken her red-legged crow from her sleeve. It sat on her fist, its beady eyes watching the hounds now squatting in a circle round them. Sabra stroked its chest. She glanced at Kodo.

'Don't be frightened, boy. Tell the Marsh Lords why you were on the cliffs.'

Kodo swallowed. 'Honey,' he muttered.

The big man nudged his horse forward. Kodo took a step backwards and stepped on the Watcher's foot.

'Clumsy boy!' She shook him. 'Tell Lord Helmek how you found the cliff bees and tried to smoke them from their nest and started the fire.'

Kodo nodded. 'Honey,' he repeated. He thought he could hear a humming. It sounded as if it were coming from the Watcher's robes. He shook his head to clear it.

'Honey. In the cliff,' he stammered.

'Fright has stolen his wits,' said Sabra. 'He'll know better than to play with fire again!'

Kodo stared sullenly at his feet. If the Watcher wanted him to appear witless he would, although he wanted to look at the gleaming lord with the tattooed thumb.

'Let the boy speak for himself, old woman.'

The man attached his helmet to his saddle and slid from his horse. He pulled Kodo free of Sabra's grip, dragged him to the edge of the cliff. Kodo wriggled. Below he could see Maia, her hair glinting in the sun, huddled on a rock staring across the sun-deeps. Why wasn't she hiding as the Watcher had told her?

'Show me the bees!' The grip on his shoulder tightened. For a moment he thought the man was going to fling him over the cliff. He tried to pull back. His feet slipped and dislodged a rock. It bounced down the cliff-face. He saw Maia glance up.

'Bee cave,' Kodo gasped. 'Honey.'

The humming was growing louder. A buzzing black column rose from the cliffs. The man swore and released Kodo. Then suddenly the air was full of bees. Kodo fell to his knees. The swarm flew over him. The Marsh Lord was cursing, waving his arms, brushing bees from his hair, his face, his arms. He ran for his horse, chased by the swarm.

Sabra knelt beside Kodo, twitching her shawl over her head, covering him with her voluminous sleeves. Kodo saw Sabra's yellow-toothed grin. Then he was smothered in stifling darkness. Bird feathers brushed against his cheek. Someone yelled. He heard a dog yelp. Beneath his knees the earth seemed to tremble as the horses took flight. Then silence and stillness.

Cautiously Kodo lifted the black cloth from his face. A bee crawled over his hand. He shook it off. The Watcher was shaking bees from her robes. They buzzed round her head as if they were talking to her. Then they flew off, chasing the disappearing swarm which was attacking the galloping riders.

The Watcher laughed. She held out her hand and pulled Kodo to his feet.

'The bees,' said Kodo.

'Have seen off the Marsh Lords.' She turned, bundling up her long skirts in one hand. 'Quickly now! Get out of sight. If they can stop long enough to look back, they must think we've fled from the bees too.'

'You called the bees?'

'Questions! Questions!' The Watcher hustled him down the track. 'I need you to look for eyebright, boy. I need to save the Sun Catcher's sight.'

Seventeen

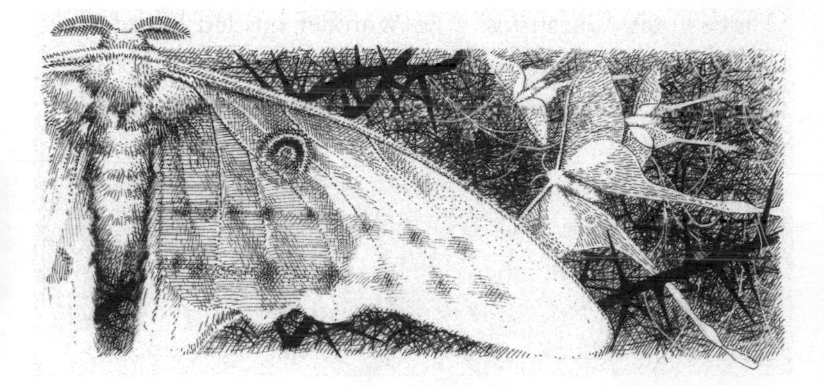

'She called the bees,' whispered Kodo. He glanced over his shoulder at the Watcher who was pounding a bunch of leaves on a rock. 'They chased the Marsh Lords.'

He seemed to have forgiven her for burning him, thought Maia. To have forgotten his fear of the fire. But she hadn't.

She shuddered. She would never, ever forget the raging fire. Never forget how sunlight had caught alight in her hands. When she shut her eyes she could still see the leaping wulfen and the gush of flames that had consumed him. Had turned him into a glass pool. How was it possible?

She was glad it was dead. Glad she had saved Kodo. But if the fate of a Sun Catcher was to burn, to destroy, then she was never, ever becoming one. She would refuse to listen to the Watcher, because despite what Sabra said, the flames had started before she'd caught the sun. The flames had begun with terror and rage inside her. And yet the fire had left no mark on her. She was a freak, a killer, a flame-thrower and she had no idea how it had happened. Maia crossed her arms and hid her face.

Kodo was still chattering like starlings roosting. 'The Marsh Lord wore a ring on his right thumb. But I could see a tattoo. It was like mine.'

He was holding out his hand. She could barely see the tattoo on his thumb.

'He was born an Untouchable. A Marsh Lord! How is it possible? He must have been a great fighter. A great leader. Sabra called him Helmek. He had a horse and a hound and he gleamed in the sun. Even the Watcher bowed to him. Does Grandfather know it's possible to leave the stilt village and live in the stone holdfast? If he can become a Lord, I can become a trader and have my own ship. All things are possible.'

Maia squinted at him. The light was dying now. Or were her eyes growing dimmer? She couldn't turn to look and see if the sun was dipping towards the rim of the sun-deeps. She didn't dare look at the sun.

'Is it getting darker?' she asked hoarsely.

'A little.'

Maia battened down a rising panic. She had stared at bright flames. She'd been dazzled. Of course her eyes were sore, her vision blurred. She rubbed her eyes and stared again at Kodo's hand.

Sabra came and sat beside her.

'I have a salve for your eyelids. It will cool them.

'They're not hot.'

'Lie down and I'll smooth it on. It will help,' said Sabra.

Maia did as she was told. Sabra's hand was like the shadow of a winged bird above her face. She grabbed it and held it tight. 'How will it help?'

'You have come suddenly into your power with no one to guide you. The fire was too bright. You looked too long. You must rest. When you wake you will see clearly again. '

Maia took a deep breath and screwed up her courage to voice her fear. 'So catching sunlight doesn't make you blind?'

'No.' Sabra freed her hand and started smoothing the salve on the skin round Maia's eyes.

Maia closed her eyes. The salve was cool on her lids. It would cure her eyes. But . . .

'That's not what you said before,' she accused.

She heard Sabra sigh. 'No.'

The silence seemed to last forever. The smoothing fingers were hypnotic. She could feel herself falling asleep under their spell. Maia grabbed at the hand that was smoothing away the memory of the fire.

'Tell me!' she demanded. 'And don't lie to me. Will the sun make me blind?'

'No.'

Maia took a deep breath.

'Not this time,' said Sabra slowly. 'But . . . a Sun Catcher cannot survive unscathed. No one can look at the sun. In the end the sun takes its payment and the Sun Catcher no longer sees as others see. They are without sight before they grow old. They don't need eyes to see what they must do.'

Maia swallowed. 'Then I won't be a Sun Catcher. I won't

look at the sun. I won't make the rage that made me burn with fire. I don't want . . . I won't . . . you can't make me!'

'Hush!'

Maia slapped away the calming hand and sat up. 'You don't understand. I can't. I won't.'

'The stones . . .' began Sabra.

'The stones are wrong!' yelled Maia. 'I'm the Weaver's daughter! I'm not a Sun Catcher!' She flung herself down, rolled onto her stomach and hid her face in her arm. 'And I'm afraid! The fire burned me. There was fire inside me. It hurt. It killed the beast and I was glad. But now . . . now I'm afraid!' she cried. 'What good is a blind weaver?'

'We all feel fear, Sun Catcher. It is what we do with the fear that matters.'

'I'm not a Sun Catcher!'

Maia felt Sabra's hand on head. 'Sleep. Let the eyebright heal. Sun-wake will bring new thoughts.'

'No, it won't!'

'Sleep.'

Maia struggled against the darkness Sabra's hand was bringing. But the effort to resist was too great. She yawned and allowed the darkness to take her.

She was dreaming. Moth wings brushed her cheeks. The black circles on the wings looked like owl eyes staring at her. Like white ghosts in the moonlight, the moths flitted from thorn bush to thorn bush. The silk shreds tied to the thorns whispered as they brushed past. Dust from the moth wings coated the torn silk. The silk shone in the moonlight. It started to sing. It was a song of welcome. The cocoons were hatching.

Maia opened her eyes. The moon hung fat and round above her. The cliffs were white in the light. A pathway of bright moonlight stretched across the black sun-deeps below.

Maia sat up. Tareth would be following the moon track. She feared for him. He would be diving for the shells. She should be there. She stood up and looked out to sea, searching for the dugout. The sun-deeps were empty.

Something stirred at her feet. Maia glanced down. It was the Watcher curled in sleep, surrounded by plump roosting pigeons, their heads tucked beneath their wings. Sabra was snoring. Beyond her, Kodo lay flat on his back, his arms flung wide. There was a movement beside her. Maia spun, her hand searching for her knife. A rabbit hopped from beneath a gorse bush and started nibbling the silver grass. Maia relaxed. Another rabbit joined it. For a moment Maia watched them and then realised that she could see. Everything in the moonlight was as sharp as if it was sun-high. She could see!

She felt the blood surge in her veins, hammering with the leap of her heart. She twisted round, taking in the small camp the Watcher had made. She could see the forgotten honeycomb oozing honey onto the large flat leaves that she had told Kodo to collect. See the shape of crows in the stunted trees. See the glow from the remains of the fire the Watcher had lit. See the shadows of rocks in the moonlight, even the dark stain on the flat rock where Sabra had pounded the eyebright leaves.

And the moths were flying. She remembered her dream. If the new silkworms hatched, the silk thread would be ruined as they gnawed through the cocoons. Tareth needed undamaged cocoons. Once he had collected and crushed the shells he would set a huge pot to boil, drop in the cocoons and start unreeling the silk thread. She had to collect the cocoons. She had to help. She had to take them to Tareth.

Turning, she saw the woven reed basket Kodo had taken from his hut to carry the honeycomb. She picked it up and skirting round him she tiptoed past the sleeping Watcher. A pigeon stirred. Its wind-flutes murmured. Maia froze. Then the night was still again.

Maia tucked her skirt into her belt, scrunched the reed basket flat until she could shove it under her tunic and scrambled along the cliff path.

Kodo sat up. The moon made it easy for him to see Maia scaling the cliff. Where was she going? The honey cave was not that way. Nor was the path to the cliff village. He got to his feet, crept past the Watcher and started to climb.

Sabra watched the two climbing figures as the stones in the bag beside her rattled against each other, then fell silent.

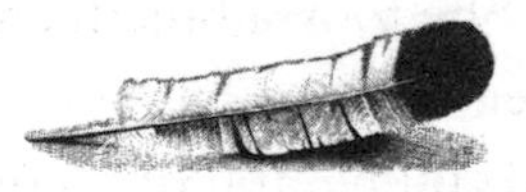

Maia paused for breath. The climb had been steep and difficult even though the way had been lit by moonlight. The opening to the moth-garden lay beyond the jutting rock. She had only to ease herself round it, ignoring the dizzying drop below as she swung out beyond the cliff-face, and she would be able to scramble across the scree into the hidden cleft where the moths lived. She massaged her fingers so that they would grip the tiny fissures in the rock. She was tired now.

A rock clattered from the cliff behind her. She was being followed. For a moment Maia forgot that the beast was dead. Fear that it was tracking her to the moth-garden closed her throat. Her limbs seemed to turn to water. She drew a deep shuddering breath and turned to face the terror that pursued her.

It was Kodo.

Fear was replaced by relief. Close on its heels came anger. How dare he follow and spy on her? Only Tareth and she knew the secrets of the moon-moths and their garden hidden in a cleft in the cliff.

She waited until he was close enough to see the anger in her eyes.

'What d'you think you're doing?' she spat. 'Who said you could follow me here?'

Kodo flinched. Maia swallowed. Did he think she was going to flame him? She took a breath and felt some of the heat welling up in her die.

'Go back,' she said coldly. 'You've no right to be here.'

She watched Kodo struggle with his uncertainty. 'You showed me the honey cave. Why shouldn't I be here too?'

'I promised you honey,' said Maia slowly. 'No more.'

Kodo looked as if he couldn't believe his ears. 'I gave you a lizard.'

'A worthless, dying lizard.' She had to be strong. To be cruel to keep him safe. Tareth had told her that the old silk in the moth-garden was not to be trusted. Had only allowed her to go there to collect the cocoons for him if she sealed her ears so that she didn't hear the silk song.

'Go back. It's not safe.'

'No one is safe with you,' said Kodo.

'This place is secret, lizard boy,' she said. 'No one knows about it. It is too dangerous for anyone to know. It's too dangerous for you.'

'Why?' asked Kodo.

Maia glared at him. 'Go back!' She glanced at the moon. Was it dimmer now? Was sun-wake close? She had to collect the cocoons while the moths danced in the moonlight.

'Why?'

'Because!' Maia hissed. 'Because the silk sings. You shouldn't hear the songs.'

She saw that she had angered him.

He scowled at her. 'Because I'm an Untouchable?'

'Yes! Because you're an Untouchable.'

She saw Kodo recoil as if she had hit him.

'Not the Cliff Dwellers, not the Watcher, not the Marsh Lords. No one,' she growled. 'Especially not you, lizard boy! Now go back to your lizards and leave me. Go!'

Kodo shot her a look of hatred. He turned and scrambled back the way he had come. Maia realised she was holding her breath. The silk was singing. She edged her way carefully round the overhang and crawled across the scree into the moth-garden.

She did not see Kodo turn back and creep to the overhang.

A moon-moth flittered by on silent wings. It brushed against her face, dusting her skin with powder from its white wings. Other gigantic moths were hanging from the silk strips Tareth had fastened to the stunted thorn tree branches. Time and weather had torn them to tatters and each strand whispered. The drowsy moths opened and closed their wings as they hung from the shredded silk; their wings moving to the rhythms of the song whispering from the silk. Two, their tails curled, were laying huge, white eggs on the leaves. The eggs gleamed in the moonlight.

Maia could feel the silk song drawing her further into the garden. She reached to stroke the iridescent blue silk hanging from a bush. It rippled as if it were moving underwater. It was beautiful. Its voice was soft and kind. It was telling her . . .

Maia stabbed her hand on the thorn bush. The thorn was driven deep into her flesh. She cried and snatched her hand away. A blister of bright blood bubbled on her thumb. The pain broke the silk-spell. She dug her hand into the pouch at her waist and fumbled for the beeswax. It was soft from the warmth of her body. She pulled off two lumps, rolled them and put the plugs in her ears. Now she was safe. The song died to a murmur. She couldn't see the colours or the pictures they sang. She had warned Kodo and forgotten the danger to herself. The old silk was strong. It had hung there for many star-shifts, tied to the bushes by Tareth when he made the secret garden, protecting the moon-moths, trapping them here. Plenty of time to make new songs.

Now the moths resting on the bushes were flying, fluttering against her face as if she were a flame. They thudded against her and fell stunned. If she moved she would tread on them and crush them.

Maia waved her arm in front of her face to fend off the circling moths and took a giant stride across the carpet of fluttering wings. She scrambled across the scree, going from bush to bush pulling off the fat brown cocoons, carelessly tearing the leaves they were stuck to, scratching her arms and hands on the thorns in her haste to collect the cocoons and drop them into the basket.

At last the thorn bushes were bare. Maia turned and slid back to the entrance of the cleft. The tattered silk seemed to reach for her. It clung to her as she passed. Maia could feel yearning, anger, demands. Somehow the silk wrapped itself round her wrist. In her head Maia heard a high-pitched sound as if crystal had chimed on crystal, a brilliant light flared in her eyes. She felt the beginning of the burn of ice. She ripped at the silk. It stuck to her fingers. The song started in her head, not even the beeswax plugs could muffle it. Maia cried out, attempting to drown the song with her shouts as she pulled the silk from her hand. At last she was free. The song faltered. Maia fled, hurling herself down the avalanching shale and scrambling from the garden.

Breathlessly she reached the overhang. She was safe. This was the worst visit. She set down the basket. It was a good haul. She scraped the wax plugs from her ears and dropped them in the basket. Some of the cocoons were moving. As the moonlight touched them they twitched. She had to stop the moonlight waking them. She looked around. Nothing but rock. She needed leaves. Anything.

She lifted her tunic, gripped it in her teeth and tugged. Eventually it tore. Maia tucked a piece over the top of the basket, hiding the cocoons. Somehow she managed to get herself and the basket back round the overhang to the cliff ledge. All she had to do now was get the cocoons safely to the cave. If she couldn't manage the basket she would just have to empty it inside her tunic. The cocoons would tickle as she clambered across the rocks. Her skin started to itch at the thought. She picked up the basket again and saw Kodo. He was sitting, his back against the cliff, staring at nothing, a silly smile on his face.

'I told you to go!' snarled Maia.

Kodo blinked at her, his eyes as wide and dark as an owl's. He was sleeping with his eyes open.

Maia shook him. 'Wake up! I told you to go! Why are you still here?'

Kodo stared past her as if she wasn't there.

Maia felt her anger flare. 'Get up.' She shook him again. 'You're lucky you didn't fall off the cliff.' He still didn't move, so she kicked him. 'Get up!'

'Ouch!' Kodo rubbed his leg.

'Get up before I do it again!' threatened Maia through gritted teeth. She watched Kodo get slowly to his feet. He yawned and stretched, took an unwary step. Maia grabbed him and slammed him back against the cliff-face. That seemed to jolt him out of his trance.

'What're you doing?'

'I told you to leave. Why're you still here?' Maia glared at him. 'What did you see?' she demanded furiously.

Kodo looked at her and then away. 'Nothing.'

Maia's eyes narrowed. 'That had better be true. You must forget you were ever here. D'you hear me? You must never try to find this place again.'

Kodo pulled his arm free and rubbed it. 'I didn't see anything,' he said sulkily. 'I fell asleep.'

'You should have gone back,' snapped Maia. 'Now come on, let's get off this cliff before the gulls come in with sea-rise and peck your eyes out because you're on the nesting ledges.'

Kodo shot her a worried look.

'They attack the Cliff Dwellers if they dare to climb up to steal their eggs. Peck, peck! Aiming for the eyes. Peck, peck! And if they don't stab you in the face they'll fly so close you let go and fall. Peck! Peck! Stab!'

'I don't believe you,' said Kodo stubbornly.

Maia shrugged. 'Wait here and see then,' she said. 'I'm not.'

She edged past him and set off along the ledge. Before she'd taken ten paces she heard Kodo hurrying after her.

Eighteen

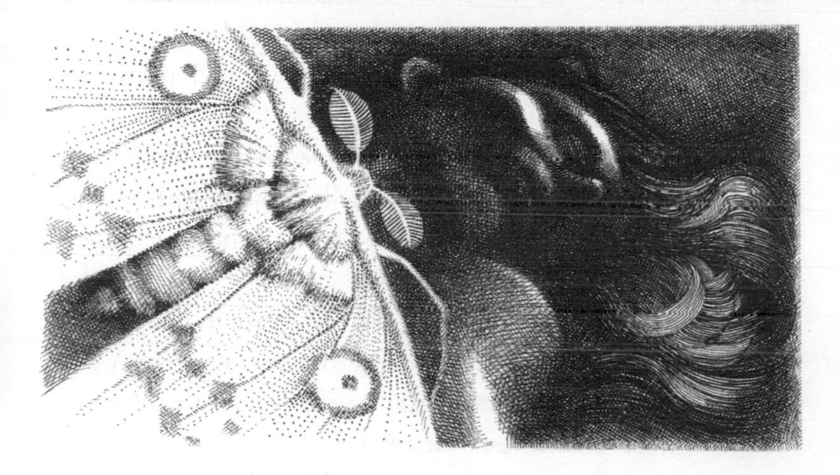

'Where have you been?' Tareth looked up from pounding shells in the dished stone outside the cave, as Maia's long, sun-wake shadow fell across him.

She limped wearily to the cave entrance and sank to the ground. 'You fished for the shells?' she asked. 'I thought I might ask the lizard boy to help.'

She remembered guiltily how she had shouted at Kodo. He had stormed off back to his village. He'd probably never be her friend now.

'I'm not so feeble that I can't dive for shells when the moon is so bright,' retorted Tareth.

He was looking at her ripped skirt, her grazed knees and the unfamiliar covered basket she had put at his feet. His gaze sharpened as he looked at her face.

'What's happened?'

Maia sighed and closed her eyes as she leaned against the rocks. She shifted her shoulders to find a comfortable spot. All she wanted to do was to sleep. She was too tired to move. She would sleep where she sat like Magnus dozing in the sun.

She sighed again and opened her eyes, squinting at the light creeping from the dark rim of the sea. It was too bright. She turned her face away.

'The beast is dead,' she said reluctantly.

'The wulfen!' Tareth dropped his heavy stone pestle. 'The wulfen is dead?'

'It was waiting . . . near the honey cave. We . . . I was showing Kodo.' She paused again, frowning as she tried to untangle the chain of events. 'I made fire. The Marsh Lords came. I've collected the cocoons. The silk was lonely. It tried to . . . make me stay.' She trailed to a halt.

'Maia!' exploded Tareth. 'What are you saying? Eagle's flight!' he swore. He grabbed her arm. 'What happened?'

Maia looked at him and then quickly away again. She couldn't meet the shock in his eyes. 'It's all right. The Cliff Dwellers are safe. The wulfen is dead.'

Tareth slammed his fist against his palm. 'That for the Cliff Dwellers' safety! What, in the name of Khandar, have you done?'

Maia made herself look at him. 'Killed the wulfen with fire. Become a Sun Catcher.' She got to her feet. She could hear the sounds of the Cliff Dwellers waking. She didn't want to see anyone. 'The cocoons were moving,' she said, remembering. 'Will they hatch before you finish crushing the shell?'

Tareth was staring at her as if he had never seen her before. Well, she'd never been a Sun Catcher before.

'Cocoons?' he repeated.

'I took them all,' said Maia. 'You didn't tell me about the fire. That I would burn,' she accused him. 'You didn't tell me that Sun Catchers go blind! What else haven't you told me?'

Maia went into the sleeping cave and slid into her furs, pulling the soft skins over her head. She must sleep. She heard the scrape of Tareth's sledge as he entered the cave.

His hand jerked the furs from her face. 'It's not possible,' he said. 'You don't have the sun-stone. You can't become a Sun Catcher without it.'

Maia looked at him blankly.

'I stole it!' protested Tareth, 'I hid it! I haven't given you the sun-stone, Maia. You can't catch the sun without it. The Watcher's wrong. It doesn't matter what the runes say. What anyone says. You don't have the sun-stone! You can't be the Sun Catcher.'

Maia held out her hands. Her right hand was throbbing where she had stabbed herself on the thorn bush.

'I made fire with these. I was fire!' she said fiercely. 'I killed the beast with fire. The sun came. I caught the sun and blasted him. I made him melt!' A sob closed her throat. 'And I couldn't see.'

She turned away, tugging up the furs. There was silence.

'It's not possible,' hissed Tareth softly. 'I hid the sun-stone!'

Silence flowed back. Then Maia felt Tareth's hand on her head.

'I hid it to keep you safe,' he said. 'I never told you about . . . my . . . your . . . our life in Khandar. I kept my promise to keep you safe . . . secret. Never to speak of it. I thought . . . it seems the Watcher was right. I have failed you, Maia.'

She hated the defeat in his voice. But she wouldn't help him. He had let her live a lie. All her life was a lie. She didn't, couldn't ever, belong. She lay rigid. Eventually she heard him leave. It was then that she felt the wet fur and realised she was crying. She didn't know if she was crying for him, or for herself.

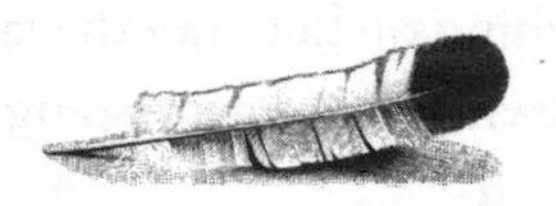

Maia had a pounding headache. She peered round the folds of fur. She could see Tareth's shadow, flowing then shrinking on the wall as he worked the loom. It was the sound and sight of her childhood when she had lain before sleep, listening to the song of the loom. If she listened very carefully, she sometimes heard the whispers of the silk he only ever wove on special, moon-bright sun-sleeps. Heard strange names weaving through the song as Tareth murmured to the silk. Names that seemed to belong to her dreams and were half-forgotten when she woke.

For a moment she was comforted. Then the throb in her hand and the hammering in her head overtook the soft beat of the weaver and the loom. Maia slipped back into a night-wake.

Icy, white wings beat frantically against her face. They splintered as they touched her. She was smothered with fat, white grubs with gaping mouths and no eyes. They wriggled over her, their mouths sucking at her skin, growing fatter as they feasted and spinning her into a web of freezing silk.

'Maia? Wake up.'

'The silk,' she muttered. 'It's talking.'

'Open your eyes.'

There was something heavy on her feet. She tried to squirm from underneath it. It shifted, then settled on her feet again. Her hand hurt. Her thumb was on fire. Fire! Terrified, she opened her eyes and sat bolt upright.

Magnus was perching on her. Tareth was by her side. The purple shadows of twilight were creeping into the sleeping cave.

'Maia?'

'Head hurts,' she muttered.

'You've slept through two sun-wakes. I couldn't wake you. The Healer said to let you sleep, that you had a fever. Yet Sun Catcher fire shouldn't cause fever.' He held out a beaker of foul-smelling liquid. 'Selora made this. Drink.'

Maia sniffed at the liquid and pulled a face. 'She's trying to poison me.'

Tareth didn't even smile. He must be worried, thought Maia. She took the beaker. Her hand banged against Tareth's.

'Ahh!' It was as if she had caught an ember from the fire. She dropped the beaker and the drink sprayed everywhere.

'It wouldn't have been that bad,' said Tareth, mopping spills.

Maia was rocking, holding her hand.

'What is it?' Tareth took her hand in his. He turned it over, holding it close to his eyes, frowning 'Have you been silk dreaming?'

Maia nodded. 'Ice and wings,' she shuddered, 'and white maggots crawling over me.'

'Wait.' Tareth slid out of the sleeping cave, returning with a small pottery bowl and a flaming twist of weed stalk. He held it up and examined Maia's hand in the pool of light. 'I'm a fool. There's a thorn buried in your thumb.'

He placed the light on the floor, taking care to keep it away from her sleeping furs.

Befuddled, Maia stared at the smoky, black stain marking the floor as the weed continued to burn.

'This will hurt,' said Tareth. He pulled a flake of flint from his belt-pouch and held it in the flame. 'I should've suspected this when you were muttering about the moths in your sleep. But,' he held Maia's hand firmly, 'I thought you were remembering going to the moth-garden.' He probed her hand with the sharp flint. 'What has the lizard boy to do with the moths?'

'Ahh,' Maia gasped. She bit her lip. 'He followed me.' Her breath escaped in a great gasp as Tareth put his knife down.

Tareth was pressing either side of the cut with his thumbs. Fascinated Maia watched green pus and blood ooze from the small wound. A thin barbed thorn lay in the mess. Tareth wiped it away.

'A heal-leaf wrapping, and you'll be as good as new.'

He stuck his finger in the heal-leaf sap in the small bowl and slathered it on her thumb. It stung. Her thumb went numb.

'No weed bed cleaning. No honey hunting,' said Tareth. 'You'll sit and doze in the sun with Magnus. The thorn trees are poisonous. I should have guessed it was thorn fever.' He was wrapping her thumb in heal-leaf. He looked up. 'I'm sorry. But you'll be well for the Solstice Gather. Although I'm not sure you should go.'

'Why not?' Everyone went to the Gather at the horse meadows below the Marsh Lords' holdfast. They went to trade, to feast, to exchange and gather news. Some even went to test their archery or wrestling skills.

'I think you should stay close until we're sure that the Wulf Kin was alone.'

'And miss the Gather?'

'Just this once,' said Tareth.

'But the Wulf Kin is dead!' Her voice shook. 'And his beast.'

Tareth frowned 'The Watcher's seen no signs of any companions. Perhaps Elder's right. That he was swept overboard in the storm. That chance brought him here. Just like us. But Wulf Kin usually hunt in packs.'

'But there's been no sign of them. I can't miss the Gather!' pleaded Maia. Suddenly it was important to see Kodo.

Tareth shrugged. 'We'll see. Wait until the thorn fever passes and then we'll see.'

'Wait,' repeated Maia gloomily.

'No doubt Selora will come fussing round,' mused Tareth.

'I'll have another fever,' groaned Maia.

'I'll leave Magnus here as guardian.'

Maia grinned. 'That'll keep away well-wishers.'

And it did. The problem was that Tareth stayed away too, rarely stopping to talk to her. Maia decided she would believe his excuses that he must use the time to weave enough cloth for the Gather. And if she pestered him he might remember that he had suggested that she should not attend. So she dozed until Tareth had bundled up bolts of cloth ready to be taken to the horse meadows, where the herders' sheep pens and the Gather traders' tents and booths would already have been set up. She sat and watched tiny boats making their way along the coast to the river which flowed into the horse-meadows. She waited for but didn't see the many-oared traders' ship. She must have missed it. She wondered, in a dream-like state, if Kodo was watching for it too. She remembered how much he wanted to become a trader and leave the stilt village. But Kodo and the honey cave, the beast and the moth-garden seemed like a dream and she was glad. Had she ever dared dream she could own a lizard? Deliberately, Maia turned her thoughts away from her thwarted plans. And as for the Watcher and her stones and the beast, she and Tareth never spoke of them at all.

Then, finding him sitting watching the last of the sun as he tossed morsels of fish to Magnus, Maia decided it was time to come back to the world. Her hand had healed. Her sleep was dreamless. And Tareth was alone. The cliff ledges were empty. Everyone seemed to be down on the beach helping with the pulling and stacking of seaweed. She could see Razek orchestrating the weed boys. Carefully averting her gaze from the flaming glory of the sun, Maia sat next to Tareth.

'The sun-stone,' she said.

Tareth threw another scrap to Magnus. 'I've explained that without the sun-stone you need never be a Sun Catcher.'

Maia nodded. 'I know. I can stay in the weed beds. I can become the Weaver's apprentice. I can even choose to become a Story Singer and walk far.' She saw Tareth start. 'The Lizard Keeper liked my tale. Even the weed children used to ask me to tell them the storm story before . . .' She decided that she didn't want to think about the time when young Cliff Dwellers had decided she was different and she'd realised that she would always be an outsider. 'Everyone will flock to hear me. But . . .'

Tareth turned his head to look at her. 'But . . . ?'

Maia shrugged, trying to disguise how she really felt about the secrets Tareth had kept from her. She wanted to know. Fragments of knowledge gleaned from the weaving whispers were not enough.

'But I'll need a lot of stories. A sun-stone sounds like the start of a good story.'

Maia watched Tareth from the corner of her eye. He was looking at her thoughtfully. She picked a scrap from the bowl and tossed it to Magnus. She saw her father turn away to gaze out across the sun-deeps.

The silence lengthened. Maia could hear the distant calls of the weed gatherers, the murmur of the sea-rise as tiny waves broke over the stone levee. Two crows slip-streamed above the cliffs, adjusting their flight to catch the up-drafts. Below on the beach someone was laughing.

Tareth sighed. 'I have a brother,' he began. 'His name is Urteth.'

Nineteen

Urteth shivered. It was freezing. Tiny flakes of snow fell over the twilight landscape, speckling his fox-fur hat. He stared bleakly from the tower, hunched deeper into the wolfskin flung round his shoulders. Below, yet another line of hungry villagers was shuffling towards the gates. Did they think there was food for all of them in the Sun Palace? Two failed harvests and now this. Was there no end to the freeze? It was as if the land was cursed.

Urteth stamped his feet to thaw his frozen toes. He narrowed his eyes to peer through the snowfall which was getting thicker and faster. There were no messengers to be seen. No riders bringing news, horse hooves drumming over the hard tracks, announcing their coming long before they were in sight. No messenger hawks. Any bird with any sense would be roosting out of the icy blasts, like his eagle,

Azara, hunkered near the fire in the solar. Even that was cold, despite the two blazing fires. Cold because the sun no longer climbed high enough to flood through the vast window that gave the hall its name.

He swore and turned away from the landscape of empty fields frozen hard enough to shatter a plough. The planting would be late again, the summer short with the threat of another meagre harvest. The sun barely rose, leaving them in this half light, its heat hardly enough to melt the huge icicles hanging like clustered spears from every roof. And any melt froze the moment icy darkness fell.

The landscape was locked in wolf-walk when it should have been green. It wasn't meant to be like this. He hadn't committed murder for this.

He made his way from the battlements into the tower, passing the huge singing wheels. No one sat waiting by the bronze wheels. There was little point. They had been silent since Elin and he had seized power. There were no more banners of singing silk to wrap about the wheels. There was no more silk. Even the story-coat had disappeared.

He had killed the Wulf Kin who had set fire to the Queen's rooms and the courtyard moth-garden. But the damage had already been done. The moths had been roasted in the fire, the cocoons fried and the thorn trees, blasted by the flames, were now no more than blackened stumps. Useless. He would order them to be dug out and create a new garden. No point in clinging to the old. He and Elin had planned a new kingdom. They would find more moon-moths and be able to replace the singing silk that Tareth had woven. Meanwhile messages could be sent by hawk or rider.

Urteth entered the sun hall. It was depressing there too. No one had bothered to light the torches; the fires were sullen stacks of wet, smoking logs. Wulfen lay, their great jaws practically in the ashes, soaking up what little warmth there was. Groups of Wulf Kin lounged throwing dice, drinking, some drifting from group to group, rousing curses as they interrupted games. The old warrior, Zartev, sat apart from the others, sharpening his curving blade. The sound of stone squealing on metal whined above the rattle of dice. It set his teeth on edge.

The door at the far end of the hall opened and a slender red-haired woman came in. 'Urteth,' she greeted him. 'Any news?'

Urteth pulled off his fox-fur hat and tossed it onto a chair, narrowly missing his moulting eagle who was dozing. Azara opened her eyes, unfolded her wings and flew clumsily towards him. Urteth held out his arm. The eagle settled on his gloved wrist.

'Nothing,' said Urteth, stoking his bird's chest feathers.

The woman was running her fingers across the narrow silk band edging her robe. The silk was worn and starting to fray. It whispered under her fingers. 'It's snowing again.'

'And there're more refuge seekers on the way,' grunted Urteth. 'Shall I bar the gate?'

The woman frowned. 'We've no food to give them. Let them stay till sun-wake and then send them on their way.'

Urteth nodded and watched her walk to the fire and nudge the wulfen aside so that she could stand close and warm her hands. She was pale-skinned and still as beautiful as the day when he had first seen her walking in the moth-garden with her sisters. Beautiful and deadly. And for some reason unusually nervous. Her hands were once more stroking the frayed silk. He saw them clench and her nails shred the cloth.

He joined her at the fire.

'Elin?' he asked softly.

She looked at him, but her eyes seemed not to see him. 'The silk is whispering. Something's happening.' She pulled her hands away from the bands. 'Is there no news from the Wulf Kin scouts?

'None.'

'Then send more! The silk is agitated. I can't tell what it is saying. Except that it repeats over and over *sun-stone* and *Solstice fire*.'

Urteth grasped her arm. 'The sun-stone. It's found?'

Elin tugged her arm free. 'It would never have been taken if you'd played your part.'

Urteth frowned. 'How was I to know that Tareth would kidnap the child and take the sun-stone? Was I supposed to kill my unarmed brother when I found him in the palace?'

'Unarmed!' spat Elin. 'He was a warrior. He was never unarmed!'

'I hit him hard enough to fell a wulfen, let alone a man.'

'Not hard enough. He stole my sister and the sun-stone.'

Urteth sighed. He had heard the complaint often enough. 'Xania escaped that night with the story-coat. How d'you know she didn't take Maia and the sun-stone too?'

'The silk would have told me.'

'It seems that the silk tells you very little, Elin. Why doesn't it tell you where your sister is hidden? Or tell you what happened to Xania, the Story Singer, after the Wulf Kin pursued her from the Queen's burning apartment and then lost her?'

He kicked at a smouldering log. A shower of sparks flew across the hearth.

'Did your silk tell you that this land cannot prosper without the Sun Catcher and the sun-stone?' he asked.

Urteth kicked the log again. The eagle pitched forward on his arm and flew back to its perch.

'We're finished if the harvest fails again. We're King and Queen of nothing, Elin. A dead land. We need the sun. And you, my dear, with your schemes to overthrow your sisters, forgot that your family, your world, was nothing without the sun-stone.' He gestured to the dim hall, the shadowy figures, the smoking fires. 'A cold, dying land and a hall in darkness.'

'Then call the palace boys to light the lamps,' snapped Elin. 'And never forget that you came from nothing. My family have ruled Khandar for ever. You and your brother were nothing, fatherless boys sent to serve us.'

Urteth smiled at her. It wasn't a pleasant smile. 'The Eagle People are not sent to serve. And you were eager enough to have my help when it came to killing your sisters!'

'I didn't mean them to die. It was your men who started the fire!'

Urteth shrugged. 'Would you have let them live? Would you really have kept them locked up? They are better dead.'

'They're not all dead! Xania escaped. Maia too. If she still lives the silk will sing on her Naming Day. It will know when she finds her power. And once we find her and the sun-stone, all will be well. Send the old one. He will find her,' said Elin.

Urteth glanced across at the lone Wulf Kin. The man, aware of his scrutiny, lifted his sharpened blade in an ironic greeting.

'Send Zartev? I thought you wanted the girl alive!' said Urteth.

Elin paced in front of the fire, her short steps signalling her anger.

Urteth shrugged himself deeper into his furs. The cold of the mountains seemed to have entered his bones. Should he tell Elin of his night-wake when Tareth had appeared and with him a flame-haired girl? They had been laughing. There was no laughter in the palace. His brother and the child had been standing in sunshine watching an eagle soaring above the sea.

Urteth stretched his hand to the fire. He must be getting old to feel the cold so. He needed a wolf-chase to make his blood sing. He was tired of the hungry, cold death of the palace. Maybe he would listen to his night-wake and ride with the Wulf Kin to seek the girl and his brother.

'She lives,' he said shortly. 'In my night-wakes she lives.'

'Good!' Elin's eyes were as sharp as a hunting fox. 'And she can do so, until she's taught me the secrets of the sun-stone.' She shoved her hands deep inside the trailing sleeves of her gown. 'I am the eldest sister. The Sun Catcher gift should have been mine. And my daughter's after me. I am the Queen. The sun-stone is mine.'

Urteth's expression softened as he thought of Caspia, their red-haired child who alternately terrorised and enslaved the palace boys. She was the one blaze of light in this dingy place.

'I thought the sun-stone chose its keeper,' he said.

'I should be Sun Catcher,' Elin spat. 'My to-come was stolen by your brother, Urteth. Find the sun-stone!'

'I will send Wulf Kin.' said Urteth. 'Have you silk for them?'

'There is no more. We need the sun-stone,' said Elin fiercely.

'And the Sun Catcher,' said Urteth.

'Find her! Bring her to me! She should be with her sister.'

Urteth laughed. 'Sisterly love, Elin?' he asked.

'Find her, Urteth, or Khandar dies.'

Twenty

The world was dead. White and silent, shrouded in curling mist. It was cold. The fog wrapped itself around Kodo, covering him with gleaming beads of water. He shivered. The mist made him deaf and blind – he couldn't see anything. He felt as if clammy hands covered his ears, muffling all sounds. He shivered again, afraid of what lay hidden in the mist. Afraid of what he planned to do.

And yet the fog was a friend. It would hide him from the piercing eyes of the eagle and the long-sighted gaze of the Watcher. If he found the moth-garden. If he tore the silk from the thorns. Why then . . . Kodo sighed. His stomach churned like maggots wriggling in dead fish. He felt bad about betraying Maia's secret, but she had it coming after her behaviour at the moth-garden. And her eagle had killed two hatchlings. He thought of the colours of the silk. It had sung to him. It had told him to set it free.

He could hear the singing now. It throbbed through the curtain of mist. The water stirred and moved to the beat of the voices, slapping against the dugout. It rocked in the long ripples. Kodo felt the current tugging the small craft. It was almost as if the silk was anxious for him to come, pulling him like sea-surge. Water splashed against the prow, spattering him with ice-cold drops.

The rhythm and the song changed. The voices grew deeper. He heard the creak of wood on wood. The voices rose. Suddenly his world was full of the crash of oars, the chant of rowers and the cry of their Oar Master. He opened his eyes. Above him, a dragon with green eyes and gaping jaws emerged from the mist to swallow him.

Kodo gasped and dug his paddle deep, driving his dugout away from the carved figurehead. Dug too deep, so that he spun and tipped, shipping water, almost overturning. A dozen, dripping, oak oars feathered over his head and thundered down alongside him. The splash as the blades hit the water drenched him, unbalancing the dugout as it took on more water. Frantically Kodo paddled backwards into the safety of the fog.

As quickly as it had appeared, the dragon vanished like a phantom, oars rising and falling in unison with the voices of the rowers. Kodo made out figures pulling at ropes, lowering the limp russet-brown sail as the boat disappeared, leaving a spreading wake and a falling song.

'Traders!'

Kodo stowed his paddle alongside his spear and, cupping his hands, began scooping water from his dugout. The traders had come in their dragon ship, rowing up to the Marsh Lord's holdfast for the Solstice Gather with their goods. He could almost smell the sacks of spices, feel the smooth cedarwood chests beneath his fingers, the sharp spear-heads and soft furs that they brought from places far away. Perhaps there would be cages of wild animals and fierce, untamed birds. He would find Maia. He hoped she would not be with the weed boys. He grimaced, remembering how Razek, the Weed Master and his boys, had chased him from the last Gather. This time he would not be so easily bullied; he was older and he would have the silk.

Kodo picked up his paddle. One day he would work on a trader ship. One day he would have a ship of his own and sail home to tie up alongside the horse meadows. And his mother would come to choose from the furs and gold bracelets he brought her. And Ootey would be silenced because he, Kodo, would be a rich trader. He knew it would happen. If he was brave enough to climb the cliff and take the bands of silk from the trees it would happen. The silk would make his dream come true. It had promised.

Moth wings brushed his cheek. Kodo touched the fine dust they left on his skin. It shone on his fingertips. He stared, mesmerised, not sure how long he had crouched, dreaming, until the large white moth had fluttered in front of his eyes and woken him. The moth flew away. Kodo followed, scrambling over the rocks, sliding down a steep fall of scree. He pitched forward and landed on his knees at the base of a thorn tree. Above him the silk hung, waiting. Kodo reached and grasped a strip, tearing it from the thorns. Suddenly the moth-garden was alive with sound. It hurt his ears. The silk was shrieking, commanding him to free it. His head was ringing. He tried to tear another ribbon from the stunted tree, but it slid through his fingers and screamed as he let it go. Another wrapped itself like stinging jellyfish tentacles around his wrist. The air was full of moths. He was suffocating in moths. He turned and scrabbled on hands and knees across the rocks. The moths streamed after him, batting against him. He beat them off and reached the entrance to the cleft. Recklessly, he clambered between the overhanging rocks, missed his footing and fell.

He tumbled, between pillows of sea-thrift and clumps of gorse that broke his fall and cracked his spear. He was bounced into a tree clinging to the cliff-face and somehow managed to grab the trunk and hold on. Slowly Kodo let go of the tree, pulled himself upright and staggered down the path, following the zig-zag track to the beach below. As he reached the wet sands, his knees buckled. He hurt everywhere, his arm throbbed, the temptation to sleep was overwhelming – but he had the silk. One piece was still wrapped around his wrist, another was clutched in his hand. He turned his head to look at them. His eyelids drooped. He mustn't sleep . . .

The screech of a gull woke him. The pain in his arm was worse. He sat up and forced himself to look at it. He was bleeding. The flesh around the wound was puffy.

Gritting his teeth, Kodo tore a finger-width strip from the frayed edge of the silk. It murmured in protest. He laid it across his thigh, listening to its whispers. He could hear the creak of oars, feel spray in his face as he stood in the bow of the boat. He was dropping a weighted, knotted rope into the water and calling out to a sun-haired man with a huge beard like a spreading lizard's crest who stood at the helm.

Blood trickled down his arm. The sun-deeps sighed beneath the cliffs. Tiny waves lapped over his feet. A tug on the mooring rope of his dugout as the water took it jerked him back from his silk dreams. He blinked at the sun. It was high in the sky.

Kodo splashed over to his dugout and dragged it higher onto the sand. Squatting in the shallows he rinsed the blood from his arm. The cut still oozed. He squeezed the sides together with his fingers then waded further out, looking for weed. Finding what he needed, he pulled a long streamer off the plant, folded it into a pad and held it over the cut. It stung as he wrapped the silk over the weed pad, tying it securely. The ends of the silk fluttered in the breeze. Kodo watched them, fascinated. He tucked the loose ends into the bindings. The silk was silent.

Now for his damaged spear. Crouching beside his dugout, he took his spear and started binding the second strip of torn silk around the crack, tying it tightly. The silk muttered. Kodo ignored it. He pulled the silk tighter, whipping it round the shaft, knotting it securely until it fell silent. It was the best he could do.

Kodo hefted the spear. It flew true. Satisfied, he stowed it in the dugout, and pulled out the lizard-skin water bag.

He drank thirstily and hunted for the flatbread wrapped in oiled cloth that Jakarta had handed to him when he had slipped from the stilt hut. It was stale but he was starving. He broke off a chunk, crumbled it between his fingers and gobbled the pieces. The growling beast in his stomach grew less demanding. He put the flabby water bag in the bow and pushed the dugout through the shallows until it was floating freely.

He was caught in the undertow and carried swiftly down the coast. Using his paddle as a rudder, Kodo steered towards a line of white breakers that marked the entrance to the estuary flowing from the marshes into the sea. Now he could see the grey smudge of the tall, square watchtower which guarded the Marsh Lords' holdfast. He would be late for the contests. Kodo sent the dugout skimming across the water.

Maia poured the tokens into the leather bag at her waist. It was heavy. Trade had been brisk and profitable. It had made no difference that the Weaver himself had not been there. She had sold all the cloth. She felt a glow of pride. It almost replaced the knot of worry that she had disobeyed Tareth and run away to the Gather.

She jingled the bag. There was no reason for Tareth to ban her from the fun. The Wulf Kin and his beast were dead. He would be furious when she returned. She had haggled for a good price for his cloth though, so maybe that would help. She'd worry about the trouble she was in later. Now she could explore. She took a token from the pouch.

Selora bustled up. 'Did you make good trade? The cloth sold quickly.'

Maia flushed. Did Selora think she had given it away?

'I asked and got what Tareth wanted,' she said shortly. 'And now I'm going to explore.'

'Razek and Laya have gone to find the hunter with a bear cub.'

Which meant she couldn't! Maia fumed. She wanted to see the bear too but there was no way she was going to trail round the horse meadows with them. She'd look for Kodo instead. She turned to go.

Selora held out her hand. 'Leave the bag with me and I'll see that it's kept safe.'

Maia frowned. She'd heard that thieves could slit the belt thongs and steal a purse without you feeling a thing. Tareth wouldn't be impressed if she lost the copper and silver tokens. She sighed. Why did Selora have to interfere and be right? Reluctantly she untied the pouch and handed it over.

'I'll take it to Elder.' Selora gestured at Maia's silver brooch. 'Be careful you don't lose that.'

Maia closed her hand protectively over the leaping wild cat. She wasn't going to give that into the busybody's safe-keeping. If anyone dared to try and steal it, she'd stick them with her knife. She scowled at Selora. She could easily have taken the bag to Elder herself.

Too late now. 'Elder will think Tareth doesn't trust me,' she thought crossly as she joined the milling crowds.

She skirted a ring of trampled grass where two half-naked

figures with gleaming, greased skin were wrestling. She got tangled up in the crowd as it surged, cheering as the men fell out of the improvised ring. She avoided a shaggy-haired hunter wearing a grey seal-pelt, who strode silently through the mob with his two hounds tugging on their leashes. She winced as she passed a fire-eater standing in a ring of flaming torches, then stopped to watch three jugglers tossing balls and knives in the air.

A tall woman, in baggy, patterned leggings and a bright pink cap, was deftly flipping six red leather balls from hand to hand. She spun them in a tumbling arc above her head. She winked at Maia.

'Catch,' she called.

The woman threw a ball at her. Ball after ball followed. Maia could hear them smacking against flesh behind her and then the balls came spinning back over her head. The crowd gasped.

Maia twisted, overbalanced and almost fell. A stout man, no taller than she was, wearing a tattered, gaudy cloak, stood behind her, grinning as he threw the balls back to the woman. Every time a ball smacked against his palm he called to the tall juggler. The words sounded strange, unlike any Maia had ever heard. More like Magnus' cries as he summoned Tareth to the hunt just before sun-wake.

The woman called back, a single command. Then the man was feeding copper discs into the mix until Maia was caught between the flow of spinning plates and balls flying past her ears. She stood feeling foolish, not daring to move. The crowd laughed and then the woman had all of the balls and discs and was tossing them higher and higher above her head.

'For blueberry bread,' called the juggler and spun a copper token out from among the tumbling objects. Maia caught it. The crowd cheered.

Maia looked at the token. 'That'll buy two,' she called.

The woman laughed and dropped the falling balls and discs into a piece of dark cloth at her feet. She strode over to Maia. 'One for you and one for me, girl.'

She looked down at Maia. 'That's a fine brooch.' Her fingers flickered and suddenly the leaping silver cat was lying in her palm.

Quick as an adder's tongue, Maia snatched the brooch back and reached for her knife. But before she could draw it, her wrist was caught in a numbing grip.

Maia glared at the woman. 'Let go!' she hissed.

The woman's grip eased slightly, but she didn't let go. She was staring intently at Maia.

'Where did you get such a fine, silver brooch?'

Maia tugged at her arm. 'What's it to you?'

'Stolen is it?'

Maia's hands curled round the silver cat. 'It's not stolen,' she spat. 'It was given to me!'

'A valuable gift,' said the woman, her eyebrows arching. 'Who gave you such a gift?' She tightened her grip. 'Tell me!' She looked at Maia's hair. 'Who are you with your red hair and this brooch?'

Maia pulled her arm free. 'Why should I tell you anything?' she demanded.

'Maia!' A voice called from the edge of the crowd. It was Razek.

'Maia!' repeated the woman. 'Your name is Maia?'

Seldom had Maia been so pleased to see Razek. She was even pleased to see Laya hanging on his arm. The tall woman was too inquisitive by far. Maia darted past her and hurried across to Razek. Ignoring his surprise, she grabbed his arm, tugging him deeper into the crowds.

'Come on,' she said. 'I've seen a trader with bead arm rings.' She peered round Razek. 'Just what you'd like, Laya. Come and see. The beads are blue,' she added.

Laya looked at her suspiciously. 'Blue?'

Maia nodded. 'Lots of women were looking at them,' she said.

Laya tugged at Razek's arm. 'Come on, before someone makes a trade,' she said.

Maia glanced over her shoulder as she hustled Razek and Laya into the throng. The woman hadn't moved, but she was staring after them, tall enough to see over the heads of the press of people.

Maia wished she hadn't been cursed with red hair. She was too easy to see.

'You owe me a flatbread!' the woman called after her.

In which case, she'd avoid the bake-man, decided Maia. She didn't trust the woman. She had thief's hands. The way she had taken the brooch! How had she done that? Perhaps she was a cut-purse as well as a juggler. The winds blew all sorts to the Gather.

Maia tightened her grip on the brooch. It was warm in her hand. She would pin it to the inside of her tunic so that it attracted no more attention. She glanced back. The tall woman was talking to the squat juggler. As Maia watched he vanished into the crowd.

Razek looked down at Maia, who was still clinging to his arm.

'I suppose you want beads,' he said.

Maia let go of his arm as if it was red hot.

'No thanks,' she said. 'But Laya will. The blue beads must be worth at least a silver token.'

She watched Razek's eyes widen in alarm. She grinned and, ducking low, twisted away from them to lose herself in the crowd.

Twenty-One

Kodo pushed his way through the crowd jostling the ale traders. The ground was soggy with spilled beer as two men dipped jugs into the vast cauldrons, scooped out the cloudy liquid and slopped it into a row of jugs. A plump woman, jug in hand, was swaying through the crowd, filling up bone beakers and drinking horns. Pouring beer with one hand, she collected tokens with the other. Kodo stumbled against her. Ale splashed onto his tunic. The woman staggered, dropped a handful of tokens and cursed. Muttering an apology, Kodo scrabbled for the coins in the mud.

'Hands off. Them's mine!'

A foot stamped on his hand. Pinned to the ground, Kodo stared up into a red, angry face.

'Get your thieving fingers off!' snorted the woman.

'I can't,' grimaced Kodo. 'You're standing on my hand.'

The woman ground her heel down hard. Kodo thought his fingers were going to crack.

'Ow! I was trying to pick them up for you!'

'Met your sort before, lizard boy. Knocking into a body so she drops her money! Well you ain't getting away with it!'

'I was pushed!' protested Kodo.

'Yeah! And I'm yer mother!'

'I'm not a thief,' protested Kodo. With a wrench, he pulled his hand free.

The woman swore and tipped the contents of her jug over him.

Liquid ran over his face, into his eyes, up his nose. Kodo gasped, swallowed and spluttered as the beer gushed into his mouth. A hand grabbed the back of his sodden tunic. He was hauled to his feet.

Kodo shook his head. Drops of beer spun from his hair, spraying the woman. 'Little thief tried to rob me, Lord Helmek!' she shrieked. The hand jerked him off his feet, and shook him like a lizard shaking a water rat. He dropped the tokens he had been holding.

'I was picking them up,' he muttered against a mouthful of finely woven tunic. He was shoved backwards and almost fell over. 'I'm not a thief!' he shouted as his beer-blurred vision finally cleared. 'I was picking them up for her!'

The woman was bending to retrieve the tokens. Beside her, a big man was brushing beads of beer from his tunic. A silver thumb ring glinted on his hand. Kodo stared.

'You!' the man said. 'The bee boy! The fire setter!'

It was the Marsh Lord. Kodo turned to run. He was too

slow. Helmek grabbed his injured arm. Kodo yelped and tore himself free. At a command, a hound bounded forward and seized Kodo's tunic.

Kodo stared down into the dog's eyes and stopped struggling. If he ran the dog would chase him, pull him down, tear his throat open. The breath hissed out of his lungs.

At another command, the dog released him. The growl still rumbling deep in its belly, it circled Kodo, nudging him backwards.

'So! What have we here? Lizard boy, fire setter and thief?'

Kodo clenched his teeth to stop them chattering. 'Not a thief,' he managed to stutter. The silk was soft against his skin. He had stolen the silk.

The red-faced woman was putting the tokens into a pouch hung on her belt.

She looked at the dog then back at Kodo. 'Scared him this has. Look at him! Got a face like mare's milk. He'll be spewing up all over your boots. Don't seem like a thief now, do 'ee? Could be I was mistaken.'

'No harm done!' she continued. 'I got thirsty men to serve.'

'No harm done!' grunted Helmek. 'A fire on the cliff. My horse stung by bees. My tunic reeking of beer.' He released Kodo to brush at the beer stains on his tunic. 'My hound,' he studied his dog lying at his feet, the tip of its tail beating a slow rhythm against the ground as it lifted its nose to sniff Kodo. 'My hound seduced.'

Could the dog hear the silk too? Kodo felt as if he was swimming through rafts of lizard-collected debris as he lifted his hand to cover the silk band, to hold the torn ends still. He pressed his hand hard against his arm and felt the soreness beneath the weed pad. It stopped him thinking about the images the silk had conjured for him.

The Marsh Lord glared at Kodo. 'What are you doing here, lizard boy?'

'Come for the Gather,' said Kodo. 'To see the trader ship. To try my skill in the contests.'

Helmek twisted his silver thumb ring. Once again Kodo could see the tell-tale swirls of the Lizard People's brown tattoo decorating the man's thumb. Then the hand was jammed in his chest, pushing him backwards. The dog growled as Kodo almost stood on its paws.

'What contest?'

Kodo gestured at boys wrestling nearby. As he did the breeze caught the silk strands on his arm. They sang. The wrapping on the spear whispered an answer.

The man took a step back. His eyes widened.

'What's this?' He touched the silk binding on the shaft of Kodo's spear. His fingers trembled.

Kodo took another step backwards. He almost fell over the dog and threw out his arm to regain his balance. The silk ends of the binding round his arm fluttered free. Helmek grabbed Kodo's elbow.

'Lizard spume!' he swore softly. He was staring at his own hand. Then he blinked and shook his head. His expression hardened. 'Where did you find this, boy?'

He thrust the spear back at Kodo. Then his hands were tugging at Kodo's arm, unwrapping the silk. Unnoticed, the weed pad fell to the earth. Helmek tore the silk free and held it up.

The iridescent strip hung in his hand. The sun shone through it and it seemed to lose all colour, to become transparent. The Marsh Lord was staring at it as if he could not drag his eyes away. He stood transfixed, listening to something that only he could hear.

'Where did you find this?' he asked slowly.

Kodo swallowed. 'In . . . in the sun-deeps.' he whispered.

'In the sun-deeps?' repeated Helmek.

'Among the storm scourings.'

The man crushed the silk into a ball, holding it tightly in his fist. 'The lizards found it?'

Kodo nodded miserably.

'Just this?' demanded Lord Helmek fiercely.

Kodo nodded again.

The man grabbed his arm. It hurt.

'You're lying,' snarled the Lord. 'No lizard found this.'

Kodo tried to meet his eyes and couldn't. 'It was twisted on a stick. Among the debris,' he muttered. 'Among the rocks. After the storm.'

The Marsh Lord opened his fist to stare at the crushed silk.

'Is there more? In your village?'

Kodo shook his head. He had a nightmare vision of mounted Marsh Lords and their hounds thundering into the stilt village, demanding information. And of the consequences when no one could tell them what they wanted to know. They would wreck the huts looking for hidden silk. Grandfather Ootey would try to stop them. He was as fierce as a lizard. He would fight. He would die.

He panicked. 'I found the silk. I didn't tell anyone. I

wanted to keep it for myself. Nobody knows. Just me and . . .' he stopped.

'And?' Like a hunting hawk on a mouse, the man pounced on Kodo's mistake. 'Me and . . . ?'

'No one,' gasped Kodo. 'I found it on the rocks.'

'Found it on the rocks? You and who else, eh?'

He lifted his fist. His ring glinted. Kodo thought he was going to hit him, but the man was looking at his clenched hand, listening.

'Who was with you? On the rocks . . . below the cliffs,' he muttered to himself.

Kodo felt his muscles tensing beneath the man's grip. Knew he was betraying his thoughts. He wouldn't think about Maia. He wouldn't think about the cliffs. He would be as dull and stupid as the Watcher had told him to be. He took a deep breath.

Lord Helmek paused. 'You were with the Watcher. And there was another. Below. Where the fire had been. The one with hair like flames,' he said. 'The girl. The one who tried to stay hidden. The one the bees protected.'

Kodo felt the blood drain from his face.

'So! Where is she, boy? She's not one of the Lizard People. Not with a head like fire. Who is she?'

'I found the silk floating in the storm-weed,' Kodo tried one last time.

The Marsh Lord ignored him. 'And I think we'll find the Flame Head here, won't we lizard boy? Everyone comes to the Gather.'

He whistled to his hound. It got to its feet, looking at its master. Helmek growled a command. The hound lowered its eyes and moved to stand behind Kodo. He could feel its breath on his legs; hear the faint whine in the dog's throat. The Marsh Lord released his grip on Kodo's arm.

'If you run, the dog will pull you down,' he warned. 'Now, where will we find the girl?'

Kodo was silent. 'Don't let Maia be here,' he thought. But if she wasn't, if the Marsh Lord didn't find her, then they would ransack his village. And hers.

Twenty-Two

Maia chose a dull brown hat made from the fleece of the small horned sheep that roamed the horse meadows. It would pass unnoticed in the crowds. She pulled it on, tucking her hair up. Her nose wrinkled. Her head smelled of sheep. She was beginning to wish that she had never come to the Gather.

'Sea shells! What have you got on your head?' asked Laya, giggling.

Maia spun round. Razek and Laya, were standing behind her. Laya had two blue beads in her hair, noted Maia, and was looking pleased with life. Razek on the other hand was scowling. Maybe the beads really had cost a whole silver token. Maia felt a little more cheerful.

'You smell like a dead sheep!' Laya smirked.

'So stay away,' suggested Maia.

Laya waved her hand in front of her nose. 'Come on, Razek.' She grabbed his arm. 'I want to see the hunter with the bear cub.'

Razek shrugged his arm free. 'I want to speak with Maia.'

Laya pouted. 'You promised we'd go back to the bronze trader. I want to barter for the shell and amber arm ring. And he'll make a good trade if you offer him the silver band.'

'I want to speak with Maia!' Razek repeated.

Maia stared at Laya's angry face in disbelief. 'You want Razek to trade his Weed Master band for shells?'

'Not that band! And anyway, what's it to you what he trades?' snapped Laya. 'I'm going to find the bear cub! Come if you want to,' she told Razek, 'but don't bring her.' She turned on her heel and swept off.

Maia scratched her head under the woollen cap. It itched. A waft of sheep smell was released.

'What silver band?' she asked. 'What's Laya talking about? You'd never trade your wristguard. Not even Laya can expect you to do that.'

Razek frowned down at her. 'You don't know anything, Flame Head.'

Maia looked down at the band on Razek's forearm. The wristguard was old and worn and beautiful with its silver chasing like fish scales.

'So if it's not that, what else have you got to barter for shells?' she asked.

'What's it to you? You gave me back my wristguard!' said Razek. 'Laya has more sense than to refuse what's offered.'

'Poor Razek!' teased Maia. 'Laya will always want more. She's used to having a Salt Holder's wealth to spend.'

'I'll soon be as rich as the Salt Holder!' said Razek. He plunged his hand into his tunic and pulled out a plain silver band. 'This will make me rich.'

Maia stared, unwilling to believe what she was seeing. 'But that's the Wulf Kin's.'

'And who pulled him from the sun-deeps? I claim his silver. His weapons and bronze tunic.'

'Tareth pulled him out!' retorted Maia. 'And he told you to drown the Wulf Kin's hoard.'

Razek shoved the band out of sight, inside his tunic. 'Tareth's not my father. He can't tell me what to do. I'm the Weed Master. The Wulf Kin was drowned in the weed beds. His treasure is mine.'

'You can't trade the Wulf Kin's silver!'

'Who's to stop me? You? Tareth? He wants nothing more to do with the Wulf Kin. And he's not here!'

'Elder said to destroy everything!' Maia reminded him. She knew in her bones that what Razek was intending to do was wrong. Worse than wrong; it was dangerous. Tareth wanted no trace of the Wulf Kin to be found. Razek mustn't trade the dead man's silver armband at the Gather.

'Elder won't know.' Razek glared at her. 'Unless you go carrying tales, Flame Head.'

Maia's eyes flashed. 'I might just do that! The Wulf Kin's silver isn't yours to trade.'

'If you do,' Razek's eyes narrowed, 'Elder will hear how you brought a lizard hatchling to the weed beds. You and Weaver will be punished.'

Maia stared in horror as he strode away. What should she do? If only she had fingers like the tall juggler, fingers like flickering fish in the shallows, she could steal the band before Razek made his trade. Well, she could try.

Her decision made, Maia darted after Razek and saw Kodo walking towards her. He would help her.

'Hey! Kodo!' she called.

But Kodo looked straight through her as if she was not there. He carried on walking towards her, a hound trailing at his heels and a man in a purple tunic striding behind him.

As they got closer she saw that Kodo was as pale as the full moon. He was holding his arm with his hand. He was hurt.

'Kodo? What's happened?' she called.

Kodo ignored her.

'It's me.' Maia tugged the cap from her hair and shoved it in her belt. 'Maia!'

'The girl!' said the Marsh Lord.

'Run!' yelled Kodo and lashed backwards with his spear. The man roared and doubled over. Kodo dropped his spear, dodged and fell over the dog.

'Run, Maia!' he screamed. He and the dog fought, Kodo kicking, yelling and punching, the dog snapping and growling. They rolled across the spear. Maia heard the crack as it broke. Kodo yelled as he was bitten. 'Run!'

Maia darted forward to help. A huge hand twisted in her tunic and yanked her back. She was jerked off balance. She heard her tunic rip.

'Got you!' rasped a breathless voice.

Maia struggled like a speared fish. Kicking and contacting nothing but air.

'Keep still! Or I'll set the dog on you too.'

Maia let herself go limp and hung, a dead weight. She heard a grunt as her attacker released her and kicked back hard. Her heel thudded into his kneecap. He yelled. She twisted. Hands like claws, she lashed upwards, aiming for his eyes. She missed, but her raking nails scored his face.

With a bellow of rage, the man lunged. Maia stepped to one side and kicked him hard again. As his leg buckled, propelled by his own momentum, he stumbled and sprawled on his face.

Faster than thought, Maia pulled her knife and slashed the belt that secured his leggings. Let him try running after her and he would find them around his ankles, tripping him up.

Suddenly, the squat juggler was there, hanging onto the dog's tail so Kodo could wriggle free. Maia hauled him to his feet.

'Quick,' hissed a voice. The tall juggler was beckoning urgently, a disc balanced in her right hand. Then it was whistling through the air. Maia heard a thud and a whimper.

'This way!' called the woman.

'No way,' thought Maia. She grabbed Kodo's arm. 'Come on!'

She pulled him into the crowd, wriggling past hands that reached out to stop them. Then they were through the press and running past a cluster of yurts. They darted back into the crowds on the far side. Maia slowed to a walk, and let go of Kodo's arm to tug her cap from her belt. She glanced over her shoulder. There was no sign of the tall juggler or the man. No one in the crowd showed the slightest interest in them. But it was best that no one remembered seeing them.

She pulled on the cap, tucking her hair up out of sight. Her hands were shaking.

Kodo was still looking dazed. His arm was bleeding. 'You're hurt!' said Maia. 'Did he hurt you?'

Kodo gazed down at his arm. He seemed surprised to see blood. He wiped it away with his hand. 'No!'

'Who was that? What did he want?'

Kodo glanced anxiously over his shoulder. 'The Marsh Lord from the cliff,' he said. 'He recognised me.' He stumbled to a halt. He knew it wasn't as simple as that. He knew he should tell Maia that the Marsh Lord wouldn't give up easily. Knew he should tell Maia what he'd done. And he had to get back to the stilt village. He had to warn Ootey.

'Maia. I . . .'

'Come on,' she said, 'We've got to find Razek.' She grabbed Kodo's arm again. He winced.

Maia, anxiously searching the crowds, didn't notice. 'We've got to stop him before he makes a trade with the silversmith.' She let go of his arm and set off.

'Maia . . . I've got to warn them. They'll be killed.'

Maia stopped mid-stride. 'What?'

Kodo was swaying. 'The Marsh Lords will attack the village. I've got to warn them.'

'But . . .'

'Maia! Look out!' Kodo lurched towards her.

Maia's world went dark and airless as a cloth was tossed over her head and shoulders. Her arms were pinned to her sides. As she was dragged backwards, she struggled to keep her feet, to wriggle free.

'Scream and the boy gets a knife between the ribs.'

Maia started to sag. She was jerked upright. 'Not this time. Now walk.'

She was encouraged forward with a shove. She staggered several paces. The world was stifling. She couldn't see, couldn't breathe. Black spots floated in front of her eyes. The ground seemed to give way under her. It was not the ground, she realised, but a pile of rugs. She tugged at the cloth and pulled it from her head. Her eyes adjusted to the gloom. The shadows moved. Someone moaned softly. She saw Kodo on his knees. A figure was kneeling by him, holding his arm.

'Leave him alone!'

'It's all right. The bleeding has stopped.'

Maia sat up so fast she felt dizzy. 'You! What d'you want?'

The woman ignored her. She poured something into a beaker and passed it to Kodo.

'Drink. You'll need to be strong enough to run later. The Marsh Lord will be looking for you. He'll blame you for the fate of his hound.'

'Have you killed it?' demanded Maia.

The juggler shook her head. 'It'll sleep and have a sore head, like its master.' She grinned at Maia. 'Who taught you to fight like that?'

Maia's eyes narrowed. 'Tareth, my father!' She looked around and realised why it was so dim. They were in a skin tent and the door flap was closed.

'Tareth, your father?' the woman sounded stunned.

Maia glared at her. 'Yes.' Her anger touched a memory. 'Tareth, the Warrior Weaver. And he will want to know who's dared to . . . kidnap his daughter.'

'I would meet with this Weaver,' said the juggler.

Kodo was gulping down the liquid as if he was as parched as the lizard scrape. 'I have to warn Ootey,' he croaked. 'The Marsh Lord will go to the village.'

'He sleeps still,' said the juggler. 'Did he keep the silk, boy?'

Kodo nodded.

Maia stared at him. 'What silk?'

'He said he would go to the village to find more,' said Kodo. 'There isn't any more. He'll destroy the village trying to find it.'

'Kodo. What have you done?' repeated Maia.

The woman was flipping a token on her thumb. She spun it in the air. 'And when the village is attacked, what then, boy?'

Kodo swallowed a sob. 'I'll be an outcast.' Maia saw him straighten his shoulders. 'I'll find the traders. If they won't have me, I'll stow away. One day I'll have my own ship and I'll return and . . . and make it right.'

'Silk dreams, boy.' The juggler caught the token and tucked it in her scarlet sash. 'The Lord will look for you. The silk will have promised him such . . . power.' She shrugged. 'He'll find you and kill you when he has what he wants.'

'I don't have anything he wants,' whispered Kodo.

'You have the silk.'

Kodo shook his head. 'No, he took it.'

The juggler's breath hissed across her teeth. She glared at Kodo. 'I must find the silk. If you want to live,' she warned, 'do not try to leave here.'

A wedge of sunlight fell across the rugs on the floor as the juggler lifted the flap and vanished.

Maia barely noticed her leave.

'What have you done?' she shouted as the flap fell back into place and the tent was plunged into gloom.

Unable to meet her fierceness, Kodo cradled his injured arm and stared at his feet.

'The silk called,' he muttered. 'I went back.'

'You stole the silk?' Maia was still grappling with the enormity of Kodo's crime.

Miserably Kodo nodded. 'The silk wanted me to take it,' he said. 'And the Marsh Lord heard it and took it.' He dared to look up and meet Maia's furious eyes. 'He'll search my village to find more.'

'You went back,' said Maia. 'Why?'

'I had to. The silk called. It promised . . . I must warn Ootey.' He swallowed. 'He'll kill me!'

'If Tareth doesn't,' said Maia. She pulled him to his feet. 'Come on . . . before she gets back.'

She tugged him towards the door flap.

Then the juggler was there, blocking the way.

'The Lord sleeps still. I've doused him with beer and left a drinking horn in his hand. He'll think he was beer-fuddled and dreamed the whole thing. We should leave now.'

Maia thought she saw the glimmer of pale silk as the woman tucked something in her sash.

'Wait,' said Maia. 'Why should we trust you?'

'I mean you no harm,' said the woman. 'I helped you escape the Lord.'

'We were already free,' said Maia.

'And were running into danger. Believe me, Maia. There were worse things waiting for you than a sack over your head.'

'We're leaving. Come on Kodo.'

He looked at her uncertainly. 'The quickest way is through the horse meadows and across the marshes. The Horse Guardians live there. They have floating shelters. Good places to hide. But we'll have to swim for it.'

Maia sucked in her breath. Kodo knew she couldn't swim. Was he telling her that he didn't want her with him?

The juggler noticed her hesitation. 'Are you going or staying?'

Maia bit her lip.

Unexpectedly the woman laughed. 'Can you swim across the marshes, Maia? Or are you afraid of water?'

Maia flushed. She turned to leave. 'Come on, Kodo.'

'Alone you'll run into danger,' said the woman.

Maia spun round. 'What danger?'

'Everyone comes to the Gather,' said the juggler. 'Even the Wulf Kin.'

'What d'you know about the Wulf Kin?' asked Maia.

'They're a long way from Khandar. Their wulfen are hidden in the woods beyond the Lord's holdfast with one Wulf Kin to guard them. Another is here at the Gather,' the juggler replied. 'They're hunting someone. The silk the boy found has brought them. He was lucky they didn't find him.'

'Who are you?' Maia whispered.

'Xania.' She swept off her cap. Copper-coloured hair tumbled over her shoulders. 'Story Singer and your sister. The silver cat you wear belonged to our mother.'

Twenty-Three

Maia clutched the brooch. 'Sister?'

'Sister,' said Xania.

'I don't have a sister,' said Maia.

'You have six sisters. Had. All older.' A cloud seemed to pass across her face. 'Only two survive. Treacherous Elin, and myself.'

'Six sisters?' Maia felt as if her legs would give way. She sat down before they did. 'But Tareth . . . my father . . . he spoke of his brother, Urteth. And the land we came from. But not sisters . . . he would have told me.' But there was so much he had not told her. He was a man of secrets, never wanting to talk of the has-been before they had settled with the Cliff Dwellers. And she had stopped asking when he had turned away from her questions, his face stern and cold. She had thought it was grief that silenced him.

'My father would have told me,' she repeated with less certainty.

'Tareth . . .' The woman's voice seemed to caress the name. 'Tareth isn't your father, Maia. Tareth saved your life. But he's not your father.'

Maia stared at her. Now she knew the woman, Xania, was crazy. Six secret sisters? Tareth not her father? 'I don't believe you!'

Xania shrugged. 'It's true. Tareth is a warrior. An eagle hunter. He's not your father. He took you the night our family was killed. He smuggled you from the palace. He stole the sun-stone and fled from Khandar.'

Not only a liar but crazy. Maia glared at her. 'Now I know you're lying. Tareth isn't a thief.'

'He was clever. He covered his tracks well. I thought you must be dead like the others. But the silk didn't sing your death song. So I have waited and listened. I knew that if you were still alive you'd show yourself on your Naming Day. I've journeyed far to find you.'

Maia wanted to leap to her feet and dash from the shadowy tent, but the crazy woman's voice seemed to pin her in her place.

'The silk sang your name, Maia, it called you Sun Catcher. It sang the song of fire.'

'You can't know that,' whispered Maia.

'The silk sang your name, Sun Catcher.'

Maia clapped her hands over her ears. 'Stop! My name is Maia!'

'I know your name.'

'Anyone could have told you that. Tareth is my father.

I'm a Cliff Dweller. I'm not a Sun Catcher. There's no such thing. No one can catch the sun.'

Xania ignored her. 'One of our sisters is always chosen. You have been chosen. Elin will know it too.'

'I'm not your sister,' hissed Maia. 'I'm a weaver's daughter.'

'So Tareth is still a weaver. Does he weave the silk? Is that why the story-coat shivers and murmurs?' she mused. 'Why I feel he is close to me. He took moon-moths too.' Her eyes were sharp as she glanced at Maia. 'Has he made a moth-garden?'

Maia felt as if she had been kicked in the stomach. How did this woman know so much? The moth-garden and Tareth's night-weaving were secrets.

'Is that where you found the silk, boy?' Xania glanced at Kodo. 'Tareth shouldn't have been so free with his secret.'

'Tareth didn't show anyone the moth-garden. Kodo followed me,' Maia leapt to Tareth's defence.

Xania shrugged. 'Then the boy better had run away with the traders. If he's caught he will talk.' She looked at Kodo. He tried to meet her gaze. 'If the Wulf Kin find you they'll torture you to learn what you know. Then they'll kill you. The silk will be found. It will sing. And if the Wulf Kin don't, the Marsh Lord may remember and look for you.' Her sharp gaze flicked to Maia. 'And Maia and Tareth will be found.'

Maia quelled a quiver of alarm. For some reason the woman was trying to scare her. 'You can't possibly know that!'

'The silk wants to be found. It wants to be free. It wants to sing. It promises the earth and the stars. The silk is ours, Maia.

Our family discovered its mystery long ago. It brought us power. It keeps our songs, our story in the story-coat. Only our sisters can keep the silk, master it, use it. And even we are not always safe from its voice.

Maia tried to laugh. 'It's only silk.'

She remembered the nights when she had fallen asleep to the sound of Tareth's sledge sliding across the stone floor. Whatever he was weaving had always been cut from the loom before she woke. He had taught her to be careful when she collected the cocoons. Had plugged her ears with soft bees wax. Had taught her never to listen to the whispers of the silk. But he had never hidden the silk from her.

'Only silk?' repeated Xania scornfully. 'Hasn't Tareth taught you anything? Or are you too blind to see what's in front of your eyes? Why d'you think Tareth weaves so little? Why does he keep the moth-garden hidden? He knows that the silk is powerful and dangerous in the wrong hands. He was wise to make his home so far from Khandar. Wise to hide the silk and you from Elin.'

'If it's so dangerous, why does he weave it?' demanded Maia. She had almost started to believe this mad woman's story, but Tareth would never do anything to put them in danger.

'He weaves it because he must, because the silk sings in his blood and demands to be born. And because he knows you will need your coming of age silk. He was chosen as a boy to weave the silk. That is why our lives are woven with his. The silk belongs to us, but its song enchanted its weaver. In Khandar the silk made him its . . . slave. Even as he fled, as the moth-garden in the Sun Palace was dying in the fire, he must have stolen the cocoons to take with him.'

'No!'

She should have refused to listen. The woman was starting to scare her again. She was like the Watcher and her runes, embroidering a story around a few threads of truth.

'And he will be weaving silk for you, sister.'

'You don't know anything about anything. You're making it all up.'

'It's true, Sun Catcher,' said Xania.

Maia felt a snake of anger uncoil in her stomach. 'Don't call me that!'

'It's what the silk calls you. I'm bound by the silk just as Tareth is. It sent me to find you. It sent me to find the Weaver.'

'I don't believe you,' challenged Maia.

Xania frowned. 'Take me to Tareth and you'll see that everything I say is true.'

'If it's true then the silk will tell you where to find him.'

The juggler's frown grew deeper. 'The silk is not a tracker hound.'

'Ha!' crowed Maia.

'And to use the silk here with Wulf Kin so close, would be dangerous.'

'So you can't prove anything,' said Maia. 'I didn't think you could.' She turned to leave. 'Come on, Kodo.'

'You're as stubborn as Elin. She has made herself Queen. She wants the sun-stone. But our mother gifted the sun-stone to you, the youngest. And when she discovered Elin's treachery, she begged Tareth to protect you and the sun-stone. Elin will have sent the Wulf Kin to hunt you. D'you want them to find you? Their beasts will show you no mercy unless Elin decides she needs you alive. And once they find you, they will find Tareth. And they will punish him for saving you. For taking the sun-stone.'

Maia froze. 'They already have,' she whispered. 'Tareth killed the Wulf Kin when he pulled him from the deeps.'

She turned to face the Xania. 'And I . . . I used fire to destroy his beast when it attacked Kodo.'

'She saved me,' said Kodo.

Xania covered her bright hair with her cap, moved past Maia and twitched the door flap aside.

'Come,' she said. 'You too, lizard boy.' She glanced at Maia. 'Cover your hair. We must find Tareth.'

Twenty-Four

Xania led them through a maze of stalls, weaving through the crowds until they reached the edge of the horse meadow. A line of horses was tethered to a rope strung between two trees. Flies buzzed round their ears. A small girl wandered along the line waving the flies away with a leafy branch. As she moved, her bangles and anklets of brass bells jingled softly. Nearby a mob of ponies grazed in a corral made from cut blackthorn. Several herders squatted at the entrance, playing dice. Beyond them stood the woven hazel sheep pens and a group of hobbled camels.

'Can you ride?' asked Xania.

Maia shook her head. She had no breath left. Xania's long legs had been hard to keep pace with.

'Only lizards,' panted Kodo. 'My dugout is in the marshes.'

'We'll slip past the horses and cut the tethers. Loose horses will distract them while we make for the marshes.'

'The marshes flood with the tide. I can't swim,' Maia confessed in a rush.

Xania grimaced. 'Then let's hope we can find the floating shelters if the water rises.' She studied the grazing horses. 'Though I never cross water unless I must. So, shall we go and free a horse or two?'

Water or horses? Maia chose and glanced at Kodo. 'Will you come with us? Or go through the marshes?'

Kodo hesitated. 'I must go home. I must warn them. If the Marsh Lord comes . . .' his voice tailed off. 'It will be faster by water,' he added.

Maia nodded. 'Go then.'

The grass tickled Maia's nose. She lay watching the girl flick flies from the face of a shaggy pony. The pony tossed its head, eyes rolling. A cloud of gnats hovered above Maia's head. She wanted to swish them away but she could see one of the dice players looking her way. She flattened herself lower in the tall grass. She hoped the bad-tempered pony was not the one the juggler had decided to steal. Even hanging on to Xania, Maia was not sure she could stay on a horse with a mind of its own. She reached for her knife. At Xania's signal, she was to slither through the grass, cut the tether ropes and startle the ponies into running.

Maia saw Xania get to her feet and slip among the horses. She seemed to shimmer softly, her bright clothes hidden beneath a coat which was almost the colour of the bleached grass. A buzzard screamed. It was the signal.

Maia rose to a crouching position and ran towards the ponies. She sliced the cords tying them to the tethering rope. They snorted and moved restlessly. Maia avoided their stamping hooves and worked her way along the line. Two to go. She heard a shout behind her and the shrill cry of the girl. From the corner of her eye she saw Xania vault onto a shaggy pony.

'Quick, Maia!'

Maia severed the remaining ropes. She stood up and waved her hands, shouting. The circle of men split apart. They ran towards her. She clapped her hands and yelled. The horses started to move. She ran forward and smacked the rump of the nearest pony. It wheeled and started to trot.

'Run!' shouted Xania. Maia glanced over her shoulder. A plunging pony was racing towards her. She caught a glimpse of Xania's face above the flying mane and saw a shimmering cloud, billowing behind her. It swirled from her shoulders, sparkling with light. Maia turned and ran.

A hand grabbed her belt. She was swept off her feet. The wild eye of the pony was level with her face. She reached and grabbed at its neck, blinded by the coarse flying mane. Then with a thud that knocked the breath from her body she was dumped across the pony's withers. Her world became the thunder of hooves, the jolting, bony withers that threatened to dislodge her, the blur of trampled grass below her and unbelievably, the high, fierce song of the juggler as she drove the herd before her.

'On, on, swift as the sun. Run, children of the plains. On, on,' sang Xania.

Maia felt the song enter her bones. She needed to run, to leap, to fly, to be free. Her whole body was jangling. Xania's silk coat streamed in the wind, calling, pleading, singing of turning stars and sunshine and shadows. She heard her name. It was singing her name. And something more. The eerie music spun in a whirlpool of sound as each voice chimed into a chord that swelled to a single high call. 'Sun Catcher.'

Heads down, manes flying, they fled beyond the horse meadow and onto the moors. The stampede slowed. Xania turned her stolen pony from the herd. She pulled it to a snorting halt.

Breathlessly Maia wriggled, trying to push herself up. She was hauled upright. She swung her leg over the neck of their mount and grabbed a handful of mane.

'Which way?' asked Xania. 'We have to warn Tareth.'

Maia swallowed. 'Was everything you said true?'

'Everything. But only the things that I know. Tareth will have his own story.'

Parts of which he had never told her. Parts of which she had had to drag from him.

'His brother, Urteth,' she forced her dry tongue round the name. 'What about him?'

She felt the sinews in Xania's arms tighten. The pony tossed its head, jerking the reins. 'Urteth is Tareth's twin. He and Elin, our eldest sister, rule what is left of Khandar.'

Maia sat silent digesting the enormity of these claims. She looked down at Xania's slender, tanned hands and for the first time saw the tattoo of a leaping cat on the back of one. The cat prowled among leaves and flowers that swirled to become the antlers of a running deer. It was the image of her silver cat.

'Are you really my sister?' she asked.

'Yes. Xania, Story Singer and your second sister.'

'I don't understand,' said Maia.

She felt Xania twist to look behind them. 'It's a long tale. And we need to be gone.'

Maia pointed to a distant clump of trees. 'We can ride as far as the Watcher's cairn and then take the cliff path.'

'Thank you,' said Xania. She flicked the reins and urged the pony on. The silk sleeves of her coat brushed Maia's arms.

'I always wanted a sister,' said Maia shyly.

'I wish I'd found you sooner, but you were hidden. I only heard your voice on your Naming Day. And if I heard you,' muttered Xania, 'perhaps Elin did too.'

Maia risked unwinding one hand from the mane. 'Tell me about my sisters,' she said. 'And my parents. Tell me about Khandar.'

'All dead or dying,' said Xania bitterly. She pulled the folds of her silk coat forward over Maia's shoulders. 'Listen,' she said. 'The story-coat will tell you.'

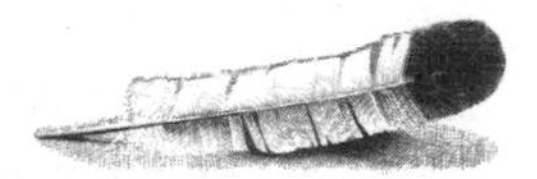

Disturbed by their approach, a flock of crows took flight. The pony shied. Maia was jolted from the dreams that held her. She was leaning against a warm body cocooned in butterfly wings. The cool silk fell from her shoulders and the vision of stone towers hewn from rock, so that mountain and building were one, faded. The great star shining in a tall column at the end of a walled courtyard vanished. A familiar stone cairn rose beside the path. She knew they were not far from home. The Watcher, her robes merging with the gathering dusk, stood waiting.

'The crows were right. The wind brings ill omens.'

She pointed a bony finger.

'Fire and death are coming, and loss and danger in a far place. You should leave,' intoned the Watcher. 'You're not welcome here,' she told Xania. 'Death follows you.'

'Death?' Xania glared at her. 'Your death if you stand in my way.'

Unexpectedly Sabra laughed. 'See how she rushes to her end,' she crowed to the wind. 'You think the Sun Catcher will save you?'

'It's told in the silk and the stars,' said Xania.

'But not for you, stranger.' Sabra gazed over the water. 'Go then, if you must.' She sniffed the salt breeze. 'The birds are unsettled. Something comes from the deeps.' She glanced at Maia. 'Warn the Cliff Dwellers to keep watch. I will light the beacons if danger comes.' She stepped closer and pressed a tiny, carved pigeon flute into her hand. 'It will sing in the wind,' she said. 'It may lighten the way. Go well, Sun Catcher.'

'Why does she think I'm leaving?' wondered Maia. Once

back in the cave with Tareth, she would be safe. There were many places to hide if the Marsh Lord came searching. Before she could ask, Xania nudged the pony forward. Peering back round her sister, Maia saw the Watcher raise her fist in farewell. Maia flicked her fingers to her forehead and the wind flute hummed. A sound echoed by the flock of pigeons that rose from their roost in the cairn.

Sabra turned and set off along the cliffs, her robes billowing in the wind. A flight of red-legged crows swooped above her.

Xania was watching the patterns made by the pigeons and crows. 'A strange old woman,' she said.

'Sabra is the Watcher. She guards the cliffs and watches over the sun-deeps. Nothing passes without her seeing,' said Maia. Even her secret forays to the lizard scrape had been seen – Kodo's too.

Maia hoped he had escaped. Had reached the stilt village. If her sister was wrong and the Marsh Lord pursued him there, that might be the destruction and fire Sabra foretold. Maia shivered.

The track wound through gorse bushes. Bees were humming around the yellow flowers in the last of the sunlight. Surrounded by the sights and smells of home, Sabra's warning seemed like the ramblings of a mad woman.

'We must leave the pony here,' said Maia. 'The way down to the caves is too steep.'

Xania reined in the pony and dismounted. The silk coat whispered as she gathered it up and stuffed it into her bag.

Maia felt the last wisps of the silk dreams fade. She slid from the pony, staggering as her feet hit the ground.

She felt as if she had been dreaming for days. Had her sister ridden far out of their way to give the coat time to tell its tales? But now, free from the dream stories of a sunlit city and laughing children, with hair as red as hers, running among flowering trees, she could hear the voices of the Cliff Dwellers returning from the Gather. Selora's was easy to pick out. She heard Laya's laugh. They had made good time. Elder would have chivvied them back to the caves – no Cliff Dweller would choose to be out in the dark.

'Maia?'

Tareth was there too. His basket scraped over the rocks of the cliff-face. Now she would have to explain why she had disobeyed him and gone to the Gather. She felt for her waist pouch and realised that Selora still had the cloth money. Her heart sank. Not only was she in trouble, but Razek's mother would witness her shame when she bustled to the Weaver's cave to give Tareth the purse retrieved from Elder. Nothing would keep Selora away, not when she could interfere in Maia's business.

'Tareth!' The whisper died in Xania's throat.

His head and shoulders appeared above the cliff-top. He hauled himself over the edge, and pushed himself upright on his crutch.

'Maia? What's this? A horse and a stranger?'

Xania was as still as the sea-stones marking the boundary of the weed beds.

'Never a stranger,' she said.

Maia watched the colour drain from Tareth's face.

'Xania?'

Xania did not move. She was staring at Tareth, at his crutches. 'What happened?'

'I fell.'

Xania managed a sound which was half-laugh, half-sob. 'Were you plundering an eagle's eyrie?'

'You know me well.'

'Like my own heart,' said Xania. She stepped forward and embraced Tareth. She was as tall as he was. His arms came round her. The crutches fell to the ground. To Maia, shut on the outside, the embrace seemed to go on forever.

'Why have you come?' asked Tareth.

'The silk brought me,' said Xania.

Maia saw Tareth shudder. 'You and who else?' he demanded.

He was looking over her shoulder. Maia could still hear Selora's voice, growing louder now. And Razek's. The Gather party were getting closer.

'You shouldn't have come,' said Tareth.

Maia saw Xania's body tense. 'I thought you both dead,' she whispered. 'You hid her well. Even the silk was silent. I couldn't find you. I thought you were dead!'

'Better dead than discovered!'

Maia felt rather than saw the shock hit Xania. She had never known her gentle father to be so harsh. She bent to pick up his crutches and held them out to him.

'Did she send for you?' Tareth demanded. 'Is this why you disobeyed me and went to the Gather?'

'No!' protested Maia.

'Why have you brought her here?'

Fear and rage and longing were all mixed together on his face. He looked terrifying.

'I'm sorry I ran off,' said Maia.

Tareth didn't seem to hear her, but he did see the approaching crowd, headed by Selora. He swore and lurched hurriedly to his basket hoist.

'Come,' he said.

Maia grabbed Xania's arm and hustled her down the path and into their cave. Tareth wasn't far behind. He abandoned the basket and swung past them, almost upsetting the cooking pot by the side of the fire. His stick scattered the wooden pieces of the gaming board. They bounced and rattled across the floor. He turned, his back against the wall, at bay in his own home.

'Leave us, Maia,' he said.

'Why didn't you tell me I had sisters?'

He didn't answer

'Her coat told me!' said Maia. 'Is it true?'

Tareth glared at Xania. 'You let her wear the story-coat?'

Xania shrugged. 'I wore it with her. The silk was kind and sang of Khandar. Have you woven silk for her? She will need its protection. The Wulf Kin are close.'

Tareth's shoulders slumped. 'Leave us, Maia.'

Maia hesitated.

Xania crossed over to her and put her hand on her shoulder. 'Only for a little while, sister. Tareth and I have much to say. And there will be pain in the telling.'

Maia looked at them. The tension was like a rope drawn taut between them.

'All right,' she said eventually, struggling to put aside the hurt she felt at her exclusion. There were answers she needed too. 'You won't leave, will you?'

Xania shook her head. 'Not without you,' she said.

'You cannot take her with you!' Tareth's voice was thick with anger.

Maia went outside and sat with Magnus. But before she quit the cave she heard Tareth ask, 'Did you lead the Wulf Kin here?' There was a pause when he must have found the answer in her sister's silence. 'How long do we have?' And then, with a groan as if the words were torn from him, 'Oh, Xania. Why did you not come? Why did you take so long to find me?'

Twenty-Five

Kodo tied the dugout to the stilt leg of the hut. Above him heavy feet crossed the overhanging net-platform.

'Useless bird! Get to your roost!'

Kodo heard Tuctuc, his fisher-bird, squawk. He could imagine Ootey waving his fist, sweeping the bird aside. He hoped it had the sense to fly to the ridge pole far from Ootey's territorial cormorant. He was bullied by the old bird. Kodo knew how it felt. He'd be lucky if his grandfather didn't kill him when he heard the news he brought.

He scrambled onto the platform, in his haste getting tangled in the drying nets. As he freed himself, Ootey's bulk loomed in the entrance of the hut. 'Back are we?' he roared.

Behind him the baby cried. 'Hush. Sleep, little one,' his mother's voice was calm. The old man's raging never seemed to worry her.

'Where've you been, boy? I needed help harvesting the choke-roots!' Kodo knew his grandfather hated standing knee-deep in the mud, digging up the roots. 'Never here when you're wanted.'

'The horse meadows.'

'To the Gather? When there's work to be done?' He saw the state Kodo was in. 'Did they chase you away, boy? The Lizard People are seldom welcome.'

'No, Grandfather.'

'Not welcome,' grumbled Ootey, 'even with one of our own a Marsh Lord. Helmek forgets where his mother came from!' Ootey frowned. 'Hides his mark with a silver ring.'

Kodo shuddered, the excitement of the escape suddenly deserting him. For a moment he wished he could change places with the baby and be rocked to sleep in Jakarta's arms. Instead he had to tell his grandfather what he had done.

'I saw him, Grandfather. The Lord with the silver ring. I angered him. I think . . . I think . . . he said the silk . . . I think he . . . ! He's com—'

'Think? Said? Silk!' interrupted Ootey. 'Your son's a jabbering idiot, Jakarta. Makes no more sense than the lizards!'

His mother, the baby on her hip, padded out onto the deck. Her smile of welcome changed to a gasp of alarm when she saw the gash in Kodo's arm.

'What have you done?'

'Nothing. I fell on the cliff. I stole . . .'

'Stole!' bellowed Ootey. He lowered his head, clenched his fists. For a heartbeat Kodo thought he was going to strike him.

Then Jakarta was tugging at his grandfather's arm, eyes wide with alarm.

'Look!'

Kodo swung round to see where she was looking. The beacon on the headland was blazing.

'Sea Thieves! Sea Thieves!' A boy paddling his dugout from the fishing ground shouted as he passed. 'They're rounding the headland. They've launched windboards!'

'Raiders!' moaned Jakarta.

Kodo heard the mournful notes of a distant shell-horn.

'They'll attack the cliffs first!' Ootey picked up his fishing trident. 'Listen, that's the Weeders' conch.' He glared at Kodo. 'Get the lizards,' he said.

'But, Grandfather . . .'

'Take the young lizards along the river. Follow him,' he told Jakarta. 'I'll bring Doon and Toon.'

'But, Grandfather . . .'

'Go, boy!' roared Ootey. 'They'll kill the lizards for meat and carry off anyone they catch.'

Kodo could see families already leaving their huts to flee into the hinterlands beyond the settlement. Ootey had told them many times that Sea Thieves would not dare to prey further inland and that the Marsh Lords would chase off the raiders. And they had believed him. After all, the Marsh Lords' protection was why they paid tithes each leaf-fall. All they had to do was flee and hide. Then return to rebuild the ransacked stilt village.

Kodo turned to do as he was told. The conch blared again. He could see smoke rising beyond the headland and it wasn't smoke from the beacon. The Cliff Dwellers' caves must be under attack. Had they set fire to the weed to try to escape in the smoke and confusion? Maia would have reached her home by now. She was in danger.

'Grandfather, we should help.'

'Help?'

'The Weaver and Maia. The Cliff Dwellers need our help. The Marsh Lord will drive the raiders back into the sea, but they'll escape to their ship. We can fight them in the sun-deeps.'

'Fight?' Kodo saw his grandfather's fists bunch. Ootey loved to fight. Even at his age he could out-wrestle all the men in the village.

'Show them we're not afraid. Show them they can't come and take us as slaves and burn our village.'

'Fight?' repeated Ootey. 'We're not Bronze Fists, boy!'

'We're better than the Bronze Fists, Grandfather,' said Kodo, fired up with the vision of the Marsh Lord with his nose in the mud. If Maia could fell a Lord, he could stop a Sea Thief. 'We can fight. We have lizards. The lizards will fight with us. They'll sink the windboards. The Sea Thieves will drown.'

'Use the lizards?'

'They would fight!'

'Fighting lizards!' Ootey's frown was terrifying. 'No one could control them.'

'You could, Grandfather!'

'No one fights with lizards, boy.'

'My father would have,' said Kodo. 'He would fight. He wouldn't run and let raiders burn the village.'

Everyone knew that Ootey's only son had been as brave

as a red-crest. He had been killed battling to save a young Doon. They remembered his courage still.

'Humph!' Ootey growled, his eyebrows jagged in a fearsome frown.

'We can scare off the Sea Thieves. No one would dare tangle with Doon and Toon when they're red-angry.'

'They would be hurt!' protested Jakarta. 'You could be hurt. We must get the lizards and find a hiding place.'

Kodo could have punched the air. His mother had wielded the perfect goad.

'Don't tell mc what I must do, woman!' thundered Ootey.

He crossed to the edge of the net platform, grabbed a fishing spear and using the shafts of his trident and spear as sticks, started drumming on the upturned dugout resting against the rail. The whole platform seemed to vibrate with the noise. Kodo could see people leaving the village stop and turn. The rhythm changed. The cords in Ootey's neck bulged with the ferocity of his drumming. The beat and its demand couldn't be denied. Kodo felt the blood roar in his ears. Men began running back towards them. In the pound the lizards bugled. Even the young were calling, their immature voices warbling up and down the scale. Above the hullabaloo Kodo heard Doon bellow.

Kodo yelled too. They were going to fight!

Twenty-Six

The painted vessel tacked across the bay. Another windboard dropped from the deck. It skimmed across the shallows. As it ground onto the shingle, the Sea Thief crouching in front of the sail sprinted across the beach. Dodging the hail of rocks hurled by weed boys skulking in the lower caves, he started scaling the cliffs. The spinning stone from Razek's slingshot hit the second Sea Thief as he was still beaching the board. He dropped like a stunned gull.

Magnus screamed and launched himself at the figure creeping along the ledge. Bird and attacker disappeared in the smoke. Maia dragged the huge jar of oil out of the cave and Tareth, his face blackened with soot, helped her tip it over the edge, tossing a flaming torch into the stream. It caught alight. They heard a shout as someone tried to get out of the way and fell.

'More oil, Maia!' gasped Tareth.

Wind-tangled hair appeared above the ledge. Maia saw Xania step forward. A spinning disc whirled from her hand and hit the intruder. Before he could recover, she had followed it with a swinging blow from the copper cooking pot. There was a yell as the attacker fell from the cliff-face.

A hand grasped the rope attached to Tareth's basket-hoist. Maia darted forward, grabbed the eagle's feeding rock and hammered it down onto the fingers. The hand let go. Clawing fingers grabbed her ankle, dragging her towards the edge. She almost overbalanced. Tareth shouted in alarm. As she lurched backwards, trying to save herself, Magnus swooped across the cliff-face, talons outstretched, and raked the clinging figure. The man screamed and let go of her ankle. Knees trembling, Maia hurled a rock after him. It bounced off his head. She heard him cry and, as Magnus swooped again, he let go of the rope. His tumbling body almost dislodged another climber, with a knife clenched between his teeth. Maia ran back to the cave entrance, grabbed Tareth's stone loom weights and, taking up position, flung them down on him. Xania joined her, her aim unerring. As long as the supply of rocks held out, they would keep the Sea Thieves off the ledge.

'More oil,' gasped Maia and dashed into the cave.

She heard a high-pitched scream.

'Laya!'

'Maia! No! Wait!' cried Tareth.

Ignoring him, Maia grabbed her knife and ran along the ledge towards Selora's cave. She could hear Selora sobbing, her hands wrapped round the legs of a burly Sea Thief who was hauling a wriggling, screeching Laya from the cave. Selora was being dragged too.

Fuelled with a mix of fear and anger, Maia launched herself. Leaping over Selora, she slashed at the Sea Thief and heard Laya scream as blood splattered her face. The man bellowed, let go of Laya and turned to face Maia. She swiped with the knife and saw his expression of surprise as she cut him again. He roared, slicing the air with his curved blade. She backed out of reach, lifting her knife ready for another thrust as he dropped at her feet like a felled tree.

Xania stepped forward and retrieved her metal disc. She hauled the Sea Thief to the edge and pushed him over, then glanced at Selora, who was trying to get to her knees.

'There are too many,' she said. 'You must hide.'

The conch bellowed again. Fish-spear in hand, Elder led a charge across the sand. A gaggle of boys brandishing weed-knives attacked the Sea Thieves beaching their windboards in the shallows.

'Look!' gasped Laya. 'Razek!'

Maia turned to where she pointed. She could see Razek, wreathed in smoke, the sun glinting on the bronze discs of the stolen Wulf Kin's cuirass, standing on the levee above steaming piles of drying weed. Someone had set it on fire.

Beyond him, swimming into the sun-deeps, were two red-crested lizards with riders perched on their backs. Strung between them was the dark line of the collecting boom. Behind them, struggling to keep up, was a raft of the smaller lizards, heads held high. As the adults passed either side of a windboard, the boom swept its two Sea Thieves into the sea. The young lizards surged forwards, mobbing them.

There was an explosion of spray and the men disappeared. The board spun, its sail submerged and was dragged down.

The red-crests swam on to attack another windboard skimming towards them. Maia saw the sail trimmer's companion, crouching on the front of the board, firing arrows at the lizards. Watched as the lizard riders wrapped their arms about their mounts' necks and the reptiles dived. Saw the flurry of foam as the young sank below the water. Then the second sail vanished. The sea churned. The lizards surfaced and were turning inshore to attack a windboard swooping towards the beach.

'The lizards,' shrieked Laya. 'They're helping us!'

Maia helped her sister pull Selora to her feet. Her face was bleeding, one eye was swollen. But she hadn't let Laya be dragged away. Maia felt a rush of respect.

'You must hide!' urged Xania.

'There's hot broth in the cave,' gasped Selora. 'Help me bring it out,' she commanded Laya.

Maia wondered if the blow to her face had addled Selora's brains. This was no time to think about food.

'We'll tip it on the next one who tries to climb onto the ledge!' panted Selora.

They heard the distant notes of a horn.

'The Marsh Lords,' said Selora thankfully. 'Let's hope they're not too late to save us.'

Maia grinned shakily at her. 'I think we may just save ourselves,' she said.

Then she heard a terrible howl. The hair on the back on her neck stood on end. Laya gasped. Selora turned pale. 'What's that?'

'Wulfen!' said Xania grimly. 'Come!' she grabbed Maia's arm. 'Hide,' she shouted to Selora as she hustled Maia to the Weaver cave.

Tareth was hastily packing a back-sack.

'The Wulf Kin are here!' gasped Xania. 'Do they ride with Sea Thieves now?' she demanded.

The Wulf Kin hunt with whoever serves their purpose. You must leave.'

He thrust the bag at Maia. 'Food and fire-maker,' he said. 'My throwing knife. And silk to give you comfort and courage. Though you have that already.' He gave her a swift hug. 'More than enough for what must come.'

She barely grasped what he was telling her. 'Silk?'

'Xania was right. I wove silk while you slept. You should have your own silk. I had hoped you would never need it, never want it. But it may protect you, as I cannot. Wear it next to your skin. Keep it hidden . . . secret.'

'Will it sing?' demanded Xania.

'It's new . . . different from the old silk . . . in ways I don't understand.' He smiled at Maia. 'But then you too are different and like the silk have grown in a different land so perhaps that's as it should be.'

'But . . .' began Maia.

His attention had switched to Xania. 'It'll be dark soon and safe to leave. There's a way up the firestack in Elder's cave to the cliffs above. Maia climbs like a goat, she'll help you.' He looked at Maia. 'If the cliffs are clear, you can hide near the cairn. Seek out the Watcher. She will take you both safely across the moors.' Then he was instructing Xania again. 'If the way is impassable, try for the saltpans.

Make your way down from the beacon, wade around the headland. Go warily. The Sea Thieves may be ransacking the salt. The Holder's wealth is well known. The Holder has a dugout. Take it.'

Xania was pulling on her shoulder bag. 'No boats,' she said.

'Now is no time to refuse to cross water!' snapped Tareth.

Xania glared at him. 'It will take more than the Wulf Kin to send me across the sun-deeps! I'll take her to Altara. The archers will shelter us.'

'To the Warrior Women?' Tareth hesitated, then nodded. 'Magnus and I will deal with the Wulf Kin.'

He flung back the lid of the cedarwood chest and pulled out a quiver. Each arrow had a narrow ring of coloured silk thread wound beneath the flight feather. He laid the bag on his wooden sledge and extracted a short, curving black bow with silver tips. Maia had never seen it before.

It seemed that Xania had. She stopped packing bronze discs into her waist pouch and leaned forward to touch the bow lightly.

'You have it still!' she murmured 'Greetings Blackwood,' she said as she stroked the wood. 'Fight well for your Warrior Weaver.' She looked at Tareth across the weapon. 'We'll meet at the Watcher's stone and make for Altara together.'

He hesitated. His eyes were dark. 'The standing stone,' he agreed.

'No!' cried Maia, afraid of what she saw in his eyes.

The silent communication between Tareth and her sister broke and they turned as one to look at her.

'I'm not leaving. Not with her. Not without you!'

'I will follow,' said Tareth.

'How?' stormed Maia. 'You can't use the basket hoist to reach the path. The Sea Thieves are still on the cliff!'

Tareth was swinging himself onto his sledge. 'I'll find another way.'

'What way?' demanded Maia.

They heard the horn of the Marsh Lords, closer now. 'The attack will be over,' said Tareth, ignoring her question.

'Then we can wait,' said Maia. 'And leave together.'

Xania was watching Tareth. 'The silk? The lizard boy said the Marsh Lord wants it.'

'No one must find it,' said Tareth.

Xania nodded and picked up a brand from the fire. 'It will be easier for me,' she said and strode into the weaving cave.

'Wait!' Maia started after her. Xania swung round, the flaring branch casting shadows across her face. 'You can't destroy it.'

Xania made a threatening gesture with the flame. 'Go back, sister. We must leave. And the silk cannot be left here. If we take it and are caught . . .'

'You can't burn it!' protested Maia.

'Tareth will find it hard to destroy. I can spare him that pain at least. Will you deny him that?'

'I don't understand,' said Maia.

'Accept what must be,' Xania said. 'Go, bid Tareth farewell. We must leave. The Wulf Kin are hunting for you. They mustn't find you.'

She turned and Maia saw her fling open a small, wooden chest and plunge the flaming branch into it. Maia heard the terrible shriek. She heard Tareth groan as the flames torched the silk. The groan became a shouted challenge. Maia spun on her heel and raced back into the living cave.

A Wulf Kin loomed at the entrance. He saw Tareth on the sledge, snarled, raised his knife and advanced. Maia's precipitous arrival distracted him.

'The girl!'

He took a step towards Maia, then staggered, Tareth's arrow piercing his bronze cuirass. He swayed, regained his balance and charged at Tareth. Another arrow stopped him in his tracks. A huge, furred shape loomed behind him. Maia heard the thrum of Tareth's bowstring as he released a third arrow and then the beast reached him, knocking him from the sledge.

Maia screamed, grabbed a smouldering branch from the fire and charged. She heard Xania shout and then she was driving her flaming torch into the side of the beast as it straddled Tareth. The stench of burning fur filled the cave. Maia saw the gleam of a knife beneath the wulfen's jaw and heard Tareth grunt as he thrust upwards. The beast shuddered and sank, burying Tareth beneath its bulk. Maia grabbed a handful of fur and tugged frantically.

At the cave entrance, the Wulf Kin groaned and tried to rise. Maia was aware of Xania stepping past her. The Wulf Kin stabbed with his knife. She saw Xania swing the flaming branch at his head. There was a bone-crunching thud. Xania followed up the blow with another. The man pitched forward and lay still.

'Help me,' gasped Maia.

Together they hauled Tareth from beneath the wulfen. He emerged, his tunic slimed with saliva and blood.

'Are you hurt?' demanded Maia.

Tareth shook his head and tugged his knife from the wulfen's fur. 'You must go! Now!'

Outside Magnus called.

'Maia . . . go!'

She hugged him fiercely and slipped from the cave. She ducked as Magnus swooped across the cliff-face.

'Farewell, my heart,' she heard her sister say, and then Xania was beside her. 'The firestack. Quickly!'

Maia didn't move. The eagle flew to the ledge, his wingtips brushing her head. He had returned to Tareth. She should be with him too. Close by a wulfen bellowed. Maia felt her blood freeze. Magnus launched himself and dived screaming towards the weed beds and a figure in Wulf Kin bronze. Talons extended, he dropped like a stone and attacked. Maia saw the figure sway as the eagle latched onto his shoulders, his beak stabbing and tearing. The figure fell, rolled across the sand and struggled to his feet. Maia saw the knife in his hand. Saw Magnus take off from the beach, bank and power in for another attack. She saw the glint of a wristguard. It was Razek, wearing stolen Wulf Kin trappings.

Maia yelled. 'Magnus. No!'

Then Xania was pushing her along the cliff ledge. 'Go! Go!' she yelled.

Twenty-Seven

Cautiously Maia raised her head from the opening of the firestack.

Xania tugged at Maia's ankle. 'Is it safe?' she whispered.

'Yes.' Maia wriggled out of the narrow opening. Xania followed.

They jogged in silence towards the Watcher's cairn, which stood like a lone sentinel guarding the track. There was no light at the cairn, no sign of birds or the Watcher. The stillness and silence were eerie. Xania held up her hand and stopped. She crouched and beckoned Maia down beside her.

'She'll still be at the beacon,' whispered Maia. The silence of the cliffs made her feel uneasy. From here she could see a windboard tacking towards the Sea Thieves' ship. A sail was on fire and the boat seemed to be drifting. Smoke still rose from the weed beds. The beacon on the headland glowed red. A confusion of horses and men was milling on the beach. The Marsh Lords, with their killing helmets and breastplates reflecting the glow of the fires were figures from a nightmare.

There was movement beyond the cairn. A figure in Wulf Kin bronze moved towards them, a huge bird hanging upside-down from his hand.

'Flame Head! I've been waiting for you.'

Xania, knife in hand, sprang past Maia.

He lifted his arm to fend her off. Her knife hit the fish-scale wristguard.

'Wait!' shouted Maia. 'It's Razek!'

Xania was crouching ready to spring again. 'He wears Wulf Kin bronze,' she snarled.

'It's Razek! The Weed Master,' cried Maia.

Razek seemed oblivious of the threat. He stepped towards Maia. His eyes were wild. His face streaked with soot and smoke.

'The weed beds are burning!' he babbled. 'The crop is lost. The weed boys are hurt . . . killed! You brought the beasts down on us! It's your fault the strangers came. And hers,' he yelled.

He held up the dead bird in his hand. Its head swung, huge dark wings hung lifeless, sweeping the ground. Maia felt the world turn black and spin.

'Magnus!'

'He attacked. He would have killed me!'

His voice was coming from a great distance. Maia heard Xania shouting. Saw her strike Razek. Through a blur saw Razek drop the eagle.

'The Wulf Kin came for you!' he yelled at Maia. 'Tareth warned that they would! All this is because of you. It's your fault!'

Rage was building inside her. Magnus! He had killed Magnus!

'The eagle attacked me!'

'He thought you were a Wulf Kin!' shouted Xania. 'You wear their clothes!'

'I fought them,' he protested. 'I wore the bronze to protect you and Tareth. I came to find you. To save you, Maia!'

'You've killed Tareth's eagle!' stormed Xania. 'Where is he?'

Maia could feel the anger swelling inside her. Her head was going to split. Fire roared behind her eyes. Her mouth tasted of ash. She fought against the need to rage and blaze and destroy Razek where he stood with his smoke-blackened face and his stolen bronze. Her eyes were burning gold. She clenched her fists and gasped for air. He had sold the silver armband and alerted the Wulf Kin. He had brought fire and death from the Gather not her. He would burn for it. Hate screamed through her.

Razek her tormenter. Razek who she had grown up with. Razek, who had wanted her to leap the hand-fast fires. Razek who had killed the eagle. Killed Magnus!

Her heart would burst with the weight of rage and grief. She dragged another painful lungful of air into the seething, roiling furnace that blazed inside her. She tore her gaze from Razek's horror and managed to turn away before the fire destroyed everything.

Her eyes fell on the eagle. Magnus would never have left

Tareth. Where was her father? The fire died, buried beneath a landslide of fear.

She looked at Razek and wished him dead.

'The Wulf Kin silver brought them here,' she accused. 'The silver you stole and sold. You summoned them! I wish they had killed you!'

'Maia!'

'I wish you were dead!'

'Please, Maia.'

'Dead!' she screamed.

He turned and ran.

She cradled Magnus, hugging him as if she could will life back into him. A stone seemed to have lodged beneath her breast bone.

Xania touched her shoulder. 'We must go.'

'Not yet!' she said. She crossed to the cairn and placed the eagle tenderly on the ground. She pulled a stone loose. Then another. Tearing at them, stubbing her fingers, breaking her nails, she ripped rocks from the cairn.

'Quickly then.' Xania realised what she wanted and joined her.

Together they lifted the eagle and placed him in the cairn.

'Sleep safe. Fly high. Hunt well, Sky Warrior,' Maia whispered as she replaced the rocks over Magnus' entombed body.

They heard the distant howl. Xania stiffened. 'We must go.'

Maia turned. Razek had stopped running. He was standing, staring back at them, a stranger, part Wulf Kin in the stolen bronze cuirass, part bullying Weed Master. Her childhood companion, Magnus' executioner. Her enemy. Laya was welcome to him. She hated him.

Twenty-Eight

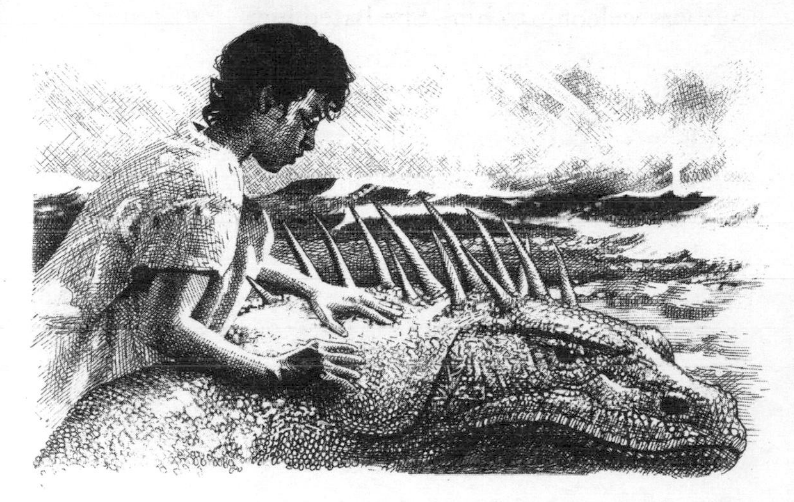

Kodo slid off Doon's neck. He landed in the shallows where the young lizards were frolicking, warbling to one another. He almost fell over as they rushed him. He staggered against Doon. Her bellow sent the juveniles stampeding back to the pen. If he'd had any breath left, he would have laughed as they tumbled over each other in their haste. He could hear Doon groaning deep in her belly. Her breath was as laboured as his. They had fought well.

He reached to pat her scaly neck. The Sea Thief's arrow wound was already sealed, but the sword slash was oozing dark blood. He threw water over the cut and ran his fingers round the edge. Not too deep, he noted with relief. He waded round Doon, checking for more injuries. There were none.

Ootey was doing the same for Toon. Ootey was grinning. It must be the first time ever, thought Kodo.

'A good fight,' gasped his grandfather. 'We saw them off, eh boy?'

Kodo looked out across the sun-deeps. He couldn't see the Sea Thieves' ship. A broken windboard was bobbing in the shallows.

'Claim it,' said Ootey. 'Jakarta will want the sail.' He grinned at Kodo. 'Well fought, boy.'

He looked towards the stilt village, frowning as he saw the group of horsemen milling on the hill beyond.

'Marsh Lords! Coming here! Well, they can expect a smaller tithe next Solstice. Saw off the raiders ourselves. The Lizard People can take care of their own. Don't need their help. Not with the lizards willing to fight.'

He watched Jakarta hurrying towards them, leaping over the shining, tidal rivulets and his frown deepened.

'Are you in some sort of trouble, boy? With the Lords?'

'Yes, Grandfather,' admitted Kodo.

'We'll see about that!' said Ootey belligerently.

And then it was business as usual. 'Stop dreaming! Get the harness off Doon and put sepweed on the cut.'

Jakarta splashed up to them. She was carrying a small clay pot, which she held out to Kodo.

'Are the lizards hurt?' she asked.

Kodo took the pot, scooped out a handful of dark green gel and smoothed it over Doon's gash.

'The Marsh Lords are coming,' said Jakarta.

'They'll search for me.' Kodo took a deep breath, 'They'll ransack the village. They want the silk I stole from Flame Head.'

'Stole!' roared his grandfather. 'Since when is Ootey's blood a thief?'

He looked towards the hill. It was empty. The Lords were out of sight, riding along the wooded valley which wound down to the stilt village.

'They're looking for Flame Head too,' said Kodo. 'And it's my fault. I took the silk.'

'Silk!' Ootey sounded incredulous.

'The silk is powerful,' said Kodo. 'It sings.'

'Sings!' spluttered Ootey, glaring at the Kodo as if he suspected he was trying to make a fool of him.

'The Marsh Lord discovered it. He wants it,' gabbled Kodo. 'The Weaver carried it in secret from Khandar.'

'From a strange land,' said Ootey, as if that explained everything; the nonsense of singing silk and a thieving grandson. 'There's none of it here, is there?' he demanded suspiciously.

Kodo shook his head. 'I told him. He didn't believe me.'

'He'll listen to me,' claimed Ootey. 'I know the secret of Helmek's tattooed thumb and his mother's shame. The Marsh Lord will listen!'

'Perhaps it would be better if Kodo weren't found,' suggested Jakarta anxiously. She looked steadily at Ootey. 'Better if he were dead.'

Kodo gasped.

Ootey glowered. Finally he nodded. He waded across to Doon and unfastened the ropes attached to the boom.

'My grandson was killed in the attack,' he said. 'Take the lizard. She'll return when you release her.' He glared at Kodo. 'The trader ship will be setting out soon. They always need willing hands.'

Kodo couldn't believe what he was hearing. 'Grandfather . . . ?'

'Always knew you wanted to leave. Never were much use with the lizards . . .' he said gruffly. 'Always dreaming. Forgetting to collect the eggs. Away for hours with the fisher-bird. Never there when you're needed.'

He scowled at Jakarta as if these failings were all her fault. 'The Marsh Lord will learn how my grandson died fighting with the lizards. How he fought bravely. How he was as fearless as a red-crest.' He turned away to unhook the boom from Toon.

'Now take your leave of your mother. Be swift. They will be here soon.'

Kodo flung himself at Ootey. Arms like knotted ropes came round him. He was crushed against his grandfather's wide chest, hugged tight and then put aside.

'Be off with you. Doon can carry you to the trader's ship. Send her back to me.'

He turned away, but not before Kodo had seen the gleam of tears in his grandfather's fierce, grey eyes.

'Go well, boy,' he said gruffly as he grasped Toon's harness and encouraged the lizard to her feet. 'I'll turn the Lords back before they reach the village. It should give you time to clear the headland.'

The last Kodo saw of him, he was striding away with Toon ambling beside him. Then Jakarta was hugging him as if she would never let him go.

And then he was perched on the long ridges of Doon's back as the lizard swam away from the lonely figure watching from the water's edge.

Once through the jagged rocks and round the long outcrop, Kodo could see along the coastline. Smoke still hung above the distant cliff village. Further away, he could make out the white gleam of the saltpans. The smudge slipping over the horizon must be the Sea Thieves' ship. Doon surged past a damaged windboard and swam on.

As the water and sky started to merge, Doon bellowed. Her crest rose. She turned back towards the shore and the red glow of the dying beacon.

Kodo drummed his heels against her shoulders but she wouldn't turn, wouldn't stop.

'No, Doon!' he shouted. 'Not the weed beds.'

A broken windboard drifted in the swell.

Kodo groaned. 'The battle's over, Doon,' Were they going to attack every piece of rubbish floating in the sun-deeps?

Doon's great jaws opened as if she was going to take a bite out of the broken board. She roared and almost submerged the board as she swam round it. Kodo glimpsed a white face, dark hair and a tattered eagle feather. As the board pitched, the sprawled figure slid into the water and sank.

Twenty-Nine

Maia watched Xania anxiously. She had driven them hard out into the Vast, barely allowing them to rest. Yet there had been no sign of Wulf Kin pursuit. Now her sister sat cross-legged, shivering. She rocked backwards and forwards. Her ragged breath hung in a small cloud. Her hand was pressed against her side, hiding the stain that flowered across her tunic. Each sun-sleep the blood-mark, which she tried to conceal, seemed a little wider.

It was freezing. Not even the silk she now wore under her tunic could keep her warm. In the still cold of sun-sleep, the stars seemed very close. Maia felt she had only to reach out to grab one. It too would be as cold as ice. She remembered Tareth's story. Were these bright, star queens, guiding nomads across the plains?

Maia glanced again at her sister. She was getting worse.

If they didn't find warmth, food and shelter soon, anything could happen. She might die. How far was it to Altara, the women's holdfast in the foothills of the Vast? They had been fleeing forever, through seven, or was it nine, sun-wakes?

Maia rubbed her eyes, too tired to count. She could feel the first stirrings of a headache. She had to do something. A little fire couldn't hurt. They had to get warm. They had to eat.

In the darkness, something furry scuttled past. That decided her. She shrugged out of her coat and slipped her knife from her belt.

'I'll be back,' she whispered. Xania, staring into the distance, took no notice.

Maia licked her finger, held it up to test the direction of the wind and slid into the dark.

She found the burrow within sight of their camp, pressed her ear to the ground near the entrance and listened. She could sense something small and warm breathing beneath the surface.

At the edge of her vision Xania was as still and silent as the rocks. Maia tried to think herself into immobility too. Time stretched. Maia wondered if she'd ever be able to move again. There was a scrabble of paws, a tiny fall of earth and a lapran scurried from the hole.

Maia lunged and struck with the hilt of her knife. The first blow missed. The lapran darted away. It was almost too quick for her. Desperately Maia managed a second back-handed strike and killed it. Hands shaking with cold she skinned the creature. There was hardly any meat on its bones.

Maia looked across at Xania. She lay in a heap. Maia

rejected the idea of going further to hunt again. Instead she collected a handful of dead grasses and hurried back to her sister.

She built a pyramid of grass and dried leaves. Now flame. She found Tareth's fire-maker. Her cold hands could barely hold the flints. The sparks were weak. The tinder too damp. She needed heat and flame. Could she make fire without the sun? Steeling herself, she held out her hand and glared at the pile. Nothing. She took a deep breath, conjured an image of the wulfen who had attacked Kodo and felt an echo of the gut-twisting fear and rage she had experienced when she saw him fall. Red roared behind her eyes. Pain stabbed her head. The kindling burst into flames. Wincing, Maia fed more twigs onto the fire. The flame seemed to burn brighter and hotter than the cooking fires of the Cliff Dwellers. She wasn't sure how real the blaze was, but if she treated it like real fire and fed it, perhaps it would cook the lapran. She speared the carcass with her knife and held it over the flames. The skin crisped and browned. Fat dripped into the flames. They popped and flared yellow. Maia sighed. She turned her knife. The smell of roasting meat filled the air.

Xania tried to sit up. 'We shouldn't have a fire. They might see.'

'You need to eat,' said Maia. She tried to ignore the grumbling hunger pangs in her stomach. 'And they're far away.'

Xania huddled closer to the fire. 'The Wulf Kin come fast.'

'I'll put out the fire once you've eaten.'

Xania coughed. 'So you managed to make fire.'

Maia shrugged. 'Needs must,' she said.

She rotated the carcass and pulled a strip of charred meat from it. She blew on it and tossed it in her mouth. She forced herself to chew slowly as her stomach growled. It was tough, burned but cooked.

She passed the knife to Xania. 'Eat.'

Xania shook her head. 'You need it.'

'I'll trap another,' said Maia. 'You need to get strong. If I have to carry you, we'll never outrun the Wulf Kin. Has the bleeding stopped?'

Xania pulled a face and tore meat from the knife. 'You may have to leave me.'

Maia stifled a stab of fear. 'Maybe. But not yet. Eat and grow strong, sister.'

Xania chewed greedily. Maia thought she could see her getting better with each mouthful. Then Xania coughed. Maia saw blood on the back of her hand where she had wiped it across her mouth. It wasn't from the lapran.

Xania ripped the last of the meat from the bones. 'We must bury the bones,' she said. 'The wulfen will scent it.'

Maia took the bones from her. She nibbled until they were picked clean. Breaking them, she sucked out the marrow. It was little enough, but at least it quietened the ravenous beast inside her. She dug a hole with her knife and buried the tiny bones. 'I'll cover the ashes when we leave,' she said.

'They'll feel the warmth,' fretted Xania.

Maia shivered as the wind fanned the dying flames of the fire. 'It's too cold for that.'

'Pile rock over the earth to hide the heat,' said Xania, 'or they'll know when we were here.'

Maia nodded. Xania was feverish and weaker with each sun-wake. It was not worth arguing with her. They must leave soon. They couldn't afford to wait until it was light. Had Xania rested long enough? Maia knew that every bone in her body would groan in protest when she got to her feet again. Her legs felt like blocks of stone. The soles of her feet burned as if they had been crisped by the sun and scoured in the saltpans.

For a moment she allowed herself to think about the cliff dwellings, the weed beds and Laya boasting about the wealth her Holder father made in the salt pan. About Magnus, hunting with Tareth across the cliffs. She heard again his whispered farewell as he had hugged her. 'Go fast. Stay safe.' Maia felt her eyes sting. She wouldn't think about Tareth.

She stabbed her knife into the ground, to loosen dirt to throw onto the fire.

'We should go,' she said.

And froze.

She heard the chink of metal.

Maia jack-knifed to her feet. The flames flared and glinted on silver. A shadow loomed. Maia leapt. Her slashing knife glanced off metal and was turned aside. With a yell, the shadow fell back, flung out an arm.

'Maia!'

She was crouching, knife raised for a stabbing thrust under the raised arm. An arm with a silver wristguard.

'Maia!' The voice yelled again.

Razek!

'Why are you here?' she hissed.

'I followed you!'

'Why?'

'You can't cross the Vast. No one can. You'll die. You shouldn't have run away. I can protect you. I stole food from the Watcher's cairn. I followed you. You belong with us. Not with her! My father saved you from the storm. You're one of us. You must come back.'

Maia stared at him in disbelief. Only one word made sense. She lowered the knife. 'Food?'

'In the back-sack.' He shrugged the bag from his back and pushed it towards Maia. 'What's wrong with her?' He nodded towards Xania.

Maia tore the bag open. Strips of salted fish, shrivelled apples and a flatbread fell out. She passed fish strips to Xania, and tore at the flatbread.

'Are the Wulf Kin following?' she asked, her mouth full. 'Is Tareth safe?'

Razek looked away. 'I don't know. I saw him fall.'

Maia choked back a sob.

'The Sea Thieves were beaten,' stammered Razek quickly. 'The Marsh Lords drove them back . . . killed them in the shallows as they tried to escape. I saw no Wulf Kin.'

'The Wulf Kin were in the caves.' Xania fingered her knife. 'We killed one. But there would be others. They're looking for Maia. If you've led them here . . . !'

'The Marsh Lords will have made the cliffs safe!'

'Then go back to them!' said Maia. 'You killed Magnus. I hate you.' She turned her back on him.

'Go home, weed boy,' said Xania.

'Not without Maia! You can't cross the Vast. You'll die. You must go back.'

'What d'you know of the Vast, weed boy? Or Khandar? Or Maia's destiny?'

'Maia belongs with us! A storm brought her to us. I saved her from death in the sun-deeps.'

'She is the Sun Catcher,' said Xania, as if that explained everything.

'You must go back! If the Wulf Kin find you here, alone . . .'

'We fight!' growled Xania.

Maia heard Razek swallow. 'Then I will too. They'll think I am one of them. That I've found you. Am bringing you to them. A trick! We can surprise them. And kill them.'

Xania laughed. 'You're mad weed boy!' She looked at Maia. 'Mad or moon-crazed, and in love with you, sister.'

'He killed Magnus,' said Maia. 'I hate him!'

'Maia!' protested Razek.

Maia ignored him. She spread the last glowing embers into the shallow pit and scattered earth over them. Filling in the hole, she piled a covering of stones over the fresh earth. It was the best she could do. Soon the ground would be too cool to tell that they had rested there.

'Should you wear the coat?' she asked. 'It'll be cold until sun-wake.'

Xania shook her head. 'The stories would distract me. And cold is good. It keeps me awake.'

Maia picked up the bag, slipped her arms through the loops and shrugged it onto her back. Xania drew a deep breath and coughed. She spat and scuffed earth over the blob of phlegm and blood. She took two hesitant steps and broke into a jog.

'Come,' she called and pressed her hand into her side as she lengthened her stride until she was running.

Maia checked that she had slipped her knife into its sheath. She glanced at Razek. 'Go. You're not wanted here.'

Razek was shrugging on the back-sack. 'I can't! Not without you.' He gestured at Xania. 'She's sick. There's death on her face. You'll be alone.'

'Go back!'

She forced herself to move. Each step was like running over hot sand. She gritted her teeth. If Xania could run through pain, so could she. She would think of something else. Not of Razek. Never of him. She wouldn't look back to see if he was following. She would conjure the sounds of home. She could count her paces to the sound of waves breaking onto the rocks at sea-high, count to the rhythm of Tareth's shuttle flicking across the loom. She wore the last of his silk and it brought memories of him. But Tareth was gone and the loom silent. A sob swelled in her throat, almost choking her. She wouldn't remember, not now. Instead she would think of Kodo and honey-hunting. But that brought images of the wulfen and Kodo falling as the beast sprang.

Grimly Maia sealed off the memories. Today there were no good ones. So she would think of nothing as she ran. The silk next to her skin grew warm and gave her a little strength.

Calves burning, her lungs raw with the effort of dragging in freezing air, a pain stabbing her side, Maia stumbled to a halt. She pushed her fist into the ache and bent double, trying to drag air into her tortured body. Only then did she allow herself to glance back. Razek was still following.

Ahead, Xania was running, light-footed as a deer, but her course zig-zagged as if she was running with her eyes shut. Every few paces she would jerk upright and straighten her course. She seemed tireless. Wearily Maia set off after her.

As she shortened her stride to tackle another incline she wondered how her sister could have described the Vast as the flat lands. The place was covered with humps and dips and stacks of jumbled rocks. Perfect places for an ambush.

Maia quickened her pace to catch up with Xania.

She was too late. A tall shape stepped from behind the rocks. Several other shadows flitted, dropping to their knees, drawing their bows. Maia heard the challenge shouted by their leader. She saw Xania leap, screaming a response. The tall figure swayed to one side to avoid her and struck out with her bow.

Maia hurled herself forward. Pulling her knife from her belt she straddled Xania's crumpled figure.

'Back!' she snarled.

She crouched over Xania's body and thrust out her left hand, fingers stretched and aimed at the tall warrior facing her. She flipped her knife, grasping the tip of the blade, ready to throw should the bolts of fire not fly from her hand. As the familiar dull thud began behind her eyes, she noticed the knotted braid on the warrior's bow tip. It was spinning. It was a blur of colour. The braid was humming and spinning faster now. Despite herself, Maia couldn't look away. It was sapping her will, but she could feel her headache dimming. Part of her was glad that she didn't have to fight with fire. Didn't have to hear the screams as she blasted and scorched the archer. But why didn't she shoot? Maia drew back her arm to throw her knife.

Xania groaned. Maia felt a hand grab her ankle.

'Wait, sister.' Xania's voice was little more than a hoarse whisper, but the archer heard it too.

She lowered the bow so that the arrow pointed at Xania and snapped a question.

Xania gasped and answered.

Whatever she said seemed to excite the archer. A torrent of words answered Xania's breathy grunts.

'What's she saying?' asked Maia.

'She'll take us to Altara, their fasthold,' gasped her sister.

The archer slid her arrow into the beaded quiver hanging from her belt. She rested the bow on her thigh, her thumb clamped across the knotted braid.

'Can we trust her?'

'Her name is Yanna,' said Xania. 'We can shelter there. They have a Healer.'

The warrior, Yanna, frowned. She glanced at Maia then, putting two fingers in her mouth, she whistled.

'Do they know the Wulf Kin are following?' asked Maia.

'They have no love for the Wulf Kin.'

The shadows swirled. Someone called out. An arrow winged past Maia, the feathered flight almost grazing her cheek. A man screamed. Struggling, Razek was dragged forward, an arrow piercing his arm. He was forced to his knees.

'Wulf Kin,' snarled Yanna, reaching for her knife. She grabbed Razek's hair and jerked his head back.

'No!' shouted Maia. 'He's with us . . . he followed us . . . me.'

'He wears Wulf Kin bronze,' spat Yanna. Razek flinched as the spit hit his face.

'Stolen. He's with us . . . he's from the cliffs.'

She might hate him but she couldn't watch him be killed.

Archers approached. Behind them were two huge spotted cats. Maia stared at them. They were beautiful, sleek, long-legged creatures. They eyed her thoughtfully while Yanna flung instructions at the archers. One was deftly tying a series of complex knots in a thin cord. Another was bending over Xania, feeling for her wound. Maia heard her sister gasp and the woman mutter what must have been an apology. A third rolled Razek onto his back and tugged at the shaft of the arrow.

Then, the first archer was tying the knotted cord to the collar of her cheetah. She pressed her face against its head, whispering in the big cat's ear. The cheetah loped away. Maia watched it gathering speed until it became a blur in the distance. When she turned back to Xania, she saw that the second cheetah had stretched out alongside her. It must be like lying next to a fire thought Maia. She shivered, suddenly realising how cold it was.

Yanna handed her a small, leather flask. 'Drink. Will warm.'

The liquid burned Maia's throat. She could feel it stinging all the way down her gullet. She gasped and took another mouthful, swallowing more cautiously. She could feel the heat spreading like fingers across her chest, down her arms.

'Drink little,' commanded Yanna, holding out her hand for the flask.

Maia nodded. 'Fire chay!' she gasped.

Yanna knelt to offer the flask to the archer beside Xania. The woman lifted her sister's head and dripped the liquid onto her lips. She licked her lips and opened her mouth. As she swallowed a mouthful a little colour seemed to return to her face. She drew a breath and started talking urgently.

Yanna looked up at Maia.

'The stranger Razek is not welcome in Altara. Altara is a woman's fasthold. You and your sister will come.' She glanced indifferently at Razek. 'We will leave him. The Wulf Kin will find him.'

'He's hurt,' protested Maia. 'You can't leave him.'

Yanna frowned.

'The Wulf Kin will kill him,' cried Maia.

Yanna shrugged.

'You can't leave him here. He'll die.' Maia swallowed. 'He's with us. He helped us,' she muttered.

Yanna unclipped the knotted braid from her bow and fastened it around her wrist. She covered it with her hand, turning it slowly, her fingers lingering on the knots. Finally she said, 'He may come. Until we decide what is to be done, he will stay outside the gates.'

'Come,' she said and set off in the direction taken by the cheetah.

Thirty

Maia awoke to the sound of wind chimes and the scent of spiced chay.

She couldn't decide if she needed to sleep longer or eat. Hunger won. Reluctantly she opened her eyes. A girl with a shaved head was squatting at the end of the low bed platform, pouring steaming liquid into a pottery beaker.

Maia pushed aside the padded cotton cover and sat up. She winced as her muscles protested.

The child looked up and smiled.

'I am Zena,' she said, mouthing each syllable as if she were tasting the strange sounds. 'Welcome Sun Lady.' She crossed to Maia, carrying the beaker in cupped hands.

As Maia took it she noticed the tattoo swirling from the child's ear, down her neck and across her shoulder until it was hidden beneath her tunic. She drank the chay in one gulp and handed the beaker back for a refill. How long was it since she had eaten? She felt as if rodents were gnawing at her intestines. Her stomach grumbled. She blushed.

The child laughed. 'Lady hungry. Sleep long.'

She passed Maia a wooden platter. Maia grabbed a flatbread. She chewed and swallowed, almost gagging in her haste.

She tore off bits of bread, dipped them in the small bowl of thick sauce that Zena had silently placed on the platter and tried not to stuff them too quickly into her mouth. She wasn't very successful.

Solemnly Zena opened the basket lying at her feet and took out more flatbreads.

'Thank you,' muttered Maia, her mouth full.

Zena grinned. 'When ready, water hot, clothes clean.' She pointed at a woven screen. Maia's tunic hung over the top of it.

Maia realised that she was naked. She hitched up the padded quilt, trying not to feel embarrassed by Zena's unblinking stare. She took another flatbread, filled it with shredded meat, folded it and managed to eat more slowly this time. She washed it down with her third beaker of chay.

'How long was I asleep?'

Zena held up two fingers. 'These sun-sleeps,' she said.

No wonder she was starving.

'And my sister?'

Zena's eyes darkened. 'She sleeps.'

'I must see her.' Maia swung her legs out of bed. She put her foot on the floor and yelped. It was like standing on a bake-stone. She examined her sole. She had a huge blister.

Zena held up a bowl. 'For feet,' she said.

Maia wrapped the quilt round her shoulders, inched from the sleep platform and hobbled across to the screen.

The deep wooden tub of hot water was bliss. Her feet stung but the warmth and comfort of the water was worth it. She rested her arms along the edge of the tub. Her feet floated. Zena padded barefoot across to her, a honey coloured chunk of scrub-stone in her palm.

Maia held out her hand. The block skidded from her hands and sank to the bottom of the tub. Well, her hair needed washing. Maia sank under the water. The water bubbled in her ears and up her nose. It filled her mouth and stung her eyes. She flailed around, bumping against the sides of the tub, trying not to panic. She found the scrub-stone and rose to the surface gasping.

Zena had disappeared. She was glad the girl hadn't witnessed her panic.

She lathered her hands, scrubbed her scalp and her body and submerged briefly to wash off the suds. Standing, she grabbed the long-handled pan lying in a small tub and threw clean water over herself. She screamed. It was freezing. She heard a giggle. She poured another torrent of snow-melt over herself just to prove that she wasn't soft, and stepped shivering out of the tub.

Moments later she had rubbed herself dry and pulled on her freshly washed clothes. They smelled of summer herbs. Maia buried her nose in her sleeve and breathed in. Memories of foraging walks with the Cliff Dwellers overwhelmed her. When she had lived there, she'd rebelled against that life. Now she would almost welcome Selora's arm around her shoulders. She shook her head. She wasn't a child anymore. She must put aside childish memories.

She shuffled on her heels to the sleeping platform, then dipped her fingers into the green gloop Zena had left. Her fingers began to go numb. Quickly she slathered the salve over her blister. Relief was instant. She examined her boots, shook out earth and small stones, then carefully eased in her feet.

She must find Xania.

Xania, her face as white as sea foam, was lying in a cell beyond a swept gravel garden. Wind chimes hanging at the window had been tied so that they wouldn't sound.

A woman was sitting beside the sleeping platform, her fingers resting on Xania's wrist. Bowls of pungent oil burned beside her. The fumes made Maia's eyes smart. As she approached, the woman crumbled dry leaves onto the burning wicks. Maia felt her eyes and nose begin to stream. Her sister didn't stir. She looked as if she was carved from stone. As if she had already set out on her journey into the dark of forgetting.

Maia swallowed. 'Is she going to die?'

The woman turned. 'It's possible.'

Xania's breath was so soft it sounded like moth wings brushing across silk. Maia felt a stab of panic. 'She can't die.'

The woman stood. 'Stay with her. If she wakes, give her this to drink and call me. I'll be close by.'

Maia sat by the sleeping platform. Xania's eyelids fluttered. She opened her eyes and stared at Maia, her gaze vague and unfocused. Maia waited as her sister came back from a far place.

Xania smiled. 'Stars,' she whispered. 'I've been among the stars with my sisters.'

Maia stamped down a shiver of fear. 'You've been dreaming. You're sick. I'll get help.'

She started to rise.

'Stay,' sighed Xania.

Maia grasped the thin, dark hand. The juggler's fingers barely returned her comforting squeeze.

'Bury me on the Cloud Plains,' murmured Xania. 'My sisters are waiting.'

'You're not dying,' protested Maia. 'I'm your sister. I need you.'

Xania's fingers quivered in Maia's hand. 'You must find the sun-stone and go to the Sun Palace. The land is cold. You must catch the sun and light the sun-crystals so they warm the land. You must use the sun-stone.'

'I can't. Not without you.'

Xania closed her eyes. A spasm of coughing wracked her. Flecks of blood speckled her lips. Maia grabbed a cloth from the bowl of water beside the sleeping platform and gently wiped Xania's mouth.

Her sister smiled. 'Thank you. The Wulf Kin was swift. The silk smoke made me slow.'

Maia swallowed a sob. Tareth had said that the Wulf

Kin often poisoned their knives. Was Xania dying from a poisoned wound? The Healer would know how to draw poison. She started to turn away, but Xania clung weakly to her hand. If it were possible, her face grew paler.

'Find the sun-stone. It's waiting for you.'

'Where? How can I find it?'

'Find the cave, Tareth said,' whispered Xania. 'Yanna can guide you. Hidden deep in the lake. He hid it among many stones where Elin could never find it.'

Maia blanked the word lake and the thought of diving for a submerged rock. 'How will I know it?'

'The sun-stone chooses the Catcher. It will know you.'

A thread of hope wormed its way into Maia's thoughts. Maybe the hidden sun-stone wouldn't choose her. She knew she wasn't strong enough to be a Sun Catcher. Look at all the mistakes she had made, the dangers she had unleashed because she'd been afraid. She had broken tabus and befriended an Untouchable and he had stolen silk from the moth-garden. And now Xania was dying.

'You can't die,' begged Maia.

'We all die,' Xania tightened her grip. 'Promise me Elin will pay for what she has done. She killed our sisters. Their silk . . . is sewed into the story-coat. Listen to the silk. It will tell their story . . . tell how Elin became a Death Bringer.'

Maia swallowed.

'Promise me!' said Xania.

'I promise.'

Xania sighed. 'Take the sun-stone. Use it well. Free our land from the curse of our sister.' Her eyes closed. 'Tareth . . . tell Tareth I always loved . . .'

Had she forgotten that Tareth was probably dead? Dead and lost forever.

'He knows,' whispered Maia. 'Sleep, sister. Grow strong.

Thirty-One

The icy wind churned through the standing horses, whipping their manes into a frenzy. Gold harness ornaments swung and glinted in the pale sunshine. The strings of pennants at the four corners of the wagon cracked in the wind. The long grey cloaks of the warriors flapped and a low, wailing dirge torn from their spinning bow-braids rose and fell.

Carefully, Maia tipped a handful of coriander seeds into the pottery dish placed at Xania's feet. Her sister was dressed in white deerskin boots and an embroidered coat. Her knife lay beside her. In her hand Yanna, the warrior woman, had placed a small, polished bronze mirror.

'Sleep well, Story Singer.'

The silk whispered as Maia gently draped the folded coat across Xania's feet. The wind lifted the hem. It billowed like a banner. As it moved it sang. The horse women groaned.

Their horses tossed their heads. The coat streamed on the wind and dropped across Maia's hand. Once again Maia tried to lay it over Xania and again the coat rippled and struggled under her hands as if it was alive.

Maia glowered at the silk, trying to shut out the voices in her head, but it was no use. If she blotted out the voices, the whisper became fragmented pictures tumbling in on top of each other in a whirl of splintering colour. The singing silk didn't want to make this last journey with Xania.

Maia sighed and twisted the silk into a bundle. The frayed raw edge of the coat lay twitching on top of the murmuring pile. She grabbed it and pulled and a thin ribbon of silk tore from the coat. Maia wound it round Xania's cold wrist. Her fingers shook. She tugged one eagle feather from her hair and tucked it into the silk band.

'From Tareth,' she whispered. 'Go well, sister.'

'Here, Lady.' Zena, the shaven-headed child, held a stalk of plaited grass with a burning end.

Maia set the glowing end against the coriander seeds. As the thread of smoke rose from the coriander and scented the air, the Warrior Women began to sing. Maia tucked the silk coat under her arm and climbed from the pit. At a gesture from the archer, four women began rolling logs over the top of the wooden tomb.

Snowflakes fell, dissolving as they touched her face so that she was crying snow-melt tears. Maia turned away and looked across the plains. The grasses were burned ochre in the wind. There were no flower-filled pastures grazed by golden horses as Tareth had promised. Just wind-burned mounds that would soon become silent quilts of white snow.

She stood in the growing blizzard as the log roof of the grave was covered with earth. She waited as stones were piled on top. Waited until the Warrior Women fell silent and the last wailing farewell was swallowed by snow and wind.

Finally as the chill of sun-sleep crept across the plains beneath the last rays of the sun, Maia stirred. The Warrior Women parted silently to let her through.

Then her way was blocked. Razek stood shivering, his arm in a sling, his face white, wrapped in a tattered cloak that looked like a find from the Untouchables' piles of debris. For a moment she felt a flicker of warmth nudge at the ice encasing her heart. She did not mourn her sister alone. He reached for her hand.

'It's over, Maia. You can come home now.'

She stared at him blankly.

'There's no reason to stay now. You can leave here. We can go home.'

'We?'

'We can go back to the weed beds.'

'We? There is no we now, Razek. My sister has left me.'

She pushed past him, clutching the coat to her chest. The silk coat was strangely silent now. The tiny crystals sewn into it glinted like tears as if the silk wept for Xania.

'Maia!' His cry was cut short as Yanna pulled him aside.

Head down, Maia walked alone. Then she felt a small hand slip into hers. She looked down. Zena's face was pale in the fading light. Her eyes were like huge dark pools. Maia thought she could see the reflections of the stars in them.

'I show the way,' said Zena and led Maia across the Cloud Plains.

THIRTY-TWO

The trader ship plunged through the storm. A wave roared under the hull like a bellowing, angry lizard. Kodo heard the foaming water hiss away behind the stern just as Doon had bugled a farewell when she turned back, heading to the stilt village and lizard-pen after he had scrambled from her back and been pulled aboard the trader vessel.

Kodo still wanted to laugh when he thought of trader Bron's face when Doon, red-crested and awesome, had reared from the water and bugled. The tremendous cry had caused the stunned oarsmen to lose rhythm and clash oars. The boat had lost way and luffed to a halt. Bron's shouts that they weren't stopping to pick up drifting flotsam from the sun-deeps had been ignored. Like eager children watching the Gather jugglers, the oarsmen had hung over the sides as Doon had surged closer so that Tareth, looking more dead than alive, could negotiate a passage. One day he would tell Ootey of Doon's heroic swim to intercept the trader vessel making swift passage away from the Gather. Yes, thought Kodo, if he had the breath he would laugh out loud.

As the full moon shrank and swelled again and yet again, he worked his passage, became crew, made friends. Now he was no longer a boy from the stilt village, a lizard boy, an Untouchable sorting sun-deep scourings. He was a trader apprentice.

'Put your back into it, boy!' roared Bron, the giant blond trader. 'Pull!'

Kodo hung on to the sweep-oar and stared across the heaving grey sea. A huge wave hit the boat. The sweep-oar bucked in his hands, slamming against his ribs. He thought they would snap.

'Hold on!' yelled Bron.

A wave roared over the side. As his feet were swept from under him, Kodo heard the oarsmen shouting. If he hadn't been clinging to the timber sweep-oar for dear life he would have been washed overboard. Before he could draw breath, another wave crashed over him. He was drowning. He felt the surge of the water wrenching his hands from the oar. The boat heeled, its leeward rail deep under the waves. He was being dragged over the side in the heart of the wave.

A hand grabbed the back of his shirt and he was yanked to his knees. Gasping for breath he swayed to his feet, as the rushing water threatened to knock him down again.

Bron, fighting to control the boat, braced himself against the water surging around his boots. 'They come in threes. Keep your mouth shut if you don't want to drown.'

Kodo spat out a mouthful of seawater. The rowers, their oars tangled like children's throw-sticks, were struggling back onto their benches. Saith, the Oar Master, lurched down the rowing deck, offering a hand here, a blow there, hauling the drenched oarsmen back to their positions. Gradually order was restored.

'Always worst near the coast,' shouted Bron above the wind. 'We might be better off keeping out in the far-deep, running with the storm.'

Kodo clung onto the sweep-oar and hoped Bron wouldn't take his own advice. The timbers of the ship were groaning with the strain of keeping course through the mountainous waves. They had been stormbound for a fistful of sun-wakes. Landfall could not come soon enough. Like everyone else, he was soaked to the skin and punch drunk from the battle with the storm. Tareth had been banished from his stints on the sweep-oar and sent below. Bojo, the black and silver long-tailed monkey had abandoned his sleeping perch high on the mast and disappeared into the hold. Despite his fear, Kodo was glad to be up in the storm instead of cowering in the dark, stuffy bowels of the boat.

Then they crested the top of a wave and he could just make out the low outline of the coast. Through the flying spray he thought he saw the finger-thin white tower that marked the mouth of the river and the port of Haddra.

'Land!' he shrieked.

If Bron could navigate the tidal race tearing across the mouth of the port, they would be safe from the storm. They had set out too late for Haddra. Only madmen would make a voyage across the far-deeps in these conditions.

They should be trading along the great inland rivers until the waterways froze over. Then Bron would leave the boat ice-bound with a skeleton crew aboard until snow-melt and new voyages. Tareth would leave and go to find Maia and her sister, Xania, if they had escaped the Wulf Kin. Should he go with him? Or stay with Bron?

First they had to make landfall. Kodo just wanted to stand on ground that didn't pitch and heave and threaten to toss him into the pitiless deeps.

Bron was gauging the roll and pitch of the boat. Short and square, as fierce as a mating lizard, he looked as if he was part of the boat. He had saved Kodo from being swept overboard more than once, his huge hands as secure as a keep-net.

Kodo looked at his own swollen hands. They were split and calloused, skin shredded and tendons torn with the strain of pulling the sheets to trim the sail. He knew if he tried to flex his hand he wouldn't be able to make a fist. It was difficult enough to curl them tight round the oar and hold on.

Life on the trader ship was hard. Even Ootey had not worked him as hard as Trader Bron did.

Across the wild water, the white watchtower at the harbour entrance was closer. Soon they would be safe.

'Jump, boy!' roared Bron.

Kodo leapt for the jetty. Trailing the line behind him, he thudded onto the planks, pitched forward and crashed into the legs of a fur-coated man waiting on the quayside.

A booted foot kicked him away.

Kodo clasped his hands over his head to protect his face. He felt the mooring rope snake away from him as the boat swung out from the quay.

'Leave the boy alone!' bellowed Bron. 'Tie the line, Kodo! The wind's taking us!'

Kodo snatched up the line and felt the rope burn scoring his palm. As a wave surged beneath the drifting boat, Kodo was dragged along the jetty. Then he was hanging face down over the edge, staring into the green water swirling beneath the wooden platform. He felt a thud as someone landed beside him. Saith, the burly Oar Master, was pulling the rope from his hand, whipping it round the mooring post. Another line came snaking through the air.

'Pull, boy!' shouted Bron. 'Don't let her escape now. Pull!'

Kodo scrambled round the booted legs and heaved on the rope. The boat bumped into the jetty and he wrapped the line tighter around the bollard. Bron leapt down with another line in his hand, pushing fur-clad figures on the quayside roughly aside and ignoring their growls as he secured it.

Then he swung round, his white-toothed grin a snarl, and glared at the strangers on the quay. Kodo saw his bunched fists and set shoulders.

'No need to kick the boy,' Bron growled. 'Nor to get in the way of the lines.'

The three strangers had formed a tight triangle. One of them reached towards his belt.

'No need for trouble, friends,' Bron said. 'We've had a hard passage.'

Kodo held his breath, unable to look away from the man fingering his knife. If he was quick, he would be able to grab his wrist before he pulled out the knife. He edged forward, eyes fixed on the hand. A hand covered with hair so thick it looked like fur.

He gawped up at the man. As if aware of his gaze the Wulf Kin looked down at him. His hand dropped from the curved knife in his belt. His cuff slid down to cover his furry hand.

He grunted and showed his teeth. They were filed into points. The Wulf Kin made a snapping movement with his jaws. Kodo took a step backwards and almost fell into the water.

'Have a care, boy,' muttered Bron, dragging him to safety beside the windbreak bulk of his body.

'Were you waiting for us? How can we help?' Bron was still trying to defuse the tension, his hand tight on Kodo's shoulder. Ready to push him out of the way if a fight broke out, guessed Kodo. He wondered if he should reach for his own netting-knife and thought better of it. Saith had joined them, standing shoulder to shoulder with Bron.

'Is it a passage?' continued Bron. 'It'll have to wait. I'll not be sailing the sun-deeps again till after snow-melt.'

A tall man wearing a black wolf-skin across his shoulder, the fur beaded with water and bristling as if alive, frowned at the Trader.

'We're looking for fugitives. A girl. A flame-headed girl. She had a companion. A woman.'

Kodo froze. Maia! They were looking for Maia.

'Woman?' Bron was shaking his head. 'A girl? Don't carry women.'

'Any strangers?'

'None,' lied Bron, ignoring Tareth, still sleeping below deck.

'We should search the ship, Urteth,' growled the tallest figure.

'We've much to trade,' said Bron. 'Ebony, oil, amber, furs, fine spear-heads, copper talents. But it'll have to wait. The men need rest and hot food.'

The crew were spilling from the boat and massing at the back of the trader. The man called Urteth eyed them and shrugged.

'Join us.' Bron nudged Kodo into the milling group. Kodo noticed how they closed in around the trader and the Oar Master, as if this was not the first time they had prevented them from getting into a fight. They moved off towards the sprawl of buildings.

Kodo found himself swept along with them.

'Close your mouth boy and stop staring,' Bron muttered. 'D'you want the Wulf Kin to notice you?'

'They'll find Tareth if they search the boat,' hissed Kodo.

'You heard them. They're not looking for him. They're looking for a girl.'

'But . . . the man . . . he's like . . .' Kodo's head whirled. He couldn't trust his eyes. He had been too long at sea.

Bron pulled the hood of his tunic over his head as if

against the cold and pushed Kodo ahead of him. Kodo risked a glance over his shoulder and wished he hadn't. The man Urteth was staring after them. Then he was distracted by the tall, old Wulf Kin.

'I'll wait and watch that no one else leaves the boat, Urteth.' The wind seemed to carry his soft growl straight to Kodo.

'Good,' said Urteth. 'And when they are gone, Zartev, search the boat. See what else he's carrying that he doesn't want us to know about.'

He hitched his wolf-skin higher over his shoulder and turned to look again at the departing group. 'Something doesn't smell right here.'

Kodo ducked his head and scurried to bury himself deep among the crowd of oarsmen. Why did the man Urteth have Tareth's face? He caught up with Bron and tugged at his arm.

Tareth smelled him before he heard him. His eyes snapped open. Wulf Kin!

Lying in the dark, listening to the groan of timbers and waiting for the ship to founder and sink, he had finally fallen asleep and dreamed of Urteth, hearing his brother's voice deep in his unconscious. He woke sweating, his clothes sticking to his body. Awoke and smelled wet fur, oiled leather and an unwashed body.

Tareth slid his knife from its sheath and rolled quietly

off the narrow sleep-bench. He heard Bron's guard-monkey gibber in the darkness. Had he smelled Wulf Kin too? Tareth edged across the filthy planks and huddled behind a bulky bale of woven rugs near the stern. Chinks of light from the battened-down hatch made it difficult for his eyes to adjust to the gloom. Even if the intruder was not searching for a crippled eagle hunter, it was best that he didn't find one on the trader ship. Quietly Tareth pulled himself up and reached for the hatch.

The intruder was making little attempt to hide his presence. It sounded as if he was searching.

He heard the man descend, grunting as he pushed past stacks of cargo. Some of it had broken loose in the storm and tumbled bales and sacks were slowing his progress. But he was getting closer. Tareth leaned into the bale, straining his ears, counting the snuffling breaths, trying to judge the distance between them. A bundle of dislodged nets thudded into the gangway, a clutter of long-handled farming tools fell, clattering nosily as they hit the floor, spilling loose from the twine binding them, blocking the space between the piles of cargo. The Wulf Kin cursed. Tareth tensed and raised his knife.

The hatch was flung open. Daylight blinded him.

'I told you to bring the sail!' complained Bron loudly. 'We can't leave while it's damaged.'

'What's the hurry?' Tareth recognised the gruff growl of Saith, the Oar Master.

'The Wulf Kin may want a passage.'

'You'll sail without me!' retorted Saith. 'If you take them aboard, you can find another Oar Master.'

Tareth heard the sound of something being dragged across the deck. He felt rather than saw the Wulf Kin move towards the companionway to investigate.

Kodo appeared over the edge of the hatch. He put his finger to his lips and beckoned. Tareth slipped his knife into its sheath. Kodo vanished. Two huge, calloused hands stretched down. Tareth grabbed them and was hauled through the hatch by Bron and dumped on the rough sail.

Kodo, his eyes bright with excitement, tossed the sail across him and then he and Bron were rolling Tareth over and over until he was not sure which way was up. He felt as if he was suffocating. The fabric tightened as a rope was tied around the bundle of sail. Then he was being lifted. He heard Saith grunt as the sail was dumped over his shoulder.

'Wait!' commanded the Wulf Kin.

'Who's that?' Kodo sounded surprised.

The Wulf Kin stepped onto the deck. 'What have you got there?'

'What's it to you?' snarled the Oar Master.

'Easy. Easy,' said Bron hastily. 'It's the sail. Got damaged in the storm. Needs stitching before we leave.'

'What're you doing aboard, Wulf Kin?' challenged the Oar Master.

'What's it to you?' mocked the old Wulf Kin.

'Ahhh!' roared the Oar Master. He dropped his end of the sail bundle and charged. Inside the bundle, Tareth crashed onto the desk and lay winded. There was a second crash as the Wulf Kin hit the deck.

Tareth could hear the sound of blows. Then Bojo's shriek

as the monkey leapt through the hatch and attacked the intruder. A voice yelled. Then Kodo's voice, full of breathless laughter was whispering. 'Bojo's bitten the Wulf Kin.'

The sail was lifted. It sagged under his weight. Tareth thought he was going to be dropped again and braced himself. Someone grabbed his feet. He was swung through the air and dumped down again. He didn't have the breath to groan. Then he was being half-carried, half-dragged along the wooden jetty, swaddled inside the bundle of torn sailcloth. Before he passed out from lack of air, the sound of the waves ceased, a door groaned on its hinges and was slammed shut. He was rolled over and the sail pulled from his face. He drew in shuddering breaths of air that smelled of rope and leather and sawdust. Sails and ropes hung from wooden pegs and lay in piles around him.

'Are you all right?' asked Kodo anxiously.

Bron grinned, hastily untying the knots which bound the sail around Tareth's feet. "Course he is. Tough as old ropes.'

The lines fell away, he offered Tareth his hand. 'Up with you. If Saith and the monkey don't flatten him, the Wulf Kin may follow.' He pointed to the platform above their heads. 'Hide yourself up there.'

Tareth squeezed the trader's hand. 'Thank you.'

'Thank Kodo . . . he wouldn't stop chattering about not leaving you for the wolf man to find, till we agreed to come and get you.'

'Then I owe you my safety again, Kodo. Not only did you and your lizard rescue me from the deeps, but now you've saved me from a Wulf Kin.'

Kodo blushed and held the ladder steady as Tareth hauled

himself hand-over-hand up to the sail-loft and collapsed on the floor.

Bron opened the door, peered out and beckoned to Kodo. 'Lose the ladder.'

Kodo nodded. He and the ladder vanished.

Thirty-Three

'Lady. Lady. Are you awake?'

Maia ignored the whisper. She sat on the cold floor and stared at the pile of shorn red hair heaped at her feet. There, she had done it. Now she was no different from the other girls. She would be like Zena. She could hide among the other new, shaven-headed acolytes. Could become a warrior like Tareth.

Maia touched her head, feeling the sting where she had snagged her scalp trying to scrape away tufts of hair. She could still feel patches of stubble and rat-tail tangles that she had missed. She sighed and nibbled the callouses on her fingers where the bow string had bitten into the skin. Soon she would be good enough to send a flight of arrows exactly where she wanted. If Yanna let her stay, perhaps she could win the knotted braid that the archer women tied to their bows or wore on their wrists. She remembered how the braids had whispered in the wind at Xania's burial.

'The braids sometimes sing,' Yanna had told her. 'Each has three silk strands tied into it. One for the Queen, from the time when the Warrior Women were her archer guard. One thread for our sisterhood, and one for our kin whom we have sworn to protect.'

If she trained harder perhaps she would deserve to wear a treasured, knotted wristband, thought Maia. And if she didn't . . .

Well, she'd leave when the snow had melted and find her own way. As did all the girls who did not make the grade and were sent away. She had asked the arrow-ward what would happen to them. The woman had shrugged, her hands busy fletching Maia's flights.

'If their blood-kin won't take them back, they will go to the Sun City. Some may work in the Sun Palace for Queen Elin. She keeps her own archers. She takes those who fail,' her voice was scornful. 'If not, they'll find work as palace girls or in the gardens.' She glanced at Maia. 'There's always women's work to be found.'

'Sun Lady? Are you there?' the whisper wouldn't go away. It was like the drip, drip, drip of the snow melting on the roof and covering the courtyard with puddles. It was as impossible to ignore as the soft shuffling feet of the girls who stared at her window in the hope of catching a glimpse of the strange flame head as they filed past on their way to the eating place or the sleeping hall. She wasn't a flame head now.

'The Sun Lady has gone,' she answered. 'She's buried beneath the snow on the plains.'

Xania's burial mound would have quickly disappeared in the snow.

The blizzard and a glacial wind that froze the breath in Maia's lungs had howled across the plains for a fistful of grey sun-wakes after her sister's final journey. They had barely reached Altara before the storms had started. The world had been buried beneath snow drifts. Nothing moved. Nothing lived. Even the stars had been blotted out by the snow-filled winds. The whole land seemed to mourn Xania's departing.

Everyone except Razek. He had not mourned. He had tried to persuade her to leave. He was relentless. Following. Watching. Waiting. She had shut him out of her thoughts. She had shut out everyone, everything until Yanna had finally lost patience with her and taken her to the arrow-ward who had armed her with a bow and taken her to the shooting field. Then the waking times had been easier. She ate alone in a corner of the kitchen, practiced at the butts and returned to her room.

The Warrior Women left her alone. And Maia had been glad of the solitude and the silence. Silence broken by Zena who guarded the door and sent everyone away. 'Lady sleep. Come back later. She sleep.' Whispers that permeated Maia's dreams.

'Lady!' The door rattled. She had jammed it shut. No one could enter. She didn't want to see anyone.

But Zena was her friend. Slowly Maia crossed to the door and lifted the latch.

Razek stepped into the room. Zena stood like a frightened lapran, twisting her hands, her eyes darting to and fro, scanning the passage.

'Not stay. Not stay,' she whispered.

'Razek! What are you doing?' asked Maia shocked. 'You're not allowed here!'

'I had to see you. They're sending hemp oil to the Sun City. Now my arm's healed, I will go with them.'

He was staring at her mangled hair. She must look like a badly-skinned squirrel. She didn't care. She hated her red hair. At least he couldn't call her Flame Head now. She was wrong.

'What have they done to you, Flame Head?'

She glared at him. 'Nothing! I want to be one of them. To be an archer.'

Was that compassion on his face? Razek, kind? Never! She spun away.

'You should go. There'll be trouble if you're found. For Zena too. She shouldn't have brought you.'

'She didn't. I followed her. I'm sick of being treated like an Untouchable. Expected to dig middens. Labouring like a lizard to earn my food and bed. Sleeping in stinking shelters. Never allowed more than a glimpse of you.'

His vehemence beat against her. She didn't tell him that she'd seen him each sun-turn. Had looked away when she saw him watching as she went to the shooting fields. Watched as the healing bindings on his arm had grown grimy and finally been taken off as the arrow wound closed. Yet still he had stayed. He could have gone with those passing Altara on their way to the Sun City and Haddra.

'Poor Razek!' she mocked. 'Why do you stay?' She turned to look at him.

'For you, Flame Head!'

Maia rocked on her heels. 'But who will care for the weed beds?' she asked.

The fire suddenly drained from him. He sank onto the sleeping bench and sat turning the silver band on his wrist.

'Elder,' he said finally. He stared at his feet. 'He was once Weed Master, before my father. He knows what to do.'

'Elder! But . . .' Maia couldn't imagine him shouting, bullying, acting as if the weed came before everything, as Razek did.

Razek didn't look up. 'The weed boys will do as he bids.' He picked up the black-handled knife she had dropped onto her sleeping mat. 'Why are you cutting off your hair?'

'All those who would train to fight shave their heads. Then, when they become warriors, they can wear their hair long again. I want to be a warrior.'

She stared at the knife. She wanted to snatch it from him. 'Tareth gave me that knife before I left.'

Razek put the knife carefully on the sleeping mat. 'I didn't mean to kill the eagle,' he said finally. 'He attacked me. He turned aside when I shouted. But I was already striking.'

'You were wearing Wulf Kin bronze!'

'I thought it would protect me. I thought I could defend the weed boys if I fought in it. Be strong . . . Like the Marsh Lords. I didn't mean to kill Tareth's eagle. I would have saved him and Tareth too, but the Sea Thieves were on the cliffs. I couldn't reach him. And then the Wulf Kin came. And I saw Tareth fall.'

He was silent for a long moment, remembering.

'I didn't think that trading the Wulf Kin's silver band at the Gather would summon them to the weed beds.'

'Tareth warned you!' said Maia coldly.

'Yes.'

He sounded almost humble. Maia stared at him.

'I should have listened. I wanted . . . I wanted to show everyone . . . to be . . . different,' he admitted.

'Different!'

Did he know how hard it had been for her among the Cliff Dwellers because she'd been different? How she had hated her red hair, her fear of the water, because it made her different from the cliff children?

'You should have listened!' She looked at the knife on the sleeping mat and sighed. 'But so should I,' she said slowly.

Her time alone had shown her many things. She was to blame for what had happened too.

'The Wulf Kin were looking for me. I went to the Gather. Tareth said I shouldn't. I didn't listen. The Wulf Kin may have followed Xania and me from the horse meadows. We stole a horse.' She remembered the silk billowing and singing behind her sister, Xania's fierce song, the wild stampeding horses, the excitement. Despite everything, the remembered thrill of it made her grin.

Razek looked up quickly, met her eyes and looked away again. 'I wish I'd seen it.'

'Laya would have said I was showing off again.'

'Ah. Laya!' said Razek. He picked up the knife, examined it, put it down. He looked up and this time met and held her gaze.

'Laya will be a good cave-mate,' said Maia. 'And when her Holder father dies you'll have the saltpans too.'

Razek hunched his shoulders. 'I hoped . . .' he began.

Maia didn't want to share Razek's hopes. 'You should go back, Razek.'

'How can I? I left the weed burning. I was Weed Master and I ran off. I abandoned the weed boys when I was needed. How can I return? The Watcher was right when she found my name.'

He scowled at her as he always had. The old, arrogant Razek was back. He had probably glared just like this when he'd refused to take the Watcher's name, thought Maia.

'She called me Storm Chaser!' he said. 'Storm winds destroy the weed beds. How can the Weed Master leave the kelp, be a storm chaser?' He clenched his fists. 'You are the storm I chased, Flame Head. I can't go back without you now! I know what they call you. A Sun Catcher could live in the weed beds. Seaweed needs the sun too! You could restore the weed beds, Sun Catcher.'

'Don't call me that!'

'The Watcher did. And Xania. Everyone here does.'

'I'm a warrior,' Maia snapped. Her anger faded as quickly as it had flared. 'I belong here now.'

'But . . .'

'I want to be here,' said Maia. 'I will be a warrior. And when the snow melts I'll find the Eagle People . . . Tareth's people. I'll bring them his story. They should know. Like my sister, I'm a good Story Singer. Ask Ootey and the Lizard People! I promised . . .' she swallowed as she remembered what she had promised Xania. She must be as ruthless as Tareth when he knifed the Wulf Kin in the weed beds. As fierce as the time she killed the beast and saved Kodo.

'But . . .'

'I'm staying here. Can't you understand? Forever!'

'Forever?'

'Yes! Here I'm like everyone else. Here I'm not different.'

Razek stared at her for so long that Maia wondered if he'd forgotten that she was there.

Finally he stirred and rose stiffly to his feet.

'Then you'll need to make a better attempt at losing that, Flame Head.' He gestured at the spiky patches of hair. 'You look more like a half-plucked pigeon than a warrior.' He held up the knife. 'Let me help.'

Maia scowled at him. He scowled back.

They must look like two sea-eagles glaring and spitting at each other, thought Maia. She grinned. So did he.

'Trust you with a knife, Razek?'

'Trust me,' he said.

Slowly Maia nodded and sat on the bench.

Razek lifted the knife. She felt the blade scrape across the top of her head and shivered. A chunk of hair fell. Then another.

'I remember the sun-wake after the storm when my father took me to the weed beds,' murmured Razek. 'And found Tareth washed onto the levees. You were tied to his back. I thought you were dead.'

The knife slid softly past her ear. Razek held out a tangled strand of hair and cut it off. 'I used my father's weed-knife to cut you free. You opened your eyes. They were the colour of the storm surge. Flecked with amber like golden weed, like the hand-fast fire flames.'

Maia felt the cold bronze rest for a heartbeat on the pulse

thudding below her ear. She turned her face to look at him. 'Razek?'

'They're like fire now,' he said. 'The weed beds saved you then. You belong to the weed beds, Maia. Promise . . .' he whispered.

Maia grabbed his wrist. Her fingers slipped across his silver wristguard. The knife jerked. A pinprick of blood beaded her skin. She glared up at him. His eyes were wide, his pupils dilated. He was looking at the tip of the knife, shocked into stillness.

'Promise . . . to return,' he muttered.

Maia tightened her grip until her fingers were claws, digging into his wrist. 'I've other promises to keep. I promised to stay!' She pushed his arm away. 'To avenge my sister.'

Fingers scrabbled at the door, like mice scurrying across the floor.

'Sun Lady! Yanna comes . . . now,' whispered Zena.

Maia thought about springing to her feet and barricading the door. She wasn't ready to deal with Yanna. She would never be ready.

The door opened. The gloom was lit by a flaring brand. Maia blinked and looked away from the light. She heard Zena gasp as she saw Razek with a knife. She fought the urge to grab the knife from Razek who was standing like Altara's wooden gate-guardian beside her. If only she could make him vanish.

'Sun Catcher,' said Yanna. She frowned at Razek. 'You shouldn't be here.' She looked at the knife in his hand and then at Maia's head. At the bright bead of blood on Maia's throat. Her hand reached for the knife hilt visible above her wide scarlet sash. 'What have you done, weed boy?'

'Nothing,' said Maia

Razek silently placed the knife at Maia's side.

'Leave,' commanded Yanna. Razek didn't move. 'Or I shall make you.' Her fingers tightened round the hilt. 'No man may come beyond the gates unless invited.'

'I invited him,' said Maia. She wiped away the dot of blood. 'It's nothing. An accident.'

Yanna ignored her. 'Your wound is healed. You will leave here, now.'

'He came to tell me he was leaving,' said Maia. Why did he stand there like a hunted lizard stunned with a throw-stone? 'To take messages home to the Cliff Dwellers,' she lied.

Yanna glanced at her. 'Since you excuse the weed boy, Sun Catcher, his only punishment is to be cast out from here.' She frowned at Razek. 'If you can reach Haddra, you will find a ship to take you across the sun-deeps to where you belong.'

Razek looked as if he was about to protest.

'At sun-wake, my archers will take you from Altara and set you on the way. Go now. While you can. Your place is not here.'

Razek didn't move. 'Maia?'

She hardened her heart against the pain in his eyes. Her hand gripped the hilt of Tareth's knife. She noticed that she was holding it so tightly that her knuckles were white. Gently she eased her grip.

'The Cliff Dwellers need you, Razek. You don't have to

chase storms.' She placed the tip of her forefinger on his silver armband. 'You're the Weed Master. It's best this way. Truly. Sun's greetings to Selora. And Laya.' She looked steadily at him, willing him to understand. 'Go well, Weed Master.'

He looked as if would argue. Maia held his gaze. She touched her forehead with her fingers.

Razek raised his fist. His silver wristband gleamed as he pressed it to his forehead.

'And a safe homecoming,' he finished the ritual parting for her. 'Flame Head,' he added. He stooped, snatched up a fallen lock of hair, stepped round Yanna and left.

Maia struggled to her feet, brushing strands of hair from her tunic.

Yanna glanced at her bleeding scalp and then at the bow propped against the wall.

'The arrow-ward tells me that you are training hard and becoming a fine shot.'

Maia shrugged. 'I'll need to be. The Wulf Kin are swift and strong.'

'The Sun Catcher has other weapons.'

'I'm not the Sun Catcher.'

Yanna ignored her. 'When the snow melts, you must go to the cave Xania spoke of.'

'I'm not the Sun Catcher,' repeated Maia stubbornly.

'That's not what those coming here believe.'

Maia thought of the half-starved girls flocking to Altara. It was an honour for a daughter to be chosen to become a warrior. Xania said she had trained here before her gift of story-singing claimed her. Sometimes whole families came and set up home outside the gates and burned offerings at the foot of the wooden gate-guardian. They came because their land was sick and they were hungry and needed shelter and the chance of life for at least one daughter. They didn't come for her. Not like Razek.

'You're wrong,' said Maia.

Yanna shrugged. 'Nevertheless, they come. Some, like Zena, have lost everything because of Urteth and his Wulf Kin. But they've never come with hope before. Now they do. And more will follow. They can read the signs, Sun Catcher. They've been waiting for you. Snow-melt is coming at last because you're here. The Sun Catcher catches the light so the land can grow.'

'No one can catch the sun.'

It was as if she hadn't spoken.

'But you'll need the help of the sun-stone. Khandar has been locked in ice for too long. But now the snow thaws. With it comes hope.'

They listened to the dripping of the melting snow. Maia could still hear the sound of Razek's departing footsteps.

'Xania asked me to lead you to the sun-stone. I can take you as far as the cave.'

Maia bit her lip. 'Xania is dead. The Wulf Kin killed her. They'll try to kill you if they track me here. When the snow melts, I'll leave.'

'The Wulf Kin don't frighten me.'

'They should! They killed Xania. They attacked my village. My father died fighting them. They're evil.'

'They are no match for the Sun Catcher.'

'I'm not the Sun Catcher. I don't know how to be!'

Yanna shrugged. 'The sun-stone will show you how.'

'I don't have it!'

'Xania told me the way to its hiding place, as Tareth told her.'

'Yes,' said Maia bitterly. 'But it is impossible to reach. Did she tell you that?'

Yanna shrugged. 'The way is hard.'

'The sun-stone's in a lake!' Maia hissed. 'Hidden in deep water. And I can't swim. Did she tell you that? It isn't mine. It's not meant for me. I never wanted it. Even if I wanted it, I can't get it.'

'I swim for Lady.' Zena stepped out of the shadows. 'Sun Lady must have sun-stone. It waits for her.'

Maia looked at the small girl. 'And will you burn for me? Will you go blind for me too?' she asked.

'Blind, lady?'

Maia felt ashamed. Zena knew all about being without. Yet fear and anger spurred her on.

'The sun makes the Sun Catcher blind.' Maia forced the words out past a rock which seemed stuck in her throat. 'The fire it makes in here,' she thumped her chest, 'And here!' she flicked her fingers across her forehead in a parody of a greeting, 'Roars and burns, hot as the sun. And it destroys everything it touches.' She swallowed, trying to blot out the memory of the wulfen killing. 'My father thought the price too high. He took me far from Khandar. He didn't want me to be a Sun Catcher.' She glared at Yanna. 'I'm afraid.' The words were sour in her mouth. 'Don't you understand? I don't choose to catch the sun.'

'The choice is not always ours to make,' said Yanna.

'It should be. I'd never heard of Khandar, nor the sun-stone until the Wulf Kin came. I grew up with the weed children. I wanted to be a weaver like Tareth. I was to be hand-fast with a Cliff Dweller,' stormed Maia. She swept aside the knowledge that she had never belonged, nor wanted to belong among the Cliff Dwellers. 'Why should I care what happens in a place I've never heard of? How is it possible for anyone to catch the sun, to banish the snow? Why should I choose fire and blindness? Why should I be the Sun Catcher?'

'When you are ready, I will take you to the lake,' said Yanna.

'I too,' said Zena. 'I swim.'

Yanna shook her head. 'No, Zena. The Sun Catcher must find her own way. Only she must enter the cave. We'll wait until you are ready. Then we'll go.'

'It'll be a long wait,' muttered Maia.

Yanna looked at her. Maia's cheeks flamed with shame.

'The sun-stone has been hidden for many snow-deeps. It can wait a little longer for you,' said Yanna.

Thirty-Four

Elin listened to the snow-melt dripping from the roof of the Sun Palace. It kept time with the gasps of the girl curled on the floor at her feet. A girl rejected by Yanna of Altara. Yanna had had no use for her. A mistake if she wanted to have secrets. The girls brought tales with them. They talked. They were useful. This one more than most. Elin stroked the old, fraying silk band. Soon she would know where her Sun Catcher sister was hidden. A sister who would have new power, new silk.

There was a shout from the courtyard below as an avalanche of snow slid from the roof and hit an unwary palace boy as he scurried from the kitchens to the great hall. The sound made the crouching girl shudder. Not long before she had been shouting as Elin had twisted her arm. Begging her to stop, promising to tell her everything.

'Tell me,' said Elin. She ran her fingers along the silk bands on the front of her gown. 'And if you lie I shall know, and he will break your arm.'

The girl's terrified eyes looked quickly at the Wulf Kin lounging by the door, twisting a stick in his hand. He caught her glance.

'Let me do it anyway,' he growled and snapped the stick.

The girl looked as if she was about to faint.

'Tell me,' commanded Elin, ignoring the Wulf Kin.

'They came . . . a flame-haired girl and a woman. The cats had been hunting for them. Yanna had been waiting for them. The woman was sick. They called her Lady. . . I helped the Healer. I heard them.'

'They called her Lady?' Elin's voice was harsh.

'Zena called her Sun Lady.' The girl flinched as if expecting a blow as Elin's breath hissed in her throat. She held her arm up, shielding her shaved head.

'The sick one was the Sun Lady?'

The girl shook her head, rocking with pain. 'The girl with flame-hair. Zena cared for her, not the sick one. She boasted that she had come to save us.'

'Save you! From what?' snarled Elin.

'Ahh!' The girl shrieked as Elin struck her. 'From the land sickness,' she moaned. 'She said that the sun-stone would be found and save us.'

Elin strode up and down the room, banging her fist into her palm. The girl watched fearfully and inched further from the Wulf Kin by the door.

'The sick one and Yanna talked about the sun-stone,' she

babbled. 'I heard them when I helped the healer. She told Yanna to show the way.'

'The way?'

'To a cave.'

Elin leaned over the girl and grabbed her chin, forcing up her head so that she was glaring into the frightened eyes. 'And where is the cave?'

'I don't know!'

'Useless!' Elin shoved the girl away.

'She will tell me,' sneered the Wulf Kin.

'She doesn't know,' snarled Elin. She pressed her hand against the silk. 'I know when she lies.' She started striding again. 'It will be close. Tareth will have hidden it near. There was no time to go far with the child and the sun-stone when he escaped from the palace. The Wulf Kin were too close behind.'

She ripped at the silk panel with her nails. 'I knew the sun-stone was near. The silk could feel it. But it's old and thin and not powerful enough to tell me more.'

Aware of the Wulf Kin's insolent gaze, she stopped striding.

'Fetch the eagle,' she commanded. 'Urteth will know of this cave. It will be in the land of the Eagle People . . . his kin.'

The Wulf Kin had made no attempt to move.

Elin drew herself up. 'You dare to disobey me?' She stretched out her hand. Tiny blue sparks were gathering about her fingers. The Wulf Kin glowered, but pushed himself upright, away from the door frame.

'Fetch the eagle!' hissed Elin.

She turned and released the sparks at the quivering figure on the floor. The girl shrieked.

'Quickly,' snapped Elin.

Carefully she tore a piece from the silk strip on her gown. Crossing to the fire, she pulled out a glowing stick and started burning a complex pattern of tiny spots and whirls into the cloth, creating the message to be sung on the bronze wheels in the white tower of Haddra.

The silk murmured, then fell quiet as the air filled with the smell of scorching threads.

Thirty-Five

The sound of an eagle's cry woke Tareth. He squirmed from the pile of ropes and sails and pressed his face against the gaping wooden planks of the Sail Maker's loft. A huge eagle was flying in over the sea. The clouds had been torn apart by the wind and shafts of sunlight gilded the bird's wing tips. His heart leapt. For a moment he thought it was Magnus. Then he remembered, and the pain in his chest felt like dying with his eagle beneath the stolen blade. Tareth cursed the Weed Master until his breath ran out. When Magnus had died from the slash of the poisoned Wulf Kin knife, something in Tareth had died too. He saw the eagle drop from the sky to perch on the posts edging the jetty. The Wulf Kin standing there cautiously lifted his arm. The eagle hopped onto his wrist. Then they turned away from the sea and disappeared into the narrow streets leading from the jetty.

Since when had the Wulf Kin flown eagles? Were the Eagle People their allies now? Had Urteth recruited them? Tareth had been away from Khandar for so long that anything could have happened.

The door creaked open. Kodo slipped into the Sail Maker's hut.

'Are you awake?' he whispered. 'I've brought food.'

Tareth slid to the edge of the platform and looked down. 'What's happening?'

'The crew are trying to drink the Wulf Kin under the table,' Kodo said, climbing up to join Tareth. 'They have strong stomachs and thick heads. They could drink the lizard pen dry! The Wulf Kin haven't a hope. The old one, who searched the ship, has a battered face and broken teeth. Saith looks worse though – you should see his fists! Trader's busy trying to keep the peace. The one in the wolf skin . . . Urteth . . . I fear him,' he looked at Tareth.

'Urteth?' Tareth dropped the bone he was gnawing. He grabbed Kodo's arm. 'Here?'

'He leads the Wulf Kin.'

'Urteth!' he muttered. 'Why? How could he have known?'

He suddenly realised that Kodo was squirming with pain. His rigid fingers unlocked. Kodo rubbed his arm. 'He has your face!' he muttered.

Tareth picked up the bone, tearing strips of meat from the shank. 'So I've been told. Urteth here! He and I must meet. And one of us will not walk away.'

Kodo stared at him.

'Why d'you look at me like that? D'you think Urteth too strong for a crippled weaver?' Tareth flung down the bone and drank angrily from the leather flask. 'That I should not dare to challenge him? I was not always like this!' He punched his twisted leg. 'And I can still fight,' he added. 'Urteth will pay for what he has done to Khandar.'

As fast as the anger had come, it left him. 'But not yet. Not until we know what has happened to Maia and Xania and why Urteth and the Wulf Kin are here.'

He looked at Kodo, wondering how much he needed to know. 'The man with my face . . . he may sense that I'm here. He was my brother. He's Maia's enemy,' said Tareth. 'I kept her hidden from him. I promised never to speak of him or even think of him lest he heard me and found her.'

'She . . . ?' Kodo swallowed the questions twisting his tongue. He decided he would get no more from Tareth even if he asked, so continued with his tale.

'The wolf man, Urteth, was angry when the old Wulf Kin came. The monkey had bitten him.'

'He should not pick a fight with a Wulf Kin.'

'Urteth said they were leaving. Then the eagle brought a message.'

'Did you see it?' demanded Tareth.

'Yes,' Kodo looked uncomfortable. 'It was . . . marks . . . burned on silk. A torn scrap of silk tied round the eagle's leg.'

Tareth groaned. 'Then they've found Maia!'

Kodo shook his head. 'I don't think so. He . . . Urteth seemed puzzled. He told the Wulf Kin to get the horses. He said he was going to the white tower.' The tower, with its only entrance a door high above the ground, was a harbour light, a lookout and pigeon loft. Kodo had seen a fistful of similar towers along the trade route. 'Maybe there's another boat. And Urteth's gone to wait for it.'

Tareth was frowning. 'The message is on silk?'

Kodo nodded.

'Urteth will need to listen to it. To make it sing on bronze.' Tareth looked at Kodo's puzzled face. 'There'll be a wheel in the tower,' explained Tareth tersely. 'You set the bronze rings and stretch the silk over them. As the wheel turns, the silk sings and gives up its message. 'Once Khandar had many towers and guardians trained to use them,' he remembered. 'And messengers to carry the silk. When she became Queen, Elin wouldn't have destroyed the wheels, not while she had silk. There must be some silk at the Palace, even though the moth-garden was destroyed. If it's a message on silk then it must be from Elin. Xania and I thought all the silk was lost when the Sun Palace was set on fire. It seems we were wrong.' He thumped his thigh with his clenched fist. 'I need to hear what the silk sings.'

'I'll go!' said Kodo. 'I'll listen to the silk message.'

Tareth hesitated. Something in Kodo's face made him nod. 'Climb well, mast monkey. Don't let anyone see you. Use the shadows,' said Tareth. 'And . . .'

But Kodo had already gone.

Thirty-Six

Kodo clung like a limpet as the wind tried to pluck him from the tower. It was like climbing to the honey cave with Maia. The watchtower was old with great holes in the walls. He climbed as far as the pigeon holes, reached for the broken edges and pulled himself into the loft. A roosting pigeon flew into his face. He almost lost his grip.

Kodo could hear the thudding of his heart. The noise of the wind. The burble and rustling of roosting pigeons. He felt dizzy, perched in the dark on the narrow stone ledges where they roosted. Maia might have felt safe up so high. He wasn't sure he did. Footsteps crossed the wooden roof above him. Urteth must be there already in the room at the top of the tower. The footsteps stopped. Kodo held his breath. Silence. Then footsteps again. He breathed a sigh of relief.

And then came the grinding, the screeching of metal. It

set his teeth on edge. The silk began to whisper and wail. Kodo pressed his hands to his ears to muffle the noise as the silk began to sing, its voice hurting his ears, making his head ache. He could feel the pigeons moving about him, moving to the sea-surge of the silk sound. He had to listen. He had to hear. For Tareth's sake. For Maia. He took his hands from his ears. The song finished. He had failed.

Then the wheels were turning again. Urteth must be listening to the message a second time. Kodo gritted his teeth and forced himself to listen too.

Kodo ran all the way back to the sail-loft and slipped inside.

Tareth was hiding among the sails hanging just inside the door. Kodo glimpsed the gleam of a knife as Tareth slid it back into its sheath. 'Well?' he demanded.

Kodo rubbed at his face. He was splodged with pigeon droppings. He attempted to pick clumps of it out of his hair and managed to smear the white slime across his cheeks.

'Why keep pigeons in a watchtower?' he complained.

'Eggs, meat, messages,' said Tareth curtly. 'Did you hear anything?'

'Pigeons burbling. Then a terrible noise.' Kodo rubbed his ears. 'I covered my ears. I thought the silk would trick me again. I missed the message.'

'Missed the message?' His eyes narrowed. 'Trick you again?' he demanded.

Kodo couldn't meet Tareth's eyes. 'I stole silk. From the moth-garden.' He touched his arm. 'I tied it over a cut.' He glanced at Tareth. 'Sometimes I have silk dreams,' he confessed. 'I should have told you.'

'Eagle's flight!' swore Tareth. 'Did you know the risk you were running when you offered to listen to the silk message?'

Kodo nodded miserably. 'I wanted to listen to the silk-song again.'

'I sent you into danger. For nothing!' Tareth rubbed his hand across his face. 'So many mistakes! First with Maia. Now you. The silk rules me.'

'But Urteth listened again,' said Kodo. 'And I heard . . . '

'You heard the message?'

'Yes. Most of it,' said Kodo. 'I know where he's going, to a lake. In a cave, near the eagles.'

The shadows, casting black patterns across Tareth's face, didn't quite hide the way his skin turned grey.

'Someone's told him where the sun-stone is hidden,' he said. 'He will take it to the Sun City. I hid the stone there and told no one but Xania, who will have told Maia.' He looked at Kodo. 'It must mean that they've been captured.'

'Maia would never tell,' said Kodo.

'How else could Urteth find out?' demanded Tareth.

'Not from Maia. Nor Xania,' Kodo insisted. 'They'd never tell. They'd die first.'

'I must go to the Sun City. If she is alive, Maia will be there. You . . .' Tareth paused. 'Trader has a place for you with his crew. It's what you always wanted.'

'I'm going with you!' Kodo said. Tareth looked at him in

surprise. 'If you're going to the Sun City, the river is the fastest way. Urteth's already leaving. So should we.'

'Trader won't wait for you. When the storms of wolf-walk pass, he'll sail.'

'There're other traders,' said Kodo, ignoring a pang at the thought of never sailing with Bron again. He'd been a good master. 'I can take you up the river. The Lizard People use dugouts to fish the sun-deeps when the shoals don't swim past the fishing-poles. I learned to use a dugout before I could walk.'

'It'll be a dangerous journey,' warned Tareth 'And who knows what lies at the end?'

'Maia will be there. I know she will. She'll never give up.'

Tareth nodded. 'Were it not for you and your lizard, I would have drowned,' he said. 'You rescued me from the trader boat. I couldn't have climbed the tower in time to hear the message. Should you choose to risk everything then join me.'

'Good,' said Kodo and left to barter, borrow or steal a dugout.

Thirty-Seven

Yanna scrambled up a boulder. Shielding her eyes she scanned the empty land stretching below them. Maia climbed up beside her. Yanna's cheetah, Nefrar, padded sure-footed to a higher ledge and sat on the rose-tinted rocks above them.

Since sun-wake they had been clambering in the barren foothills towards the cave. The sun was hot. The snow had melted on the low hills. The quartz veins in the rocks gleamed like silver snail trails over the pink stone. Maia shrugged off her back-sack and flexed her shoulders. Yanna had pushed on hard and fast, using the stars to navigate, resting only as sun-wake rubbed out the stars, or at sun-high when the dazzle of sun on snow had hurt their eyes.

By second sun-wake she had huge blisters on her toes. Yanna had watched her limping without comment, but with

Maia trailing behind her, had set off in a new direction. As the shadows lengthened she found what she was looking for – a yurt, smoke trickling from its smoke hole and a stone corral packed with shaggy ponies.

'The People of the Running Horses,' explained Xania, as they climbed over the stone walls. 'When the wolves are running they use the corrals to protect the ponies.' She bartered with a woman, whose grubby-faced child clung to her mother's embroidered tunic, gazing shyly at Maia. A small lapis lazuli bead cut from Xania's bow holster was exchanged for hot, spiced mare's milk, flatbread and two ponies. 'To take us as far as her herd-share's corral,' explained Yanna as they left on the stocky ponies. 'And save your feet. It sends us a little from our path but . . .' She shrugged.

And it had saved her feet. When they left the ponies in the second wolf-proof enclosure sheltering in a hollow within sight of the distant hills, Maia's blisters had popped and dried to hard skin which rubbed off inside her boots. It had made the journey into the foothills bearable.

Maia pulled off her hat and rubbed her spiky scalp. It was wet with sweat. Her hair was growing in a golden fuzz.

A shadow drifted across the rocks. Nefrar growled softly. Maia looked up. There was an eagle high above. She watched it spiral lower, wing tips spread like fingers as it banked and pirouetted in the air currents. She felt her heart leap. This was the land of eagles. Tareth's home.

Yanna almost knocked her off her feet as she pulled her into the shadow of the overhang.

'What?' demanded Maia, rubbing her elbow, which had smacked against a rock.

'Eagles have far sight!' muttered Yanna.

'Am I to be frightened of eagles too?' demanded Maia. She wiped her head and pulled on her hat.

'Urteth was an eagle hunter before he lived in the Sun Palace,' explained Yanna.

'Did you see anyone following us?'

Yanna shook her head. 'No. But our tracks are clear where the snow lies.'

Maia felt as if Yanna blamed her for the drifts of calf-deep snow still clinging to the tundra. Maybe the tardiness of snow-melt would convince the warrior that she was not the chosen Sun Catcher. She sighed. Once she found the sun-stone everyone would know the truth.

Yanna pulled a strip of dried meat from the leather pouch tied to her belt and handed it to Maia. Maia chewed and tried to swallow.

Yanna passed her the water bag. It was almost empty even though she had stuffed it with snow before they started to scramble uphill. Maia wet her lips and sucked up enough water to dampen her mouthful of leathery meat. Her boots would have tasted better. She managed to swallow and thought wistfully of eating a huge bowl of Selora's fish stew with soft flatbreads, and then honeycomb. The thought brought with it the memory of Kodo. He had loved honey as much as she did.

'Is it much further?'

'We'll come to the cave before sun-sleep. I'll wait for you and guard the way.'

Maia felt a stab of panic. 'How will I find the right place?'

'You will know. The sun-stone will call.'

She made it sound so simple. If only Xania were here to tell her what to do. If only Tareth had told her where he'd hidden the sun-stone before he fled Khandar. If she had brought the story-coat, maybe it would have told her what to do.

Nefrar stretched and flowed like water from the shelter and began leaping among the rocks.

'The eagle must have gone,' said Yanna.

Together they toiled up the rocks until Yanna called a halt at the dark mouth of a cave. The cheetah nosed past Maia and sniffed at the entrance. Then he sat, wrinkled his nose and bared his teeth in what looked like a grin.

Yanna removed her back-sack and unhitched her bow holster. 'This is as far as I may go. Only the Sun Catcher may seek the sun-stone.'

'I could wait until sun-wake,' Maia said in a small voice. 'Then you wouldn't have to stand guard alone in the dark.'

Yanna stared at her. Nefrar butted Maia's leg.

Maia sighed.

She pulled a flint and a wedge of dried fungus from her back-sack. With shaking fingers she struck the flint and trickled sparks onto the fungus. It began to smoke. Gently she blew until the dried plant began to glow and burst into flame.

She took a step towards the cave. The big cat stood and pushed his head under her free hand. She could hear him purring. She glanced at Yanna.

The archer shrugged. 'Nefrar chooses his own path,' she said. 'I know only that I may not enter.'

Side by side they stepped into the cave and followed the

narrow tunnel that led into the side of the hill. The air grew cooler. Maia was glad of the warmth of Nefrar's head under her fingers.

Then Maia could smell water. Nefrar's fur stood up in a prickly ruff under her hand. The torch flared. They clambered over a rock fall and suddenly stood in a huge cavern. Maia lifted the torch above her head but couldn't see the roof. The space seemed to stretch forever. She was dwarfed by slender stalagmites that stood like guardians on the edge of a vast, dark expanse of water. Stalactites hung from the cavern roof. Glow-worms of light gleamed on the rocks as her torch illuminated them.

Nefrar stepped forward and put his foot delicately in the water. He pulled back. Ripples curved from the edge, vanishing into the darkness. The cheetah coughed, sat and began licking his paw.

Maia stared into the blackness. How was she expected to go further with the way completely blocked by water? She could see seven shadowy columns far from the shore. Was that where Tareth had placed the sun-stone? Could she wade that far? Or was the water like the sun-deeps, plunging, bottomless. She lowered the glowing fungus and sank cross-legged on the shore of the huge underground lake.

'Where are you?' she said to the darkness. 'If I'm the Sun Catcher, show me where you are.' There was no reply.

Maia sat and waited. Waited until she felt as if she too was stone and Nefrar's breathing had changed to a gentle snore. Then, soundlessly, a light fell through the edge of the darkness and spread swiftly across the water to where she sat. Maia looked up. Now she could see a circle of light above. There must be a hole in the cavern roof. And the moon was shining in, making a track across the water to the middle column in the lake. It was like the track Tareth used to find the shell beds at home. The moon track she hated, always afraid that he would be drowned as he dived beneath it.

Maia glanced at Nefrar. He was lying, stretched, the tip of his tail twitching. He opened one eye.

'I don't suppose you like swimming any more than I do,' she said, as she got stiffly to her feet and stepped into the black water.

It was warm. It lapped round her knees. Then she was up to her waist and still the columns were far away. Maia looked back the way she had come. The cheetah was sitting now, watching her. She hadn't gone far. She could still wade to the safety of the shore.

She turned. One step at a time. She took a deep breath. And almost fell as the ground dipped sharply beneath her feet. She was up to her neck in water. She bit back a cry. Took another step. It didn't seem to be getting any deeper. Then another. The water swirled around her. It was difficult to stay on her feet. The water lapped her chin, covered her mouth. She tried to stand on tiptoe and lifted her chin until the bones in her neck creaked with the strain.

She struggled on, creating expanding circles of ripples as she wallowed forward. Now the stalagmites were almost within reach. The middle one seemed to be in a circle of light. Maia reached out. The surface was as rough as the weed bed levees. She almost went under the water as her fingers scrabbled for a hold. There wasn't one. Nor a ledge to hold the sun-stone.

Maia clung to the stalagmite. It scratched her fingers, her chin and cheeks. Her fingers were glistening. She was bathed in moonshine. She dared to look down and saw that the track of light went on beneath her. She took a deep breath. Tareth had hidden the sun-stone here. He had wanted to protect her, to hide her among the Cliff Dwellers so that she need never know that her destiny was to be a Sun Catcher. He had placed the stone where he knew she couldn't reach it. She took another sobbing breath, let go and sank.

Water streamed up her nose, roared in her ears, filled her clothes. Bubbles streamed above her as she slowly let her breath out until there was nothing left, and she felt the blackness pressing at the back of her eyes and knew she was going to drown. Still she sank, and as her mouth opened to draw in breath and filled with water, her feet touched the bottom.

Maia panicked, kicked hard and struggled to the surface. Choking, she grabbed at the stalagmite. Hugged it. She couldn't do it. She couldn't follow the moon track.

She'd failed. And then, beyond the columns of stalagmites, she saw another small beach on the far side of the lake. In the sheer wall beyond was a narrow hole.

Somehow Maia launched herself forward, kicking, arms thrashing and clawing at the water, and floundered into the shallows above the sloping beach. She crawled from the water and lay like a beached seal on the shore, coughing and shivering with fear. But she had done it. She sat up and stared.

Each stone on the pebble beach gleamed. No, not pebbles, she realised, but tiny mirror stones like the tiny crystals in the silk coat. Sharp-edged crystals. She carefully brushed the crushed rock from her hands and stood up. She crunched across the beach and stepped through the dark tear in the rock wall.

And felt like an insect among giants. She was standing among huge tumbled spars of crystal. Some climbed to the ceiling of the cavern, others lay on their sides. Several fallen crystal pillars rested like glass bridges spanning the towering columns. Maia stared. The whole cave glowed with a faint blue light which seemed to come from far above. She turned slowly. She was in a crystal forest. How was she expected to find one stone here?

She walked to the nearest fallen giant. She could see a tiny figure approaching. Fearfully she stopped. So did the figure. She reached out her hand. So did the figure imprisoned in the crystal. She leaned closer. It was a reflection. A movement seemed to flicker across the crystal bridge. Maia looked up. And in the crystal shard which leaned against the bridge she saw Tareth.

'Tareth!'

He didn't hear her. He was turning away, looking behind him. Maia glanced that way too. Nothing! When she turned back, Tareth had gone. Instead Xania, gleaming golden in her story-coat was standing there, eyes closed, her arms raised like wings as her coat billowed about her. Behind her, a family of flame-haired girls was laughing and running through an orchard of trees hung with moths opening and closing their wings. She was singing. Maia couldn't hear her.

'Xania?'

The Story Singer opened her eyes. She held out her hand to Maia. A wind seemed to take hold of her until she and the coat dissolved like smoke.

Then there were eagles, diving and fighting in the sky. They plunged so close to Maia that she flinched, even though she knew they were caught in the crystal. Now Tareth was there again, struggling with himself. No, fighting a man with his face. In a fight to the death, while their eagles battled above them. Tareth fell. Maia rushed forward and beat at the crystal with her fists.

Tareth turned his head. His dark eyes smiled at her. Then he was gone in a swirl of blood-red smoke and in his place stood a beautiful woman, with eyes like blue ice and red hair that tumbled down her shoulders. She held herself like a queen, but her robes were worn, the fabric frayed. She reached out, trying to touch Maia.

Maia backed away. She saw a slender, red-headed girl, sitting at the feet of the tall woman, feeding an eagle. Saw the man with Tareth's face, a wolf skin slung across his shoulders, a bloody knife in his hand, come to stand by the woman. They both stared at Maia. She saw their lips move. She read their lips. They were calling her Sun Catcher. They stepped towards her.

Maia grabbed a handful of sharp pebbles and threw it at the crystal.

The crystal chimed like a soft bell. A sound which rolled from one gigantic shard to another, deepening as it travelled until the whole cave was vibrating. Vibrations which forced Maia to her knees and made her cover her ears with her hands. Even that did not block out the sound. She curled into a ball. Her head would burst with the noise. She heard the stalactites groan and crash about her. Felt the ground shudder beneath her.

Someone was screaming. She heard Tareth bellow. Shock brought her to her knees. Crystal was cracking and tumbling about her.

'Run! Run! Maia, run!' chimed unseen voices.

'The sun-stone!' screamed Maia. 'Where is the sun-stone?'

'Run!' wailed the crystal voices.

Chunks of glass were raining on her. If they didn't bury her, she could be sliced in two. She folded her arms protectively about her head. The cave rocked. Maia staggered to her feet. She turned and faced the tumbling columns.

'The stone. I claim the sun-stone. The Sun Catcher claims the stone!' she shrieked.

The crystals sang. The eerie high-pitched wail almost burst her eardrums. The ground beneath her feet heaved and cracked. A smooth, grey stone rolled to her feet. Another stone, gleaming blue in the strange light, tumbled after it. Maia stared at them. Behind her the water shifted, shushed over the beach licking at the entrance to the cave.

Which one? There was only one. The Watcher had known that there was only one stone. Had known that the sun-stone would choose and burn.

Maia stepped forward.

'I choose the sun-stone,' she shouted and, bending swiftly, grabbed the grey stone.

Maia heard the wave coming, roaring into the sudden silence. The stone lay inert in her hand. There was no flame.

The ground shifted, twisted and heaved. She turned and ran back through the narrow entrance.

Then a wave was upon her. She flung up her arms, clutching the dull, grey stone and, twisting like a dolphin, leapt into the curling foam.

Thirty-Eight

A rough tongue rasped her face. Maia opened her eyes. A heavy weight pressed her into the ground. Whiskers tickled her chin as the pink tongue licked her again.

'Uh,' muttered Maia, wiping her face on her sleeve. It was sopping wet. Her hand still clasped the grey stone. She looked round. The dark water was smooth, as if the wave had never been. The moonlit path across it had gone. Instead tiny, torn patches of sunlight shimmered on the water.

She looked at the wet cat. 'You must have pulled me out. Thank you.'

Nefrar ignored her now.

Carefully Maia put down the stone and squeezed water out of her clothes. Then she tried to stand and realised that her knees felt as wobbly as a pot full of eels so she sat down again. Obligingly Nefrar sat next to her and she leaned gratefully against him.

'We should probably go and find Yanna,' said Maia.

Nefrar yawned.

'Before we fall asleep again,' said Maia firmly, and using the cheetah as a prop, levered herself upright.

It seemed a long way to the entrance. Then she was walking along the blade of light cast into the cave by the setting sun. And against the red sky a silhouette waited. A figure too broad for Yanna. A shadow she had seen a thousand times waiting for her in their cliff cave. Tareth! She stumbled forward.

'Greetings, Maia.'

Maia stopped dead at the entrance of the cave, blinking in the light that danced off the burnished bronze cuirass of the man blocking her path. She felt the muscles along the big cat's back ripple as he tensed. She twisted her hand firmly in Nefrar's plaited collar. Her other hand slid to her shoulder until she could feel the hilt of the knife she wore in a sheath under her tunic. It was still there.

Outside the cave, Yanna was sitting cross-legged on the ground. She could not see Yanna's bow holster. Behind Yanna stood a hobbled horse.

A shadow fell over Maia. There was a flurry of wings and a huge eagle landed on the gloved fist of the man. A man who wore a wolf pelt across his shoulders. A man with Tareth's face. But who was not Tareth.

Maia swallowed. 'Greetings, Urteth.'

'You know me?' Urteth sounded surprised.

'My father told me about his lost brother.'

'My brother,' Urteth nodded. 'But not your father.'

'In everything but blood,' said Maia.

Urteth shrugged.

Maia felt her heart twist. Why did he have to look so like Tareth? She knew she mustn't trust him. He controlled the Wulf Kin.

She studied the tumbled rocks around the cave entrance. She could see no sign of the Wulf Kin. It didn't mean they weren't there. Her fingers tightened on her knife. She needed to stay strong.

'Then does that make us kin?' mused Urteth.

'Never!'

'A brother, since your sister Elin and I are hand-fast.'

'A sister who's a stranger,' said Maia.

'Which is why I'm here,' said Urteth smoothly. 'To take you to her.'

'You came without your Wulf Kin?'

The raptor on his wrist shifted and glared at her. Urteth however didn't seem upset by her tone. He stroked his eagle's head.

'Azara and I don't need the company of Wulf Kin to greet family.' He nodded to Yanna. 'Nor her bodyguard.'

Yanna spat on the ground. Her hands were tied.

'Yanna is a friend. Is that how you treat friends?' demanded Maia. She loosened her fingers in Nefrar's collar, but did not release him. 'However, the cat, also my friend, is my bodyguard.'

Nefrar purred. His tail twitched. He stared steadily at Urteth. The eagle leaned forward, glaring now at the cheetah. Maia saw Urteth's arm move as if he were about to cast Azara at the feline.

Warrior-swift, she slid her knife from its sheath. 'Release your eagle and you'll be dead before it reaches Nefrar,' she threatened. 'Tareth taught me well!'

Urteth smiled. He seemed to relax. 'Evidently. But not how to greet your kin.' He slowly spread the fingers of his swordhand wide. 'I come in peace, Maia'

As if to prove it further, his fingers stroked the breast of Azara. It was a caress Tareth had often given Magnus. Maia blinked away the memory.

'Your friend attacked me,' continued Urteth. 'She wouldn't listen to me, so I had to restrain her. I wish neither of you harm. I've come with greetings from Elin and to escort you to the Sun Palace where she's waiting for you.'

'Waiting to kill you!' said Yanna.

'Waiting to welcome you,' corrected Urteth. 'She thought you dead. She was overjoyed when the silk told her you were alive. She sent me to find you. She misses her sisters. She sometimes wishes the plague which killed the family had taken her too.'

'Plague!' snarled Yanna. 'She was the plague.'

A frown darkened Urteth's eyes. It was gone in an instant. Maia wondered if she had imagined it. But he was too plausible. She mustn't think of him as Tareth's brother. He was an enemy.

'You shouldn't believe all the words spread about Elin,' said Urteth. 'She longs for this land sickness to end. She longs for your help, Maia.'

'My help?'

'Aren't you the Sun Catcher? Have you found the stolen sun-stone?' His voice was casual but his eyes were eager.

'You shouldn't believe all the words spread about me,' mocked Maia.

Warily she stepped round Urteth, keeping the cheetah between them. She cut Yanna free.

'He has my bow!' Yanna said.

'Which I'll return once I know you won't try to kill me,' said Urteth. He looked steadily at Maia. 'Despite everything, I come in peace.'

Should she trust him?

'It's time the Sun Catcher returned. The land is sick,' continued Urteth. 'The sun-stone should be returned to the Sun Palace.'

Maia suddenly felt weary beyond belief. Everyone seemed to know what she should do. Everyone but her. 'We will come,' she could feel Yanna's angry eyes, 'and accept your word that you intend us no harm.'

Urteth nodded. 'You have the sun-stone?'

It was the sun-stone he needed, not her. Until he had it, she and Yanna were safe. Maia tried to imagine away the hard lump of stone pressing against her side, beneath the silk Tareth had made. Could Urteth see it under her wet clothes? And had she chosen the right stone? She stifled a yawn that was part anxiety, part exhaustion.

'The sun-stone is safe, as it always was,' she said.

She looked at Yanna who stared impassively back. Would she guard the sun-stone with her life? Did it demand lifeblood as well as destruction and fire? Tareth had never wanted her to find out.

'We'll leave after sun-sleep.' She didn't manage to smother a yawn this time.

Yanna nodded. 'I don't trust him,' she whispered. 'I'll keep watch while you sleep.' She glanced at Urteth's horse. 'It'll be a long journey,' she said loudly.

'The Sun Catcher shall ride with me,' said Urteth.

Maia decided she would argue about that later. There was no way she would ride and leave Yanna to run alongside Urteth's horse.

She didn't have to argue. She woke stiff yet warm, with Nefrar stretched alongside her. Yanna was leaning against a rock watching Urteth tend a small fire with a blackened pot set in the flames. The smell of cardamon and warming mare's milk tickled Maia's nostrils.

Nefrar stretched, rolled over and padded across to Yanna. Maia sat up. Her ribs hurt where she had lain on the stone hidden under her tunic. She jiggled it into a better position. Somehow she would have to find a safer place to hide it, but she needed to keep it close. The sun-stone felt warmer today. Was it a sign or just the warmth from her body? If only Xania and Tareth had told her more.

'Sun's greetings, Sun Catcher,' said Urteth, and carried a bone beaker of mare's milk across to her.

'You drink from it first,' commanded Yanna.

Urteth shrugged, smiled at Maia and drank. A line of

foaming milk patterned his top lip. He wiped his sleeve across his mouth, just as Tareth would have done and handed Maia the beaker.

'Thank you,' Maia watched him across the top of the beaker as she drank. Now she studied him she could see the difference between the brothers. Tareth, even when angry, had never looked as dangerous as Urteth. There was something behind his eyes that sent a frisson of panic pricking the hairs at the back of her neck. And yet, part of her wanted to like and trust him.

'We'll leave when you're ready,' said Urteth, and turned to throw the padded felt saddle on the back of his horse.

Yanna crossed to Maia to share the milk. 'You ride. He and I will walk,' she said. She lowered her voice. 'You found it? I felt the earth tremble when you were gone.'

Maia wondered if she should confess her doubts about the stone she had chosen but decided there was no point in worrying Yanna. She knew she could never force herself to return to the cave. The lake had tried to drown her, to keep her forever in the hidden place. And anyway, the tumbling crystal pillars would have blocked the entrance. She just hoped that the stone had recognised her as Xania had promised and that she had chosen well.

'It's safe,' said Maia.

'The Warrior Women will join us as we go to the Sun City,' Yanna promised Maia. 'I will send a message with Nefrar.'

'We're going in peace!'

'I don't trust him. Where are the Wulf Kin?'

Maia glanced at the cheetah who was gazing at the sky. 'Would Nefrar know if they were close?'

Reluctantly Yanna nodded.

'Then perhaps it's as he says and that Elin needs a sister's help.'

Yanna made a rude noise. 'He's tied my bow to his horse. Free it and drop it as you ride.' She looked across at Urteth. 'See. He's untying it. He's taking it. He doesn't trust us!'

Despite her anxiety, Maia laughed. 'With good reason!'

Yanna's reply was lost in the sound of wings as three eagles flew overhead and circled. Urteth's eagle hunched her shoulders and screamed a challenge. Calling to each other, the eagles swooped lower, then broke formation, winging towards three riders galloping towards them. Surefooted, they seemed to float across the tundra. Sunlight glinted on the golden fur hats the riders wore. Two of them rode with a spare horse running free beside them. Their coats gleamed like new copper tokens. Maia drew a quick breath. They were beautiful. These must be the fabled horses Tareth had remembered.

'Eagle Hunters,' confirmed Yanna, as each eagle flew onto the upraised fist of a rider.

Maia saw Urteth shrug on his black wolf skin and hold out his arm for his eagle. Then he was striding to meet the riders.

They swept past him, the leader flicking his fingers in a brief greeting as they urged their horses up the slope towards Maia. She heard Yanna gasp and put her hand out to stop the archer stepping in front of her. Nefrar strolled forward to stand at her side as the horses were reined to a halt in front of her.

'Sun Catcher!' called one of the men. He swung from his

horse and strode towards her, his eagle balancing, wings outstretched on his arm. When he reached her he dropped to one knee.

'I am Egon. The eagles brought news. And the snow-melt told us that it was true, though the old men muttered in their beards that it was a false tale. We bring an escort to the Sun City.'

Maia touched her forehead. 'Egon.' She stared at the top of his golden hat. It was the colour of flames in sunlight she thought. The man rose to his feet. At his gesture a smaller hunter dismounted and delved into woven saddle bags. He carried a long bundle towards Maia. It was almost as long as he was tall.

'My son has gifts,' the eagle hunter continued. 'So the Sun Catcher can ride with pride into the Sun City with the Eagle People.'

The smaller hunter grinned at her and she saw that he was not much older than she was.

'I am Huan. The Story Singer told us to watch for you. We've waited many star-shifts.'

He opened the bundle and shook out a long, padded, embroidered coat. Bewildered, Maia allowed him to help her put it on. When he handed her a golden fur hat she tugged off her cap and pulled it on over her spiky hair. It was like being Flame Head again. She smiled at him. He leaned forward to ruffle the fur of the hat, spoiling the solemnity of the moment.

The third man led forward one of the horses.

'This is Fionn, the fair one,' said Huan 'She will carry you well.'

'She's beautiful,' said Maia.

The horse lowered her head and snuffled at Maia's outstretched hand, then blew gently on her face. Maia laughed. Fionn backed away, shaking her long mane. When Maia held out her hand, Fionn stepped forward again and stood still as the Eagle Hunter cupped his hands, waited as Maia put her foot in them and threw her up into the saddle. The horse nodded her head. Small golden ornaments on her bridle glinted in the sun – a deer, a camel, and hunting cat and a running deer. Maia touched the hunting cat and felt for her silver brooch, pinned to Tareth's silk inside her tunic. Perhaps she did belong here. She gathered up the reins and hoped she would not fall off.

She glanced at Yanna who was already swinging herself into the saddle of a bronze coloured horse. The Eagle Hunters remounted. At their word, the horses wheeled and clattered past Urteth, who was vaulting, stony-faced, onto his own pony.

With their eagles flying ahead, calling to each other, the hunters fanned out in an arrow wedge behind Maia and Yanna. The cat bounded alongside Yanna's horse. Maia turned in the saddle to see Urteth riding behind them, clear enough to avoid the flying stones kicked up by the horses' hooves.

As the horses picked up speed, the hunters started to sing. The wind stinging her eyes, Maia risked loosening one hand to clamp it over the stone jiggling under her tunic as she rode. She mustn't lose it. When she had the chance, she would put it in the deep pocket of the embroidered coat. She looked across at Yanna who was urging her horse on, her head thrown back, singing too. A song that turned to a yell of defiance as they passed a rocky outcrop and a Wulf Kin on a shaggy pony, his wulfen running free alongside joined the wild ride at Urteth's side.

Thirty-Nine

Maia watched the tall figures, their beasts padding alongside, disappear into the darkness, making for the cluster of fires that marked the boundaries of the Wulf Kin camp.

'More Wulf Kin!' said Maia. 'How many will Urteth summon?

At least they had kept themselves apart, she thought. A gang of armed thugs prowling among the Eagle People's cooking fires would have made everyone edgy. As it was, Yanna posted an archer guard each sun-sleep. She still didn't trust Urteth.

Yanna poked the fire. Sparks flew into the sky. 'We'll still be more.'

Each sun-wake brought more people to swell the ranks of the escort. First the archer guard with their cheetahs had arrived. Yanna had been delighted and had instantly rearmed herself with a bow. Nefrar had coughed a welcome and returned to Maia's side. He seemed to have adopted her. She hoped Yanna wouldn't be jealous. The archers had strung out behind the original Eagle Hunters, pinning the Wulf Kin inside their circle. Then another small band of Eagle People arrived, among them women and children, astride bronze or golden horses. All wore brightly-embroidered, belted coats over baggy leggings tucked into leather boots. Some like Tareth had eagle feathers plaited into their dark, shoulder length hair. They wore a leather gauntlet and carried an eagle on their fist. Maia saw a small girl who rode with the children, a young half-fledged eagle balanced on her arm. As a boy, Tareth must have ridden so. She remembered her dream to fly her own eagle. She sighed. Her destiny lay elsewhere even if she felt ill-prepared to answer its call. Well, she'd worry about that later.

What worried her now were the small family groups who were joining them. What would happen to them if, as Yanna feared, Urteth broke his word and the Wulf Kin attacked?

Somehow she must find a way to protect them.

She slipped her hand inside the deep pocket of her padded coat. She'd moved the stone there, where she could touch it. The sun-stone was smooth and cool, just like an ordinary pebble. She felt another dizzying surge of self-doubt. What if it was just a stone?

'How far to the Sun City?' asked Maia.

Yanna threw a handful of shrivelled berries into the water simmering in a pot on the fire. They scented the air, making

Maia think of the wide pans of berries and honey stewing over cave fires.

'Near,' Yanna was saying. 'You'll see the towers between sun-wake and sun-high.'

So little time. Maia swallowed. She wasn't ready. Would never be ready.

The snow had finally melted in most of the hollows which lay deep in the shade. The fierce heat of the sun was drying the earth. New growth sprouted among the bleached grass stalks.

'We'll camp outside the city walls,' added Yanna. 'I'll send archers ahead to search the city.'

'She's my sister,' protested Maia.

'She wants to be Sun Catcher.'

Elin was welcome, thought Maia. 'I need to be alone,' she said. 'The sun-stone . . . calls.'

Terrified though she was, she had to learn more about the sun-stone. She didn't need Yanna or the cat anywhere near when she tried to summon sun-fire. She could still remember how she had burned Kodo. And she would never forget the smell of scorched fur as the wulfen died.

Slowly Yanna subsided by the fire. Nefrar blinked and stayed where he was. But as Maia set off into the darkness, she could sense him following her. She stopped and turned. Nefrar stopped too.

'Go back!'

The cheetah's tail twitched. He yawned, his teeth white in the darkness, and sat.

She set off again. This time she couldn't hear anything. She suddenly felt very alone. But she wouldn't go too far, she promised herself. The darkness thickened. Soon she wouldn't be able to see the camp fires if she tried.

She almost screamed as something touched her leg.

Nefrar's purr came loud and strong close by her knee. She reached out to touch his head.

'You're as stubborn as Yanna,' she complained, but was glad, when she continued into the darkness, that Nefrar went with her.

She had noticed a tumble of rocks earlier. Now she almost twisted her ankle as she stumbled over them in the dark. On hands and knees she scrambled around them, slid into the hollow they made and sat on the edge of a patch of snow.

'It could be dangerous,' she muttered.

The big cat breathed on her face.

'Uh!' Maia wrinkled her nose. He had obviously been hunting with the others. 'Don't go to sleep,' she warned and reached into her pocket for the sun-stone.

If she cupped her hand, the sun-stone fitted perfectly. Maia sighed. So far, so good.

Gingerly, she placed her left hand over the right, holding the sun-stone between her palms. Nothing. A cool, smooth nothing. She closed her eyes and concentrated, summoning pictures of the Crystal Cave. Still nothing. She placed it on the ground and leaned forward to stare at it. She felt a bit silly, glaring at a rock. Nefrar batted it with his paw.

'Don't,' gasped Maia.

But still nothing happened.

She explored the stone with her fingertips. It was just a water-smoothed, grey stone.

She *had* made a mistake! She felt sick. Xania had promised

her that the sun-stone would know her and this rock had been waiting. 'But so was the crystal stone,' nagged a voice in her head, 'and you ignored that one. You never wanted to find the sun-stone, did you? You took the wrong one . . . on purpose!'

'Maybe everyone's wrong about me,' she muttered to silence the inner voice. 'Maybe my gift is different. It's only what the Watcher called me when she saw how the runes fell.'

She remembered the smoke and burning and Sabra's hand taking the pain for her when she had picked up the grey stone on her Naming Day. If she made fire and touched this stone with the flame, perhaps it would know her.

She heard a soft footfall. She grabbed the sun-stone and shoved it in her pocket.

'You shouldn't walk alone in the darkness,' said Urteth. His voice chilled her bones. 'Who knows what dangers await?'

Maia stood, cursing the stiffness in her legs. She must have been sitting for ages while the moon rose and bloomed. She could see it hanging above the tallest rock, casting Urteth's black shadow across the patch of snow.

'Who knows,' she agreed huskily. 'But I'm not alone . . . I brought my shadow.'

She saw the fur pelt on Urteth's shoulders bristle as he tensed.

Beside Maia, Nefrar growled softly.

'Good,' said Urteth. 'But you should return to the fires. The wulfen are let off their leashes at night.'

Involuntarily, Maia's eyes searched the darkness. She

suppressed a shudder. 'Then hope they don't fall foul of Yanna's archer guard,' she said.

Urteth eyed the cheetah. 'A beautiful pelt,' he said. 'Were you hunting? I've food at my fire.'

'I needed to be alone.'

He didn't take the hint, walking beside her as she set off towards the fires.

He nodded. 'Elin too walks alone in the darkness of the Stone Court watching each sun-wake for the sign that the Catching is to come.'

Maia's brain buzzed with the implications of what he was saying. Maybe the sun-stone was powerless in the dark and needed sunlight to make it strong. The Watcher's stones had reacted in sunlight, she remembered. Perhaps she was wrong to expect the sun-stone to do whatever it did in the dark after being hidden in a cave deep beneath the earth. She hadn't had time to examine it in sunlight. She would have to find some way of going off on her own after sun-wake.

'When the sun reaches the catching-stone,' said Urteth. 'Then people will gather in the Stone Court and the Sun Catcher will catch the sun.'

Maia walked on in silence. She would have asked about the Stone Court and the catching but she was afraid to show her ignorance. She would ask Yanna when the Sun Catcher was supposed to go there and what she did.

'Before the Catching, Elin and Caspia will welcome you,' continued Urteth.

'Caspia?'

'Our daughter.' Pride softened Urteth's voice. 'She already shows her gift. The light follows her.'

Did he think his daughter was a Sun Catcher? Did he want the sun-stone for her? How could he love her and wish such a fate on her? Maia shivered.

'Pass, Sun Catcher,' a tall archer stepped from the darkness. 'Do you wish this . . . man . . . to reach the fire also?'

'Yes.' She laid her hand on his arm. He touched her hand. Then he looked at her strangely.

'You are cold,' he said. 'You should return to your fire.' Ignoring the archer's threat, he walked away.

He knows, thought Maia. He suspects that I'm afraid to use the stone like the true Sun Catcher. If he thinks that he will kill me and the Wulf Kin will attack the camp. He will take the sun-stone.

Forty

Maia stared up at the stars. It would be sun-wake soon. Urteth had not used the darkness to try and seize the sun-stone. But he would. He wanted it, if not for Elin, then for his daughter. Before they reached the Sun City, he would strike. Many would die. Urteth would never allow her to live. Unless Elin, her sister . . .

Maia clenched her fists. Xania had said that Elin had killed her sisters to become Queen. There was no escape unless she left them all. She had to get Urteth away from the Wulf Kin.

She rolled over and buried her face in her arms. Nefrar, stretched across her feet with the tip of his tail almost in the fire, got up and strolled off in disgust. She heard him settle beside Yanna, and her sleepy greeting. That was good. The cheetah would keep Yanna safely, warmly asleep until she was gone. Maia lay still and waited. When she heard their snores she sat up.

The darkness cloaked her as she crept through the sleeping bodies towards the horses. Even the archer guard seemed to be dreaming, asleep on her feet. The horses stirred restlessly as she slipped between them, but they didn't make a sound.

She led Fionn to the edge of the herd and struggled to haul herself onto her back. There was no time to collect her saddle. Yanna might wake at any moment. She hoped she wouldn't fall off and laced her fingers through the coarse mane. This must be the worst planned escape ever. But Fionn seemed to sense what she wanted. The mare moved almost silently, skirting the fires and not snorting at the flames. The hunched figures curled by the fires didn't stir as they passed. Maia tapped her heels into Fionn's flanks and they turned to step towards Urteth's fires. Not too close. Her flight mustn't seem obvious or he might suspect.

He hadn't posted a guard. He must know that no one would dare to try to ambush him. Nothing stirred in his camp. She could see dark shapes lying by the fires. She twisted her hands tighter into the mane, squeezed her trembling legs against the sides of her horse, and felt a tremor across Fionn's skin.

Then they were past, and the empty plain stretched in front of her. And somewhere beyond, the Sun Palace. She forced herself not to look back, and sent Fionn trotting into the dark.

At first Maia thought she had failed. Then she heard the sound of something following. Please let it be Urteth and not a vigilant Wulf Kin with his beast, she thought and urged Fionn into a gallop.

The Eagle People had chosen well. Fleet-footed, as swift as the wind, Fionn outpaced her pursuer. Risking a glance over her shoulder, Maia saw that a single horse was following – Urteth's black pony. She urged Fionn on towards the sliver of light edging across the horizon and rode towards the dawn.

When the semi-circle of light was too bright to stare at, Maia slowed her horse. She smoothed her hand down the sweat-darkened neck and turned Fionn, the rising sun behind her, to wait for Urteth. Urteth's wild gallop slowed to a canter when he saw her waiting, easing to a walk within speaking distance.

'You're far from camp,' called Maia.

'As are you.'

'I wished to be first to see the Sun Palace,' said Maia.

Urteth gestured behind her. 'The sun is glinting on the towers.'

As Maia turned to look, she realised her mistake. Urteth used the distraction to move closer. Maia stared at the point of the stabbing spear, the blade angled towards her chest.

'Why are you here?' he demanded.

'I'm going to the Sun Palace – to meet my sister,' said Maia.

'Alone?' Urteth glanced over his shoulder. The plain was empty.

'As are you,' she responded.

Urteth grinned. 'My brother reared you well, wild cat. D'you think you could best me?'

'I am the Sun Catcher,' said Maia coldly. 'My family has

the gift. As Tareth found, even though he hid me and my destiny away among the Cliff Dwellers.'

'Tareth wanted your power,' said Urteth. 'That's why he stole you and took the sun-stone.'

Maia bit back the denial that sprang to her lips. Urteth must crave power. That was why he accused Tareth of the same ambition. He didn't know that Tareth had thought the sun-stone a burden. That he had wanted to save her from herself.

'It's true.' She forced the lie from dry lips.

Urteth nodded. He seemed to be considering. 'I told Elin that the Sun Catcher is chosen. And that even if Caspia grows into her powers she may not be chosen.'

'Just as Elin wasn't!' Maia hazarded a guess.

Urteth was silent. 'Perhaps,' he acknowledged.

'But a gift can be trained. Can be strengthened,' taunted Maia. 'Tareth understood that.'

Warring emotions chased across Urteth's face. 'What do you want, Sun Catcher?'

'To meet my sister. To return home.'

Maia allowed herself to think of the Cliff Dwellers living on the fringes of the sun-deeps. She dreamed of flying an eagle and watching it on the thermals above the cliffs. She wanted to crawl across the warm sands and watch the lizards laying in the lizard scrapes. To climb and steal honey from the bees as she had with Kodo. Even to see Razek, his silver wristguard glinting in the sunshine as he strode along the levees. She set the pictures free, hoping that Urteth would feel them and believe her. 'I miss the sun-deeps,' she said and suddenly realised that it was true.

'And when you meet Elin?'

Maia shrugged. 'I'm a stranger in the land of my birth. Tareth ensured that when he stole me from the Sun Palace. But I've learned that my family are trusted with the gift of sun-catching. That it's the duty of the Queen to catch the sun. Elin is Queen.'

Urteth's eyes narrowed. 'And you would give the sun-stone to Elin?'

'The sun-stone belongs in Khandar.'

'You'll share the ways of the sun-stone?'

'Everything can be taught to those who are willing to learn.'

'Can you teach me?' Urteth tried to keep his voice even, but his eyes were greedy and his breathing quickened.

Maia felt a blaze of triumph. She had him! She nodded thoughtfully. 'If you're willing to pay the price.'

'I have weapons and men. I can pay the price!'

Maia shook her head. 'I have weapons and women warriors,' she said.

'What then?'

Maia glanced at the sky. Urteth's eagle was high above, almost a dot in the sky. There was no danger there.

'An eagle,' she said.

Urteth glanced aloft. 'Azara?'

Maia smiled. 'No, Urteth. An eagle of my own. Your eagle is old.'

He frowned at the slight.

'Old and wise,' said Maia quickly. 'But I want a young eagle.'

Urteth smiled. 'Old, but not as wise as you, Silver Tongue.

My brother had a silver tongue too, but it won't save him. He will die in a strange land. Eagles won't hunt over his grave.'

Maia clenched her teeth. She was making this too easy for him. Tareth had died, killed on the cliffs because of Urteth and his ambition. He deserved to suffer. 'A young eagle, of my choosing. And . . .'

'And?'

He was wary but eager too. He would promise her anything. She almost laughed.

'Safe passage in Khandar.'

'I've given my word already!' His voice told her that he thought her gullible.

'And Yanna, her archers, the Eagle People and the families who have come to meet the Sun Catcher left free to return home unharmed.'

He frowned.

'Your word that they'll remain safe. And that the Wulf Kin won't hunt again among the Lizard People and the Cliff Dwellers.'

He nodded slowly. 'Done.'

'And Caspia's company on my journey to the cliffs.'

His face darkened. 'Not Caspia!'

'So that I may show my . . . niece . . . the secrets of the sun-stone,' continued Maia as if he hadn't spoken. 'As a token of good faith between us.'

She watched him struggle. Finally his need for power won. Poor Caspia! Maia was glad that it had been Tareth who had found and rescued her from the burning palace and not Urteth.

'Agreed,' said Urteth. 'Show me.'

Maia reached inside her deep pocket.

Urteth's eyes widened. He looked from the dull stone to her face and back again. 'That is the sun-stone?'

Her gaze never leaving Urteth, Maia held the stone up to the sun. 'See how it drinks the sun,' she commanded.

Urteth gazed at it. She saw his fingers tighten around his spear. Was he going to stab her and grab the sun-stone? She managed not to back Fionn away from the spear-point. He mustn't think she was afraid. Urteth only understood strength.

'The sun warms the sun-stone and kindles its power,' Maia's voice took on the lilting cadence of a Story Singer. 'See how the sun touches it.'

'I see nothing,' said Urteth. 'Merely a stone.'

Maia was desperately afraid that he might be right, but pushed the fear down inside her. 'Perhaps you're not chosen to see,' she challenged.

'I will see,' snarled Urteth.

'Then you must wait,' said Maia. 'The sun's still low. The sun-stone needs the sun high to gain all its power.'

Urteth nodded. 'So Elin told me. But the sun has been too low in the sky to reach the catching-stone. The sun must strike the pillar and pierce its eye. As a boy I was taken to the Stone Court to witness the catching. The ground beneath our faces was warm as we lay and waited. Your mother was the Sun Catcher.'

Maia tried not to think about the sun piercing her eye.

'She screamed as she caught the sun,' said Urteth cruelly. 'Will you scream?'

She glared at him. 'The sun is low. The sun-stone will stay cool. I won't scream when I show you how to catch the sun.'

'Nor will I,' said Urteth. He pushed his spear into its sheath on his saddle and reached out his hand. 'Let me feel the sun warm the sun-stone.'

'The sun-stone is linked to the Sun Catcher. It feels and wants what the stone holder wants. That is its power,' said Maia.

'Give it to me!'

Maia sat down firmly on her horse. Fionn backed several strides away from Urteth's outstretched hand.

'What does Elin want with the sun-stone?'

'To warm the land. To light the great stones.'

'And you? What do you want?'

'What use is a country starving because the crops don't grow, because the sun comes too late and departs too soon? The land is dying. I can make it richer and stronger than it ever was when it was ruled by women. Your mother let the land wither. She grew too old to catch the sun as she ought. Your sisters were weak. They deserved their fate. Elin and I will make it a kingdom that will outlive the songs they sing about us.'

'And the sun-stone will give you this?'

'Yes! I want the sun-stone!'

Maia could feel the sun on her back. It glinted on the bronze discs of Urteth's cuirass. She could see it flaring in the mare's eyes. The horse lowered its head. The sun must be a red ball climbing above the edge of the plain. The tips of her fingers which held the sun-stone were warm. She hoped it was enough.

'Then you shall have it, Urteth. Learn what it is to be a Sun Catcher.'

She tossed the sun-stone high. It hung in the air. It was still grey, tinged pink with the new sunlight. Urteth urged his horse forward. The sunlight seemed to hold the spinning stone. Maia glared at it, channelling all her anger and fear into it. Pain shot through her head, stabbing her eyes. Urteth leaned forward, reached and caught it.

'Ha!' he shouted in triumph.

Then the sunlight hit his eyes, dazzling him. His pony reared. Urteth lost his balance and fell. The pony turned, trampling him, and shot away. Above him an eagle screamed, echoed by Urteth as burning light filled his hand and ran up his arm. He rolled over and over trying to quench it, beating at it with his other hand. Smoke began to spill from his fingers. There was the smell of burning leather. The grass caught light.

'Drop the sun-stone,' shouted Maia.

But either Urteth didn't hear her or he couldn't let go. He staggered to his knees. Sunlight streamed into the sun-stone. The rock was smoking. Urteth's hand was turning black.

Fionn, frantic to get away, wheeled and tried to bolt. It took all of Maia's strength to stay on, to turn her and try to ride back to Urteth. The mare dug her heels in, and stood head down, trembling, refusing to move. Maia slid off and ran towards Urteth. He was still on his knees, staring blindly at the sky.

'Close your eyes! Drop it!' shrieked Maia.

There was a crack. Parts of Urteth's hand seemed to be

falling away. He pitched forward and lay still. Maia leaned over him. The sun-stone had cracked. The outside had broken away. It was flakes of rock that had split off, not Urteth's flesh. She could see a white crystal glowing in Urteth's blackened hand.

Ignoring the pain in her head she prised Urteth's fingers open and pulled the sun-stone from his grasp. It was cool in her hand. She almost dropped it in surprise. Urteth groaned and rolled over, staring sightlessly at the sky. One side of his face was blistered. His breath bubbled in his throat.

A breath of wind caught the tiny flames in the grass. Maia shoved the sun-stone into her pocket. She stamped on the flickering flames and stumbled towards her horse. Fionn seemed to be standing in a haze of smoke. Maia rubbed her eyes. Surely the fire had not caught that quickly?

This time Fionn wasn't so cooperative, shying every time Maia tried to catch her. Just as she got a hand in Fionn's mane, something plummeted from the sky and thudded at her feet. Fionn took fright and pulled away from her. Urteth's eagle, Azara, lay dead at her feet an arrow through her chest.

Yanna and two archers arrived in a thunder of plunging hooves. Yanna flung herself from her horse.

'Are you all right? We saw the sunlight fall.'

'Urteth is hurt. Dying!' She managed to say. 'The sun-stone has killed him.'

'He was an evil man,' said Yanna. 'He would have killed you.'

'He wanted the sun-stone to heal the land,' said Maia.

'He would have killed you,' repeated Yanna stubbornly.

'The sun-stone protected you.'

'And I killed his eagle,' claimed one of the archers. 'It would have torn your eyes out when Urteth fell.'

The ground was trembling beneath Maia's feet. She could see flying horses stampeding across the plain. Hear the whoops of the Eagle People. The scream of eagles. The baying wulfen. Maia staggered towards Fionn. 'I need water. And my horse . . .' She gestured at Fionn a hundred paces away.

Yanna unhooked her water-pouch from her saddle and handed it to Maia. Trying not to look at the dead eagle, Maia turned back towards the place where Urteth had fallen. The wind had risen. Flames were crackling. The thin ring of fire round Urteth was spreading. The smoke was not just the haze in her eyes. Tearing off her coat, Maia ran towards the blaze. She whirled her coat above her head, slamming it down on the flames. The water-bag fell from her hands, spilling in the grass. Water hissed. Maia beat at the fire. She saw an archer dancing in the smoke trying to stamp out the flames as they ran in flickering lines across the grass. Stampeding horses circled her. Men were shouting, leaping from their horses, kicking earth across the flames. She saw the old Wulf Kin racing towards her, fire licking at his pony's hooves. He was stooping low in his saddle. Yanna shouted. Maia darted aside as the pony thundered past her. Then Yanna was at her side, bow in hand, firing arrows. Maia inhaled smoke. She could smell singed feathers. Her eyes smarted and ran with tears. The world blurred. Yanna was smothering the fire. Others joined her and as suddenly as it had started the stone-fire died.

Wiping her streaming eyes, Maia shook the smuts of soot from her coat and unwillingly looked to where Urteth had lain in the path of the blaze. She stared at the crushed, blackened grass. Small pieces of cracked stone and burned leather lay in the grass. But Urteth had gone.

Forty-One

'Urteth is dead!'

'The sun-stone killed Urteth!'

The whispers spread like wildfire around the encampment. Rumours confirmed by Yanna.

'But he only disappeared,' objected Maia.

Yanna had shrugged. 'The sun-stone destroyed him. Urteth is dead.'

Maia wasn't convinced. She rubbed her forehead. The headache had gone and her eyes no longer looked through smoke. 'The Wulf Kin have gone too.'

When they had returned to the camp, there had been smouldering fires but no sign of the Wulf Kin.

She wondered why but first she needed to know everything Yanna could tell her about the Stone Court and the role of the Sun Catcher.

'I've never seen it,' admitted Yanna. She saw the dismay on Maia's face. 'But Xania told me parts of the story.'

'Tell me.'

'The catching-stone in the Stone Court is the heart of the Sun Palace. The sun falls through the eye of the catching-stone. The light is like a great star.'

Maia nodded slowly. The story-coat had once shown her a star in a stone, when she and Xania had ridden away from the Gather to find Tareth. Memories of what had happened later, when the cliff village had been attacked by Sea Thieves and then Wulf Kin, flooded into her mind. Images of the desperate escape and Razek waiting on the cliff and Magnus and Tareth had . . .

She slammed the door shut on her thoughts.

'The sun-stone becomes the sun,' Yanna was saying. 'The Sun Catcher throws its rays to the far corners of the Stone Court. And the light warms the land and the land comes alive,' she finished confidently.

Maia sighed. So much for Xania's song-story. Crafted for firelight, it contained no useful detail.

One of the eagle women approached, dragging a wriggling bundle.

'We found her creeping into camp.' She let go and a muffled figure fell to the ground. The woman held up a long curved knife. 'With this!' She grinned and held up a flat, blackened pan. 'And this! We couldn't decide if she came to knife you or beat you to death with the cooking pan!'

'No mess with me!' growled the bundle. It writhed, sat up and a red face appeared in the folds of a voluminous cloak.

Maia's lips twitched. 'Zena! I thought Yanna told you to stay in Altara.'

'Lady! I find you!' Zena struggled to throw off the cloak. She beamed at Maia and then stared fiercely at the eagle woman. 'I told you Lady know me!'

Maia tried to look stern and failed. 'What're you doing here?'

'Snow-melt. Many people crossing plains. I go too. I bring Lady's coat. She need coat when catch sun.' She looked at Maia's face and her grin faded a little. 'Lady pleased to see Zena?' Her eyes flickered to Yanna. 'Yanna not!' she whispered.

Maia hauled Zena out of the cloak and held her tight. 'Very!'

Zena hugged her back, then wriggled out of Maia's arms and burrowed among the folds of the cloak to pull out a soft drawstring bag. She held it out to Maia.

'Here coat. Zena keep safe.'

She grabbed her flat cooking pan from the eagle woman. 'Now Zena make flatbread just as Lady like. Then Zena can stay with Lady. Lady not let Yanna send me away?'

Maia took the bag. It seemed her fate to have Xania's story-coat, just as it was her burden to keep the sun-stone.

'No one will send you away,' she promised and crossed her thumbs. She glanced at Yanna, who was trying hard to frown and not smile. 'Yanna's pleased, not angry, that you were brave enough to follow and bring the coat.'

And since there was no one to tell her how or what she was to do in the Stone Court, she could at least wear Xania's silk coat.

'I'll wear the coat when we ride into the Sun Palace.'

Zena nodded with delight. 'Sun Lady look beautiful, like a queen,' she said.

'And will lead us into the Sun City,' said Yanna. 'Elin will tremble at the sight of you and all your followers.'

'Many, many people,' agreed Zena.

'All of whom will need feeding,' said Yanna. 'I'll send the Warrior Women to speak to herders and barter for animals from their flocks. We must hunt. Gather food. The Eagle People will ride with us. The eagles and the cheetahs will enjoy the chase. The people in the Sun City shall not go hungry when the Sun Catcher arrives. There is always feasting after the Catching. We must bring food for the feast.' She looked at Zena. 'A pity you did not come with a wagon and food. I will have to send messages to Altara.'

Zena hung her head.

'Will you hunt with us, Sun Catcher?'

Maia shrugged. She pushed the bag containing the story-coat into her back-sack. 'I don't have the skill to hunt Nefrar. Nor to ride Fionn with the eagles,' she admitted reluctantly. 'I would be of little use. I can help with foraging.'

Yanna nodded. 'Urteth is dead and the Wulf Kin gone but I will leave archers and an eagle to protect you.'

The camp seemed empty once the hunters had left whooping with delight at the prospect of the thrills of a hunt. It took forever to start those left moving towards the Sun City. Impatient to see her first glimpse of the Sun Palace, Maia rode on, her followers strung out across the grassland behind her. Beneath the dead, wheat-coloured stalks, a green haze of new growth was spreading like a carpet across the plain. She could see Huan, the eagle boy, riding far out on the left flank of the untidy procession. He cast his eagle into the sky. Its wings beat powerfully, black tips almost touching the top of the tall grasses, as it skimmed the plain and suddenly dropped. Eagle breakfast.

Maia urged Fionn into a canter.

They breasted the rise, saw the sun glinting off distant roofs, and then they were racing down into another long decline filled with sunshine and cloud shadows. Down in this dip, it was as if they were alone in the world. It was warm and still. The crowds behind them had disappeared. The Sun Palace and her future were out of sight. It was good to be free of the sideways glances, the greetings and the heavy weight of everyone's unspoken expectation that she would save them.

She heard hooves behind her – she might have known that she would be denied her escape, would have to wait for the others to catch up. No doubt Yanna would have told Huan to keep her always within sight and reach.

Maia was tempted to ride on. She sighed. She shouldn't but . . . she a drew a deep breath and smelled . . .

'Wulf Kin.'

Too late. Tall figures rose from the grass. She was surrounded.

Fionn reared as a Wulf Kin grabbed at her mane. Maia

felt herself sliding out of the saddle. The mare was pulled squealing to her knees as another Wulf Kin leapt at Maia, dragging her from Fionn's back.

Maia crashed to the ground. She tried to roll away from her struggling mount and was grabbed and flipped onto her back. The stench of the Wulf Kin hit her as a huge hand came down to cover her mouth. Her stomach heaved. She was going to vomit.

Then her feet were being bound in cutting cords. She kicked and wriggled, but she was being dragged feet-first through the grass. A snarling wulfen leapt across her, splattering her with strings of saliva.

The world swung dizzily as she was lifted and slung over the saddle. The ground seemed to rise to meet her as she hung head-down. Hampered by the hand pinning her to the saddle and the pony's bone-jolting run, she tried to reach for the sun-stone. She needed to make light and fire to resist her attacker. Then something thumped against her head and all was darkness.

Forty-Two

Groaning on their giant hinges, the great gates swung open. Maia, her head still throbbing from the blow, shook the sleeves of her padded coat down over her hands so her wrists were hidden. She wouldn't ride into the Sun City looking like a captive.

Ahead, a wide sweep of shallow steps led upwards to a gleaming silver gate set between two white towers. High walls curved away from the towers. Behind them a jumble of turrets and domes glinted in the sun. And rising above it all, a slender obelisk, pointing like a finger at the sky. The Sun Palace. The catching-stone.

Maia felt her stomach plunge.

Her captor urged his pony across the square towards the wide sweeping steps. Then they were riding into a vast stone courtyard, past the towering stone obelisk. Stable boys ran to take the ponies. Before she could be pulled from the saddle, Maia slid to the ground.

'Climb. The Queen waits,' growled the Wulf Kin.

He propelled her up the steps and into the Palace. Their footsteps echoed along a cloistered corridor set round a small courtyard planted with stunted trees. They were burned black. Maia stared. It was a dead moth-garden. Now she saw that the walls were streaked with soot, almost obscuring a mural of flowers and moon-moths. She had just deciphered the painting of a girl collecting cocoons when they entered a room beyond the dead garden.

The room was filled with shadows. Huge pillars supported a painted roof. Carved and decorated with patterns of animals and plants, they were like trees in a stone forest. Even in the gloom, Maia could make out the gold of stars and moons gleaming on the domed ceiling. A wide avenue stretched between the pillars, past a vast hearth. On the walls, banners shivered in tiny eddies of air as they passed. At the far end Maia could see a round window filled with swirls of dark glass. Below this was a dais with three steps leading to a stone throne that gleamed with gilded decorations. And on the golden throne was a woman with Xania's eyes, whose red hair hung almost to her waist. A jewel of white light blazed on her hand, which rested on the shoulder of a thin titian-haired girl sitting at her side.

Maia felt a knife-thrust of hate.

Elin. And Urteth's child, Caspia. She looks almost my age, thought Maia, surprised.

The girl was scowling at her. Maia scowled back.

'You found her!' There was satisfaction, but no joy in Elin's exclamation.

Maia noticed that her hand had tightened on the shoulder of the girl, who wriggled in protest.

'Where is Urteth?' demanded Elin, her voice rising.

The Wulf Kin shrugged. 'Elsewhere. With the old one, Zartev.'

A flush stained Elin's cheekbones.

She's afraid, thought Maia.

'Has she got the stone?'

'She wears it.'

The Wulf Kin strode back to Maia, grabbed her bound wrists, holding them up for Elin to see.

Elin moved down the steps. She was not as tall as Xania, Maia noticed, but power and authority seemed to shimmer from her. Released, the girl, Caspia, sullenly rubbed her shoulder and, seeing Maia watching her, clicked her fingers. A wulfen ambled towards her. Caspia slid to her knees, her long green skirts puddling around her and, buried her fingers in the shaggy fur, caressing the creature's head. As if it were a tame hunting hound thought Maia, and felt slightly sick. Caspia looked up, saw Maia's expression and smiled.

Elin strode across the floor. Maia could hear the frayed silk on her gown whispering. She hoped the coat bundled into her back-sack and her own silk wouldn't respond.

Elin looked directly at Maia for the first time. Her gaze was like ice, her voice just as cold. 'So you are the missing sister.'

Maia forced herself to stare back. She could feel the silk

Tareth had given her warm against her skin, comforting her.

'Xania. Is she with you?' demanded Elin. She glared at the Wulf Kin. 'Did you find the Story Singer?'

'They killed her,' retorted Maia.

Elin's expression didn't change.

'She died from a poisoned blade. A Wulf Kin blade,' said Maia.

Still Elin showed no emotion. Her hands uncurled and she stroked the silk panel at the front of her robe.

'Dead?' she mused and shrugged. 'A matter of so little consequence that the silk didn't sing her passing.'

'Then your silk's weak and confused,' taunted Maia. 'Even the stars wept when Xania was laid to rest. If it didn't tell you that, what else has it kept from you? Your silk is not to be trusted, sister.'

Elin stepped closer. She reached into the open neck of Maia's coat, found the twisted leather thong and ripped the bag from its hiding place. Her eyes glowed with triumph.

'It told me that you would bring me this,' said Elin.

Maia felt as if she had lost part of herself. The sun-stone was hers.

'Easy to tell when the plains are full of rumours and the snow starts to melt,' Maia hissed. 'Did your silk sing Urteth's death-song, too?' she goaded.

Elin's arm fell slowly to her side. The bag hung loosely from her fingers. She turned and walked to the dais, climbed the three steps and sat on the throne.

'Urteth?' Her fingers trembled across the silk panel of her tunic. 'Dead.'

Maia felt no pity. 'He wanted power. He held the sun-stone and died.'

'I would know if he was dead.'

'He tried to use the sun-stone. He failed. It killed him.'

'You lie,' Elin's voice rose. 'The sun-stone needs the sun in the Stone Court. It's powerless until then. It must wait until the Catcher wears the sun-helmet and summons the sun. It wouldn't have harmed Urteth.' She glared at the Wulf Kin. 'Anyone can handle it. Even a child.'

She tossed the sun-stone into Caspia's lap.

'See. Touch it. Show them how they all fail me, Caspia.'

The girl stopped fondling the wulfen and reached out.

'No!' shouted Maia.

Caspia glanced at her, grinned and took hold of the sun-stone.

Maia closed her eyes and waited for the scream and the smell of burning. Nothing happened. She heard the Wulf Kin exhale beside her, as if he too had feared for the girl. Maia opened her eyes. Caspia was dropping the sun-stone into her mother's lap.

'You see?' said Elin. 'Neither you, sister, nor the sun-stone, are any danger to me.'

Her hand hovered over the sun stone, almost, but not quite, touching it. Maia wondered if she was imagining the strange, blue flickering light which seemed to come from Elin's ring and trickle over her questing fingers. A bead of light dropped onto the sun-stone and extinguished.

Elin held out her hands. Now Maia could see the light clearly, it was sparking, leaping across her sister's fingers. What power did she have?

'Release her,' commanded Elin. She seemed to be playing with the blue light, tossing it from hand to hand. The jewel in her ring glowed.

The Wulf Kin pulled out his long-bladed knife and cut Maia's ropes. Maia rubbed her sore wrists. She didn't understand. The sun-stone hadn't flared with light and burned Caspia when she held it. Was it too dark in the hall? Was her family immune to the sun-stone's fire?

As if she had guessed Maia's thoughts, Caspia grinned at her. Her eyes were dark, deep as the lake in the cave. Maia felt herself drawn into the depths. Felt a probe, nagging like a sore tooth. Tiny, dislocated images seemed to travel across the back of her eyes. Was Caspia's gift thought-stealing? She shut off her thoughts to break contact. Maia felt a jolt and then, like sea-fall, a sighing retreat.

'Sun's greetings, sister's child.' Maia touched her fingers to her forehead and held out her hand.

Caspia reached out. Their fingers touched.

'You like lizards,' said Caspia slowly. 'And eagles. You want an eagle.' She smiled. 'I like wulfen. And Azara, my father's eagle, although she's old. Urteth has promised me my own eagle.'

Remembering the eagle's fall, Maia glanced up.

Caspia gasped. 'Azara's dead?'

Maia hid her thoughts. Caspia was dangerous.

'And Urteth?'

Try as she might Maia couldn't ignore the look of devastation in Caspia's face. Her fight was with Elin. 'The eagle died. Urteth fell. The sun-stone burned him. He vanished.'

'Vanished?'

Reluctantly, Maia nodded, remembering the mayhem – swirling, circling riders, screaming eagles, baying wulfen. 'The old Wulf Kin was there. Urteth died.'

Caspia's eyes flashed. 'Zartev would never let my father die!' she retorted. 'He would have returned to the Sun City to tell me. The old one is loyal to me and my father!'

But not to Elin, thought Maia.

Caspia turned to Elin. 'Mother, let me . . .'

'Enough!' said Elin. She was frowning, her hands clenched over the carved, snarling cats on the arms of the throne. 'Leave us!' she commanded. 'All of you.'

Caspia scowled but walked slowly towards a low door in the wall to the side of the central hearth. The wulfen padded at her heels.

'Come, Vultek,' said Caspia, as she reached the Wulf Kin. 'And bring Jadhev.'

'Leave us,' said Elin.

The Wulf Kin turned insolently to follow Caspia.

Vultek glanced at Maia. 'Sun Catcher,' he said, flicked his fingers in a mocking salute, his silver armbands glinting as, with his companion, he strode from the hall.

The only sound in the room was the faint hiss of the fire as a damp log fell into the flames. Maia moved towards the fire, slipped off her back-sack, disguising the action as she held out her hands to the flames. She dropped the bag.

Elin, entranced with the sun-stone, did not notice. She held it up, turned it in her fingers. The edges of the crystal were tinged with rose. She placed it on the floor in front of the throne.

'Now, sister,' she said. 'What shall I do with you?'

'Surely, sister,' Maia retorted, 'the question is, what shall I do with you?'

She crouched in a fighter's stance and slipped a knife from her boot. 'Your Wulf Kin are careless. They should have searched me. I promised Xania I'd avenge our sisters.'

Elin laughed. 'You cannot harm me,' she crowed and flicked her fingers.

Maia felt as if her hands had been struck by a falling bolt of light. Her fingers tingled with pins and needles. The knife fell from her hand and lay in a ring of blue light at her feet. As she watched, it seemed to distort and began to melt.

'The sun-stone is mine, sister.'

Maia sucked in a deep breath and glared at her sister. If her knife was no use against the blue fire in Elin's ring, then she'd find another way to defeat the Queen.

'Urteth's dead,' she said. 'I saw him die. He tried to take the sun-stone. He burned. And the old Wulf Kin will take your daughter. Is it worth the loss of Caspia and Urteth?'

Elin's face went blank. She looked beyond Maia towards the door. Maia took her chance and charged.

Forty-Three

Kodo had never seen such a fine city. Warning him to be careful, Tareth had sent him to listen for any news. The market-place was alive with gossip. People started hurrying from the square. Kodo followed and was pulled along on the coat-tails of a crowd running along the narrow streets. Ahead of the mob he could hear voices calling.

'Sun Catcher! Sun Catcher!'

Maia? Here?

Instead of fighting against the tide, Kodo ran with it, tripped and was flung against a tall figure, who cursed and fell with him. The crowd flowed over them. Pummelled by stampeding feet, bruised, and breathless, Kodo uncurled as the mob disappeared. He sat up, feeling his ribs. His companion, still flattened on the ground beside him, groaned and swore.

'Lizard spume!'

'Weed boy? Razek?'

Razek groaned again and staggered to his feet. He stood rubbing his shoulder and glaring down at Kodo. He saw Kodo's tattooed thumb and remembered him.

'Lizard boy. What are you doing here?'

'Trader now,' retorted Kodo. He scrambled to his feet. The stabbing in his ribs seemed insignificant compared to the shock of seeing Razek. He pressed his fingers gingerly against them. They didn't move. Not broken then. He stared at Razek, still not believing his eyes. 'I sailed with Tareth. We're looking for Maia. What are you doing here?'

Razek went white. 'Tareth? He's dead! I saw him fall from the cliff!'

'Jumped more like,' said Kodo. 'Doon found him floating in the water. A trader-ship took us aboard.'

'Alive?' Razek grabbed Kodo's arm. 'Tareth?'

Kodo pulled free. 'And waiting for me. Did you see Maia? They were shouting "Sun Catcher."'

Razek didn't seem to hear.

'Maia!' Kodo shook him. 'Did you see Maia?'

'Maia! She thinks Tareth is dead.' Razek looked around wildly. 'I must tell her.'

He turned as if to follow the crowd. Kodo grabbed him and held on. It was like snaring a wild fisher-bird.

'Razek!' he yelled, kicking him as Razek's wildly swinging fist, hit him in the ear. 'Stop. Where's Maia?'

'With the Wulf Kin. She was riding with the Wulf Kin. I tried to follow. They were too quick for me. The crowds came. I shouted, "Sun Catcher". Then you knocked me down, lizard boy!' He clenched his fists.

'We must tell Tareth,' decided Kodo. 'Come on!'

He turned and after a few steps realised that Razek wasn't following.

'Come on! Tareth's waiting near the market.'

Razek shook his head. 'I can't!'

Kodo ran back. He twisted his hand in Razek's tunic and yanked him along the alley. 'Come on! Tareth will want to hear the news.'

'Let go, lizard-breath!' Razek buffeted Kodo round the head.

Eyes blazing, Kodo backed away. 'Don't you want to help Tareth find Maia?'

'I can't. I . . . killed Tareth's eagle,' he gabbled.

Kodo stared at him in disbelief. He rubbed his stinging ear, trying to clear the buzzing flies of his thought.

'Maia needs our help,' he said eventually. 'Come on.' He turned and ran. He heard Razek stumble a few steps after him. 'Hurry.'

They matched each other stride for stride even though Razek was a head taller. He glared at Kodo as he ran.

'You kicked me, lizard boy!' he panted.

'Trader to you, weed boy,' retorted Kodo, pleased that, unlike Razek, he was not in the least out of breath. 'Come on! You're slower than an egg-bound lizard.'

They raced through the twisting streets descending to the gates. As they emerged from the labyrinth Razek grabbed Kodo and yanked him to a halt.

'Wait! There's Yanna!'

Kodo saw a tall woman riding from the gates. She had a bow holster strapped against her thigh. A sleek, spotted feline loped beside the horse. This time Kodo was dragged across the street by Razek as he waylaid the rider and grabbed the horse's reins. The woman glared down at them. Kodo felt the burn of her gaze but Razek seemed immune.

'Wulf Kin,' he panted. 'They've got Maia!'

'Where?'

Razek gestured back the way they had come.

Yanna looked up towards the gilded tips of spires visible above the rising tangle of streets. 'The Sun Palace? She's gone to Elin!'

Razek tugged at her bridle. 'A captive! Against her will!'

'We've got to help her!' added Kodo.

'Help's coming. The Eagle People are coming. My archers are coming.' Yanna gestured back through the open gates.

Kodo looked out across the vast plains. His eyes widened as he saw the approaching throng.

'Come on,' he said. 'We must tell Tareth.' He looked up at Yanna. 'Maia's father is here.' He saw the disbelief in her eyes. 'Tareth, the Warrior Weaver, has come to rescue his daughter,' he said proudly. 'And so have I.'

He glanced at Razek. 'So have we.'

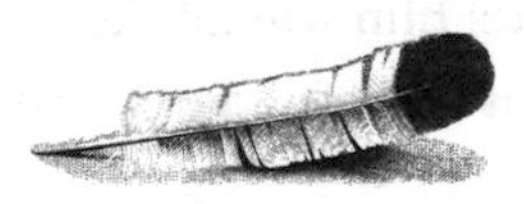

Tareth was seated at the table shuffling tokens across a board.

'She's here!' said Kodo. He grinned at Tareth's startled face.

'She rode in with the Wulf Kin.' Yanna strode in behind him.

'Who are you?' Tareth was already reaching for his knife. Then he realised what Yanna had said. 'You saw her?' he demanded.

'I saw her. She was a prisoner.' Razek entered the room. He glanced at Tareth and then shamefaced, down at his feet. 'I saw her with the Wulf Kin. I followed.'

'Eagle slayer!' hissed Tareth. 'Why are you here?'

Razek flinched.

Yanna's gaze flickered between them. 'He followed Xania and Maia to Altara.'

'Xania. She's with Maia?' demanded Tareth.

Yanna shook her head. 'Xania lies on the Plains.'

Tareth moaned.

'She brought the Sun Catcher safely to us,' said Yanna softly.

Tareth glared at her, his face a mask of pain. 'Yet Maia's with the Wulf Kin?'

Yanna met his gaze. 'They'll have taken the Sun Catcher to the Sun Palace.'

'To Elin!'

Yanna nodded.

'Then we're too late! Elin will kill her!'

'The Sun Catcher is strong,' said Yanna. 'She'll fight. She has the sun-stone.'

Tareth's hand tightened around the handle of his sheathed knife. 'Elin will force her to use the sun-stone, to catch the sun. Or she'll kill Maia and try to use it herself.'

Yanna shook her head. 'Only the Sun Catcher can use the sun-stone.'

Tareth's face was harsh. 'Who knows what Elin can do, or thinks she can do? The sisters' gifts are strong.'

Yanna nodded. 'Truly. Maia brought snow-melt. Even now the plains are green. And the first flowers have appeared. The land grows warm with her touch. The sun will be caught.'

Tareth turned away. 'Kodo! We have to get into the Stone Court.'

'At sun-wake everyone will be in the Stone Court,' said Yanna.

They looked at her in surprise. 'It's Solstice,' she reminded them. 'And the Sun Catcher must catch the sun. All follow the Sun Catcher, even the Eagle Hunters. They'll be here before sun-sleep.'

Tareth grabbed Kodo's arm. 'Eagle Hunters?' he asked. 'Does Urteth ride with them?'

Kodo winced. 'There were many eagles!'

'Urteth is dead!' said Yanna. 'The sun-stone burned him.'

Tareth gazed at her in disbelief. 'Dead?' He shook his head. 'I would have felt his passing.'

'The Sun Catcher destroyed Urteth,' insisted Yanna.

'Then Elin will be beyond reason!' said Tareth. 'There's no time,' he said. 'We must go now!'

'I'll open the gates for you,' said Kodo.

'How?' demanded Yanna.

'I'll get over the walls with this,' said Kodo as held up the large three-pronged hook he had taken from the trader ship. He pulled a ball of fishing twine from the pouch on his belt. 'Tareth and I have a plan. I'll tie the line to the hook, throw it over the wall, knot on a rope.' He glanced at Razek. 'Razek can carry that, wrapped round his middle under his tunic. He's thin enough for it not to show,' he added. 'And then we climb. Into the bees' nest. Good honey-hunting,' he grinned, as he carefully hung the grappling hook onto his belt and hid it beneath his cloak.

'I'll climb the walls,' said Razek.

'And me,' said Kodo.

'And me!' said Tareth. He was glowering at Razek.

Kodo held his breath. Surely Tareth would not refuse Razek's help? If the Wulf Kin held Maia they needed all the help they could get.

Tareth glanced at Yanna. 'And if you will lend me your bow . . . ?'

Yanna was adjusting her quiver strap. She stabbed herself and yelped. Sucking her finger, she stared at Tareth. 'My bow?' The silk braid on the bow whispered. Yanna stilled it with her thumb and handed Tareth the bow and quiver.

'When we meet again you will return them,' she said.

Kodo glanced from one solemn face to the other. 'That's settled then. Are we going? Or must we wait until Trader and his ship arrives after new-leaf?'

'Fire-brand!' said Tareth. 'Did you drink the red-crest's milk as a pup?' Despite his anxiety he smiled at Kodo.

'I'm a trader now,' said Kodo. 'But I'm a lizard boy too. And the Lizard People are strong and fierce, like the lizards.'

Razek's head came up like a hunting hound. He stared at Kodo. 'Your tribe fought well, lizard boy. So did the weed boys.' He looked at Tareth. 'I will come and fight for Maia's freedom with you.'

Tareth remained silent.

'I will fight,' continued Razek, 'because my father and I once saved Maia from the sun-deeps.' He raised his chin, his eyes never leaving Tareth's cold stare. 'I am Weed Master. Maia is from the weed beds. She is my . . . friend,' he added. He drew a deep breath. 'Let me come with you.'

Slowly Tareth nodded. 'Come then,' he said. 'We've Wulf Kin to fight.'

Forty-Four

Kodo clung like a monkey to the archer as her horse raced through the streets. Ahead, Tareth, astride a bronze horse, was riding in tandem with Yanna, his crutches lashed to his back, her bow in one hand, the other twisted in her tunic. Razek clung to another rider, his face grim, his grip a stranglehold. Not used to riding lizards, or anything else, guessed Kodo. Yanna's cheetah bounded alongside as they joined the vanguard of mounted archers Yanna had sent ahead to the Sun City.

'We cannot wait for the others,' Yanna had said. 'We will have to storm the Sun Palace, disarm the guard and find Maia.'

But storming was unnecessary. As they clattered into the square, the palace gates opened and a small party of Wulf Kin rode out. At their head was a flame-haired girl on a black horse.

Kodo's greeting died in his throat as he realised that this red-haired girl was not Maia. As the party swept past them, the girl looked directly at Kodo with bright blue eyes. He felt the shock as their gazes locked. She had eyes that looked straight into his head. She turned in the saddle as she led her troop across the square, prolonging the bond. He felt as if he was sinking beneath the keep-nets, his eyes waterlogged, a jagged pattern like the criss-cross ropes before them. He couldn't breathe. He gasped for air as the girl vanished into the maze of streets leading from the square and he was free.

'On!' urged Yanna. And the horses swept up the steps through the open gates into a square, riding over the two men in grey tunics who tried to stop them and on up shallow steps leading to huge metal doors, standing ajar. An arrow ricocheted off the door. Tareth twisted in the saddle and retaliated, aiming high. Kodo heard a cry as three of the archers turned their horses and sent a flight of arrows towards the top of the wall.

Then he was through the door and into a courtyard, charging in pursuit of Tareth along a covered way, the sound of hooves deafening in the confined space. A Wulf Kin appeared. Yanna yelled and rode straight at him. Tareth fired another arrow then tumbled from the horse as it swerved to avoid the wulfen springing from among blackened tree stumps. The Wulf Kin fell before Tareth hit the ground.

Kodo threw himself from the horse, rolled and came to his feet dragging the grappling hook from beneath his tunic. Razek was also down and running towards a man who had appeared at the doorway, knife in hand. They crashed together. Kodo saw Razek's blade flash as he struck.

Then the hook was free. Kodo swung it in an arc and flung it at the wulfen. His aim was true. The heavy hook struck home. Kodo yanked it back, tearing flesh. He thumped it down on the dazed beast's head. As it reeled, Yanna was there, plunging her knife into the wulfen. She sprang past him to reach Tareth, dragging him to one side. Pulling two arrows from the quiver strapped to his thigh and dropping to her knees, she fired them at the Wulf Kin running along the far side of the burned trees. He dropped like a felled tree. One of the archers slid a knife from her boot, leaned over him and cut his throat.

Kodo helped Tareth to his knees. Tareth pulled his crutches free.

A scream of rage rent the air.

'Maia!' Tareth spun and lurched towards the door behind them. Kodo and Razek hurled themselves after him.

Forty-Five

Maia's whirlwind charge took Elin by surprise. She screamed as Maia leapt, her left foot thudding into Elin's chest. The right crashed into her jaw. Elin went flying.

Landing like a cat, Maia stamped on her sister's seeking hand. Blue sparks spat from Elin's ring. Maia gasped. It felt as if thorns from the moth-garden had stabbed her foot. She stooped and bowled the sun-stone out of reach across the flagstones, sprang after it and fell flat on her face as Elin grabbed her foot. The fall winded her. She twisted, kicking at Elin's face.

Lurching to her feet, Elin ran towards the sun-stone. Maia flipped onto all fours and sprang. Grabbing Elin's long hair, she twisted it round her hand and pulled. Elin yelled as she was jerked to a standstill. Shrieking, she spun on her heel. Maia hung on as Elin's hair ripped through her fingers.

Howling with pain and rage, her fingers like tiger claws, Elin attacked, aiming short stabbing blows at Maia's face and throat. The ring flared. The speed of her ferocious attack forced Maia backwards. Off-balance, she kicked, catching Elin in the thigh. Blue light swirled around them as Elin's hands clamped onto Maia's throat. She squeezed. Maia felt as if her eyes were popping from her head. She punched and kicked. Elin absorbed the blows. Gasping for breath Maia sagged. As her weight dragged at Elin, Maia's foot swept away Elin's lead leg. She lost balance and they tumbled to the floor.

Then Elin was slithering towards the sun-stone. She grabbed it, lifted it and tried to use it. Maia saw blue light in her ring flare and die. Elin screamed in outrage and backed away like an animal at bay. She flung out her left hand. Nothing happened. Had the sun-stone drained the ring?

Vicious, dangerous, desperate, Elin fought on.

Maia rolled away from a final bruising encounter which left Elin spread-eagled. Something wasn't right. She couldn't summon up fire to destroy Elin. Nor could Elin deliver a killing blow. And if Elin couldn't kill her, had she really murdered all her sisters as Xania claimed?

She crouched, gasping for breath, ready to attack again if Elin moved. She had never felt so tired.

'How did my sisters die?' she panted.

Elin crawled towards the throne and rested against the dais. 'The plague.'

'Xania said you killed them!'

Elin was silent for a long time. 'When the plague came to the city, I locked them away. They died one after another.'

'You wanted them dead!'

'I saved the Sun City from the disease. I saved you. Xania never believed me. But she wasn't here. She was singing stories in the mountains when the plague came. I sent messages to the Eagle People, warning her to stay away. But she returned to be with Tareth.' Elin's voice was tinged with contempt. 'She would have freed the sickness. We would all have died. I did what I had to.' She coughed, holding her ribs. 'I cleansed the palace with fire. Flames destroy the plague. It was the only way.'

'Leaving me to burn!' said Maia.

'I sent Urteth to find you.'

Maia drew in a shuddering breath and felt the slow burn of power returning.

'To find me – or to kill me?'

Elin ignored the question. 'You were gone. So was the sun-stone.' She glared at Maia. 'Its gift should have passed to me. I was to be Sun Catcher after my mother, not a wailing child too young to hold the stone. But Xania didn't care. She wanted the sun-stone for you – a child! She said you were to be Sun Catcher. That the silk told her. You, not me – the eldest sister!'

'So I had to die?'

'I would have saved you from the plague and the fire. Would have reared you like a daughter. But Xania and Tareth stole you and the sun-stone and Khandar grew weak.

'Each snow-deep, my gift faded. The harvests failed. The cold lasted too long. The sun was too weak. I needed the sun-stone to catch the sun.' She twisted the ring on her finger. The jewel was dull. 'My gift and yours are the two halves that will make the land whole again. I need your power, sister. The sun-stone is mine.'

The same story, a different slant. Where did the truth lie, wondered Maia. Who did she believe?

'The story-coat,' she said suddenly.

Elin started. 'The coat?' she echoed.

'The silk knows the truth.'

Maia couldn't read the expressions chasing across Elin's face like wind ripples across the weed beds. 'It is lost,' said Elin slowly. 'Burned in the fire.' She sat up and smoothed her silk panel, seeking reassurance.

'It didn't burn,' said Maia. 'Xania was the Story Singer. She had the story-coat all the time. She hid the knowledge from you and your silk.'

She saw uncertainty darken Elin's eyes.

'I thought the story-coat should be buried with her,' Maia added slowly and watched relief flood like the sun rising from the deeps across Elin's face. So, Elin was lying. She must have feared that the story-coat held the truth of that time. Feared that her sisters' silk was stitched to the coat. With the story-coat lost, she thought she was safe.

Now Maia knew what she must do. What she had always had to do. The Watcher had known it. Tareth had feared it. Xania had demanded it. She had denied it. But the knowledge had been growing in her since Zena had braved the journey across the plains alone to bring her the coat. Since the hungry had started flocking to Altara and had followed her with hope in their eyes. Since the Eagle People had left their hills to ride with her. She breathed slowly, gathering her strength.

'A pity,' said Elin slowly, unaware of the change that was taking place in Maia. 'The coat was . . . powerful. It chose Xania. It's good that it lies with her now. She'll have its tales to keep her company on her last journey.'

As if you care, thought Maia.

'I tried to give Xania the story-coat for her final journey,' she explained. 'I tried not to listen to Xania or the silk. I didn't want to hear the song of my eldest sister, the Death Bringer.'

She pulled the coat from the bag. It tumbled like a waterfall from her hand, murmuring with joy at being freed. Elin shrank against the stone steps. An invisible draft touched the coat, the mirror stones glittered and the silk sang. And threading through the song Maia could hear Elin's name as tiny shadows shivered across it, changing the colour of the silk as they passed.

'Listen,' said Maia. 'It knows you.'

Elin's face was the colour of milk.

'It has stories to tell you, sister,' Maia advanced across the hall and the story-coat sang as she went. 'It knows what you have done, Death Bringer.'

'No!' Elin cowered against the dais.

'Xania's story. And your sisters' death songs. The truth in the fire. Xania stitched her sisters' silk into the coat. Listen to the story of Khandar and your treachery!'

Elin rose to her feet. 'No!' She drew herself up, her right hand fumbling for the large jewel on her finger.

Maia's laugh was cracked, but it was a laugh nonetheless. Her legs were trembling, but still she stalked Elin.

'I am the Sun Catcher!' said Maia. 'You cannot harm me.'

'No!' howled Elin.

The door was flung open, and crashed against the wall. Figures poured into the room.

Maia spun on her heel. The coat flared out, the silk brushed against Elin. She moaned, but Maia didn't hear her. She lowered her arms and the silk pooled around her feet.

She stared at the group swiftly crossing the hall towards her. At one tall, dark-haired figure swinging on crutches, as if blown by storm-winds. A man with eyes of fire and an eagle feather in his hair.

'Tareth!'

'Maia! Look out!' shouted Kodo.

Kodo? Here? Taller, older, weather-beaten, a boy-man, he was leaping at her, knocking her aside as Elin sprang for the last time. Maia staggered, heard a bowstring twang and a woman shriek.

Elin slumped, grasping her arm where a feathered arrow quivered in her flesh.

Yanna strode up to her, bow in hand, fitting another arrow as she moved.

'Stay still if you value your worthless life,' she spat.

Then Maia was grabbed and enveloped in strong arms. Tareth's crutches crashed to the floor as they clung to each other.

'You're not dead. Not dead.'

'Kodo found me. You're safe!'

'Safe. Not dead!' The words reversed themselves. 'Kodo. Not dead! Safe!'

Then she was tumbled and passed from one set of arms to another, pounded on the back, shouted at until her world wheeled like the turning stars around her. And Razek was there too. His face drawn, his hug tentative and brief. And then he was gone and Tareth was in his place, hugging her as if he couldn't bear to let her go. Nefrar twined round her legs, a welcoming growl rumbling deep in his chest. And finally, she and Kodo faced each other. They grinned a little self-consciously.

Kodo flicked his fingers to his forehead. 'Sun Catcher!'

'Lizard boy,' she teased.

'Trader!' He shrugged. 'Almost trader.'

'And the juggler?' he asked.

Maia felt a stab of anguish. She shook her head. 'A Wulf Kin blade,' she whispered.

'We feared you were both dead,' Kodo said.

'We ran and ran,' remembered Maia. 'And hid in Altara. Razek followed us. Yanna sent him away.' She glanced at Yanna and her archers, who still surrounded Elin. Someone had removed the arrow and her sister was standing, holding a bloodstained pad to her arm.

'Is the arrow poisoned?' Elin was demanding.

'Only the Wulf Kin poison their weapons,' snarled Yanna. 'This wound won't kill you. But you will die. You have taken life. You will give your life!'

Tareth was slumped in the chair on the dais.

'I agree. She would have killed Maia. Xania accused her of killing her sisters.'

'Xania lied,' spat Elin defiantly. 'The plague killed them. You brought ruin to this land, eagle thief. You stole the sun-stone. You stole my sister. You brought us hunger when you took them. You who are nothing now Xania is no more!'

'Nothing,' said Tareth. 'Yet more than you can know.'

'The evil on this land is you,' hissed Yanna. 'And only the Sun Catcher and your death can remove it. You'll die before sun-wake.'

'I am Queen! You cannot decide my fate, archer.'

'But I can, sister!' said Maia.

She moved to stand beside Tareth. He would have risen. She placed her hand on his shoulder.

'You!' hissed Elin. 'You are merely our mother's afterthought. You will all obey me!' She glared round the group of condemning faces. She was dangerous and magnificent.

Maia sighed. What a queen Elin could have been.

'I am the Sun Catcher,' Maia said quietly, and felt Tareth's hand stiffen in protest beneath hers. 'And at sun-wake I will catch the sun, as Xania knew the Sun Catcher must.'

'Yes!' cried Yanna.

'And my sister will stand in the Stone Court beside me.' She looked at Elin, whose face had grown pale. 'And when it's over, she's free to go.'

'No!' protested Yanna. 'You can't let her go. She must die for what she has done.'

Tareth held up his hand to silence her. 'Free to go, Maia?' he asked quietly.

'She is my sister. I will not be a Death Bringer. I will not be like her.'

Elin laughed. 'Xania was wrong, sister. You will never catch the sun. You are weak. A Sun Catcher brings death fire as well as life. The stone burns and brings light. Give the sun-stone to me.'

'Free to go,' continued Maia. 'But never free of the silk.

She must wear the story-coat and listen to its song.'

'You cannot give her Xania's coat,' protested Yanna.

'You must not,' warned Tareth. 'The silk is powerful. And has a will of its own.'

'It was Xania's silk. She will have her revenge,' said Maia. 'Elin will never escape it for as long as she has breath to sing them.'

Tareth shook his head. 'Elin is not the Story Singer. That was Xania's gift. She kept the stories safe.'

'Xania told me she stitched her sisters' silk into the coat,' said Maia. 'We can find and unpick the story. That is the only silk Elin will wear.'

'And will always hear the stories of her treachery and the death of her sisters?' asked Yanna.

Tareth nodded.

Maia turned away. The room suddenly seemed stifling. She escaped through the doors behind the dais and out into the air. There, from the balcony, perched like an eagle's eyrie above the city, she could see the plains ablaze with lights. A broad, winding river of flaming torches was snaking towards the gates.

Kodo had followed her. 'The Eagle Hunters are arriving,' he said.

'And a few others,' said Maia. She stared at the lights until they blurred and danced in front of her eyes. 'I'm afraid,' she said. 'Afraid of sun-wake. Afraid I'll fail.'

She glanced at Kodo and then away again, ashamed that he could see her brimming eyes and her dread. 'I've no idea how to catch the sun . . . What I'll have to do.'

'Tareth will know,' said Kodo. 'He'll have seen it before.'

Maia nodded and was silent so long Kodo wondered if she had fallen asleep on her feet. He stood there trying to count the lights. The Stone Court would be full to overflowing at sun-wake.

'I'm afraid of going blind,' said Maia out of the darkness. 'Sun Catchers lose their sight. No one can look at the sun unharmed. I think that's why Tareth hid the sun-stone. He didn't want it to happen to me.'

Some part of Kodo had been waiting for this and he was ready. 'On the cliff, after the beast died,' he said, 'the Watcher found eyebright. She said it would help.'

'It did. The first time.'

'And that won't be the only thing that will,' said Kodo. 'I've heard and seen many strange things since I left the stilt village. And Trader Bron tells such tales of the places the ship has still to visit when the storms are over. I'll ask in every port. Somewhere there'll be a cure.'

Maia gulped. 'D'you think so?'

'Bound to be,' said Kodo. 'I can search until I find plants and potions that soothe sore eyes, like the Watcher made, and I'll bring them to you.'

Maia slipped her hand into his and stood silently watching as the gates below opened to allow the torch-bearing crowds to enter. A thin, golden light began to flow through the streets, climbing the hill towards the Sun Palace.

'Like gold rivers of honey,' said Kodo. 'Beautiful.'

They glanced at each other, remembering.

'Beautiful,' she agreed.

Forty-Six

The sun-wake was beautiful.

Maia watched as a band of light inched above the edge of the distant hills. Soon the Stone Court would turn pink with the rising light. And when the light spilled through the top of the tall column, she must try to catch it.

She shivered in the cool air and stood still as Tareth placed the heavy helmet on her head over her ravaged hair. He left the visor up. His face was drawn. He tried to smile and failed, so she smiled for him.

He had worked throughout sun-sleep, seeking out and unravelling all of the tiny fragments of old silk left in the palace. He had sent Kodo running to tease threads from the giant bronze wheels in the message tower. He had untwisted the bands that tied his eagle feather in his hair.

Yanna had watched him, then summoned her archers.

Each one unravelled their knotted braid and teased out the three silk strands tied into its core.

When there was still not enough, Tareth had torn a strip from the hem of the story-coat. But he refused to touch the worn silk on Elin's robe.

Every shred had been unpicked and the threads rewoven into translucent eye pieces, as thin as moth wings, which Tareth had fitted over the eye sockets of the helmet as the moon sank behind the mountains.

'It might be enough. It must be enough!' he had muttered ceaselessly, as he worked. He repeated it now.

'You don't have to do this,' he told her, yet again.

'What will happen if I don't?' she asked him, just as she had as they argued long into the dark when she had made him tell her how she was to catch the sun.

Tareth battled with himself. 'Poor harvests,' he said eventually. 'An empty land. Famine.'

'Well, then,' she said. Finally.

He fastened the chin strap of the helmet.

'The silk will protect you,' he promised.

'I know.'

'Xania's story-coat will protect you,' said Tareth.

'Yes,' said Maia. 'And your silk too . . . the cliff silk.' She touched his hand and turned to face the Stone Court.

The obelisk on the opposite side of the square was black against the rising light. She could just see the dark hole, like an eye, near the top. Once the sunlight reached it, she had to lift the sun-stone and hold it until it caught the sun and blazed with light. Then she must twist the glowing crystal and throw the light to the four corners of the square to the catch-stones placed in the carved pillars that encircled the Stone Court. She could see them, like huge lizard eggs glimmering in the pink light, reminding her of those she had seen so long ago in the scrape. As they caught the blaze from the sun-stone, the catch-stones would bounce the sunlight out across the Palace. Warmth and light would leap like her silver cat from each slender stone tower to the next until a necklace of sunlight rimmed and protected the wide valley, banishing the long shadows and warming the cold earth. Finally, she must climb the stone cairn behind her and fit the stone into its niche. Each sun-wake it would begin again and the land would grow warm.

Maia sighed. At least that was what Tareth had said as he had tried to persuade her to give up the ritual. He had begged her to place the sun-stone in its niche before the sun reached the obelisk in the hope that the sun streaming through the eye would bounce against it and light the other stones.

She glanced down at the distant faces turned up towards her, waiting for her to lift the sun-stone. Somewhere among them was Kodo. And Razek, who had hovered, an outsider, after that first hug. She hoped they would remember not to look up at her when the sun came. She knew Tareth was close by. He wouldn't go far, had refused to wait with the others in the open square below. Beside her stood Elin, silent and blank-faced, but holding herself like the Queen she once was.

Maia felt the sweat prick her scalp. Even with her short hair it was hot inside the helmet. The sun-stone was warming in her hand. While she had been dreaming the sun had been rising. Below her the crowds were stirring. The colours of their clothes shifted and ran, merging and bending like the seaweed in the shallows as the wind blew across the water.

Would Selora and Laya ever hear of this? Maybe they would, if Razek found the courage to return. Or if Kodo's trading ship made the journey to the horse meadows below the Marsh Lords' holdfast in time for another Gather. She had no doubt that Kodo would become a trader and would make the journey back to the stilt village with the gold earrings he had promised his mother.

The silk whispered as Elin turned away from the rising sun. A whisper that grew like the sound of sea-rise sighing over the stone levees protecting the weed beds as, in the courtyard below, the crowds lowered themselves to the ground and hid their eyes in their arms.

It was time.

For a heartbeat Maia crossed her thumbs and wished hard. Wished that Razek would find his way home. Wished that, this time, the sun-helmet with its woven, silk eyes would defuse the harsh sunlight. Wished that Kodo's search for an eyebright cure would not be needed. Wished that the story-coat could sing Xania this ending. This beginning.

She lowered the visor. Holding the sun-stone with her fingertips, she watched through the thin gauze as the ray of light crept towards the eye of the needle. Her breath sighing inside the helmet sounded like the sun-deeps in a shell pressed to her ear. The sky was streaked with pink and gold. A shaft of sunlight pierced the stone like a gold blade. Light fell over her hands, trickling down her arms, running into her, warming her, cool and hot at the same time.

The sun-stone blazed.

Maia raised her hands. And caught the sun.

ACKNOWLEDGEMENTS

The journey from a story to a book is almost as long as Maia's travels. It's as exciting too, although luckily not as perilous as her adventures. Like Maia, I had help and made friends along the way, so there are a lot of people to thank for making this new adventure happen.

First of all Dave and my amazing family, who are always there as inspiration and cheerleaders and who brought buns in paper bags to feed me when I trudged across the Vast of ideas to complete the story. Thanks, guys. Maia wouldn't have left the cliffs without you. Maia, together with Kodo and Razek also needed the enthusiasm and input of the students on the MA in Writing for Young People at Bath Spa University and the encouragement and creative skills of the tutors – Course Director Julia Green, Steve Voake and Lucy Christopher who manage to tease stories from their students while writing their own books. Read them, they're great. Many thanks too to my agent, John McLay, who believed, took a deep breath and leapt into the sun-deeps. A special thank you to Orion. You wouldn't be reading this without their wonderful children's books team, and especially my editor Fiona Kennedy whose encouragement, eagle eye and pencil have made this a better book than it was when it arrived on her desk. She also found Geoff Taylor and his illustrations are a joy. Huge thanks to you all. It's been fun.

Lots of other people contributed in ways they'll never know. All those friends who listened; Lizzie for light bulb moments, the hut and that fish; Tina for long distance walks and fire fungus; Peter for the first word; Pen for checking most of the others and showing Maia how to fight; the crew of Spirit of Australia whose epic adventure across the Pacific on their way to winning the Clipper Round the World Yacht Race inspired Kodo to take to the sea; and last but not least the amazing children I've had the privilege to meet, teach and share stories with. Like Maia, even when the going is tough and the words don't make sense, they try again and never give up. This is for you all, with thanks. Enjoy.

Sheila Rance
West Sussex
November 2012

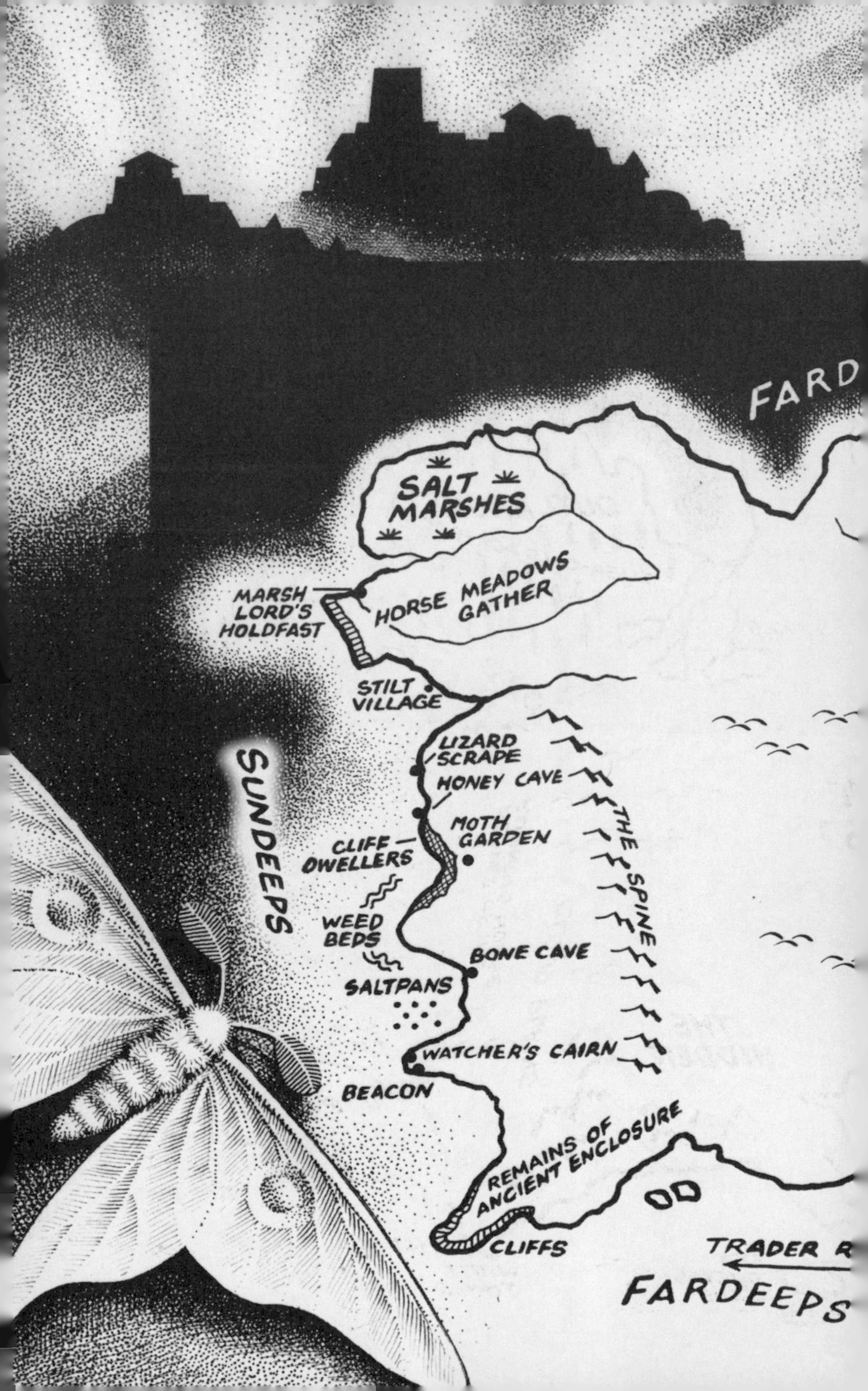
FARD
SALT MARSHES
HORSE MEADOWS GATHER
MARSH LORD'S HOLDFAST
STILT VILLAGE
SUNDEEPS
LIZARD SCRAPE
HONEY CAVE
MOTH GARDEN
CLIFF DWELLERS
THE SPINE
WEED BEDS
BONE CAVE
SALTPANS
WATCHER'S CAIRN
BEACON
REMAINS OF ANCIENT ENCLOSURE
CLIFFS
TRADER R
FARDEEPS

The lump of coal did what it was told, and began to grow very despondent, a word which here means "certain that a miracle would not occur after all." "Perhaps miracles only happen to human beings," it said, "or maybe miracles are only as genuine as Mr. Wong's Korean Barbeque Palace and Secretarial School. Perhaps I should just bury myself and become a diamond after thousands of years of intense pressure."

When the lump of coal rolled inside, however, it discovered that Mr. Wong's Korean Barbeque Palace and Secretarial School was not a miracle after all. The air was filled with the smell of oregano, which is not a Korean spice, and the owner was wearing a pair of very ugly earrings and a rude scowl on her face. "I don't need any coal," she said. "I get all my coal from a Korean restaurant supply factory. Everything in this restaurant has to be one hundred percent Korean."

"But Wong isn't even a Korean name," the lump of coal said. "And judging by the smell, I don't think you're using proper Korean spices."

"Please go away," said the restaurant owner, "and don't leave smudges on my Korean floor."

Just when the lump of coal was ready to return to its bag in the backyard, however, it ran into someone I'm sure I don't have to introduce. He was an overweight man with a long, white beard, dressed in a very bright red suit.

"Santa Claus!" cried the lump of coal. "It's a miracle!"

"I'm not a miracle," said Santa Claus, "and I'm not really Santa Claus. I'm an employee of the drugstore, dressed up and giving out coupons. The real Santa Claus is at the mall."

"Do you have any use for me?" asked the lump of coal. "I'm an artist at heart, but I'm very helpful when cooking meat."

Santa Claus sighed. "Well," he said, "my stepson is a very disobedient boy named Jasper. His mother used to say he had an artistic temperament, but I think he's a brat. You're just the thing to put in his stocking as punishment."

"I guess that's better than nothing," the lump of coal said, and when Santa Claus put him in Jasper's stocking, the lump of coal found that being in a cozy sock was, in fact, better than nothing. And when Jasper found the lump of coal, things became even better than better than nothing.

"A lump of coal!" Jasper cried. "I've been wanting to create some abstract art featuring rough, black lines!"

"I'd be happy to be of assistance," said the lump of coal.

"Egad!" cried Jasper. "You can talk! It's a miracle!"

It was a miracle, although the miracles didn't stop there.

Jasper and the lump of coal collaborated on a number of remarkable objets d'art, which the art gallery sold for an enormous fortune. That was a miracle.

Jasper and the lump of coal used this fortune to visit Korea, where they had always wanted to go, and when they came back they bought the restaurant and turned it into a proper place, known as Yi Sang's Korean Barbeque Palace and Secretarial School, after the famous Korean poet who was unfairly imprisoned for crimes he did not commit. That was a miracle too. In the daytime the two friends cooked genuine Korean food, and in the evenings they produced works of abstract art, and they never saw Santa Claus again, although they heard he had been fired from the drugstore for making fun of someone who was buying a certain ointment.

All these things are miracles. It is a miracle if you can find true friends, and it is a miracle if you have enough food to eat, and it is a miracle if you get to spend your days and evenings doing whatever it is you like to do, and the holiday season—like all the other seasons—is a good time not only to tell stories of miracles, but to think about the miracles in your own life, and to be grateful for them, and that's the end of this particular story.